RAW MEAT

A stunning left hook caught Major Cliff Breen on the cheekbone and smeared his nose across his face. Breen sat down hard on his butt, feeling the tears come to his eyes.

"Goddamn, you broke my . . ." He held his hands out. "Look at this." His hands were wet with blood.

He heard a growl. He looked up. The soldier fiddling with the rifle had thrown it to the ground and began advancing. The other soldier stepped up beside him and the two began moving in on Breen.

Breen remembered his pistol. He grabbed for it, but his hands were slippery with his own blood. He was trying to squeeze the trigger when one of the men grabbed his leg and yanked hard on it. He was thrown on his back . . . and felt one soldier biting into his leg, savagely, deeply.

Breen shrieked in agony . . . as they began to feast.

Other Dell books
by James V. Smith, Jr.:

BEASTMAKER

BEASTSTALKER

THE LURKER

ALMOST
HUMAN

· · · · · · · · · · · · · · · · · ·

James V. Smith, Jr.

A Dell Book

Published by
Dell Publishing
a division of
Bantam Doubleday Dell
Publishing Group, Inc.
666 Fifth Avenue
New York, New York 10103

ISBN: 0-440-20450-X

Printed in the United States of America
Published simultaneously in Canada

May 1990
10 9 8 7 6 5 4 3 2 1

RAD

To Senior Editor Brian DeFiore
and to Lori Perkins—
my heartfelt thanks.

For Chris

Prologue

· · · · · · · · · · · · · ·

The terrier rammed the fence muzzle first, the impact tearing the dog's lips, loosing flows of scarlet down its teeth. The animal bore into the wire, gnawing on the diamonds of the fence, clamping and shaking himself like a shark feeding on a carcass, finding a purchase with its jaws, throwing its body into contortions that rippled cables of muscles along its head and back.

"My heavens," whispered Edward Gates. "It's as if . . . as if he's trying to snip his way through to get to us."

"That's precisely the case, Mr. Gates," said the second man. Quist stood by calmly, dressed in a white laboratory smock, his hands casually in the pockets of the coat. But this man was anything but calm and casual. In his sweaty right fist he clutched a pistol, a 9-millimeter automatic with hollow-point slugs. He'd personally tested the bullets for stopping power against such dogs in case there would ever be instances where fences did not bar animals from humans.

"Its mouth . . . all that blood. The damned creature appears oblivious to pain that would stop a normal animal. Doesn't that hurt?"

"Perhaps, Mr. Gates. But this animal is quite single-minded." He shrugged as if this should be obvious to anybody, especially the man responsible for this operation. "It simply wants to kill us. We have bred it and trained it—not to sing for its supper, not to sit up for its supper, not to beg or bark for its supper, but to kill."

The dog whimpered, tearing at the fence in a renewal of rage.

"There!" said Gates. "He hurt himself that time."

"Not necessarily, sir. That's more likely a sign of frustration that he can't get to us."

"No," said Gates in disbelief, shaking a full head of slick black hair, shooting off blue reflections.

In confirmation, in contradiction, the terrier backed off a few yards and ran at the fence again, with an explosive burst of speed. Again its muzzle took the brunt of the attack. Its body whipped around stiffly. The dog pulled away, leaving tufts of fur in the twists of the storm fence. It whimpered impatiently.

Gates stepped backward. "What the hell kind of canine *is* that?"

"American bull terrier. It's usually called a pit bull, owing to its reputation and use in—"

"I've been apprised of that. But how? Why? What possible motive could it have for attempting to kill us? Is it some kind of guard dog? What has made it so vicious?"

"Our training techniques are really quite . . . brutal here. I mean, for our purpose they are appropriate, but to the uninitiated—"

Gates held up an open palm in a traffic cop's signal.

"Don't squander your defensive arguments on me, Mr. Quist. Answer my question. Why is that damned brute of a dog trying to kill us?"

The chastened Quist stuck out his multiple chins, pulling bunched neck skin from beneath his collar.

"Sir," he said, "this dog and many like him have never been visibly nurtured by humans. It has never been trained to commands of the human voice. Humans have taunted it and even used some mild physical abuse. Mostly, though, it's been abuse of another kind. You could even call it psychological abuse, a deprivation of any form of companionship, a training program that teaches the animal to hate humans, to attack any living thing, in fact. This dog will attack its mother—"

"You mean *would.*"

"No, sir. In fact it *has* attacked its mother, but she being much the superior animal and he, the runt of his litter, nearly—"

"Never mind. I get the idea. The training program. Go on."

"Only when the dog attacks a living thing is it fed. These terriers have never eaten dry food. They kill to eat. Live animals. Fresh kills. I . . . er, might suggest this is one reason the budget for The Ranch is so . . . extraordinarily large."

Gates waved his hand impatiently. "The breeding, Mr. Quist."

"This lack of human contact. It's a kind of de-evolution to the wild for the dogs. They spend much of their time either in famine or in brief periods of feast. We have cultivated this behavior in order to test a pure dog specimen against our . . . other specimens bred here."

Gates was transfixed by the dog worrying the wire. "It isn't even barking or growling," he observed.

Quist raised his chins again, this time with an air of superiority. He brushed a hand over his bald pate, fluffing up the the two shoe brushes of hair above his ears.

"Mr. Gates, barking . . . roaring . . . growling . . . these are all—at times—unproductive behaviors for the hunter-killers of the wild. Lions or wolves will engage in it during mating or play or squabbles or when dominating another of their kind. But stalking and hunting are quite demanding of stealth and earnestness. Believe me when I say that this animal would kill you in minutes and devour you entirely over the course of several days—and the only noise would be the sounds of teeth cracking bone and tearing flesh."

Gates shuddered and backed away another step.

The terrier tried another tack. It backed off and leaped at the fence, paws, nails, and teeth hooking into the mesh.

"Christ, it's climbing out." Gates backed up farther, looking over his shoulder to find the gate to a second, taller fence that surrounded the inside pen. His alarm was apparent in both voice and expression. Beneath heavily oiled black hair his face had grown pasty white.

Quist held his ground, although his wrist now showed from the pocket of the smock as he withdrew the pistol an inch.

Gates saw the action and remembered the gun that had been issued to him on entry to this complex called The Ranch. He patted his own jacket pocket.

"Never turn your back on either the dogs or other

experimental subjects in this facility, sir." Quist took a step backward toward the gate even as he spoke.

The panting terrier worked its way up the eight-foot fence.

"Surely it won't escape the barbed wire," said Gates.

"Concertina," corrected Quist. "Get out of here— through the gate, sir. *Now!*"

The terrier reached the top of the barrier. It barely slowed for the concertina, with its razorlike butterfly wings of steel welded to galvanized wire.

Gates ignored his guide's instructions. He turned and ran to the opening and let himself out.

Quist kept backing.

"Shoot it!" Gates ordered.

"No," snapped Quist. "I want you to see this."

Gates saw. He felt his stomach lurch.

The terrier threaded his head between the coils of razored wire. It might have just as easily been pushing itself through all grass in a meadow, so unaffected was it by the wire. Except for the blood. The hooks and blades of the concertina caught on the hide of the muscular beast, slicing, tearing, and ripping it.

The dog pushed its hind quarters over the fence and struggled to free itself from the coils, without even a yelp or bark as it hung impaled on a hundred steely points.

"Quist, for crying out loud, evacuate the area. I command you, dammit."

The dog started to fall. But the coils and barbs held it atop the fence.

Gates heard the sounds of rainfall on the asphalt walkway between fences—scarlet rain splattering from eight feet.

Again the animal uttered that minute squeal of frustration. Again it renewed its struggle, wriggling between razored coils.

Gates saw the animal would be free of the concertina in seconds.

Quist put his hand on the gate.

"Get out of here," said Gates, straining the words between his clenched teeth.

The next sound was the splat of the dog on the ground.

Next came the scrabbling of dog nails on concrete.

Quist stepped out and slammed the gate, pulling the latch down to keep a barrier between men and dog. Gates had drawn his pistol. He held it in a shaking hand. He flinched as the dog stumbled and smacked wetly on the ground, sliding into the fence, leaving a wide skid mark of blood.

"I ought to kill *you*, Mr. Quist. Taking chances like that. If I knew how to use this thing . . ."

Quist stuck his multiple chins out defiantly. "Hyperbole, sir, with all due respect. Had you really wanted to kill me, you'd have shut the gate before I got here, locking me inside with that."

He pointed.

They both looked at *that*.

That was the terrier, its sliced muzzle thrust against the fence. One eye had been drained of the fluids that kept it inflated, rounded, and shiny. It pooched from its socket like a tiny deflated balloon. Strips of hide and flesh had been sliced from stem to stern as if its coat had been run through a paper shredder or a pasta cutter. The tendon above the hock on the left rear leg had been cut through, causing the paw to dangle uselessly. All four legs sluiced blood silently from the body to the ground, where four puddles grew into one as Gates watched.

"I get your point, Mr. Quist. Now, suppose you put the animal out of its misery so we can get on with this orientation."

"Misery, sir? No, this animal is not in misery. It is delighting in the pursuit of its supper—perhaps a bit disappointed at the short-term outcome of the hunt. But he's hardly discouraged. Watch."

The dog put a front paw into a hole in the fence and pulled itself upward. Soon all three good legs and the animal's teeth began working together in an awkward, fumbling climb.

Gates looked to the top of the fence. This outer fence stood ten feet tall. And the top split into two curves, one to the inside, one out. The bows of the curves were filled with concertina.

Quist said, "This fence was designed to keep things in *and* out, as you can see."

Gates grimaced weakly, his face gone even paler.

The dog fell backward six feet and splatted back down to the asphalt like a pile of wet towels.

The warm, muggy stench of gore hit him in the face, and Gates turned to vomit.

Quist smiled at the convulsing back of the man who'd been too distracted in Washington, D.C., these last months to even know what had gone on at The Ranch. He'd thought he'd been wrestling with monsters in the press and on Capitol Hill. He even thought this measly twit of a dog was a monster. Yet he hadn't even seen a monster—he wouldn't even know one when he did.

"This animal's sire actually climbed both fences and had to be killed by the security reaction squad."

Gates straightened up, turned, and peered over his handkerchief to see whether Quist was exaggerating. He shook his head in disbelief.

Quist nodded in contradiction, reflecting brilliant Nevada daylight off the shiny cap of skin covering his skull.

"Come, Mr. Gates. Now that you've seen this preliminary display by a relatively inferior animal, I want to show you a *real* beast."

"Later. I still feel . . . ill-disposed."

"Later, then."

Gates turned his back on the animal inside the fence and walked toward the clinic observation room. Quist took his own advice and kept his eye on the terrier as he walked. Again the dog climbed, this time to no more than four feet before it fell again. The dog tried to launch another climb. But weakened by the blood loss, it could do no more than bite into the wires.

Quist heard the crisp, hard snap of teeth breaking as the animal exerted its last in a frustrated death grip.

Only then did he finally turn his back on the terrier and enter the laboratory buildings.

Book One

". . . Their faces were as the faces of men . . . and their teeth were as the teeth of lions."

—REVELATION, Chapter 9

1

Images of Men

When the radio call rose up to his ears, Josh Avery was lying on his back, star-gazing. He had always found day skies boring. But the skies of night had intrigued him all his life, from the time he was a boy and used to find excuses to sleep outside to the time when he was a teenager and no longer made excuses, to the time he was an infantry private in Vietnam on his first tour. Later, as a warrant officer pilot on his second combat tour, he found he had not lost his fascination for the night skies. Now, though, when he was far past the age that he should have been a dreamer, he still gazed at stars, soaking up the tranquility radiated earthward by them. The stars perhaps were the guides to activity on Earth, Josh sometimes thought, when he had fallen deeply into one of his spells.

Any radio call would have broken the spell. But this faint, insistent droning sound was a call to battle. Josh bolted erect, forgetting about his night-daydreaming, instantly on alert. He slid his butt across the roof of the Huey and rolled over onto his belly all in one motion. His right hand found and gripped the metal handhold on top of the cabin. His left hand found the second grip a little lower. One boot kicked the right side of the fuselage, pushing in the hinged, spring-loaded door to the toehold built into the fuselage. Hanging by one arm and supporting himself by one foot, Josh opened the pilot's door and clambered inside, dropping into the pilot seat.

"Ingalls," he barked. "Are you untied?" Of course, the blades were not untied, and Josh knew it. It was his way of waking the staff sergeant, who should have already heard him climbing down from the cabin top, and if he had been alert enough, he would have already been running back to the rear to untie.

Meanwhile, Major Cliff Breen uttered a "roger" into the boom mike of his communications helmet and looked over at his mission commander, who was strapping into the armored seat of the UH-1H Huey.

"How did you know? You sure as hell must have good ears, Colonel."

"I didn't hear the words. But I was listening to the tone of the voice leaking out of your helmet."

"Eh?" Breen had leaned over and pulled away the ear cup of his helmet so he could hear what Josh was saying.

"Never mind." Josh pulled on his own helmet and stamped the intercom button on the floor. "Major, you should have had the engine cranking already."

Breen pointed at the tip of the main rotor extending out over the front of the cabin and opened his mouth as if he would say that the helicopter was still tied down. But even as he pointed, the blades began to move to the side, and they both knew that Ingalls was swinging the blade, pulling as fast as he could away from the tail rotor, trying to give it momentum for the start.

Josh reset the helicopter's throttle and squeezed the starter trigger, checking the pre-start setup as he went. The Huey's turbine began ticking faster and faster as the early stages of the start progressed. Then, as fuel began to ignite and spin the turbines faster with the expansion of the gases, the engine began to whine, whistle, and then to roar huskily. Josh saw the sparks of half a dozen cigarette coals being stripped from cigarette butts and being stomped into the dry Texas earth of summer a dozen yards away. So Josh knew the Special Operations team had shaken off their own sleepy vigil and begun their final preparations for the mission.

Breen read off the essential parts of the checklist as the main rotor blade began picking up speed and shaking the cabin. "N1 at forty percent. 'Start' switch off . . ."

"Get the radios," Josh ordered. He shut off the "start" fuel and advanced the throttle to the idle position.

He was all business now, no longer the daydreamer, no longer the stargazer. He felt the bootheels clumping around the cabin floor behind him and knew that Ingalls, the crew chief, had climbed back inside, had already made his check of the engine compartment and beneath the helicopter to make sure all things were functioning, and that there were no oil leaks. He checked the N1 tachometer and saw that it was sixty-eight percent.

In minutes the Special Operations team, nine enlisted men and a captain, would be climbing aboard with their weapons and night-vision devices.

Engine and transmission oil pressures were in the green.

He felt the helicopter begin rocking as men climbed on board, scrambling to predetermined positions.

The electrical meters read the proper voltage. He increased engine RPM to a full 6,600.

So far, so good. No delays of any kind. Josh began pulling up the collective pitch lever on his left side. As the helicopter grew light on its skids, he heard Breen sounding off in low tones the pre-takeoff of the instruments. He glanced over to his left and saw that his copilot had pulled down his night-vision goggles. Breen's hands poised near the controls, waiting for Josh's command.

"Clear left, clear right, clear behind, all passengers tucked in," said Ingalls.

"You have the controls," said Josh. He glanced over and saw Breen take the cyclic in his right hand. He felt the light touch on it and the collective pitch lever on his left.

"I have the controls."

"Let's get with it," Josh ordered. He turned off all interior lights and pulled down his own night-vision goggles, blinking rapidly to try to orient himself to the clear vision it gave him. He found that he did not care for the stark clarity, the two-dimensional greenish cast picture that he was able to see through the NVGs.

As the Huey swept up and out of the clearing, accelerating to about forty knots of airspeed and settling into an easy, loping cruise at the level of pin oaks and pecan trees of Fort Hood, he punched the start button on the sweep second hand of his clock and adjusted his knee board so that he could hit the time/distance milestones he and Breen had plotted earlier.

"I've got the controls," he said. Breen acknowledged and released the controls, then picked up his map to navigate. Josh knew that the men in the back would be navigating as well, each member of the Special Operations team responsible for himself in case the aircraft crashed and evasion was necessary. Every man aboard was responsible to take this practice mission as seriously as the real thing.

In any case, all the map reading was a redundancy to Josh Avery's knowledge of the Fort Hood training area. In five years of flying assignments here, both in conventional and non-conventional aviation units, he had acquired an uncanny sense for the terrain and could navigate entirely without reference to a map. Only in pre-flight preparations for a mission did he use one.

After fourteen minutes from the very southernmost tip of Fort Hood, Breen began reading the pertinent checkpoints as they grew closer and closer to their destination drop zones.

"Cowhouse Creek."

Josh rogered. In another four minutes of carefully picking their way among the trees, often flying with the rotor blades below the level of the treetops, Breen called off, "Shell Mountain Road just ahead." Josh accelerated to dash across the road at low level and continued navigating north-northeastward until the terrain began to rise sharply.

"Shell Mountains," said Breen.

"Ingalls, get ready to push them out in thirty seconds. Make damn sure there are no ropes trailing behind when I turn this thing around."

Josh came to a hover below the top of the cliff and grunted for Ingalls to disgorge six of the special troopers. Three went out each side of the Huey, rappelling down the sides. Josh watched through the chin bubble between his feet, observing the tips of their ropes through the cargo mirror that had been fixed in advance to give him a rearward, downward view. He had to make sure the ropes were touching the ground so none of the soldiers depending on him would come to the end of the rope before their feet touched earth. When he saw the ropes being reeled back up into the cabin, and as he felt the effect of more than half a ton of men and equipment dropping off, he adjusted power to maintain the altitude.

"Ropes are in," said Ingalls.

Josh began backing away from the hill, simultaneously pivoting the Huey around its mast until he had reversed the helicopter and was now flying out of the valley. He circled around the ridge, continually flying to his right until he had covered about another mile, and repeated the maneuver, dropping off the remaining four men. When the ropes had been hauled back in and he had turned the helicopter around, he noted with satisfaction that the clock's second hand was just now sweeping past the appointed time for the delivery for his second batch of men. He accelerated to sixty knots and turned the controls over to Breen to fly them on a course that would bring them back in ninety minutes, enough time for the Special Operations team to perform its mission and rally at the predetermined pickup point.

"Pretty much like clockwork, huh, sir?" said Ingalls.

"Everything exactly on the time hack," said Breen.

"Yeah," said Josh. "By my count this was the twenty-first time that we've done it this month without a hitch. Seems to me that we're ready for whatever operation these boys are supposed to be pulling. I think it's time we got our boss to let us know just exactly what we're up to."

• •

In ninety minutes, exactly on schedule, the Huey screamed over the treetops and settled into the low grass, the nose of the helicopter coming to rest just above the specially designed beacon that could only be seen through night-vision goggles and only from the air along the flight path the Huey had flown on its final approach. Josh gritted his teeth as he saw a rotund body rolling away from the beacon as their rotor wash caught up with the helicopter just before the skids touched down.

"Chrissakes, Cliff, you nearly crunched one," he muttered.

"Here come the rest," said Ingalls.

"Count 'em."

"I've got eleven."

"We're out of here," said Josh, and the Huey lifted off after spending less than fifteen seconds on the ground.

Within another ten seconds, Josh heard a static click as a headset microphone was keyed, releasing a growl into the crew's headsets.

"Who the hell was hotfooting it into that LZ? Was that you, Avery? Breen? Ingalls, these two birdbrains been letting you fly?"

Josh purred into his mike, "That was me, sir. We ran a little late on our course so we had to make up some time at the very end. We came in at about ninety knots, but we were landing right on a button, if I recall."

"On a button, my ass. You almost set it down on top of me. Do I look like a damned button? I had to leave the signal beacon on the ground."

"Hazards of combat, Colonel Vickers."

• •

They sat huddled over sweating mugs of beer at the West Fort Hood Officers' Club.

"Hazards of combat, my ass. Avery, you were fifteen seconds late and you overshot the LZ by a good ten feet because you were too hot on the landing approach. Fact is, the helicopter skidded about six feet once it touched down. I don't like that cowboy shit."

"Sorry, sir."

The sloping shoulders of Josh seemed to slump even more than usual, and his head sagged. But in contrast his bushy, wild-haired eyebrows ascended, revealing mild defiance in smoky blue eyes.

Colonel Tommy Vickers lifted his beer mug and drained half the contents, never taking his own gray eyes off Josh's. When he had slugged down his drink and rattled the mug off the tabletop, he said, "I ain't buying it."

Josh's long face broadened into a smile. "Buying what?"

"I ain't buying shit, Avery. You ain't sorry. You ain't serious about that military-courtesy *sir* stuff. And if I were to get that airheaded Cliff Breen into a corner and lock his heels together it wouldn't take me thirty seconds to sweat it out of him that it wasn't you at the controls at all. It was him. You're protecting his flaky ass. I've yet to see you drag the skids of a Huey six inches, let alone six feet."

Josh shrugged. "So you got me, Tommy. Don't make a federal case of it. Cliff was flying, but I take responsibility. We were shooting the bull out on the course and got a little behind on the clock. But I have to tell you, boss, this crew is getting a little weary of repetitive training. We had it down pat about fifteen nights ago. I don't know why we're still doing the same things. Is there something that you can tell us?" Again the bushy eyebrows rose up, stretching Josh's face into a caricature of himself. Above the eyebrows, his forehead rose tall and rounded. Below the curly, haphazard hair of those eyebrows, his nose came down straight and long. Josh's chin was rounded and strong and, like everything else about his outward appearance, long.

Vickers snarled, "We're soldiers, dammit. We train until it's time for the dress rehearsal to be over."

"Seriously, Tommy, we've gotten about as much value out of training here at Fort Hood as can be gotten. I'm not saying we should go to some exotic site, but it ought to be different. Do you realize I flew the entire mission tonight without once using a map? I've got this fort memorized. It's making me—the whole crew—lackadaisical. That's not good."

Vickers's expression softened. He nodded. "Josh, we've known each other for a long time. If we weren't such good friends, I'd be nailing your ass to the wall for your insubordination and familiarity with an inferior commissioned officer." He bared his teeth—evenly worn and small like baby teeth—in a mock smile. Josh acknowledged the weak attempt at humor with smile of his own. But he said nothing.

Vickers's neck—rather the swollen juncture of head and shoulders that passed for a neck—puffed out of the collar of his fatigue jacket.

"I wish I could give you more details, Josh, old

buddy. I can't. I can't tell you what we're doing or why we're doing it or when we're going to do it. It ought to be enough for military officers to know we got our orders. You've been on enough missions to know those orders don't always include giving out information, even to the mission pilot. I'm the only one allowed to have this information. It's compartmentalized down to me and me alone."

Josh nodded thoughtfully and swigged his beer. "I don't want you to give the mission away, for chrissakes, Tommy. But I do think that we ought to go someplace else for a couple weeks. Even if we fly the same kind of mission, at least it would be more of a challenge because it would be unfamiliar. Another thing—why can't Cliff Breen and I have a Blackhawk? Surely the U.S. Army is not going to fly a mission like this in a helicopter left over from the Vietnam War. If this thing is so damned important—"

"Who said it was an army mission?" Vickers opened his eyes wide in an exaggerated look of astonishment.

"So it's not?"

"I ain't saying it is, and I ain't saying it ain't. Now, you know better than to try to play games to get information out of me, Josh. I will tell you this, and I don't expect to hear it coming out of every crew chief's mouth on the entire damn flight line—we ain't going to get any Blackhawks. The UH-60 is not in the game plan."

Josh opened his mouth as if to protest, but the only sound that came out was a throaty hiss as something had suddenly occurred to him. "Ahhh . . ." He clamped down on the sound. Vickers had just revealed a key intelligence clue to the mission. If the aircraft used in this project was no longer in production for U.S. military forces, then it was to be a covert operation that couldn't be tied to the army.

Vickers seethed in anger. He struck the tabletop with a meaty fist, causing the two beer mugs to jump. "Now, goddammit, you stop trying to pick my brain for classified information." His tone became threatening. "Avery, it wouldn't matter to me if I went out and found another pilot to do this mission. I could do it because I like you and don't want nothing to happen to you, or I could do it because you're pissing me off. It don't make no mind to me. Look at us."

Vickers waved his hand back and forth between the two of them. "We're just like a couple of those old Hueys, and you know it. I'm fifty damn years old and in my last year of active duty. My thirtieth damned year. I know I'm never going to make a star. I been knowing that for the last ten years. So what I been doing is taking on missions to try to keep some interest in my life, to try to make some kind of contribution, to try to keep away from some broke-dick staff job."

He jabbed a finger at Josh. "Don't you be looking away from me. I want you to look into my eyes so you know I'm telling the truth, so you know I know. What I know is, you're on the same career track as me. You're just like one of those goddamned Hueys that you're always flying. You're obsolete. If you were so damned hot, you'd be commanding an aviation battalion instead of being out here pulling duty like some young warrant officer flying around the fort. Don't shake your head at me. You know damned well I'm telling the truth."

Josh looked the shorter man in the eye. What he saw was himself. No, he wasn't the short, squat, tough-talking, brash, red-necked infantryman as Vickers, somebody who'd as soon fight as shake hands. But he was the same leftover relic of a previous war who could never quite adjust to the modern developments in the army, the computers, and the constant peacetime preoccupation with reorganizing, renaming, and relocating. No denying it. Something had happened to him after Vietnam. And it was not the lack of a parade or other recognition. He was not offended by the lack of respect from the citizenry. Nobody had ever spat on him.

Fact was, he didn't even notice pacifism, or if he did, it didn't seem to matter. All his friends were hard-drinking, tough-talking Vietnam veterans still in uniform. They clung together like a brotherhood, thereby insulating themselves from what was happening in the mainstream of American society. They didn't care about long-haired veterans always whining about not being appreciated. Besides drinking and getting laid now and then, they had no interest in anything.

Vickers was right. Josh knew that as he squinted hard, even angrily into the eyes of the short, overweight colonel. They were both the same thing. Same as the Huey. "Anachronisms," he murmured.

"Don't use ten-dollar words on me."

"Sorry, Tommy," he whispered. "You're right."

"Damned right I'm right. The whole damned rest of the army is flying around in those new Blackhawks and Apaches and experimental stealth helicopters and whatnot. But remember one thing, Josh. Those bastards are flying around in circles. Pretty soon they'll be flying up their own asses. They're never going to get any action unless there's a war. So that leaves them either hoping for a war so they can test out all their tactics, or praying for peace, which is the wimp's way of looking at the world. Me and you, boy . . . we're going to get some action. You're going to get your pants lit on fire before long. I tell you, we have found us a real, live enemy that needs killing, and somebody has given us the green light to take him out. Now, don't that make your pecker grow?"

Josh nodded thoughtfully. Another lie. He didn't get excited about risking his life anymore. He'd found something in his life of more lasting value than dangerous thrills. Like most everything else of value he'd ever encountered, he didn't even know how to deal with it . . . her.

• •

At midnight, Josh wheeled his sports car into the driveway of her Copperas Cove home. He began unpiling his lanky, unwieldy body, six feet four inches tall, from the driver's seat. He had loved the hot wheels, the feeling of almost-flight the turbo-sport gave him. Usually. But tonight it seemed like such a literal pain in the back to be peeling himself out of the car's cramped cockpit. Suddenly, all the things that Vickers had said—all the painfully truthful things that Vickers had barked at him in the club—seemed to drain his enthusiasm and not a little of his self-respect right onto the ground, as if someone had opened the petcock to his soul. What a prospect! Here he was, forty-two years old, and a flop. What a time to discover that he'd wasted most of his adult life, and his childhood, too, for that matter. He'd advanced so far in his career as a lieutenant colonel pilot that he was now pulling the duty any warrant officer right out of flight school could be doing. He was an airborne taxi driver, just as Vickers had said.

And what was the payoff? A few thrills. Imagine. At his age. A thrill-seeking forty-two-year-old, slightly potbellied, partially arthritic, over-the-hill army lieutenant colonel who probably wouldn't advance as far as that troll, Vickers. Times had changed. The army had changed. And he'd found himself completely left behind. A modern dinosaur.

He'd known it since Vietnam. All memories about things that really counted in his life had stopped running on the videotape replay in his mind after his third combat tour in Vietnam. In reality, he had known then that he had learned all he could learn in that war experience. For the war was ending, and he was leaving early on this last tour, among the last of the American soldiers to depart. The army that he was returning to was going to be peacetime baloney. Everything had turned to sham. He knew he should have hung up the uniform then. He knew he was a has-been. He had suppressed that knowledge, as if he could deceive himself. But he hadn't been able to deceive Vickers. Vickers knew. Vickers had lived through the same damnable and damning experience. At least the old semi-alcoholic was honest about it. All that was left was to seek thrills. Drink a few beers. Brag with the other dinosaurs. Get a stray whore to listen now and then to the farfetched tales that shouldn't have even been told for security reasons.

It didn't matter anyway, Josh realized. Nobody—not even their drinking buddies—believed the damned war stories. Lately, nobody even wanted to hear about Vietnam flying stories.

Admit it, he told himself. *You're washed up.*

Never had that become more apparent than in the last sixty days or so. He had completed his twenty years in the army. He could have retired if he wanted to. What did that mean?

It meant that he could no longer use the excuse to himself that he was just marking time, just putting in his years to get to the pension. He had always said before that he could stand on his head for the years that it would take to get to his retirement. Then he wouldn't have to put up with the pretense anymore. Then he could hang up the fatigues and start a new career.

But he hadn't given the first thought to that new career. All that lay ahead of him was this mission and perhaps some vague notion of a mission beyond that. All he had wanted to do in those years since Vietnam was find something adventurous to do. He was constantly seeking thrills. What did it amount to? Nothing.

There was no sense of achievement. He could not even tell his new woman. . . .

He opened up the door and dropped his flight bag in the closet. He found her waiting, sitting in the dim light beside a lamp, reading. She looked at him and smiled, her bright teeth catching the light and gleaming like some glitzy toothpaste commercial. It was a genuine smile because she didn't feel as sorry for him as he did for himself. Marilyn. *Poor woman,* he thought. *Poor, pathetic woman. She loves me.*

2

. . . .

THE RANCH

The desert wind had been blowing all day long, leaving clouds of dust and sand suspended thousands of feet in the air. So the sun settled over the horizon, bright red, slinking out of sight, leaving fiery orange streaks across the dirty sky.

Edward Gates stood watching the sunset out the window of his quarters, feeling absorbed by the red glow to the west. A vast, empty expanse of land unfolded before him to the west, rising into the hills. All the earth that he could see was bathed in a monochromatic blue-gray. The edge of the sky was a brilliant, fiery line of gold that turned into an orange-red glow. The colors grew even more brilliant as the sun sank lower. Nothing he'd ever seen on the East Coast had compared to the glory he now witnessed. It almost made him forget why he was here.

When he heard the knock at the door it startled him, although he had been expecting it. He turned and spoke at the door, "Mr. Quist?"

"Mr. Gates. Time for you to meet the laboratory staff."

After a brisk walk down stark, white-tiled hallways, Quist opened a door that looked like all the other doors in the hallway, and stood back for Gates to enter. As he walked into the room, Gates found it more hospitable, perhaps because it had carpeting and a couple of department-store prints hanging on the walls, giving a touch of color to the room—although nothing would ever match the scene he'd just experienced outside, his first desert sunset. The briefing room was a large conference room with a semi-oval table twenty feet long. Around the table stood twenty chairs at comfortable intervals, and at each chair stood a member of the laboratory staff.

Quist showed him around the room, introducing him to each man, giving their names and titles. Gates knew he would never remember the names; he would have to learn them. What did strike him was the monotony of this crew. Each was formal, addressing him as "Mr. Gates." Each had a handshake that was too nervous and far too clammy. Obviously, each was anxious at meeting the boss, who had been merely a name from afar in the past year and a half. The only other impression that he got was an odd one—that each man kept his left hand in the pocket of his lab coat as he shook hands.

Well, he thought, he had given Quist free rein to staff The Ranch and to oversee all the engineering projects. So it should be little wonder that each member now being introduced seemed to be a stuffed-shirt, cookie-cutter image of Quist himself.

All but one.

Finally Quist introduced him to a man who stood shorter than all the rest. He looked as though he were cut from the same academic mold as all the others.

This man was even shorter than Gates himself. He had a plastic smile, but a warm hand. Because of that, his was the only name Gates remembered.

"Gregor Munn."

"Nice to meet you, Mr. Munn," Gates said. He shook his hand a little longer to indicate that he was sincere. Besides, it was kind of a relief to be shaking a warm hand.

"Gregor is a German-born researcher," Quist informed him.

"Really?" Gates replied. "I've a German background myself. We'll have to converse about all things German sometime."

"Indeed," said Munn.

Gates hesitated a second, wanting to say something else in the way of small talk but realizing that wouldn't be fair to the rest of the crew, with whom he had not shared even a moment's conversation. He immediately liked Gregor Munn. Among other things he had the self-assurance to keep his hands out of his pockets.

He turned to the table and took the spot indicated at the head of the table. He waved his hand, signaling the rest of the men to sit.

"Gentlemen, I deeply regret that I have been unable to pay closer attention to the worthwhile and industrious activities that have been going on here in the past year to two years. Unfortunately, matters in Washington have demanded my attention. The activities of a certain quasi-governmental organization were brought to the attention of the administration and Congress. Only an industrious effort by many patriotic people was able to prevent the judicial branch of government from becoming deeply involved in settling the issue.

However, let it be said that the existence of a domestic intelligence organization—alleged to be called The Corporation—has been found to be unsubstantiated."

Gates watched as men nodded and murmured assent and faint praise. Then he continued speaking.

"What I have been able to determine . . . is that a great collection of scientific research materials has been misunderstood, but now, at least in Washington, no such record of scientific data or The Corporation exists. Your data are well protected and very much appreciated. As of this moment, all the activities that are legal and worthwhile have been salvaged from the earlier, misunderstood operation. I'm happy to say the genetic research that you all have been involved in— research that will be put to good and everlasting use for the welfare of our country—now resides here at The Ranch."

Gates moved away from the table and indicated that the rest of the group should do the same. "I'm not one for speeches. It's going to take me a few days to get my feet on the ground and understand exactly what you've been doing. I will want to meet each of you and learn how you fit into the overall picture. I will need to be briefed in great detail in order to catch up with what is going on. I assure you that I will not be insulted if you should treat me as one who knows absolutely nothing. My activities in Washington have greatly reduced my ability to keep up with what has gone on out here. However, in the coming weeks I intend to be briefed fully and to make an active contribution to your own scientific endeavors. And now, if Mr. Quist will show us to the cocktails and buffet, we'll no doubt become better acquainted."

Gates drank his gin and tonic, savoring the bitter

taste of the quinine water. "Mr. Quist, this is certainly a somber group you have assembled here, present company excepted." He nodded toward Quist and Gregor Munn, exempting them from his appraisal of the group.

Quist gazed around the room, nodding here and there to groups of men standing around with their hands in their pockets, some snacking, some drinking. "I would say that the researchers are quite preoccupied, Mr. Gates."

"Well, I suppose it has something to do with the boss swooping into town—if you could call it that," said Gates. "My former superior would have had a more vulgar phrase to describe them."

Quist's eyebrows went up.

"He would have, citing his crude vocabulary, called them a bunch of tight-asses."

Quist smiled, straining the expression through his own taut facial muscles.

Gregor Munn took a drink of his club soda, a thoughtful expression working its way down his wrinkled forehead to his pursed lips. Finally, he said, "Tight-asses? I don't believe that expression has any meaning to me in a practical sense. However, it does conjure up a visual image that's somewhat odd. Is this like . . . constipation?"

Gates laughed, in part because Munn's expression had remained so deadpan. Maybe he was as tight-assed as all the others, after all.

Quist did not laugh. He said, "Mr. Gates, I believe that the group will relax after we are able to give you our demonstration tomorrow. Right now the staff is extremely nervous. Everyone believes quite a lot is riding on our ability to impress you."

"Rest assured, Mr. Quist, I was more than impressed by this afternoon's demonstration. However, I fail to see what that dog and its violent behavior has to do with the kind of scientific endeavor we're sponsoring here. I'm more interested in observing the highly touted creation you have led me to believe now exists."

"Tomorrow you will see the creation in action," Munn said.

Gates laughed nervously. "Ordinarily, I would not appreciate the mysterious air that all of you have generated about this demonstration tomorrow."

He stepped over to the sideboard and set his glass down at the edge. "But I have to tell you that I am really quite enjoying the suspense."

The glass tumbled off the side of the counter and shattered on the floor.

"How clumsy of me." Gates squatted and reached for the glass fragments.

"No!"

The outburst startled Gates, causing him to jerk back involuntarily from the glass.

"No," Quist repeated. "No, Mr. Gates, don't bother with that. We have employees who can take care of it. You might . . . cut yourself."

Gates stood and brushed his hand off against his pants, although he had not touched anything. "I . . . you terrified me with that shout."

Quist smiled nervously and when he spoke, he actually quivered. "I'm sorry, Mr. Gates . . . I assure you I was only thinking of your best interests."

Gates looked at Munn, exchanging a nervous smile for a plastic one. "It was nothing, really," Gates said. I . . ." He gazed around the room suddenly feeling uneasy. He saw that from every knot of men, some-body was watching. He felt self-conscious and nervous —and something else. He felt gooseflesh on the back of his neck, as if something had gone terribly wrong. Certainly more wrong than a simple broken glass. He looked at Munn and smiled as falsely as the German. It occurred to him, as another chill ran down his spine, that it was not so much the attention of the others that had upset him. Something about Munn, something extraordinarily odd in the German seemed to be generating the chill he felt.

COPPERAS COVE, TEXAS

The warmth of the morning sun on the east side of the house, the master-bedroom side, baked Josh awake. The hour was midmorning, and already the sun had been heating the house, overpowering the laboring air conditioner for about six hours. Somewhere in the house Josh heard a telephone ringing. He rolled over, tossing off the sheets and pulling at the boxer shorts that had bunched up in his crotch. *Why do you wear those things at all?* Marilyn would ask him about once a week, usually after making love, usually when he got up to put them back on before going to sleep. *Don't you realize,* she said, *that modern man doesn't wear those lousy things? Look at you.* She would point at the part of him pointing back at her. *Look at those things. They don't even stay closed. They don't even keep you in. They must be horrible to sleep in. Every morning you wake up pulling them out of the crack of your . . .* His part in the conversation would be to say, *Leave me alone. I'm not an eighties kind of guy, anyhow. Besides,*

*what do you know about the shorts mankind wears?
You some kind of expert on men's shorts?*

It was their form of post-lovemaking non-intimacy.
Nothing so straining as romantic talk, yet something
more intimate than sweet nothings. He didn't know
what it meant to her, but he had the feeling that the
growing dialogue on boxer underwear, a dialogue built
upon week by week as another brick of conversation
was added, actually kept him from having to talk
about things like love and marriage, things that he had
no time to contemplate, let alone talk about.

"Quit playing with yourself."

He straightened out his shorts and closed the opening. A smile tugged at his lips, letting them peel apart.
He lay there with his eyes closed. "It gets my circulation going. It's my way of waking up," he said. "If you
were the kind of woman who could give me real satisfaction, I wouldn't need to play with myself."

"We can talk about whose inadequacies are worse
another time," she said. "The phone's for you. Vickers." The last word, the colonel's name, had a way of
escaping with an extra bite of hardness from her
mouth.

"What's he want?" Even as he asked the question,
he sat up on the bed knowing what the answer would
be.

"He wouldn't say. He never says. The man's a jerk.
He's crude and corrupting."

"As if I need to be saved from corruption," Josh
murmured. "Are we leaving, do you suppose?"

"As if the poisoned old toad would tell me . . . as
if you would."

Josh finally unglued his eyelids and shook his head
at the bedside clock, as if he could not believe its dig-

its. "Too early. We're not scheduled to even be at the airfield until after sundown. Wonder what's on his mind?"

She was out of the bedroom, already walking down the hall toward the squeal of a child in the distance. "Why don't you answer the phone and find out, instead of sitting there playing with yourself?" The playful tone had crept back into her voice. He picked up the phone.

• •

"Eat your salad, Josh." Vickers stuffed a forkful of lettuce into his own tiny-toothed mouth as if to demonstrate.

Josh watched the food disappear and saw an image of himself pitchforking hay into the giant maw of the barn back home. When was that? How old had he been? Twelve? And how long would it be before he'd be just like this? What had Marilyn called him? Poisoned toad? The no-neck look certainly gave that impression.

"Don't you want to know why I got you out of bed? Eat your salad. What're you grinning about?"

"Nothing . . . I just can't think of eating this. It's breakfast time for me. This salad doesn't cut it, Tommy. Besides, I'm getting a case of the nerves. You were excited. You don't get excited over nothing. And you don't wake me up when I've not gotten all my crew rest unless there's something we're supposed to do. My guess is that we're going to leave, and you're going to sit there and play games with me until you're perfectly ready to tell me. Fine. I can wait. I can watch you stuff your face like a bovine milk generator. I've got time if you do."

Vickers's face darkened for a moment. He squinted

at Josh for a full ten seconds, a fragment of lettuce wadded in the corner of his open mouth. Finally he shrugged. "Bovine, my ass." He snaked his tongue around the lettuce, drew it into his cavernous mouth, and swallowed. "All right, I can tell you we're leaving this training area. I want you to get ready for duty just like you do every day. Only this time when you report to the flight line on the south ramp you'll be boarding an airplane instead of pre-flighting a helicopter. We won't be back for a while. Don't make any phone calls and don't tell anybody in advance. Everybody else that is going to show up down there is not going to get this kind of advance warning. We can't trust anyone else. Got that, wise guy? Now, what are you smiling about?"

"I didn't realize I had so much influence over you, Tommy. I mean, after I give you a hard time last night about getting a real live mission for us, getting us moved off Fort Hood, you deliver within hours."

"My ass. It's nothing to do with you. Just make sure you're ready to go when you get to the flight line. And by that I mean don't be prepared to come back for a good long while. If that means you have to make some excuses to your woman, you do that. But don't give anything away."

"I love it when you get nervous, Tommy. It just absolutely thrills me to see you so anxious about something like this. When was the last time I gave anything away on a secret mission, anyhow?"

"I'm not nervous, Josh. You just can't tell the difference between nervous and deadly."

"My ass," said Josh, tossing Vickers's own expression back at him.

• •

Vickers strutted around the flight line nervously, paying attention to every trivial detail, from the appearance of the men to the loading of the helicopter. Once again, Josh felt a twinge of disappointment that it would be a Huey, an H model converted from the D model, one difference being that its pitot tube, a dull spear essential to measuring air speed, poked out its nose instead of the cabin top.

Josh climbed up the ramp into the military cargo plane and found a place that would give him some leg room. Best thing for him to do now was stay out of the way of the enlisted men loading the craft. He strapped his gear to the spot, taking up enough room with his flight bag, his helmet, and some extra clothing he had packed in another bag so that he would have enough room to stretch out and sleep on the fold-down jump seats. No telling how far they would have to go, how long they'd be in the chilly, drafty cargo compartment with their helicopter.

He pulled his cap down over his eyes and leaned back, his chin on his chest as if dozing. But he was not sleepy. In fact, this was his usual time of day for awakening. He hid his face, partly to shut out the others, to be left alone, and partly to savor the recollection his last frantic hour with Marilyn.

She was warm and giving, urgently so. He'd only told her that he'd be going and that he wouldn't be returning for a while. She took it as a permanent departure. That was her inclination every time he left. She believed that without the wedding band she had no real proof he'd ever come back.

Normally, her way of keeping a hold on him was giving him absolute freedom, a leash so long that he wouldn't feel trapped. "I know it wouldn't take much for you to feel as if I was trying to trick you into getting married." Of course, it wouldn't. She had two children. She was the widow of a warrant officer pilot whose helicopter had exploded atop a training area of Fort Hood one night three years ago. She had two daughters, one ten and the other barely three. It would not be easy for a woman who taught business courses at Central Texas College to snare a husband from the available men in this area as long as she had those children.

So he knew it must have been difficult for her to give him the freedom she had granted. When he left for overnight trips, even when those trips lasted a week or longer, she did not quiz him. She accepted his explanations that he was involved in flying missions that couldn't be talked about. He couldn't tell her a thing about them, and she would not be allowed to ever indicate that he flew missions that couldn't be talked about. "It's really that serious? That sensitive?" she had asked him once. He had looked at her and said, "Yes," and she had never brought up the subject again. But she bit her lip often in the hours before he left, nibbling at her flesh the way anxiety nibbled at her soul.

Every time he told her he would be leaving, she clung to him in an explicit show of a basic insecurity. She felt that he might leave her. Or else she felt that he might be going off to crash his helicopter just like another man she'd loved.

Of course, he did know she loved him. But couldn't say for sure whether he loved her. Love. It was a question he had never before been preoccupied with. Until Marilyn. She often made him wonder what this thing called love could really be. She seemed to be so capable of it with her children. She acted as if she loved him; she told him often enough, too. It scared the hell out of him, just as making a career decision would have scared him if he'd ever made one on his own.

He had said he loved her. The words came almost exclusively at moments of high passion. Afterward, he felt guilty about saying them. *You shouldn't tell somebody that as a way of manipulating them,* he told himself. He tried to say the same words later, when his emotions had flattened out. But he couldn't. The three words would rise up into his throat, but then his neck would double-clutch, suffocating them. He wondered what that meant.

The jabbering of Vickers in the distant reaches of his hearing rose to a new, urgent pitch. Josh could not hear the words, but he could tell from the tone that someone was getting an ass-chewing. He opened his eyes and cocked his head toward the flight line a hundred yards away, where Vickers waved a jabbing finger under Major Cliff Breen's nose. Josh turned his wrist to look at his watch. Breen was late—that is, he was exactly on time, which was late according to Vickers's watch, perpetually set to ten minutes ahead of the rest of the world.

Josh shook off his preoccupation with Marilyn. He tenderly put her away on a mental shelf that he could come back to later. He would come back to relish the memory of their last hour together. He stood up and strode off the back of the airplane, walking his long-legged gait toward the shouting colonel and the nodding major. The remainder of the ground and aircrews bustled about finding work to do, even when there might not be any. Everybody understood that when

Vickers flew into one of his rages, furious activity remained the safest refuge.

By the time Josh had reached the pair, Breen had been dismissed. He scuttled toward the aircraft hauling his baggage away.

When the major had scurried out of earshot, Josh said, "How is a guy supposed to get any sleep with you screaming out here on the flight line, Tommy? You really ought to relax. The man wasn't even late."

"Listen, you SOB, don't you stick up for him when you don't even know what all that was about."

Josh bit down on his lip. He could see that Vickers was in no mood for familiarity, let alone argument. He nodded thoughtfully. "What did he do?"

"He *wasn't* late. He was here fifteen minutes ago and then disappeared after he found out we were deploying. When I nailed his ass, he said he had to run back up to flight operations and get something from the snack bar. Snack bar ain't even open."

Josh cocked his head and raised an eyebrow. "So?"

"He showed me a fistful of candy bars, like that was some kind of excuse. The somebitch probably made a phone call."

"Colonel, you need to relax. Everything is under control. I know Cliff. He wouldn't let our little secret slip. He's a good man and a reliable officer. If I were you, I'd take a quick walk around the flight line to release some of that energy of yours before we get on the plane. You're going to be like a caged tiger by the time we—"

"Don't patronize me, Avery. This is an important mission, goddammit."

One of the plane's engines began whistling. Then another let out a groan. As the engines fired up, Josh turned to watch currents of heat roiling from the exhaust openings.

Josh moved toward the plane. He looked over his shoulder and saw Vickers running heavily toward a staff car. The car tore out, leaving the flight ramp, sprinting up the road toward flight operations. Josh thought it strange that Vickers would dash off at the last minute, after getting so upset with Breen about a handful of stupid candy bars. He stood on the ramp for ten minutes, enduring the acrid fumes of the plane until he saw Vickers's car racing back toward the flight line. Then he shrugged and boarded. Maybe the burned-out old toad got hungry thinking about those damned candy bars. He strapped himself in and settled down to reminisce taking Marilyn off the shelf again.

3

• • • • • • • • • • • • • • • •

LAWRENCE, KANSAS

He tried to hug her, to calm her, but she wouldn't stand still for it. She stiff-armed him in the chest to ward him off. She left him standing as she went to gather more of her belongings to throw in the suitcases she had splayed open across the living-room floor.

"PJ," he called after her, "how can you just run off? You're halfway through a graduate program. I'm just getting started on the faculty. For the first time in my life I'm happy. How can you just throw all of that up into the air and run out from beneath it before it hits the ground?"

He could tell by the sounds of drawers and doors opening and shutting that she was ignoring him. She burst back into the room, a strong, angular woman now, having grown lean, even gaunt, since he'd met her a year and a half ago on that mountain. Indeed, PJ Payne had hardened since the night her husband was killed on that peak in Montana. He wondered if she'd begun to petrify.

She dumped a load of toiletries into the smaller of the two suitcases.

"PJ, I said—"

"I heard you, Grayson. You don't have to go. You don't have to run off from all the things that have become dear to you here." She folded her bony arms into acute angles and stood looking directly into his eyes. Her green, piercing eyes penetrated to his very core. The look corresponded to the tone in her voice that served notice she wouldn't relent.

Grayson Kirk felt his own brown eyes begin to flicker in the heat of her stare. He drew his eyelids down in an intentional blink, a pair of eye shields that released her grip on him for a moment. "All I meant was, why can't we let it go? We've made a new start. Nothing we can do can bring back—"

"I'm *not* trying to bring Mark back. My only reason for existence now is revenge. Grayson, all those times I told you I loved, *love* you in the last year and a half, I wasn't lying. But I also loved Mark. They killed my husband, dammit. I'm going to get even somehow. I'm going to bring them down."

"For all we know, they've already been shut down. After the mountain blew up, after the operation was exposed, after Congress began investigating, things happened—you know they did. We heard from more than one source that there is no longer a group called The Corporation. They've been eliminated."

"In that case, I'll just be taking a short vacation in Texas. I'll look around and, finding nothing, I'll return. I'll be back in a week."

He grasped her shoulders and tried to pull her toward him. She stiffened, refusing to be comforted. In a way, Grayson Kirk knew that this kind of reserve overtly demonstrated her feelings for him. She would never really love anybody the same as she had loved

Mark Payne. She would always hold that little something in reserve. Nobody would resuscitate the part of her that had died atop Judith Peak.

Kirk's own manner hardened a bit.

"PJ, you mean you're going to run off just because you got a telephone call from one of your so-called spies? Are you going to drop everything for the rest of your life each time you receive a mysterious message? Is this the kind of life you want us to lead?"

"Not us. Not you, Grayson. Me. It's the kind of life I'm going to lead until I'm satisfied. Up there—in Montana, you got your revenge."

He bristled at the suggestion that his only concerns were selfish ones. His face contorted with his anger, the muscles, shortened by surgery and tightened by scar tissue on the right side, pulled up into that wiseacre grin that had gotten him into trouble so often in the past.

"Bullshit, PJ. You got all the revenge, all the satisfaction you ought to be entitled to here on Earth. Nobody has been after us in more than eighteen months. This is no more to you than an obsession. I've been in the spook business, PJ, remember? I spent most of a career pulling sneaky stunts for my government and the army. I've got contacts, too, and as far as anybody knows, there is no longer any such thing as The Corporation. It's *over.* Can't you just let it die? Can't you go on with your life?"

She braced herself, hunching her shoulders, refusing to engage in the argument. "I'm going to Texas." She turned and walked toward the bedroom. The phone rang, stopping her in mid-stride. They both looked at it. Finally he picked it up. Without a word he extended the receiver to her.

She took it and gave her false name, the one assigned to her in the witness-protection program. She listened for a second, then said weakly, "I see . . . yes . . . yes . . . right away . . . thanks."

She held out the telephone to him but dropped it before he could take it.

"Rogers. The man who called last night. He . . . they found him dead this morning."

"Oh, my God."

"They're after Rogers's contact. And they're after us. Again."

THE RANCH

Edward Gates felt a twinge of discomfort when people kept opening doors for him. He preferred results to servitude. Gregor Munn and Quist, the chief researcher, stood outside a pair of double doors waiting for him to enter a cavernous room. Gates realized he'd stepped into the mouth of an amphitheater. Terraces of chairs rose up from a children's gym in the center of the room. A large cage was situated on the stage. In it were monkey bars, an overhead ladder, and an obstacle course made up of cement blocks big as coffee tables. It was a stark metal-and-concrete setting with a drain in the center of the gently sloping floor. It looked like a cage in the primate section of a zoo.

Gates did not start walking down the stairs into the heart of the room until he saw that the wire enclosure around the cage included a roof. He didn't relish the idea of watching another crazed dog trying to scale a fence after him.

"No more dogs?" he asked hopefully.

Quist swept a hand, indicating they should descend

the stairs. "Mr. Gates, the rest of the research staff is awaiting us. I think you will find this demonstration to be considerably more striking and more substantial than what you saw yesterday."

"No more dogs, then."

Quist remained noncommittal. Gregor Munn grasped Gates's elbow and gently urged him into the cavern. Gates walked reluctantly down each step toward the cage, not wanting to get close but realizing the seat of honor was only six feet from the wire.

"Mr. Gates, I'm going to be running the show today," Munn said. "You will find the quality of research that I am going to be demonstrating today intense and dramatic. Please indulge the mysterious nature of this exercise till now; for its purpose is about to be revealed in full."

Barely reassured, Gates moved into his chair, nodding at the other researchers. Again he noticed they all seemed tense, all with their hands in their coat pockets. Suddenly, he felt chilly. So he put his own hands into his jacket pockets, feeling a pale comfort as his fingers closed on the grip of his pistol.

Instead of taking a seat beside Gates, Gregor Munn walked down to the locked gate of the enclosure and reached inside the neck of his shirt. He withdrew a loop of string with a key tied to it, and unlocked the padlock. He swung the cage door open and stepped inside. Reaching through the access holes in the wire, Munn inserted the padlock back into its hasp and locked himself into the enclosure.

Unaccountably, Gates felt a sudden wave of relief wash over him as the padlock mechanism snapped home. Certainly, he reasoned, there'd be no dogs in that cage now. Not with a man inside.

All at once Gates realized that the assembled research staff had been affected by the same feeling of relief. Shoulders that had been hunched were now relaxed. Hands emerged from pockets. Men wiped their palms on their thighs to dry them. He looked at Quist, who smiled. Gates realized it was the first time he'd seen the chief researcher at ease.

Quirst said, "Now, please watch the video screen."

Gates tried to focus on the television that hung on the wall, but the sight of the German inside the cage stole his attention.

Munn stripped. He shed his jacket first, folded it, and laid it on the floor next to the wire. He kicked off his shoes even as he was unbuttoning his shirt.

The black screen flickered to life, distracting Gates for a moment. This picture showed a hallway with barred doors along its length and a larger door at the far end. He heard the scratching of static from speakers beside the screen.

He watched Gregor Munn step out of his trousers, fold them, and place them on top of his jacket and shirt. He peeled off his socks, and clad only in a pair of gym shorts and the loop of string that held the key around his neck, he spoke to Gates.

"The graphic demonstration which you are about to see, Mr. Gates, is not intended to fill you with revulsion, although it might, anyhow. In fact, this entire demonstration has been replicated a number of times and, as scientific experiments go, it has been established with absolute certainty that your hypothesis about military applications of genetic engineering was valid. While you were preoccupied in Washington, your staff here has justified the effort and resources expended at this laboratory site."

Munn's orientation speech was cut short by the sound of a dog's bark. Everyone's attention, including Munn's, snapped to the video screen above the cage. A metallic click and the singing of a spring being stretched preceded the picture of a door snapping open. A dark rectangle appeared in the center of the screen. Then again came the scratching sound, and Gates realized it was not static in the audio system. Somewhere off camera was a dog, its claws scraping at cement.

"Not another dog," he murmered. Suddenly the dark spot on screen burst to life as a black-and-brindle bull terrier exploded from the opening and dashed down the hallway toward the camera. The violence and suddenness of the attack caused Gates to recoil in his chair. He secretly glanced sideways to see if others had been affected by the dog. Most of them had seen this demonstration before, he realized. Hardly anyone seemed startled. Instead, each sat grimly, jaws set.

The dog leaped directly at the video camera lens and Gates recoiled again. The impact of a body against a metal door came across both the video sound system and a metal gate against the back wall of the enclosure.

Gates was galvanized as this door also flew open. The dog disappeared from the field of view of the television's eye and squirted through the doorway into the cage with the German researcher, Gregor Munn.

Gates felt the electricity of fear jolt him to his feet. He hollered, "Quist! Get him out of there!" His voice skipped to a higher pitch even as the dog sprang from the floor at Munn. Everybody in the room froze— except the pair inside the cage.

Munn offered his left wrist to the dog as it exploded

from the floor. The dog's mouth gaped open, exposing jagged mountains of teeth.

At the last second, Munn jerked his wrist straight up out of the dog's reach and sidestepped the trajectory of the hurtling animal. The animal threw its head back even as it was passing under the wrist and tried to grab the man.

Like a matador using his own arm as a cape against this bull terrier, Munn raised the arm another six inches and the jaws snapped shut with a metallic pop. The dog landed awkwardly, hitting the floor on his rump and flopping over on his back. But even as it skidded along the floor into the enclosure, the animal twisted, trying to regain its footing. Its front claws tore at the cement, leaving white marks as its back legs pushed off from the wire for another run at Munn.

Again Munn offered the arm and withdrew it. Again the dog's teeth popped, and the animal flew against the wire wall.

"What the hell is going on? Quist, get him out of there! Munn, get out of that cage before that dog . . ."

That dog abruptly changed its tactics after its second crash landing. This time it ignored the hand, offered waist-high, and bore in, its head low, its teeth slashing left and right, going for the man's bare leg. Munn extended his right leg away from his body, offering the new target. As the dog went for it, Munn suddenly pulled it back.

The dog tried turning. Its momentum carried it past the target, into one of the cement blocks. But this time its dash carried the animal only three feet past Munn and he came back again, slashing faster, this time closer to the center of the man's body. This time not making a dash for either leg, ignoring the hand and the feet, the bull terrier came in with all four paws on the ground as if to run between the man's legs.

Munn countered by reaching overhead and grasping a rung of the horizontal ladder, launching his body into the air. He encircled the sides of the ladder with his legs and rolled over on top. He came to rest sitting on top of the horizontal ladder, his legs dangling, the angry bull terrier leaping five feet into the air snapping at empty air just below the heels of the German researcher. Munn's mouth hung open as he labored to breathe.

"Thank goodness," Gates murmured. He looked around and realized that he was standing, although everyone else had remained seated, their eyes fixed on the scene. He saw that everyone else, however, was just as grim and nervous as he. Apparently, although they had seen this exercise before, it disturbed them.

"What's the point of this?" he demanded. "I'm disappointed in the behavior of this group. This is not research. We cannot afford to let our researchers be injured in some kind of barbaric daredevil scheme. I came here to see a genetic creation, not a reproduction of the Roman Colosseum. Have you been spending our budget just to breed vicious dogs, Mr. Quist? Now I command you, get that man out of the cage."

"But, Mr. Gates." The protestation came from Gregor Munn inside the cage. The man spoke raggedly as he gasped for breath. Below him, the dog had suddenly adapted to a new tactic. It began climbing the vertical rungs of the ladder to get to the man.

"Mr. Munn, unless you use that key to let yourself out of the cage right now, before that dog should shed even a drop of your blood, you are fired."

Munn spat in answer.

Gates flapped a hand ineffectually at the researcher. "Do you hear me? You are fired unless you use that key right now. Someone get that dog—"

"Mr. Gates," shouted Munn, "pay attention to this demonstration. It is quite impossible for anyone to let me out of this cage. You see, I am the only one who has a key. After this demonstration, the lock will have to be cut off." He held out the string looped around his finger, the key dangling down toward the drain in the center of the room. Munn let the loop slide off his finger and the key tinkled on the floor about six inches from the drain grate.

The dog had reached the top of the ladder and was straining to reach the man, its stout jaws extended, an impatient whine escaping its throat. It gathered itself for a leap from the top of the ladder across the horizontal rungs. Suddenly Munn dropped through the horizontal rungs to the floor, his feet barely making a sound as he crouched. With one bare foot he swept at the key, pushing it into the drain. Gates heard the tinkle as it fell to the bottom.

Suddenly, his knees felt weak as it dawned on him that the demonstration would not end at his order. In fact, he realized, it had just begun. He found himself pressing into the seat of his chair, pulling away from the cage. The dog tumbled off the side of the ladder and fell heavily to the floor. It let out a yelp and streaked across the floor toward the man, avoiding the chunks of concrete. Munn let out a curdling shriek and ran away from the dog. Again, Gates found his legs and stood up, holding out a hand as if somehow he could help or stop the events before him. But Munn's cry was not one of fear. It was a scream of triumph. The man leaped at the fence and climbed up a full six feet. He hung there like Spider-Man as the dog hissed in growing frustration below him. Then the dog began climbing the wire. As it did, Munn worked his way higher until he came on a level with Gates sitting in the elevated amphitheater.

"Mr. Gates, look . . . look at me. The key to this room is down that drain behind me. And the key to this project is here in front of you. And any case, I am not a man. *I am your genetic creation! I am the experiment!*"

Gates crumpled into his seat. He shuddered at Munn's face. He slumped back in his seat, as fearful now of the man behind the wire as of the dog. His spine rippled at the memory of that plastic smile last night. Munn . . . a creation? An experiment?

The dog had closed within inches of Munn's feet and stretched out his corded neck as if to nibble on a heel. He was reaching farther and farther but suddenly Munn came alive and clambered higher up the wire until he hung horizontally from the cage top. His toes released the wire. He swung twice, then dropped to the floor. Again, his feet barely made a patter as he touched down.

The dog looked back over his shoulder and seemed to sense that his quarry was no longer going to run. It loosened itself from the wire, falling awkwardly to the floor. It walked brazenly toward the man, its head held high, almost a swagger to its gait.

Munn held out a hand and waved it off to the side of the dog's head. But the pit bull would not be distracted. It kept boring in on the man, so Munn slapped the dog's head savagely. Angrily, the dog snapped again, closing on the air. While he was distracted, Munn swung a right hook and punched the dog soundly in the ribs, causing an expulsion of air from its lungs. Like a snake, the terrier snapped back to the right unexpectedly. One fang slashed across Munn's forearm, drawing blood. A rivulet of scarlet poured from the wound.

Munn grunted and swung again with a left hook, catching the dog behind the ear, bringing an exasperated bark of pain. The dog seemed to be confused but it knew nothing else than to continue its attack. It pressed harder, throwing its head from left to right.

Munn stepped away from another of the dog's lunges and slipped in his own blood, which had began collecting in tiny puddles on the floor. He lost his footing and went down to one knee.

The dog struck while his weight was on that knee, and slid inside Munn's grasp, closing down on the inside of his right thigh. It burrowed into the meaty part of the leg.

Munn let out a little cry, but Gates was astonished to see a plastic smile wrapped around his teeth instead of an expression of pain. The dog meanwhile began to twist and throw itself around violently, trying to pull chunks of flesh off its victim.

Gates gasped, "Save him." Quist, like all the others in the room, had his attention frozen on the bloody scene unfolding before their eyes. Collectively, the men began breathing rapidly. Gates was aware of his pulse throbbing in his temples.

"Save whom? Gregor Munn or the dog?"

Gates tried to turn his head to see what kind of expression on Quist's face would back up such an outrageous remark. But he could not wrest his attention from the cage. Munn bent over and bear-hugged the dog. He stood up abruptly. As he did, he pulled the dog's teeth out of his own leg, taking with it a wad of flesh, leaving only strands of tissue joining man's leg and dog's jaws. He flung the dog against the fence headfirst.

The pit bull crashed to the floor. He whirled but did not attack right away. He cast his head back and forth as if to find the man. The dog's mouth hung open, dripping strings of Munn's blood. A hunk of tissue fell from the bleeding, seething jaws.

Gates saw why the pit bull acted so confused. The blow against the fence had drawn the animal's blood, tearing a flap of skin loose over its brow. Curtains of red blinded him.

Gates heard a savage growl. He kept staring at the dog but suddenly realized the sound had not come from the animal.

"He has drawn blood on the pit bull," whispered Quist.

Gates heard Quist's remark repeated under the breath of half a dozen of the men in the amphitheater. He looked up at Munn in time to hear the last of the rattling, threatening growl die in his throat. This was not the Gregor Munn that he had met last night. This was an altogether different picture of the man, if it *was* a man. His face had contorted. His lower jaw had dropped open, hinging impossibly wide. Munn had somehow grown long canine teeth. His lips were drawn back into a savage grin, as if to get them out of the way of the teeth.

The dog was not bested. It finally penetrated the clouds of blood and fixed on the form of the man. It attacked again.

Munn did not feint one way or another. He

crouched lower as if to get down on the level of the animal. By the time the dog lunged, it only had to clear the height of a foot to come face-to-face with the man. The room reverberated with the collision. Clattering teeth to teeth, the dog and the man met. Munn's mouth closed on the smaller jaws of the dog. He tossed the animal to the side with his teeth, catching its body with his hands. He hurled it across the room again into the fence, the effort bringing bestial grunts from his throat.

A chilling howl filled the room. The dog whined in pain, dragging itself by its forepaws across the floor.

"Broke its back," somebody in the gallery whispered.

The dog's next feeble attack came painfully, determined as ever to finish its kill. It dragged its useless rear quarters across the concrete, leaving a wide, wet streak of himself on the floor as his head and neck wounds leaked in torrents.

This time the dog did not have to travel far to meet the man. Because this time the man attacked the dog. This time Munn battered the animal's head against the concrete, and hunkered down over the top of the dog, biting into its back. The dog flattened on the concrete as the man pressed on him, slashing and tearing at the back. Munn tossed his head and scattered bits of fur and hide.

Gates could no longer watch. He turned his head away and saw that the men in the room were transfixed by the scene. For Gates, the sounds coming from the cage were enough—the noises of body fluids being splashed around, the sounds of teeth tearing into bone and flesh, the beastlike grunting and growling. Next came the fragrance, the bouquet of opened skin, blood vapors, and body fumes. Gates felt sick.

Gates struggled to his feet, being careful to keep his head turned away from the gory scene enacted in the cage. To Quist he said, "I'm leaving now. Come, I want to know what's at the bottom of this . . . genetic creation."

As they were leaving the room, Gates heard the squeal of the dog and then a gurgle. He knew the battle was over. He did not look back; the sounds were enough for him. He could not rid his nostrils of the smell of gore.

It took longer than he had thought to regain his composure. He felt chilly and faint, so begged off further briefing by Quist to take a walk outdoors. After he had been outside in the hot, dry sun for an hour or so, the nausea passed. He returned to the compound's main building and asked for the briefing to resume.

• •

In the chief researcher's office, Quist had regained his sense of pomposity. He leaned back in his chair, his fingers intertwined across his belly, and began telling Gates the background that had been withheld until the previous hour's demonstration could be completed.

"Gregor Munn, of course, is not a real name. It was a name we assigned to him. Ordinarily we give them numbers. We call them Descendants."

"What happened to Munn?"

"The dog was killed, of course. And Munn was mortally wounded. The tear in his leg opened up the femoral artery and he bled to death as he was continuing to . . . to consume the carcass."

Again Gates felt ill, his stomach lurching as he

thought about the image he had last seen, an image that had branded itself into his mind and his nasal memory. "Why didn't Munn stop and get medical care once he had finished the dog?"

"He couldn't. If he had not been fatally wounded, if he had not bled to death at the supper table, we might have been able to treat him. In any case, there's not much point in spending too much effort or medical resources trying to repair our . . . goods once they have been damaged. It's much more economical to simply use another one of our resources. Besides, once the Descendant has been involved in such combat, they're really too dangerous to handle. Mr. Gates, in the time it would take for Munn to heal, we could easily create a copy of him."

Gates stirred in his chair, his mouth opening soundlessly. After a full minute's silence, he said, "This business of grandstanding . . . actually, that was quite dangerous, wasn't it?"

"Yes," said Quist, "I suppose it was a little less than prudent for us to take Gregor to the reception last night and introduce him to you. We did it for the effect it would have on you today."

"Effect, indeed."

"Well, yes. You see, Mr. Gates, there are a couple of . . . flaws in our genetic creations that we've been able to bring to the level of development of Gregor. Of course, there are extraordinary advances in the science of genetic engineering that I would be most eager to brief you about. For example, the life span—"

"What flaws?"

Quist doodled on the notepad before him. "Well," he said, "the first is the limitation in intelligence."

"Limits on intelligence? Why, it seemed to me that

Gregor . . . that thing . . . was quite human. If there's any flaw in the genetic research, it's that we're not creating at a level low enough. It's one thing to develop a subhuman species that can be put to use in various ways. But it's quite another to simply develop a race of almost-human beings and try to enslave them. That's not what we're striving for at all. That's not . . ."

Quist was shaking his head throughout Gates's speech. "Sir, the gentility that Gregor Munn displayed last night was the absolute limit of his ability to be trained. And believe me, these are not human beings. If there was ever any doubt of that, I would think that the experience you witnessed in the center of the amphitheater this afternoon would be testimony enough."

"You mean to tell me his language facility and the behavior pattern were trained?"

Quist was nodding now. "Yes. It took us the most of six months to be able to bring Gregor Munn to the stage where he could be trusted outside the security that's normally accorded these . . . Descendants. But his purpose was only that one thing, to serve as an imposter to . . . well, to deceive you, sir. These things can only be trained for a few functions. Teaching them language uses up some of their capacity for intelligence. But you see, that's the beauty of the entire experiment. You only have to teach them special skills. They will perform those few skills to perfection time after time after time. They have no expectations."

Gates stood up and leaned over Quist's desk. "Wait a minute, Mr. Quist. What did you mean about the first time one of these things has been accorded the freedom to mingle with men?"

"Well, Mr. Gates, the most serious flaw in the research so far is that streak of violence that you witnessed today. You'll recall that the earlier strains of these mutant beasts looked like things out of science-fiction movies. The one element that was common every time the experiment was tried was that these things were exceedingly violent. Well, there are still traces of that violence in our Descendants."

Gates backed up until he felt his chair at his calves, and sat down. "What brings it on?"

"Blood. These Descendants are utterly without fear. They seem impervious to pain. And even the loss of their own blood has no effect on them. This is precisely the quality that makes them most effective for a variety of extremely hazardous missions. Can you imagine the kinds of hardships you could send these Descendants on?"

"Mr. Quist, of course I can imagine. It's the reason for our existence. It's the reason nobody in Washington asks any embarrassing questions about our so-called covert-ops budget. But you were saying about blood."

"Yes, blood. It seems that our Descendants, while not immediately affected by the loss or sight of their own blood, fly into an extraordinary rage whenever the blood of another is spilled. The rage almost always ends in a feeding frenzy. But that's quite another problem. At any rate—"

"The glass!"

Quist nodded emphatically.

"The glass I dropped last night," Gates said. "If I had cut myself . . . You bastards. Do you mean to say that thing could have flown into a rage last night?

This kind of thing could happen if someone should get
a sudden bloody nose?"

Quist's head bobbed continually to each question.

"Someone could pick a scab? Someone could nick
themselves shaving and have a trickle of blood flowing
down his neck?"

Quist nodded still. "And believe me, sir," he said,
"each of those things has happened to someone on
staff while we've been here. The accident rate has been
astronomical."

"You mean to tell me that, all of those experiences
to the contrary, you let one of those things loose
among us last night?"

Quist held up a hand in interruption. "You may
have noticed last night that each of us was on constant
alert. You may have felt at times that people were
staring at you. Believe me, sir, there was never a moment when at least half a dozen of us would not have
been able to immediately save you from our Descendant, the late Gregor Munn. Besides, with every generation we breed we're able to reassure some form of
improvement."

Gates's open mouth formed a question. He tugged
on the pistol in his jacket.

Quist reached into his pocket and withdrew his own
pistol. "Nobody around here is really permitted to be
without one at any time. It's a 9-millimeter. The bullets have been especially drilled to make them hollow
points. Then the hollow points have been filled with
plastic and capped with a thin shield of plastic. Quite
illegal, of course. Should the bullet ever—"

"Never mind, Mr. Quist. If we ever run into legal
problems here at The Ranch, I'm quite certain that
hollow-point bullets will be the least of our worries.

Just assure me that there will be no further surprises of the sort I've just seen. Give me your word that I won't be victimized by any more of these games."

"You have my assurances, sir. From now on, Mr. Gates, we are engaged in nothing but very direct methods to bring you up to speed for our first experimental mission. I suggest we spend the rest of today and indeed the rest of the week giving you a full orientation about the facilities here on The Ranch, the research that we've under way, and an introduction to the population."

"Fine. Tell me, what is the extent of the military application of this research? After all, it's entirely the reason for the existence of The Ranch."

FORT IRWIN, CALIFORNIA

Lieutenant Colonel Josh Avery lifted his night goggles as Major Cliff Breen flew the preplanned route. Josh wanted to test the darkness on his naked eyes. His NVGs seemed willing to show him a reasonably crisp view of the desert floor. Somehow the picture seemed clearer and sharper than what he had been used to at Fort Hood. Perhaps it was the altitude. However, without the NVGs, the blackness outside the helicopter dismayed him; even with all the instrument lights inside the cockpit, he felt as if his eyes were not open at all. He had to blink and wave his fingers in front of his face to get even a sensation of light. It unsettled him so much that he slid the night-vision goggles back into place. He scanned the instruments and his map. "Everything in the green," he said.

Breen grunted into the intercom.

"You know what, Cliff? This is the same old stuff. Even out here in California."

Breen sighed. "Same shit, different day."

In fact, Josh knew, this was really not the same old stuff as they flew in Texas. Things had changed. Vickers exhibited far less patience with the crew, especially the Special Operations team now packed into the cabin behind them. And the old curmudgeon had instituted a new set of rules. No lights of any kind were permitted. Even emergency flares had been outlawed. He banned use of the helicopter's anti-collision light. The red rotating beacon used to warn off other aircraft in flight had been disconnected. In fact, Vickers told them, all exterior lights in the fleet of mission aircraft had been disconnected, including the green and white running lights.

He sounded serious. Josh began to realize that this whole mission was serious. He thought about Marilyn back in Texas, about her concerns, about her clinging to him as he was preparing to leave. Then he shook his head to clear his mind of the distraction of Marilyn.

The fluorescent-painted needles of the instruments glared at him from the dash, their glow magnified by the NVGs. For the dozenth time tonight, the instrument needles were not where they should have been.

"Keep your airspeed up, Cliff. The altitude, the DA." Breen grunted at him again. The helicopter was laboring and so was the major. "You're not concentrating full-time."

Josh made a mental note to brief Vickers that the Special Ops team carried too much gear. Their equipment and body weight didn't make a lot of difference in Texas, where the altitude was much closer to sea level. But at these higher altitudes, where the air was thinner, the helicopter had to labor much harder to get the same amount of lift.

During the day the heat would thin out the air even more, raising the density altitude, making it a critical factor. Already, Breen was struggling with the Huey. He could only imagine how it would be on a hot afternoon with a full load and full fuel tanks. In fact, Breen's concentration had been wandering ever since they left Texas.

For tonight he wasn't worried. The later it got, the chillier it would be, and the better the density-altitude factor would become. What's more, after they dropped off the troops and flew around, they would burn up a few hundred pounds of fuel and have an even wider margin for error.

Josh's suppositions about the mission becoming easier came true. Breen's landing was a little hard, but even at Fort Hood that was the rule rather than the exception for the major. He seemed to have difficulty with his depth perception at altitudes from three feet on down to the ground. He had a tendency to be too eager to get the aircraft on the ground at any cost. Sometimes this was offset by the troops stepping off the skids at the last second and lightening the aircraft just before touchdown, but not always.

Although the specialized landing beacon had been banned with all the other lights, the Huey landed at exactly the right spot, according to Josh's navigation, and within ten seconds of the LZ time. They were on the ground less than ten seconds. They dropped the team and flew their holding pattern route, becoming better acquainted with the features of the California desert.

Forty-five minutes later, when they made the stop to pick up troops, they were again on time.

Their only indication of trouble came fifteen seconds after they lifted off, heading toward home. The intercom snapped, and Josh expected to hear Vickers's gravelly voice bitching about some trivial detail or other.

"Uh-oh, we got us a problem, Colonel." It was the voice of Ingalls, the crew chief. "Head count is off. We're one short."

"Don't tell me," said Josh. "Don't tell me the one short is the fat, short one."

"All right, Colonel, I won't tell you. I'll let *him* tell you when he gets back out of this godforsaken desert."

"God," Breen sighed over the intercom, "and everything was going so damned well."

"The torture never stops," said Josh. "How could the guy get lost?" His tone was light, his radio manner meant to be reassuring. But inside, his guts were churning. He uttered an obscenity to himself.

• •

They didn't have long to wait in the debriefing room to hear from Vickers. An hour after he was due to have met up with the Special Operations team at the rendezvous site and be taken out by Josh's helicopter crew, he called base on his own survival radio and demanded that a helicopter be sent to him. "Any helicopter," he ordered. "Any helicopter but the one flown by that bunch of bumbling idiots that was supposed to pick me up in the first place. I want somebody who can read a map. I want somebody who can navigate and fly and get me out of this desert. Everygoddamned-body else, stand by for me to get back."

Vickers's debriefing was a picture of rage. Even Josh, who had been in the army twenty-plus years heard words used—not just one word but many—in more creatively vulgar ways than he had ever heard before. At first, Josh folded his arms and lowered his head, unwilling to lock eyes with Vickers. Like everybody else, he stared at the floor. Vickers would regard looking at him as a gesture of defiance. Except for those few new word usages, Josh had heard this sort of pep talk before. The idea was to get everyone's attention. He'd used the same kind of strategy himself. Basketball coaches used it. Parents used it. And army officers and non-coms resorted to it quite frequently. Josh knew that Vickers simply meant to refocus everyone's attentions. The possibility for error in a dangerous mission in a new environment was greatly increased. Furthermore, it was fairly obvious that the real mission for which they had been training was getting closer and closer.

So the locker-room motivational speech began to run its course.

Half an hour into the tirade, Josh began to get uneasy. This was no ordinary motivational speech. This wasn't even a crotchety colonel's angry outburst at having been left in the desert. This was an outrageous display of temper. Nothing good could come of it. Vickers had begun to sacrifice a lot of respect over this. Certainly it wouldn't help the morale. Much more of such a violent tongue-lashing would backfire against his precious project.

Forty-five minutes into the harangue, Vickers was still going strong, except that his voice had become as coarse as his vocabulary. His audience kept staring at the floor, but every now and then a head would turn to catch the eye of someone else. The men smirked at each other. They rolled their eyes as if the old man had snapped. They were beginning to regard the whole thing as a joke.

Vickers might have sensed it, too, because he stopped talking. For a full three minutes he just stood with his hands on his hips. Josh watched him. He could see the man's pulse throbbing in the veins of his temples. His neck had swollen against the collar of his jacket, cutting off his circulation until the red face had begun to turn blue. Josh remembered Marilyn's characterization as the poisoned toad, but bit his tongue sharply to keep from smiling.

When he finally spoke again, Vickers's voice was low and threatening. The men stopped shifting around in their seats, stopped clearing their throats, and stopped breathing. "Flight crew dismissed."

With a collective sigh of relief, the two pilots and crew chief stood up. "Not you, Avery. Sit down. You're the senior officer of that bunch of pansies. I want you to hear the rest of this."

When Breen and Ingalls had cleared the room, a different, calmer Vickers spoke. "You're through," he said to the infantrymen sitting on benches. The men stood up to leave the room. Vickers shouted, "Sit down! I didn't dismiss you. What I told you was, you are through on this mission. There's a plane waiting for you outside at this moment. I want your asses and all your gear on it in fifteen minutes. It's flying you back to Fort Hood. The lucky ones of you bastards are being reassigned to mech infantry units. The rest will be marooned on staff jobs until your butts rot off. You're through in Special Operations. You're done with this mission here. Now get out of my sight. I don't want to see you anymore. You make me sick."

Vickers crooked a finger at Josh Avery, who was as stunned as any of the Special Operations team members. Josh followed Vickers out of the briefing room.

At the door, the mild, timid, pleading voice of the commander of the Special Operations team called after them, "Colonel Vickers? Sir?"

Vickers slammed the door in the captain's face. As they walked down the hallway from the briefing room, Vickers threw an arm around Josh's shoulder. "Not a bad show, eh? Well, Josh my boy, when the going gets tough the tough go drinking. What do you say we go quaff a few beers?"

4

• • • • • • • • • • • • • • • • • • • •

THE RANCH

The skull, translucent white and soft to the touch,
rested in Gates's hands. At first he had recoiled from
its satiny feel. But when he held it, feeling the weight
and smoothness of it, he found it not altogether unpleasant. He turned it over to examine the pins inserted in the hinge of the jaw. As he did so, the jaw fell
away. He grabbed for it and scraped the back of his
hand on the two-inch-long canine teeth exposed when
the jaw dropped. The four fangs were wrapped with
rubber bands to hold them into the jaw.

Gates grimaced. "Is this a plastic model?"

"No, there is hardly a need for models here at The
Ranch. We have access to large numbers of experimental parts."

"I hope that doesn't mean there are literally grave-
yards all over this place. We couldn't afford—"

"Rest assured, Mr. Gates, we have no intention of
these sorts of skeletons being exhumed from our
closets. In fact, we have a licensed, federally approved
biological-hazard waste facility. All experimental subjects are reduced to ashes, which are buried off site."

"Incinerator?"

"Mr. Gates, that is an item for another part of our tour. For now, I want to begin building a case using this model to show that our Descendants are less than human. It is a distinct species that is clearly less than human."

"And that is an important distinction," Gates said, pointing a finger toward the ceiling.

Quist took the skull from Gates and manipulated the jaw, demonstrating the set of double joints that allowed the lower jaw to become unhinged and drop nearly vertical, although the head stayed horizontal. "Like a human jaw, this one is hinged at the temples of the skull," he said. "The second joint, however, is distinctly unhuman, formed here at the point of the angle just behind the wisdom teeth of the jawbone."

Gates leaned in closer, squinting to see every detail pointed out to him.

"Now, sir, a hormone that we have isolated in the Descendant is released when the blood of an adversary —or for that matter when the blood of any other animal is drawn. Then the thing goes into a killing frenzy, then a feeding frenzy. It's a well-defined form of a survival instinct triggered by an external force. It's rather like the release of estrogen from a female animal in heat, a scent that stimulates the male to an erection and to the acts that conclude in reproduction."

Gates nodded his head, absorbed. "It's like an exaggerated form of salivation in normal animals, isn't it?"

"Exactly, Mr. Gates. The hormone triggers changes that include the involuntary constriction of the upper and lower jaw muscles. As you can see, the lower jaw in a normal situation is very similar to ours. But when upper and lower muscles here close to the ear are constricted, it forces this hinge forward and drops this rear socket of the jaw downward, allowing it to be elongated." He manipulated the skull bones to demonstrate as he talked. "This is not much different from the activity in the jaw of rattlesnakes and similar reptiles allowing them to swallow animals even bigger than their own circumference."

"Is that the purpose of this? To allow the Descendants to swallow larger food?"

"Somewhat. The throat and mouth do become enlarged and the lips do stretch over the teeth to allow chunks of food to be swallowed with very little chewing. However, there seems to be much more of a purpose of aggression served by the jaw dropping down and exposing the fangs like daggers. Watch."

He manipulated the forward part of the jaw, releasing the rubber bands to snap around the elongations of the roots of the canine teeth. The teeth snapped into the mouth cavity, meshing like scissors.

"The hormones also activate the musculature of the canine teeth, permitting the fangs to drop into the mouth cavity and to hold them there, where they become deadly weapons for slashing and tearing."

"It's like the claws of a cat. Retractable fangs. Imagine."

"Not quite. The display of these teeth is not something these animals can voluntarily control. Normally the teeth recess into the jaw, hidden in the musculature of the neck and face. It gives the animals almost a double chin."

Gates's eyes flicked a look at Quist's own multiple chins.

Quist didn't notice. He continued. "As far as we are

able to tell, only the sight or smell of blood is able to cause these fangs to extend. As you can see, the characteristics that I've just described on this skull are really quite animal in nature. It's the first of a long chain of evidential arguments that discriminate this Descendant from the human race."

"Again, an important distinction, Mr. Quist. Let us never forget that while we're here."

As they left Quist's office, Gates looked into the amphitheater and saw a crew of men hosing down the interior of the cage, scrubbing the concrete floor with stiff, long-handled brushes and soap suds. The smell of acrid ammonium wafted into the hallway.

"Quist," said Gates, "was Gregor Munn consumed by fire? And have his ashes been buried?"

"It's safe to say, Mr. Gates, that Gregor was consumed. At least in part. The skull you just examined—that was Gregor's. The rest I'll tell you about in a little while."

Gates rubbed his hands down the sides of his pants, remembering the size of those fangs.

FORT IRWIN, CALIFORNIA

Josh slammed on the brakes of his jeep and skidded to a stop against a telephone pole laid down as a sort of desert curb. The drifting sand would have obscured painted lines in a matter of days. Then the continual wear and tear of sand on the pavement would grind away the lines; so posts and blocks of cement delineated parking spots.

He leaned back to pull out his flight gear from the rear of the jeep and then strode across the sand toward the flight operations building. He strode purposefully,

fully intent on finding out what had gone wrong last night He had called Breen earlier.

In a just-awakened whine, the major had protested over the telephone that there was no reason for them to fly today. In fact, there was not even a mission scheduled for the night, because a new Special Operations team had not been designated. No mission order had come from Vickers, Breen had griped.

"This mission is from me, Cliff. Now, roll your butt out."

Vickers had been all too facile last night after dismissing the Special Operations team and sending them back to Fort Hood to punitive assignments. Josh had declined to have a drink with Vickers, begging off to say that he was too tired and too upset over screwing up the night's mission. Vickers had insisted that it was not his fault; Josh thought otherwise.

Bicycle Lake was a dried-up bed of alkali that had been converted into parking spots and an airstrip for helicopters and light aircraft. Josh detoured toward the rear of the building so he could pass by the coffeepots on his way to check the weather and his flight plan. After he had poured himself a cup of the black liquid, an oily sheen floating on its surface, he walked into the flight planning room. Immediately his eyes met Breen's. The major held the telephone to his ear and began talking a little too loudly, Josh thought. In a moment he hung up. Josh saw a flicker of guilt pass across the major's face.

"Looks like the weather is going to be fine today and on into the night. Clear blue and twenty-two. Far as I know, it will be like that for the rest of our lives around here."

"Your mood has changed since I woke you."

"I don't mind flying, after all. Besides, I think that means we're going to get the night off, doesn't it?"

"That's right, I guess. Vickers isn't likely to be able to get a new Special Operations team here in time to fly tonight. Meantime, I want to retrace our aerial steps from last night. I want to see what actually happened. I want to find out where we screwed up."

"Well, I've already pulled a pre-flight and filed the flight plan for the rest of the day. Ingalls has pulled a fuel sample and added some hydraulic oil. We're ready to go as soon as you get out there. Coming?"

Josh eyed his copilot closely. Seldom did Breen show such animation. It aroused Josh's suspicions all the more than if he'd just gotten up and left glumly. Had he broken the prohibition about calling home to family?

Family. The word hit Josh. Maybe he should call Marilyn. What harm could it do?

"Cliff, go on out and take it up to pre-start . . . no, go ahead and pull the trigger. I'll be there before you get it up to operating RPM. I want to update my map."

Breen smiled, his head bouncing nervously. Then he marched out of the flight operations building. Josh watched him go, wondering if it was his own imagination or if it was just Breen's excitement at being able to fly during the daytime, when they could actually see to the edge of a more distant horizon than night-vision goggles accorded. Or maybe it was just that they were going to be able to do some drinking, maybe have some fun tonight.

He looked over at the telephone where Breen had made the call. Surely the major would not have made an unauthorized call. Surely after the ass-chewing they'd gotten last night he would not risk picking up a telephone to call his wife. Surely not.

Josh walked over to the telephone and looked down at it.

Marilyn's number came to mind. It wouldn't take but a few seconds.

The telephone was a new model, one with an automatic redial button on it. That feature gave him another idea. It was wrong of him to think ill of Breen. It would be even more wrong to check up on someone he should trust to the fullest. On the other hand, he could satisfy his curiosity about whether Breen had dialed the flight service station for a weather report or . . .

He found himself short of breath as he realized he was picking up the telephone, listening for the dial tone. He touched the redial button. The telephone tones scurried into his ear faster than human fingers could have dialed the number. Still, by the number of beeps, Josh knew that it had been a long-distance telephone call. It had not been to the flight service station at all. Breen had lied.

A phone-company recording answered.

"The number you have called"—the woman's voice gave the number—"has been disconnected." The woman's voice repeated the number and Josh copied it down on a scrap of paper on the desktop. He folded it and stuffed it into his shirt pocket. He didn't recognize the area code of that number, but he knew it was not the central Texas code, 817. Josh walked out to the helicopter, his mind whirling with all the puzzling behavior of the people around him lately. He thought of Marilyn. He thought of Marilyn's two daughters, Jill and Katy. Damn, they were coming to mind often lately.

THE RANCH

"Mr. Quist, said Gates, "I insist on getting the whole story about these Descendants."

"Descendants. Good name, isn't it? In the first place they are descended from those early beasts created by the original researcher on this project."

Gates nodded. "Yes, those were some rather primitive specimens, at that. Based on what I saw yesterday with Gregor Munn—or whatever it was—you've come a considerable distance while I was back East keeping the dogs of Congress at bay."

"Yes, and there is another aspect to the name Descendants. Instead of the ascent of man, these . . . things represent a descent. A reversal in the process of evolutionary development."

They entered a wing of the building that Gates hadn't yet seen. It was one of three protruding from the back of the main facade of the building.

As they walked into the broad boulevard of tile, Gates continued his briefing. "The Descendants are a distinct species. Like many other subspecies of animals, we created these using selective breeding techniques. We use drugs to lower the natural barriers that prevent mixing of the proteins between species."

Gates only half listened. The sounds and smells in this wing distracted him. "Where are we going now?"

"Now we are in the nursery wing of the building. At the farthest end is a laboratory where eggs are harvested and fertilized in vitro. About half the fertilized eggs survive for being carried to term."

"How . . ." Gates bit off his question. He had become increasingly more cautious about asking questions, as though there were some answers he did not necessarily want to hear.

Sensing this, Quist said, "In time, Mr. Gates, you will be taken through the entire process and learn the entire sequence of our research. You'll find that it's quite a significant operation and quite capable of growing to much greater proportions within the facilities that we have already built. In fact, we're only operating at about ten to twenty-five percent, depending on the particular mission that we're preparing for. Should we decide to enlarge the operation, it can be done with the minimum of capital investment."

Quist stopped in the center of a crossroads of hallways. "Down there," he said, pointing toward the end of the wing, "are the laboratories. Those we will tour later, when there is more interesting activity going on. Down this way is the nursery. I warn you, Mr. Gates; what you are about to see you will find startling, even electrifying. You might opt to avoid this part of the orientation if you like. I could simply brief you in the office."

Gates held up a hand. "It's all right, Mr. Quist. I want to see it. I know that there are things that are unpleasant. I know that the Gregor Munn demonstration was certainly one of the most unpleasant things that I ever expect to experience, but our purpose in getting involved in this kind of research transcends the day-to-day detail, gruesome as it is. We are in the performance of research that is essential to the national security of the United States—even though most Americans would abhor it. These are things that, ugly as they seem, are essential to our ability to stamp out warfare and terrorism in the world. I won't put my own comfort above the distress of things like warfare and terrorism, Mr. Quist."

Quist pursed his lips and nodded, flapping his chins, indicating his agreement with the director.

The first nursery bay Quist led him into was anything but electrifying, Gates thought. It looked no more nor less exciting than an ordinary nursery at any ordinary hospital.

Except for its sheer size. The room opened on an enormous bay, a sea of floor tiles covered with formations of baby cradles on carts.

Inside the doorway of the nursery, Gates stared around the room, amazed by the number of cradles. "More capacity than all the maternity wards of all the hospitals in a major city," Quist said.

A security guard in surgical dress handed them masks and surgical caps. She helped Gates put them on. Then she held a paper gown for each of the two men to slip into.

"Put your right hand into the pocket of this gown and you will find a slit instead of a pocket," she said. "Reach inside that and feel your pistol inside your coat pocket. That's how you get to it if an emergency occurs."

Gates nodded hesitantly, a question forming on his eyebrows.

Quist answered the question before it was asked. "Yes, even in here. In fact, this has a tendency to be one of the more dangerous places."

Altogether there were five hundred cradles in this bay, one of six on the wing, Quist explained. He noted that most of the cradles were vacant, but judging from the sounds of crying and the size of the support staff moving around in the passageway between formations of cradles, Gates realized that at least a fourth of the cradle beds were filled.

"It smells sweet . . . like a nursery."

"Yes, of course, Mr. Gates. We do maintain high standards for our sanitation and medical care. After all, we could not afford to run this place like a stable."

"Of course."

As they approached the occupied cradles, Gates saw an infant in each bed. Each infant seemed perfectly normal, perfectly human. Each was covered with new bed clothing. The cradle, however, was more than normal. The slatted sides were welded steel bars with wire screens that allowed air circulation, but prevented infant arms from reaching out. Acrylic glass covered the tops. Each cradle was actually a locked cage with a combination padlock securing it. On the cart below each cradle were shelves for the individual diapering and other nursery supplies that might be found in any home or any hospital.

Quist pointed at the main doors they had used to enter the nursery. "We take extraordinary security measures to protect the staff and infants. The way this room is arranged, the newborns are brought in and kept closer to the door. Then, as they develop, they are moved down week by week, closer to that far door. Finally, they are moved over into the toddler nursery."

"You mean to tell me they stay in this room for years?"

Quist smiled, and the security guard laughed until Gates's harsh stare and angular bend to his eyebrows restored the woman's sobriety behind the mask.

"Mr. Gates," said Quist, "these Descendants have an accelerated developmental stage. Their entire life cycle is extraordinarily short by comparison to ours. You'll remember that the earliest generations of beasts included an incredible metabolism and enormously fast growth rates. These Descendants grow to maturity faster than dogs, in fact. They consume mountains of food. The cost of this growth is a short life span of no more than one to two years. As a rule of thumb, one week in a Descendant's life is equivalent to one of our years. So the life span ends up being just over seventy weeks. And the effective productive life is from eighteen to fifty-two weeks."

"My God, Gregor Munn."

"Thirty-two weeks old. You're remembering he told you his age was thirty-two. There was no way for you to know he meant weeks, not years. So you see, the infants in this room will be here only three to four weeks before being moved into the next stage."

"Except for the time compression, are the other developmental stages similar to human beings? Is the mortality rate the same as human infants?"

"No. In fact, the mortality rate is quite high; and I'll be showing you why in just a little while. In fact, these animals are really quite a lot less than human when they are born. In fact they are somewhat beastly. They are delivered with a vestigial tail and quite animallike behavior. In the first hours after birth, our doctors remove the tails of all specimens and castrate all the males. This castration is done as a safeguard to prevent accidental breeding. We found quite early on that test animals left with their gonads continue producing a testosteronelike hormone that leads to extreme body hair, distorted features, permanently extended fangs, and much more aggressive behavior— something akin to human behavior on extended, massive steroids. If it were to be simplified to the most elementary discussion, I would say that males left to develop their own adult hormones appear a more Neanderthal-like species, something between man and baboon. But without that hormone being produced, they really come along quite nicely, like the specimen that Gregor Munn represented."

Gate's face contorted. "And the females?"

It was Quist's turn to grimace. "Most females are disposed of, except for maintenance as possible breeding stock or for experiments. We find that very few of them have the application for military requirements such as we are training for here. I'm happy to report that a new branch of inquiry will permit us to determine the gender of our creations so we can avoid the seemingly brutal culling of our stock."

Gates shook his head and bit a lip. "Has it ever occurred to you that . . ."

"That what we're doing is unethical? Immoral? Of course, Mr. Gates. But as you yourself say, is terrorism any more ethical? Should all moral men be laid waste by terrorists, religious fanatics, and warmongers? When do we stop being moral? When we are eliminated as a race?"

Gates waved his hand impatiently. He didn't wish to hear any more, because he had been engaged in the same kind of argument with himself over the years. He had already settled the discussion with himself. Except for the stark realities that he was seeing come to fruition before his eyes, those questions would not have cropped up in his mind again. He realized that it was the stark, naked brutality of his very rational and intellectual argument that was causing him to hesitate. "I don't want to discuss morality right now, Mr.

Quist. I want to see what happens with these Descendants."

Quist nodded enthusiastically. "Right now it is feeding time, Mr. Gates. Now you will see why we do have some difficulty with mortality among these little animals. Actually, one of the flaws of these creations is their astonishing appetites. As you might guess, the kind of growth rate that I have described would require an enormous intake of calories. They have extraordinarily well developed digestive systems in order to keep up with the growth rates. They have voracious appetites, comparable to that of a mole. At this age we have to feed them hourly. Adults we feed six times a day. I assure you, that creates a significant logistical problem."

"I'm almost afraid to ask—what do they eat?"

"Watch." Quist slid his hand into the pocket of his paper coat. Gates saw that he was reaching for the comfort of his security blanket, the grips of that pistol. He did likewise, finding the heft of the pistol comforting.

Quist pointed to a glassed-in enclosure that was the control booth for the nursery, a high-security nurses' station. A security man in medical gowns waved in acknowledgment and touched a control pane, activating a set of lights and other security equipment. Gates heard electric door latches snap shut, locking the two men into the nursery room. At the far end of the nursery, a pair of oversized doors slid open, revealing a stainless-steel feeding chamber. A formation of medical personnel filed into the nursery and lined up to wheel the carts toward the feeding area.

Gates watched in fascination as the hourly feeding of Descendants began.

THE CALIFORNIA DESERT

"When we get to the pickup point, I want you to set it down. Then shut it down," said Josh abruptly. His manner with Breen had become clipped, as his anger had steeped. He felt a twinge of regret that a good deal of his irritation stemmed from jealousy. He wished he'd been able to make a call to Marilyn. Breen had wasted an unauthorized call, not even phoning his wife.

They were hovering along about ten feet above the ground and at the speed of a horse's gallop. It would not be long.

Up close, the desert dazzled Josh. At altitude it seemed to be a brown, irregular sand table with dirty, itchy connotations, as if somebody had strewn ashes and gravel over the earth. But down low, the brown cast gave way to a mosaic of individual colors: of white sand, of black lava gravel, of individual plants and shrubs of a hundred, if not a thousand, species.

Now and then he could see signs of animal life, reptiles darting from shade pool to shade pool. Rabbits darted like pinballs, and here and there a coyote slunk, flattened by the Huey's noise. The desert was alive and vibrant when he didn't have to view it through night-vision goggles or from an altitude of a hundred feet. He shook off the mesmerizing feeling that seeped into his body, threatening to make him a day gazer.

He should be paying attention, he should be focusing, he told himself. He studied his map closely, scrutinizing the ground outside, matching ink symbols to the earth's features. He navigated by day exactly to the same spot as he had last night. The overall scene looked different in the harsh sunlight. But when he told Breen to make his approach, they came to a hover. He could see last night's skid impressions in the crusted outer skin of the desert. He pointed out the windshield, and Breen hovered the Huey over the spot. Faint footprints led off in two directions back toward the drop-off points.

Josh directed Breen to follow one set of footprints, tracking down the exact path the men had followed on the ground. As he went, he followed with his finger on the map, moving it painstakingly slowly. In less than ten minutes they had covered the same terrain it had taken the men forty-five minutes to cover last night. There, at the end of the trail of footsteps, two more parallel depressions in the sand indicated where their helicopter had set down. The tracks they had been following and another set of tracks coming from another direction led up to the two parallel skid marks in the gravel. Josh indicated that Breen should return to the pickup point.

Breen landed on the spot, setting down in almost exactly the same position he had last night. As the copilot began going through the shutdown procedures, Josh opened his door and climbed out, taking his map and his mission sheet from the previous night. Minutes later, the blade of the Huey had coasted to a stop and teetered down momentarily for Ingalls to catch it. Breen sauntered up to a position Josh had selected on a gentle knoll about a hundred yards from the parked helicopter.

"What did you find out, sir?"

"I'm checking my orientation here." Josh had spread his map onto a flat place in the sand and gravel, crusted to an inch deep like snow in winter. He laid his military compass out on top of the map, orienting the paper magnetic north arrow to the compass arrow. Using several fist-sized chunks of lava, he pinned the map to the ground and stood up, squinting through the aiming sights in his compass toward the prominent landmarks on the terrain—a mountain peak to the east, a faint crossroads to the north, and the convergence of two dry streambeds to the southwest. After each sighting he copied the magnetic reading on a scrap of paper. Then he knelt and used the edge of his notebook as a straightedge to mark the back azimuth from each of the prominent land points. Where the three lines intersected, he pointed a finger and wrote down more figures.

"Here, Cliff. Take my compass. Use your own map and shoot this spot on the ground. I want to compare your answer to mine."

Breen, excessively meticulous in Josh's opinion, took all of five minutes before he grunted, meaning he had arrived at a solution. Josh looked at the circled spot on the map and the X drawn inside a circle indicating the spot. "Colonel," he said, "we are exactly on the pickup point . . . certainly no more than the width of a grease-pencil line, a hundred lousy meters from where the helicopter is parked."

"Exactly. The exact spot we were supposed to occupy last night. If there is any reason in the world why Vickers didn't get picked up last night, it was because *he* was in the wrong place."

"Do you think if we got back in time he might allow the Special Operations team to stay on here?"

Josh wagged his head.

"Something odd is going on here. I've been in the army twenty years and I've seen dozens of petty, arrogant senior officers who couldn't read a map any bet-

ter than they could memorize a telephone book. . . ."
He paused. "Telephone book," he repeated. He shook
his head as if dismissing a thought. "But Colonel
Tommy Vickers is not one of those. The man can read
a map. I've never known him to be lost. If he had been
even anywhere nearby, he would have been on the
radio, bitching for us to come pick him up. Even if you
grant the remotest possibility that he might have mis-
placed himself last night, he would never have gone
through that outrageous act. He'd have been too embarrassed."

"Act?"

Josh brushed aside the question. "What about your
own act, Cliff? What about that telephone call back at
base-ops?"

"The flight service station call? I got the
weather . . ."

Josh grimaced to show he was not buying.

"I . . . it was my girlfriend."

"You've got a girlfriend? What does your wife think
of that?"

"She doesn't know about . . . but of course you
would know she doesn't know. Otherwise I wouldn't
have a wife anymore."

Josh still wasn't buying. "Tell me more about this
mistress."

Breen chose his words carefully. "She was threatening to confront my wife. I've been promising to bring
it out in the open. I begged her not to while I had to go
on this mission; that was before I left. That was why
Vickers was chewing me out for being late back there
at the flight line at Fort Hood. I had to beg her to give
me a chance to return from this mission before we—I

—told my wife. I didn't want to leave her and the kids and then just leave things up in the air."

"Go on." Josh wanted to know why Breen's mistress wasn't in the same telephone area code as his wife. He wasn't about to believe the major was carrying on a long-distance affair.

Breen studied Josh's face carefully before answering. "I . . . my girlfriend decided she would get out of town, too. She . . . left me. She went to Kansas City. She said she was going to stay away for good, so I called her this morning and begged her to give me a chance. Colonel, she's threatening to start a telephone harassment campaign against my wife. I have to get some control of that situation. Maybe that's why I was flying so terribly last night."

Josh didn't like it, any of it. Casual adultery exposed a serious flaw in an officer's character, he believed. He never wanted to be around people like that. He waved his hand in a motion to cut off the whining which he detested even more than the disloyalty. "Can it, Cliff. Let's get back to Bike Lake."

THE RANCH

Gates watched in fascination as the feeding of the Descendants began. The majority of the corps of security and medical personnel assigned to this ward began wheeling carts and cradles toward the feeding room at the far end of the nursery. A pair of attendants hauled a train of linked food-service carts up to the front of the nursery. The doors slid up and Gates felt the heat escaping. He also smelled the sweet, cloying scent of warm, sugared milk.

"It's cow's milk. We fortify it with sorghum and vitamins."

The workers assigned to the feeding of the youngest of the Descendants began moving to the carts and picking up bottles. Except for their size, the containers looked like ordinary baby bottles.

"Each bottle is a half gallon's worth. They're made of plastic, of course, instead of glass. We have to maintain a huge herd of cattle in order to obtain this much milk. As you might imagine, the cream is not separated out. It's necessary to have as rich a product as possible to feed these infants in their first week. But after a week—you'll remember that one week is the equivalent of a year of human's growth—they are quite ready for solid food."

Gates shook his head even as Quist spoke. "Solid food after a week? I imagine that requires vegetable gardens as well?"

"Hardly, Mr. Gates. The Descendants prefer meat. It requires that we sustain quite a large supply of beef cattle as well as a dairy herd."

Gates stretched as far as he could on his tiptoes to see over the shoulder of one of the attendants preparing to feed a Descendant infant. Quist motioned him to go closer. "They are relatively safe at this age; dangerous still, but not requiring nearly the precautions that will be required in the next few weeks of their lives."

As Gates watched, the Descendant infant began sucking greedily upon the bottle, draining it in long, steady pulls.

"Watch," said Quist. He reached over the top of the cradle and tried to wrest the bottle from the baby's mouth. He could not pry it loose. The attendant reached in to help the chief researcher pull on the bottle. The infant's cheeks formed two deep hollows as it sucked, clutching harder on the bottle. The baby wrapped his arms and legs around it and the researchers' arms as they heaved the bottle upward. The infant rose up into the air with it, continuing to suckle, barely seeming to strain, showing no emotion.

"Except for that strength, they look so human," Gates said.

Quist nodded at the attendant. The chief researcher held the bottle as the woman unfastened the Descendant infant's diaper. She lifted the legs so Gates could see.

Beneath the mask Gates bit his lip. Below the Descendant's penis was an angry red scar in the scrotum, indicating where the castration had taken place. At the anterior lower part of the spine, there was a welt of fluorescent pink with a black scab centered on it.

"That bump at the end of the coccyx would be invisible on a human being. We took off a six-inch tail that has a tendency to curl between the legs of these animals as they grow. Lift him up farther."

As the infant was practically stood on his head, Gates saw a black sheen along the lower back of the animal.

"Looks like fur."

"It is fur," said Gates. "Many human babies have it when they are infants, a fine pelt that disappears or turns to blond as the baby grows. In these things, this patch of fur would continue to thicken and blacken throughout life. Feel it." Gates did so gingerly.

Quist continued, "If we did not emasculate them, they would develop pelts over their entire bodies. Actually, it's as soft and thick as a short-haired dog."

The attendant lowered the baby and refastened the tape on the diaper.

By now the Descendant had drained the bottle and continued to suck eagerly on the air, the first signs of distress showing.

"He's still hungry," said Quist. "He'll be needing a second bottle right away." The attendant had already retrieved one from the cart.

The Descendant infant's face grew red and pinched with pain and looked as if it might cry. Still, Quist could not pull the bottle away. Finally, when the attendant waved the fresh bottle over the top of the cradle, offering another half gallon of the warm, sweet liquid, the Descendant released the empty bottle and opened its frothing mouth to receive the nipple. Again Gates was startled. Four needles meshed in the baby's mouth.

"Baby teeth like none you've ever seen before, eh?" said Quist. "The canines are the first to descend in these infants. They are fixed into position until the infant begins to lose them in a month to two months. The adult teeth that descend through the gums then stay retracted unless the animal is distressed, and are activated by the hormones that appear at about the same time."

Gates's eyes opened wide over the top of the mask. He shook his head as he said, "I'm just amazed at these things. I want you to accelerate the tour, yet I'm utterly fascinated by every phase of it. I keep thinking of all the moral implications of this research. I keep remembering that our ends will certainly justify the things we are doing here today. Show me more. What about those others, those . . ."

"Those juveniles? Actually, they are still infants. It's just that their behavior at two to six weeks seems juvenile in human developmental terms."

The mechanics of the feeding process for the older Descendants contrasted considerably from the bottle feeding in the nursery. Gates saw at once that the crews for this feeding were organized into groups of four. Three of the attendants were each responsible for removing one toddler from the cribs and placing each one of them at a feeding trough. These were stainless steel and enclosed completely on all sides. At one end of the enclosure was a stainless-steel depression, a trough that was fed from a channel that ran down between two rows of the enclosures. At the other end of the feeding enclosure, another depression was actually a gutter. Gates didn't immediately see the purpose of it. Each infant was stripped of its baby gown and diaper and placed inside the enclosure on its hands and knees. Then the attendant tugged on a stainless-steel handle at the top of the enclosure, and the gate fell open at the far end. A mound of raw meat slapped in a heap on the metal floor.

"It's beef," said Quist. "Ten to twenty pounds, according to the infant's weight. At this age, they eat their own body weight twice a day."

"It's not cooked."

"They prefer it raw, and as you will see later, the beef is really quite freshly killed. Within the hour, in fact." Gates leaned forward to see over the enclosure and felt a hand on his shoulder. He turned to look into the eyes of one of the attendants—the fourth member of the crew, who stood behind the other three, pacing back and forth from side to side as the attendants watched their charges feed.

"It's all right," said Quist. "You'll have to be very careful, Mr. Gates. This team leader is responsible for the security of everyone here. I'll remind you now that you do have that pistol in your right-hand coat pocket. However, I caution you not to use it unless you are actually attacked by one of the little Descendants. The fourth member of each of these feeding teams is responsible to the other three for their security."

"How is that done?"

As if in response, one of the Descendants shrieked. The attendant at the enclosure reached quickly with a gloved hand to the feed lever to let out another ration of beef. But before he could pull on the lever, the Descendant leaped a full three feet in the air from its squat and grabbed onto the gloved hand. The attendant let out a cry of pain as the Descendant bit into the thumb of the glove and began shaking its head back and forth. The man turned, holding the Descendant toward the fourth member of the feeding team. The fourth member drew a black instrument from a holster around his waist.

Gates ducked away.

"Don't worry, Mr. Gates. It's not a pistol."

The fourth member punched the Descendant in the back with his instrument and the little beast suddenly went spread-eagle, its arms and legs flying outward, its mouth flying open, releasing the third attendant's gloved hand. One of the other attendants caught the animal and lowered it into its enclosure. Gates watched as the third attendant pulled off the glove and showed the indentation between the thumb and the wrist. "No damage," he said. "There will just be a bruise; the gloves did the job again."

Quist said, "The glove is stiff leather on the outside, and on the inside, a finely woven chain mail, then another layer of leather. It positively would not do for any of those little beasts to draw blood at feeding time. Fresh blood—fresh human blood—would elevate the feeding frenzy to a dangerous high."

"What was that . . . thing he used on the animal? I think I'm going to begin calling them animals. I see no reason but to call them anything but beasts or animals or Descendants. It's clear to me now. I'm completely satisfied that we're not dealing with humans here, after all, but another species altogether. But what was that thing?"

"A stun gun. A charge of electrical current immobilizes its victim instantly. It will be all right momentarily. There, see it's already back to feeding."

"More a feeding frenzy," Gates murmured. He looked into the feeding enclosure and saw the Descendant pulling itself forward on its belly, unsteadily getting to its hands and knees, dropping its face into the pile of warm red meat. Even as it did so, it relieved itself, and the attendant used a warm spray to wash down the enclosure, squirting waste and excess blood into the tunnel. A stream of water swept the waste away from the feeding enclosure.

"The efficiency, Mr. Quist. I really admire the economy and efficiency that you have put together here. I only wish I could have been here from the beginning."

"Mr. Gates, your being here now is sufficient. Because all we have done in the past months is put this program into place for launch. The mission tonight is an extraordinary test of whether all the things we have prepositioned are going to have any hope of being carried out in a practical, useful sense for the security of our country."

FORT HOOD, TEXAS

"Bring back anything?" asked Grayson Kirk.

Indeed, the inside of the West Fort Hood Officers' Club brought back wrenching memories with every dank smell that wafted to PJ Payne's nose. Here, she had spent heart-galloping times both happy and terrifying. Here, she had longed like a high school girl for just a word or glance from Captain Mark Payne. In the raucous after-work party atmosphere, she had nursed drinks and gazed into his face, feeling an electricity passing between them, a connection that shut out all the other partying officers. She had been chased by police and by shadowy agents from here. She had accompanied Grayson Kirk here once before to begin the search for her missing husband.

Her pulse fluttered a second. And yes, they had found Mark, had found him dying in Montana.

Now they were back at the beginning. Square One. The smell of spilled beer souring in the carpet and the braying of drunks leaked from the bar to the entry of the club, where PJ stood before the pay phone.

"Are you all right?" Kirk asked.

She nodded, her answer belied by the gray pallor of her face. She sniffed deeply, stiffening as she inhaled, dropped the coins, and tapped out the numbers on the touch-tone pad. She held the receiver away from her ear as it emitted a recording. Over and over, the blasé voice repeated the number as PJ counted silently. Then, with a snap of static, the recording stopped. Ten seconds of silence. Then a whisper.

PJ spoke into the phone.

"Any further word? . . . Nevada? . . . No . . . How could they know? . . ."

A crowd of rowdies burst from the bar, hugging each other, bellowing drunkenly into each other's ears. PJ cupped her hand over the phone. "Wait . . . I can't hear you. Just a second." She took an impatient breath and studied the floor until the mob passed behind on their way to the latrine. She felt Grayson Kirk press nearer to make way for the drinkers.

A snide, offensive remark whispered from one of them caused her to flinch. She closed her eyes hard, determined to ignore the group. She felt Kirk stiffen at her side, and she reached for him, digging her nails into his forearm as an entreaty to ignore the drunks. He relaxed.

She pressed the phone into her ear angrily as the group seemed to want to stop and chatter boisterously in the entry. She leaned closer to Kirk and whispered closely into his ear. "The contact says they are following us already. . . ."

At first it felt like a pinch, and she reacted hotly, turning to swing the phone receiver at the offender. But then she realized the sting had come from a needle as she felt the cold liquid pooling in her buttock.

She gasped, more in frustration than pain. "Grayson, it's . . . them. . . ."

He didn't need to be told. Three of the drunks had instantly sobered and slammed Kirk against the wall.

"I got the needle in him," said one gruff voice.

"Got them both," answered another.

PJ felt her knees buckle. She drew a breath to scream, but her exhalation was a moan.

The commotion had drawn the attention of some officers from the bar. "What's going on here?"

"Nothing, Major," muttered the gruff voice. "Our friends just had a little too much to drink. We're going to buddy up and get them home safely before they get into trouble."

PJ wanted to protest. But her body would not cooperate. Indeed, she felt her lips numbing, her vision blackening, shrinking rapidly into a narrow tunnel. She heard a moan and realized it had come from her. She tried to call Grayson's name, tried to apologize for dragging him into this.

No words would form in her tingling mouth. She tasted a bitterness in the back of her throat. Then she was out, her last conscious thought one of regret that they had fallen into the hands of the very people she had vowed to bring down.

5

. . . .

The late-afternoon sun had begun falling from its apex in the sky. The shadows were lengthening, stretching eastward. Lieutenant Colonel Josh Avery and Colonel Tommy Vickers stood well away from the other clutch of men who huddled against the side of the building, finding whatever shade they could. The two senior officers stood out in the heat.

Josh felt the sun trying to penetrate his clothing and body, trying to suck the fluids and the very life out of him. In the meantime Vickers was giving him an oral beating at the same time. "Crew rest, my ass. We've got a mission to fly tonight. We are going to fly to Nevada. We are going to pick up a new Special Operations team. And we are going to drop them in on an exercise. There is no argument about this, Avery. I won't accept an argument."

"Colonel, I'm not trying to argue with you. I'm just trying to point out that we flew until very late last night. And then you kept . . . we had to stay up a little later than ordinary for the mission debriefing.

First thing today I was out flying again to try to check out the route from last—"

"Who gave you permission to do that?" Vickers's eyes narrowed and he stepped closer, invading Josh's personal space. Josh stepped back, feeling the heat of his superior's rage as well as the bright, breathless sun, which was beginning to make dots float before his eyes.

"Colonel, you've got to get away from this notion that I am trying to deceive you or defy you. All I'm telling you is I assigned my crew some additional training today. We went out to refly the mission in order to discover what we had done wrong. I was under the impression that there would not be another Special Operations team, that there would not be more flying tonight. If there is any problem here, it is simply that I misjudged the mission requirements. And all this crew-rest business is to say that we will have overflown our time in the cockpit by the time we are midway through tonight's mission. That is not a big deal, unless something happens. If we bend a tail rotor or get a blade strike or stretch a couple of skids, then there will be hell to pay."

Vickers slung a hand in the air absently. "Fine. You done your duty, mister. Now, I'm taking full responsibility if anything should happen to those helicopters or to you. You just give me your assurance that you will do your very damned best and won't let anything go wrong, that you won't sabotage the goddamned mission or something."

Josh took a step backward as if to get a better view of the squat colonel. "What do you mean, sabotage the mission, goddammit? Colonel, I don't know where you got a notion like that, but I don't appreciate hearing it."

"Don't you talk to me like that, Avery."

Josh felt a surge of heat from within, a heat that minimized the burning of the sun on his damp back.

"I'll do better than that, Tommy, you little son of a bitch. If you ever challenge my honesty again I'll knock you on your goddamned ass. Understand that, Tommy?" Josh stood, his feet spread and planted, his knees slightly bent. He realized that his arms had tucked a little and that his hands had clutched themselves into fists. He'd assumed a combative position.

Vickers glared at him a second, then began laughing. "Fine," he said. "I like to see that in you, Josh. I like to see a little life once in a while. I'm not so sure you could beat my ass, but I'm damned happy that you'd be willing to try it for having your honor insulted, you little weenie pilot." He turned his back and stomped away.

Josh flinched as if he would grab the colonel's collar and haul him back. But then he froze there in the sun, feeling foolish for letting Vickers get to him.

The flight to Nevada was uneventful and enjoyable for Josh. The sun was at their back the entire time, letting the shadow of the helicopter lead the way across the mountains and into Nevada. The terrain slid by underneath, as if the earth had become a treadmill for their aircraft's shadow.

From altitude there was nothing interesting to see except for the passage through the mountains. Josh let Breen fly until they reached the mountains. Then he took control and put the helicopter into a zigzag climb, keeping a constant distance between the craft and the rising terrain. Instead of picking a saddle between two peaks, he chose one of the highest peaks and attacked its summit. As he gained altitude, the helicopter began slowing as the climb angle grew steeper and steeper. Josh adjusted power, aiming the skids of the helicopter for the jagged boulders on top.

As he flew, he felt himself being invigorated with the excitement of precision flying. The others in the craft watched forward as the peak grew larger, more detailed, more deadly. But nobody said anything, except Josh, when he asked for the wind direction. Breen made a radio call to confirm what they had already heard on their initial flight weather briefing: a twenty-knot tail wind blowing steadily east.

Josh cut his margin of clearance of the peak even slimmer. Had the wind been blowing into his face, he knew there would be an invisible downdraft on their side of the mountain. As the air came across, it would be suddenly lowered in pressure and forced downward. It would rob the helicopter of a few feet and force it onto the rocks.

As the Huey crested the peak, Josh anticipated the downdraft and lowered the collective, lifting everybody's belly, giving a sudden rush of excitement. The barren rocks that had been growing in the windscreen suddenly dropped away. Josh nosed the helicopter over, again trying to regain the closeness to the mountain as he flew downward at 120 knots, struggling against the impulse to push the nose over faster than the helicopter had been intended to fly.

The downdraft, the sudden drop in power, and the pushing of the cyclic forward in the cockpit caused the helicopter to scream down the mountainside at a dizzying pace. Josh found a valley that was cut deeply into the side of the mountain and flew down into it, continuing to descend, the sides of the valley rising up above them to the left and right, twisting and turning as if inside the screen of a video game.

Within fifteen minutes the excitement was over. They had flown out of the valley, which had expanded before them into another large desert floor.

He turned the helicopter back over to his copilot, Breen, and hunkered back into his own seat. He tried to stay alert, checking instruments and making radio calls as the flight progressed. But he was distracted, preoccupied with the strange feelings he had been having about this mission ever since they had assembled on the south-ramp flight line at West Fort Hood, Texas.

It was after nightfall when Josh saw the lights in the black distance, somewhere near a horizon that he could not see. "There's The Ranch," he said into the intercom.

"Roger," Vickers rasped. They were the only two who had been permitted maps, so Josh had to do the navigating from the front. But he knew that Vickers, as was his continual habit, had been navigating from the rear, checking him along the way.

The spot on the ground had been designated only as The Ranch—"capital T, capital R"—by Vickers. As they flew toward it with the last lights of twilight dimming, Josh wondered how any ranch could exist in the terrain he was seeing below. He had halfway expected that somewhere along the line the ground would begin greening or that he'd see some sort of irrigation system scratched into the earth, to grow alfalfa or hay. How it was possible to have a ranch in the desert, he did not know.

When they had flown in for their landing in the spot

that had been designated by Vickers, lighted by yellow beanbag lights, Josh and his crew began looking over the aircraft, readying it for the night flight. Then the crew ate and rested.

• •

Vickers set the time for the night mission at midnight. As the hour approached, so did the troll colonel. Before he had even reached the helicopter, he shouted for them to "fire it up."

Josh looked at his watch. Fifteen minutes early. Vickers pulled him aside as Breen and Ingalls began the start up.

"Ingalls," Vickers said, "he's not going with us. You tell him. Somebody will meet him and take him to his night quarters. I doubt if he'll bitch."

Josh nodded. "It would be helpful to have somebody back there making a head count on the pickup," he said.

"Fine, I'll make the goddamned head count. Here." He held out a pair of belts. Immediately, by the heft of them, Josh knew that they were gun belts, and was able to see and feel the pistols in the light that reached them from across the ranch's out yard.

"They're loaded. Strap them on. You and Breen both. You may have to use them tonight."

"Are you bullshitting me, Tommy?"

Vickers leaned in extremely close to Josh's chest, thrusting his chin upward toward his subordinate's face. "Do I look like I'm bullshitting you, Avery? No, I'm not."

"How? When? . . ."

"You'll know when. *Goddamn,* you *will* know when."

"Over there," he said, pointing to a group of outbuildings in the distance, surrounded by bright amber mercury-vapor security lights. "Beyond those lights is a helipad for pickup. You'll meet your Special Operations team there."

Josh could see that the colonel was distracted and unusually tense, even for Vickers. Josh found the intensity infectious. He concentrated all the more on the start as they readied to launch the mission.

On the helipad a squad of intense, earnest soldiers climbed into the cabin with Vickers. Josh saw they were armed with a hodgepodge of weapons—AK-47s, M-16s, Uzis—and he was certain the variety was not due to accident or lack of funding.

The cold night temperature lessened the effect of the high altitude. Josh found that Breen was flying at less than full power. He navigated as usual, unwilling to trust anybody else over terrain they had not seen before. Occasionally he looked into the back and saw the men hunched sternly and soberly over their weapons.

Just a half hour after takeoff, Breen began lining up the final leg of the approach path to the landing zone, dropping to an altitude below twenty feet, sometimes brushing the skids on the scrub brush.

"We'll be touching down in four minutes, thirty seconds, Colonel," said Josh.

"I know. You don't have any lights on anywhere, do you? No rotating beacons, no red-filtered flashlights?"

"No, of course not. We haven't been able to use any on any other mission. Why would we begin using them tonight?"

"Don't start with me now, Avery. Standing out in the middle of nowhere, where no one else can hear is one thing. But you're not going to start talking to me like that on the intercom in the middle of a mission. Do you got that?"

"Roger, about two and a half minutes now."

"After you touch down and drop off these troops, we're going to pull off a ways and shut down the helicopter."

This was a new twist to Josh. By now, he'd begun to get accustomed to Vickers's twists and turns. But he was beginning to wonder if the erratic behavior of the colonel could be traced to mental instability.

Breen set the helicopter down gingerly, dancing the skids among the hard stones that protruded from a shallow covering of soil at the spot where the LZ was designated. A tiny ridgeline of stone high-centered the right skid, causing it to shake, making the helicopter seem as if it were tap-dancing on the rock. As the soldiers began jumping from the helicopter, their weights kept rocking it back and forth as well. But in seconds they were gone, sopped up by the blackness of the night. Vickers gave Josh a set of map coordinates. Josh gave a course, and Breen set the Huey down less than a minute later.

"Shut it down," Vickers said, then disconnected his communications headset and jumped from the cabin to the uneven ground. Josh, watching him through his NVGs from the cockpit of the helicopter, did a double take. He thought Vickers was drawing his pistol from its holster. But no, the colonel was putting his pistol back.

Vickers ordered them to leave the blade untied. He also instructed them to get the helicopter preset for a quick takeoff. When this had been done, he handed each of the two men an oversized binocular case.

"Night-vision binoculars." He pointed past the nose

of the helicopter. "Let's go watch these guys fumble around in the darkness."

In minutes they had settled along the edge of a ridge. They put the binoculars to their eyes. They were about two hundred meters away from a steep drop-off. That fell away about one hundred feet and leveled off into a valley floor that was only half a mile wide. In the center of the valley was a mound of earth that looked like a scoop of ice cream dropped on the desert floor and gently melted away, except for that round top.

Josh said, "Where is the rally point going to be?"

"The rally point is right here," came the growl from beneath a set of the binoculars. "But there ain't going to be no pickup."

"You going to make them walk out?"

"Listen to me, Avery. If you could see my face I'd have you read my lips. But since you can't see, I'm going to ask you to open your goddamned ears and listen. This is the rally point that ain't no rally point. There ain't going to be no pickup. There ain't gonna be no troops walking out. This is a one-way mission."

Josh shook his head, unable to think of a question to ask, considering the bizarre circumstances that Vickers had just laid out.

"Any questions, Avery?"

"Listen, Tommy, why don't you knock off the bullshit and tell me what's going on?" Josh saw Vickers's hand being raised toward him. Vickers flapped it in his face and then pointed down the hill into the valley. Josh picked up his binoculars and focused on the spot. He saw the two groups of soldiers they had dropped off. He saw half of them approaching the mound directly between their position and the objective. About one hundred meters beyond that, approaching from the valley, five other men crawled on their bellies.

"Here, hold these." Vickers brandished his own night-vision binoculars. Josh took them. He watched the colonel fumbling around inside the binocular case. "A radio," he explained unnecessarily. He telescoped an antenna up and barked into the set. "Charlie Battery, are you up and ready?"

"Roger," came a crisp reply.

Vickers took back the night-vision binoculars, snatching them from Josh's hands.

"Now, watch closely," he said, the growl in his voice rising a pitch higher in excitement.

Below, the men continued pressing toward the mound. For the first time since this training had begun, Josh saw defenders in position. Then he saw several other figures take shape. Now he began to understand a little more about this mission. Vickers had preassigned an aggressor force to begin testing the Special Operations team. Apparently, all the flying requirements had met with Vickers's satisfaction. No wonder they didn't have to worry about rallying or picking them up. These soldiers would be graded on how well they were able to sneak up on the objective. Josh realized then that Vickers probably intended to be flown down after watching the training engagement to debrief both teams. That's why a rally point was not necessary. That's why it had only been a one-way.

• •

The single pop of a rifle startled him. He looked carefully and saw other flashes. Moments later he heard the rapid popping of automatic and semi-automatic fire.

"Blanks?" Breen whispered.

Vickers barked a sarcastic laugh.

Josh watched one of the men on the mound fall backward and roll ten feet into the desert. Pretty realistic, he thought.

Out on the plain, two of the attackers writhed in the dirt, acting as though they'd been shot.

"Have you got umpires down there telling those men that they've been removed from the combat, instructing them to act like they've been wounded or killed?"

Vickers snarled through another sardonic laugh, "Umpires, hell! They're using live ammunition."

Josh laughed, believing that his ears had played a trick on him. "Paint balls? Laser lights? How are they—"

"Fire for effect, Charlie Battery. Fire for effect," Vickers growled into his radio.

Josh heard Vickers laugh wickedly. "Umpires, huh? You think umpires, Avery. You just go ahead on and think it. You two are about to see something that is going to knock your dicks stiff. It's a damn shame that you can't ever repeat what you see to anybody else in the world, understand?"

Both men nodded.

"I say again, do you understand?"

Josh and Breen grunted at once, now aware that Vickers could not see them nodding in the dark.

In seconds Josh heard a swishing shriek above them in the air and ducked involuntarily.

"Incoming," Vicker said. "You can put the binoculars down. I've got white flares mixed in." The pop in the air above them confirmed it. A brilliant white flare lit up the scene.

The blast of artillery rounds exploding above the

desert floor cut off a wicked giggle that Vickers had uttered. Josh threw down his night-vision binoculars and saw in the dancing light of flares the speckles of dust being raised off the earth. All of a sudden everything became clear. Vickers was calling in live artillery. There was no way to simulate what was happening below. One section of the firing battery had exactly preplanned its fires for the exact spot that the one team of soldiers had crawled into. The men vanished in a cloud of dust and shrapnel. Josh knew that there was no way that men lying in the open on the desert floor could survive air bursts at a hundred feet above the ground.

"My God," he shouted above the sound of gunfire screaming overhead. "My God, Tommy, you've called in artillery on your own team. Shut it off! Shut it off, goddammit!"

"*You* shut it off, Avery. Shut off the chatter and watch."

Josh did watch—in horror. One team had not been affected by the artillery, and Josh realized that they had not yet been noticed by the defenders on the hill. They acted completely unconcerned about the artillery. They continued to advance toward the hill. When they were within fifty feet they abruptly rose up and began firing their rifles at the defenders.

Josh realized that there were in fact no umpires down there on the ground, that these men were firing live ammunition at each other. He'd never heard of such a thing. He'd never seen such a thing, except in combat. What kind of crazy training mission was this?

"Colonel, are you nuts?" he shouted. "You are killing your own people and they are killing each other. What kind of soldiers are those?"

Vickers mumbled into the radio. The artillery firing, except for the periodic flares, stopped seconds afterward. "Too accurate," Vickers complained. "Goddamned ragheads wouldn't be that precise with their own firing batteries. Goddammit, I broke the attack before I had a chance to see the bastards test each other out. But have you ever seen anybody that cool under a battery artillery attack?"

Josh watched as half a dozen men ran down the side of the mound toward the attacking force. Two of them were shot down immediately by the attacking force, and one of the attackers was bowled over by a sniper's round from on top of the hill.

Suddenly, the two forces met in bloody hand-to-hand combat. Josh saw them grappling on the ground. He realized that they must be biting each other as well. Within minutes the attacking force was completely overcome. Another half dozen soldiers ran down from the mound carrying their rifles. The troops began fighting among themselves.

Breen, who had never seen combat, suddenly left the two of them and ran off a dozen feet to begin vomiting into the sand.

Josh realized that Vickers was on his feet, hanging the strap of the night-vision binoculars over his shoulder. He stood up. Vickers said, "We've got to get out of here. We've got to evacuate immediately."

"Evacuate? Why?" Josh asked.

"Because the counterattacking force had too easy a job of it. They are going to continue pressing their counterattack and mop up the area. They are going to be searching the area and killing anybody in it. And the attackers are going to be retreating back to here."

"Goddamn," whispered Josh. "What kind of soldiers are these? You don't mean . . ."

Vickers punched him in the arm. "Wake up, Avery, Yes I do mean. They are going to search this area and kill everybody in it, including us, if we are still here when they arrive."

Vickers put the radio to his mouth and mashed the button. He gave several commands indicating that other targets should be fired, beginning immediately. "Fire for effect, and don't stop firing until I tell you to. I want you to walk that artillery up the hill toward the landing zone."

Josh picked up his binoculars and looked over the edge of the hill. He saw that at least a dozen men in groups of twos and threes were running toward the hill.

"They must have heard me, for crying out loud," Vickers shouted. "Let's go. Josh, you stay here with me. We'll protect the rear while Breen gets back there to fire up the chopper."

He pulled his pistol and ordered Josh to do the same. "And you, Breen, you get your ass back to that helicopter. I want to hear it firing up seconds after you disappear from my sight."

Josh heard Breen's bootheels clumping on the hard ground as he disappeared behind them. Then he thought he heard the sound of his heartbeat. He reached down and extracted his pistol from the holster. A 9-millimeter. He was used to the weapon. He'd been in similar combat situations—but not in the United States.

"Do you want me to shoot to kill?"

"What the hell do you think?" growled Vickers. "After what you've seen, do you really have to ask that question? Affirmative, I want you to shoot to kill. Don't get any attack of compassion now. Those troops that are coming up here are every bit as deadly and ruthless as any Vietcong you faced in Vietnam. They are worse than the NVA. Worse than all the mean somebitches you ever met in the world. They are the baddest troops you ever seen or heard about. They will kill you and then eat you for breakfast."

Josh believed the hyperbole. He hunkered down among the rocks, cradling the pistol in both hands, getting the feel of it. The artillery began firing, but he saw that it was striking the area where the hand-to-hand combat had been over for more than a minute now. Already, soldiers were climbing up their hill. He was grateful to see that the artillery had begun walking its way up, closing behind them.

"Here," Vickers said. He handed out a heavy bag and Josh took it. He opened up the noose of the sack. Another one of Vickers's bag of tricks. This time a bag of hand grenades. He whistled under his breath and uttered an obscenity. What the hell had Vickers gotten him into now? He had to shake his head to realize that once again he was not in a combat zone in a far-off land. Instead, here he was digging into a bag of live grenades while under attack by a group of bloodthirsty American troops gone berserk.

• •

Major Cliff Breen had just seen as much of combat as he ever wanted to see. It had been a relief to him that the American withdrawal from Vietnam had prevented him from going there. He was not one of those soldiers who believed he needed a war to make a career. And now, with fifteen years in the army, he believed he might make it to the end without a war.

That was, until tonight. Then something worse than his worst dreams had happened. He was witnessing combat. He was practically engaged in combat. And now he was running headlong through the night to avoid combat.

The ground was uneven, alternately rock hard and sandy soft. And the drifting shadows cast by the flares floating across the skies made him lose his balance. He stumbled frequently but did not fall. Finally in the light he saw the the black Huey. He dodged two tall spires of brush. But surprisingly the brush dodged, too, and he crashed into it. The grunting and cries of surprise meant that he had run into men. He rolled over and came up between them and the helicopter. He was close enough to see that they were American soldiers.

"Damn, what a relief," he said. "What the hell are you two people doing here?" Both of the strangers were out of breath, gasping for air.

"We landed in a helicopter." They, too, were out of breath.

Breen leaned in to see if he could identify the men, but could not. "Great, I'm one of the pilots who flew you here. I've got to fire it up right now and be prepared for our mission commander to come back." The shooting behind him grew nearer. Then a grenade exploded, making him duck. Intermittent artillery bursts kept rolling closer.

One of the two men was on his hands and knees, fumbling around for the rifles they had dropped; an M-16 and an AK-47. The other circled, facing Breen, moving around to get himself between the helicopter and the major.

"What the hell are you doing? I've got to get to that helicopter. You're in my way."

"You can't pass by here. We have orders. We have to wait for a helicopter to land for us."

"Fine, fine. Great, you've done your job. I'll make sure you get a commendation for it. But this is your helicopter and I'm your pilot. I'm supposed to start this helicopter, so get out of my way so I can . . ." He tried to sidestep the soldier before him. The man pushed him back.

"But that's the helicopter that's supposed to take you out of here," Breen whined.

"You can't pass by."

The other soldier on his hands and knees stood up, grunting in satisfaction, shaking sand out of his M-16 rifle, trying to work the action. Breen heard the sand grinding in the metal parts and felt relief that it was not working and that the man had not gone for the AK, which tended to be less affected by grit.

"Look, I'm a major in the United States Army. I'm the pilot of that helicopter. And both of our colonels, the guys who are in charge of you two assholes, told me to get back here and start this helicopter, and that's what I'm going to do."

He stepped forward and the man shoved him back. Breen heard a grunt and turned around. He saw that the other soldier had the rifle pointed at him and was trying to pull the trigger.

"What the goddamned? . . ." He felt a sudden chill as he realized the man was trying to kill him. In a cold, calculated fashion, he was trying to get his rifle to work so he could shoot him. The man had had orders and now he was going to carry them out. Quickly, Breen turned to the other one. "Get out of

my way, soldier, before I have you thrown in the
stockade." He shoved the soldier to the side. He did
not see the blow coming. A stunning left hook caught
him on the cheekbone and smeared his nose across his
face. Breen sat down hard on his butt, feeling the tears
come to his eyes.

"Goddamn, you broke my . . ." He held his hands
out. "Look at this." The hands were wet. He could see
that it was blood from his broken nose. He could smell
the blood. He could taste the warm flavor of liquid
copper trickling down his throat. He heard a growl.
He looked up. The man fiddling with the rifle had
thrown it to the ground. He began advancing. The
other man stepped up beside him, and the two began
moving in on Breen. Breen remembered his pistol. He
grabbed for it in the holster and had it out. But his
hands were slippery with his own blood. He was trying
to squeeze the trigger when one of the men grabbed
his leg and yanked hard on it. He was thrown onto his
back, his head smacking against the hard earth. He
leaned up on one elbow and pointed the gun down
beyond his knee where the man . . . where the man
was biting into his leg, savagely, deeply.

Breen shrieked in agony. The soldier looked up,
turning his head toward him in a wicked grin, baring
four huge canine teeth, like something out of a vam-
pire movie. The other man lunged for Breen's chest
and shoved him back toward the earth.

For the second time the major's head hit the earth.
He tried to work the pistol around, tried to shove it
against the body of the man pulling back on him, but
he couldn't twist enough.

Suddenly he felt the same kind of excruciating pain
that he had felt in his legs; the puncturing, stabbing,

and tearing as the soldier on his chest clamped his jaws on his throat and cut off the air supply, ripping into Breen's neck.

• •

Vickers threw a grenade as far as he could down the hill and watched it bounce once as it disappeared into the darkness, where he had seen a couple of soldiers advancing. When it went off he heard shrapnel singing through the air and then heard simultaneous screeches.

"Two more down. Goddammit, Josh, this is almost fun, ain't it?"

Josh Avery fired a couple of rounds from his pistol at a fleeting shadow across the barren landscape below him. "No. I don't hear that helicopter starting up. Tommy, this is crazy. Is there any way in the world for you to call this off?"

Vickers chuckled savagely. "Avery, my boy, we are in the shit. There is no way out of this except to fight our way out of it. There is no surrendering to these bastards. They are going to cut you to pieces and eat you alive if we don't get to that helicopter in time."

"That goddamn Cliff Breen must have gotten lost. He probably couldn't find his ass with both hands. I can go if you want me to, Tommy."

Vickers grunted with the effort of tossing another grenade, the spoon flying off musically. "Get going, Avery. Keep your pistol ready. Don't be afraid to use it." Josh turned to run, hesitating a second until the grenade had gone off.

"Avery, goddammit, I mean it. If you see anybody —I mean goddamned *anybody* out here, you have to consider them the enemy. Shoot first, ask questions later, unless you run into Breen. Wait a second. He's

such a simple-minded bastard, anyhow. Shoot anybody, including Breen." Vickers laughed sardonically
but it was lost on Josh, already running toward the
helicopter.

By force of habit, Josh had memorized the terrain
on the way there. Always concerned about being lost,
he never went anyplace in the city or even in a new
building without imprinting the route in his head. As
he broke into the tiny clearing near the Huey, he realized at once that something was out of place. The light
of the flares was dimming. He saw a lump of boulders
that weren't there before. When one of the boulders
moved he pointed his pistol and hollered, "Don't
move, you bastard. I've got you covered."

A fresh flare popped high above them, casting his
shadow across the men on the ground. The shadow
stretched all the way to the helicopter. Josh stepped
aside to move the shadow. He saw Cliff Breen lying
bloodied and torn on the ground. Two men adminis-
tered to him.

He immediately saw that Breen was torn so badly
that he probably couldn't survive. His throat had been
torn away and his head lolled back at an odd angle. In
the wavering light of the flair, Josh could even see the
vertebrae in the neck and the dark holes of the trachea
and esophagus bleeding down into the torso. Below
that, Breen had been partially disemboweled.

"What the hell happened to the major?"

No answer. The pair simply stood up, shaking blood
from their hands, wiping their faces. Josh saw teeth
that he could not believe existed outside a zoo.

"What happened to . . . ?" His voice trailed off
as he realized that these two had not been administ-
ering to Breen at all. They had been *feeding* on him.

He knew he could not get to the helicopter with these two blocking his path.

They advanced toward him, exposing the teeth. One of the man's jaws dropped down on his chest so that his mouth was open inhumanly wide. Josh remembered Vickers's warning about using the pistol.

Josh lifted the 9-millimeter. He'd never shot somebody so coldly. His warning, though, was brief and to the point.

"You take one more step, you silly bastard, and I'm going to blow your goddamned head off." The man took another step. Josh hesitated. The man bunched for a leap.

Josh didn't so much pull the trigger as flinch, firing by reflex. The bullet struck the thing in its open mouth, splattering blood, throwing the thing's head back as it leaped. Josh's hesitation cost him. The dying figure, a cavernous hole blasted from the back of its skull, hit Josh full in the chest, throwing him to the ground. His hand hit a rock, paralyzing his grip on the pistol. He tried to turn the gun, but the hand would not work properly. He felt those fangs stabbing him through his shirt. He tried to push the head away, but the effort brought a cry to his lips. It felt as if those teeth had lodged between his ribs. Josh couldn't breathe, the pain clutched his chest so tightly. He tried to squirm loose. Fortunately for Josh the second figure, seeing the blood, attacked its mate, pulling it backward, yanking the fangs free painfully.

Josh dragged himself from beneath the pair. He felt around for his dropped pistol but could not find it. So he struggled to his feet and dashed toward the Huey. Josh's chest was wet, sopping with his own blood. He painfully climbed into the cockpit, afraid to glance down at his shirt.

For a moment, in his panic, he couldn't remember how to start a UH-1H helicopter. He tried to think his way through but could not. It seemed as if long minutes were passing, although it could only be seconds. Where was his mind? What was he doing?

He backed up mentally and emptied his mind of the checklist, stopped trying to figure out which button to hit next, which trigger to pull, which switch to flip. He put his body on automatic and told himself to start the helicopter. Instantly, things happened the way they should. The starter motor began to tick. All the power gauges and tachometers were correct. He watched the exhaust gas temperature rise and prepared to shut off the start fuel as the helicopter's turbine engine was prepared to take over powering the blades. It seemed to take forever. Josh felt his chest tighten, a constriction in his throat, and a dryness in his mouth. He felt as if he would vomit.

Josh wrapped the throttle full to the stop, and the RPM leveled off at sixty-six hundred.

The second of the two soldiers, seeming to take offense at the Huey blasting the wind in his direction, looked up from its companion. He turned and ran at the helicopter, but Josh picked it up out of reach. All he would have to do now is ease the nose forward, pull collective pitch, and make an awkward takeoff, turning away from that artillery. But he knew he couldn't leave without Vickers. Where was the SOB? Surely he could hear the helicopter noise and head in the proper direction.

Josh began hovering toward the spot where he had left Vickers. He couldn't recall having seen anyplace clearly that would be suitable for landing. The terrain sloped too severely.

As he was thinking about how this whole mess was going to be sorted out—with the wild man in the clearing below him and the artillery growing closer and closer—Vickers burst into the edge of the clearing and ran across, oblivious to the creature below.

Vickers threw a hand grenade behind him to hold off his pursuers. Seconds later, the grenade's explosion attracted the creature's attention below the helicopter. It pursued Vickers, who dragged a foot as he tried to circle around the clearing. Josh could see Vickers had been wounded, too.

Josh pushed the cyclic forward, dropping the Huey's nose, making the helicopter dash across the clearing. He felt the jolt as one curved tip of the skid struck the thing in the shoulder and bowled him over. Josh set down the helicopter roughly on the uneven ground and Vickers struggled toward the aircraft.

Josh screamed at Vickers to hurry, although he knew his voice couldn't possibly be heard. The colonel struggled to climb over the edge of the cabin, but finally he rolled over on his back on the deck, and Josh picked up the helicopter.

He began another dash toward the edge of the clearing in a quick takeoff run. As he did so, a soldier burst out of the brush and leaped straight for the helicopter, both hands in the air, his mouth wide open. Again Josh saw the vicious fangs, the fierce inhuman expression. He flinched, feeling the pain in his chest again, hauling back on the cyclic, pulling the collective up to get an immediate climb.

There was a moment's hesitation before the blades gripped the air and pulled the craft up. In that moment, the creature bashed into the Huey's nose door with his chest. As the helicopter finally swooped up and to the right, Josh expected the thing to fly off and fall down. Instead it started pounding on the windshield.

The extra weight of the thing on the very front of the helicopter caused the center of gravity to shift far forward—too far forward, Josh feared. He felt the nose dropping and the helicopter falling toward the ground, even after he had pulled the cyclic back to the rear stops. Still the helicopter kept dipping.

He heard a clicking in the intercom. "Fly back over the clearing," Vickers ordered, his voice filtered through painfully gritted teeth.

"Tommy, get as far back in the cabin quickly to offset the weight."

"I said, fly over the—"

"Goddammit, Colonel. If you don't get back there right now to offset this out-of-balance condition, we're going to crash and burn right here, you son of a bitch. Now, you get back! Get back! *Get back!*"

Josh felt the clumping of bootheels on the cabin floor. Immediately, the nose began to ease up, and the cyclic control was gradually given back to him.

He flew a circle over the clearing and spoke over the intercom. "Whatever you are going to do, hurry up, Tommy. Do what you're going to do so we can get outta here."

"Okay, let's go."

Josh looked out the side and saw four figures dash from the edge of the clearing to the center of it.

Vickers called an artillery firing mission on the clearing. Josh realized the last of the creatures down there would soon fall victim to incoming artillery. Finally he leveled out on a setting that would take them directly back to The Ranch's headquarters.

"What are you going to do to that sombitch hanging on to the front of the aircraft?"

Josh shrugged, sending sparks of pain shooting across his chest. The creature no longer pounded on the front of the helicopter. It had simply seemed to be embracing the nose of the craft. "There is nothing to worry about," Josh said bitterly.

"Why is that, Avery? When we land on the ground, what's that bastard going to do? Give us a shave and a haircut?"

"By the time we get back he'll be dead."

"How do you know?"

"Look at the airspeed indicator."

"What the hell does that got to do with anything?"

Josh pointed at the instrument indicating zero.

Vickers got the point. "He's impaled on that thing. That tube?"

"The pitot tube."

Back at The Ranch, Josh set the helicopter down with enough forward airspeed to keep up the nose of the craft. They skidded across the sand to the helipad for about twenty feet before he finally dropped the collective. The helicopter rocked forward and then stopped. Before it had stopped bouncing, the figure clinging to the front of the craft had fallen backward.

After the shutdown, the two men got out and finished peeling the figure off the craft, laying him on the ground.

"He's dead," said Vickers.

Josh wasn't interested in the creature's condition. He stepped up to the head and put the toe of his boot on the jaw, pressing it downward. It fell open on his chest. The harder he pressed downward on the chin, the longer the lower canines grew as the chin pressed on the jaw from below.

"What the hell is that thing?" he asked weakly. As he stood there, his wounds still seeping, he suddenly felt faint from the aftershock, the loss of blood, and the scene he had just witnessed. He knew he was experiencing the after effects of combat. He'd been through it before, plenty of times.

"Vickers, you know what the hell is going wrong here, don't you? What kind of men are these? Are they even men?"

Vickers stood up, himself a bloody mess. "Welcome to the zoo, Avery. Welcome to the zoo."

Josh dropped to his knees. Slowly he toppled over, unconscious, his face in the sand.

Josh vaguely heard the arrival of an ambulance and dreamily felt himself being handled. He realized he must be dreaming. He felt the prick of a needle and the numbing warmth of anesthetic drugs coursing through his veins. He remembered he had been wounded, then realized he was being patched up. He experienced a sensual, erotic sensation and visualized himself in bed with Marilyn. As his dreams slipped into even foggier depths, he decided that this evening's terrors had been part of the dreamy unreality. That thought gave him some peace. He felt satisfied in every way, knowing that when he awakened he would be back at Fort Hood, Texas, and in the arms of his lover, Marilyn.

Book Two

*"Who is like unto the Beast?
Who is able to make war
with him?"*
—REVELATION, Chapter 13.

6

Slaves of Men

THE RANCH

Josh seemed to be half-awake, half-dead in a fogged state of consciousness. At times the mist seemed so thick he felt as if he were drowning in it, suffocating, gasping for air. At other times he floated above the fog and bobbed there on top of the waves of the ethereal. At those times he felt hands, cold and powerful, working his body over, lifting him, holding him, suspending him from sinking back into the fog. And he heard voices, urgent voices, commanding voices talking to each other in brisk, businesslike terms. He could not understand their language, and he did not feel at all acquainted with this situation.

Then, despite his best efforts to open his eyes, he would sink down into the hazy cloud again, his vision shut out, his hearing fading until no sounds but the distant yelps and barks of excited, businesslike people reached him.

Then he was painfully awake.

He opened his eyes, staring at a stark, flat ceiling with no texture, no holes. A white nothingness. He had no sense of depth or vision as his eyes cast about wildly, looking for a spot of color. Was this blindness? He'd always expected blackness. Was it instead like being trapped in a fog?

The room began to take shape. He saw that it was daylight, and that bright sunlight streamed into the room, whitening the ceiling, so that he could not make out its texture for a long time. Finally, his pupils narrowed so he could even see the strokes of the brushes that had painted the ceiling.

When he had looked up as far as his furry eyebrows would allow him, he could see no more than the ceiling. To the side, all he could see were white walls. When he looked down and squinted one eye at a time, he could see tubes protruding from his nose. He tried to utter a grunt but found that he had no vocal cords. He realized that the tubes had gone down his throat. He gagged, and in panic tried to grasp the tubes and pull them out, but he could not. His hands were leaden. His arms were weighted down. He could not move.

"Well, ain't you a sight?" came the husky growl of Colonel Tommy Vickers. "Hey, doc, we got us a live one here."

Josh's eyes moved around as far as his eye sockets would allow. Finally the head of Vickers came into his field of vision. From the other side of his bed came a younger-looking face, the mouth and nose covered with a surgical mask. Josh felt the cold chill of a stethoscope against his chest and a firm squeezing of his wrist.

"Rapid pulse. He's excited."

Josh tried to lick his lips, but could not even move his tongue. He felt another moment of panic and strained against the enormous gravity holding him in place.

"Hold it, boy. You're hog-tied so the IVs and tubes won't come out. They've even got one stuck up your dick." Vickers laughed in that savage tone of his. Somehow the familiarity and the vulgarity acted like a relaxant, soothing Josh. If Vickers could joke about his condition, he must be confident Josh would survive.

"You're going to be all right, Avery. We didn't realize how hurt you was until you conked out on us. Seems like one of those Descendants bit you right in the titty. Broke one of your ribs and poked a hole in a lung. It went flat as a goddamned empty pig bladder. For a while there it didn't look like you was gonna pull out of it. But now you're going to be okay. You'll be back flying in no time. We need you right away. So get your ass better."

Josh tried to signal with his eyes by blinking wildly, making zigzag movements from side to side.

"Boy, you got to speak up. I can't hear a goddamn thing with all those tubes in you." Vickers laughed again and Josh felt a poke in his thigh. "They are going to be pulling all these tubes out of you this afternoon now that you are awake. You should be on your feet by the end of the day. Couple weeks and I'm going to be showing you around this place, introducing you to some of the staff. You are going to like it here, Josh. You are going to feel pretty damned good about it."

Josh suddenly felt a sense of peace and relaxation. He rolled his head to the left and saw that the doctor was injecting a syringe into his IV tube. In seconds he was asleep, this time floating on top of his fog cloud.

When he awakened, the tubes were gone, and he

was propped partially upright in his bed. He tried a
little groan to see if his vocal cords worked. It gave
him great satisfaction to hear the reedy whine. "I'm
stiff," he croaked, simply trying to see if he had his full
powers of speech restored. He couldn't help smiling at
such a little success. He checked himself over visually
and saw that no longer was he strapped down, and no
more tubes invaded his body. He touched the sore
black spot where a needle had entered his arm. His
throat ached when he swallowed. He felt he had to
urinate, but knew he would be reluctant to do so for
the dull, burning sensation there. He remembered
Vickers's remark and the sadistic laugh. In an almost
slow-motion shudder, he moved all his limbs and muscles, including those on his scalp, and found that he
was a whole person suffering mainly from stiffness and
shortness of breath. The only wounds were covered by
a square bandage the size of a chess board, which was
stuck to his chest across his right pectoral muscles. He
touched it and it was tender. He started to pull back
the bandage but it stung so much and felt so hot that
he decided to leave it alone.

He sat up on the edge of the bed and swung his legs
over. It took so much strength to get that far, he felt
like lying back down to rest. But he didn't. Instead, he
slid down to the cold floor and shuffled across the tile.
He made his way to the window.

He remembered as the vast expanse of nothingness
opened up before his eyes. He saw a huge courtyard
below him, surrounded by the walls of the building
and filled in with concrete and a few potted desert
succulents and bushes. Beyond that courtyard was the
outer yard that he had seen when he landed in with
the helicopter. Even farther he could see that there

were fences and guard towers. Whatever cattle or other livestock was being raised here at this ranch, it didn't seem likely that any of it would ever get out.

The desert floor spread out for miles. In the distance, jagged, low mountains, barren of any vegetation rose up to form an irregular distant horizon. Everything began tumbling back to him through the tunnels of his memory. He'd hoped to see the contonement area of Fort Hood, Texas. Instead he saw the Nevada's desert.

Josh remembered how he had gotten here. He remembered the flight, and most starkly of all, he suddenly remembered that . . . thing clinging to the front of the helicopter as he flew without an airspeed indicator back from the battle site to here.

Breen. Those soldiers had been feeding on his corpse! The little war fought that night, how long ago was that? And in Nevada? Had he dreamed all that?

"So glad to see you're up and about, Colonel Avery."

Startled, Josh tried to whirl and nearly lost his balance and went down. He grabbed the window frame to steady himself and turned more slowly. Before him stood a slight man with slick black hair.

"Edward Gates. I'm the director of this ranch. The attending medical personnel said it wouldn't be healthy for you to continue lying on your back. It's best that you be up so that normal drainage will occur; that you won't have as much of a chance of developing any of the various forms of pneumonia that bedridden patients often have."

"How long have I been here?" Josh cleared his throat to punish his unsteady voice. His vocal cords stung him back.

"A couple of weeks . . . you've been kept sedated."

"Weeks? God . . . Where am I?"

"Why, I'm certain that you remember your coming here. You flew in. If your map navigation is as good as Colonel Vickers says it is, you know perfectly well that you are in the state of Nevada, United States of America."

Josh nodded. He strained hard to keep his face neutral. He wanted to lash out at this little oily-mannered bastard with the arrogant, superior attitude. But he knew that would do no good. Certainly not in his weakened condition. The underdeveloped nerd could probably whip him in a wrestling match. So Josh kept his face blank. He knew that any kind of outrageous behavior would get him in deeper difficulty. Whatever this situation was, it began dawning on him as his head cleared, it was a grave one. It would not be helped by his showing high emotions.

He said calmly, "When you have time, sir, maybe you and Colonel Vickers could brief me on what my . . . continuing role will be here."

Gates bought the act. He relaxed and smiled as he said, "Why, Colonel, we fully intend to brief you. The events that you have seen—indeed have participated in—have made you a part of the innermost circle in this . . . project."

"And what is the project?"

"You will be briefed, Lieutenant Colonel Avery. And I will personally give you a tour of the entire facility here. I want you to feel comfortable with all that is going on and with your ability to make a contribution to our project, an undertaking that will in turn be an enormous boon to the security of our country."

"What is my schedule for rehabilitation? I'd like to get started if I could, Mr. Gates. Sir."

Gates had prepared for such a start. He told Josh to shower and shave and to dress in fresh clothes. With the assistance of a medical aide pushing Josh in a wheelchair, he was to join Vickers and him in the courtyard below. There, Avery would be allowed to walk about to get some light exercise. "Most of all," Gates said, "You will be able to enjoy the fresh air."

When Josh's wheelchair rolled out into the courtyard an hour later, he felt as if his rehabilitation program had taken giant steps forward. Although he still felt weak and hungover from pain-killers, the shower washed away the days of staleness acquired in bed. His stiffness had slackened. His head had lightened. The latter was a mixed blessing—on one hand Josh had regained his senses; on the other, he found his memory restored. He knew the events of that night did not belong to the dreamworld he'd been floating in. They were part of a nightmare he'd lived.

Vickers stood up and shook hands. He showed him to a chair. Josh noticed the colonel's limp and remembered he'd been wounded, too. Although the courtyard was half in the sun, it was cool and fresh beneath the umbrella.

"It's almost like being at the seaside in the evening," said Josh.

Gates smiled and puffed up. "We're obviously proud of this facet of the facility. Those grates you see up on the walls are air-conditioning vents. Actually the air is blown down from the second floor, sucked out, and recirculated from the opposite side of the courtyard into those vents over there. Otherwise we'd be suffocating in here."

"Artificial fresh air," Vickers observed dryly. "Nothing too good for our wounded soldiers."

"Would somebody mind telling me what's going on?" Josh said, trying not to let his impatience show through. There must be a purpose for this enclosed courtyard to look so much like a prison exercise yard, he deduced. There had to be a reason why he couldn't get fresh air and a view of the great outdoors. There had to be an explanation for there being no windows into the building from out here except at the third-floor level and higher. There were no ledges, no drain-pipes, no rain guttering. Nothing. Any man that was left in this courtyard to his own devices—locked out by steel doors without knobs on the outside—would be as much in a cell as if there were bars keeping him in. He took a deep sip of the iced tea before him and waited for the men to speak.

Gates nodded at Vickers. The colonel said, "Avery, you are a smart boy. I'm going to cut straight through the shit. You been handpicked for a special mission. I . . . we know everything about you from your high school days until now. We know about your capabilities, we know about your loyalties, we know about everything. We know about Marilyn, Jill, and Katy. We practically know when you started having sex. You shouldn't be embarrassed by this kind of scrutiny. You know perfectly well it is the kind of thing that has to happen when you get a top-secret clearance and then some special compartmentalized positions, which you have. You are now so deeply involved in it that you can no longer say no to it. It's a military mission. It's an order. It's a command, a request, a goddamned holy crusade for the church. Whatever you want to believe it is, you're part of it."

"Can you tell me what happened last . . . that last night? Who are those things that attacked us?"

"Think of them as a new brand of Special Operations team. Think of them as a special kind of . . ."

Josh waived a hand impatiently. "Tommy, you said you were going to cut straight through the bull. Now where did you recruit men like that? Is this some kind of 'Dirty Dozen' mission?"

A burst of laughter escaped from Vickers's throat. "Well, I'll be goddamned. I never even thought of it like that. But yes, that's *exactly* what it is. We got us a Dirty Dozen operation going on."

"But where did you find them? In prisons? Are they some kind of foreigners?"

Vickers laughed again, more savagely. "No, boy, we found these people in a wholly different place."

Gates held up a hand. He'd been listening intently, but he interrupted now. "Not people. Emphatically *not* people."

"Not people," repeated Vickers. "That's the project, boy, it's a scientific project. It's combining science with the military arts, if you want to look at it that way. This Special Operations training is the final answer to terrorism in the Middle East. We finally got something to kick some Eye-ranian ass. This is a force of terrorists sponsored by the United States military. Think of it, Josh; we finally have a military force of suicidal fanatics. Even more suicidal and fanatical than the goddamned Revolutionary Guard."

Josh shook his head to settle his thoughts swimming back and forth. For a moment he was wondering if he had not slipped back into that white fog of semiconsciousness that he had experienced after surgery. "Whoa. There's an awful lot going on here that doesn't seem right to me. What do you mean they are not people? What do you mean suicidal? Are we talking about the same United States here?"

"One thing at a time. Let's start with suicidal. Let's start with maniacal. Wouldn't you agree that those soldiers attacking the hill the other night and the defenders were suicidal? Weren't they maniacal? When's the last time somebody attacked your helicopter with his bare body and got himself skewered on it like a barbecued hot dog?"

Josh sat in stunned silence, unable to give an answer to any of those questions.

"Officially, the United States has never sponsored any form of terrorism. Officially, the United States has never pulled off a coup in a foreign country, not even in Eye-ran to install the Shah there. Not even in South Vietnam to get rid of Diem. Not even in the invasion of Cuba. Not any attempts to assassinate Fidel Castro. Never has there been an attempt to unseat a dictator in Central America, in South America, or in Asia. Officially. Got it?"

Josh nodded dumbly.

"And as for the people—*people,* they ain't. These are a highly refined form of animal, my boy. You know animals, don't you? As in vegetable, animal, mineral, people. These are war animals. Armies all the way back to the Crusades and beyond used pigeons to carry messages. Even up into World War Two, reconnaissance planes were throwing them out of the cockpit. You know, animals. The United States has used dogs. The navy uses dolphins to plant mines on enemy ships. Animals."

Josh finally found his aching voice. "But these looked like men more than animals."

"That's the beauty of them, boy, that's the beauty of them."

"Jesus, it sounds so immoral. What if the press . . . what if Congress?"

Gates spoke up. "Genetic research has always been controversial, Colonel Avery. In fact, any kind of experimental research has come under the scrutiny of all sorts of forces who would limit progress in the name of animal rights or—"

"Or even human rights," Josh countered.

Gates was not flustered. "Is it humane to allow human terrorists and human armies to wreak havoc on our civilian populations?" Josh wagged his head ever so slightly, as much in astonishment at himself for agreeing with that kind of reasoning so easily.

"And is it any better to send human beings to almost certain deaths or to counter such acts of terrorism, including war?"

Vickers said, "Josh, looks like you got a question on your mind. Spill it, boy."

"I just want to know . . . can I un-volunteer for this project?" Josh looked back and forth at both men. Their reactions were instant smiles. Then they looked at each other and began to chuckle and finally to laugh.

Josh stood up, pushing himself away from the table, feeling the stiffness in his body. He was tired, but the adrenaline these two generated in him was enough to stoke the fire of his anger. There was no point in trying to remain calm with these two. "I quit," he said.

His remark simply tickled the pair all the more. Vickers clutched his sides and rolled in his chair. Gates merely laughed into a half-open fist.

"You guys are pissing me off. I've got people back at

Fort Hood who will be making inquiries after me. I've got family. I've got Marilyn. She will be wanting to know where I am. I want out. If there was any way that I could do this legally I would expose the whole crazy scheme to the country. Maybe I can't do that. But I sure as hell can tender my resignation. I'm eligible for retirement. I quit, goddammit."

The renewed gales of laughter eventually subsided and the two men sobered up, their faces overcome with sternness in place of their humor.

"How you gonna quit, boy?" Vickers asked rhetorically. "You're dead."

Josh froze.

Vickers growled, "Now, sit down before you piss me off."

7

· ·

Grayson Kirk stopped feeling sorry for himself the moment he heard the whopping sounds of a helicopter descending somewhere outside his cell. *A Huey!* He knew it by its characteristic sounds. It was like an old friend calling to him. It had lifted him clear of his morass of despair.

As long as a helicopter was coming in, it could be flying out someday. At the very least, it meant that a pilot was somewhere inside these grounds. Probably two. There was some kind of kinship in that. In the simple sound of a landing helicopter—once at dusk and again in the wee hours of the morning—Kirk had found cause to kindle hope for an escape from this place.

But in the ensuing days, he never heard the helicopter start up again or leave. He knew it could not have done so—he didn't sleep hard enough for the sounds of it to escape his hearing.

Gradually he lost track of time. His room had no windows or clocks, so he couldn't tell day from night. With the loss of sensations of time, he began to lose hope that he would ever escape. He had no idea what might have happened to PJ. He had not seen her since Texas. He didn't know whether she was alive or dead. That uncertainty was most depressing of all.

He decided to stop eating. They continued to bring him food every six hours or so, but he refused to eat or drink. He became weaker, sleepier, less pained by his stark physical surroundings and a lot less discomfited by his emotional deprivation. He'd never before experienced such exquisite agony, heightened by caring so little about what happened to him. As in some kind of fairy tale, he'd die of consumption, pining away for his love.

• •

In three weeks, Josh finally began to regain his health. The stiffness and nagging aches and pains in his body had all but disappeared, leaving the painful surgical wound on his right side as the only reminder of his night of terror with those subhumans.

He had taken to a regimen of walking around his room in a horseshoe fashion, up one side, across the end, and down the other. He would turn and reverse the pattern again and again for two hours a day. Jogging in place had simply proved too painful, the bouncing tore at his insides. Even the walking at first had tired him after only three circuits. Vickers had granted him an hour outside in the courtyard, and every day two security men led him there and back to his room.

No more word had come from Gates and Vickers. A pair of courteous but formal attendants brought meals every day. The food, like the people here, was bland. He ate it with a spoon. Just as in a jail, he thought. Apparently, they had decided that he was not going to cooperate in their scheme to train these sub-humans to perform terrorist acts, national security notwithstanding.

They were right, goddammit, he told himself. There was no way that he was going to get involved in such a harebrained scheme. In fact, it surprised him a little that he had found such determination, considering the circumstances. He was virtually under arrest if not actually in prison. Even if he were able to get out of this room, this building, this compound, there would be all that distance across the desert that he would have to travel. He was as good as dead. He had no illusions about what they meant when they said that he was dead that day in the courtyard when they laughed at him. Somehow he had just disappeared from the face of the earth. Somehow they had made it happen. Surely, anybody who could create a completely new subhuman species to inhabit the planet could make one individual of the human species disappear.

A knock at his door interrupted his walking circuit. Gates and Vickers entered the room before he could signal them to do so. The two chose a pair of straight-backed chairs that Josh had pushed against the wall to clear a lane from his exercise path.

"C'mon in," he said, his voice tinged with irony.

"Thanks," answered Vickers in a like tone. "Sit down on the bed. I want to show you something." He motioned to the door. Another expressionless assistant guided in a cart with a rattling, wobbly wheel.

On the cart was a television set with a VCR. The assistant plugged in both devices and left the room, quietly closing the door. Josh stood at the foot of the bed, his arms folded in front of him.

"I said sit down, Avery. Don't be such a hard-ass. I know you are not going to want to participate in this research project without some inducement from us. And I know now that even if we get your cooperation, either by coercion or not, we probably couldn't trust you."

Josh had bent into a zigzag to sit on the bed. He stiffened, standing straight on his feet at the challenge from Vickers. "What the hell do you mean?"

"Is that any way to talk to your superior officer?"

"To use an expression of yours, Vickers, *my ass.* If I'm dead, I'm not in the army and I'm not playing your goddamned military courtesy games. What do you mean I can't be trusted?"

Vickers smiled and squinted, trying to read Josh's face. "You know, I halfway believe that innocent act, but I think you are more the type that places his faith in the hard-ass routine. I think that you are going to have to be busted like you were in basic training, just like OCS. Yep, we need to break you down and build you up all over again. At your age I don't know if the building-up part can be done. But believe me, Mr. Josh-hard-ass-Avery, I can do the busting-down part, if necessary. I'll bust your hard ass to dust if I have to. Either you're going to do the training or somebody else will. And if you don't do it . . ."

Josh opened his mouth to retort, but Vickers poked the remote control savagely at the television and again at the VCR. In a few seconds a tape began to roll.

The first scene was a kick in Josh Avery's guts. Marilyn's face filled the screen. She cried into the camera, her face contorted, not at all as pretty as he remembered. The image zoomed out, showing the scene was outdoors. Marilyn sat in a folding chair. On either side of her sat her two girls tucked under her elbows. Using an arm to comfort each of them prevented her from hiding her own anguish. The camera lens zoomed farther back to a long shot so that Josh could see the location. He had already known what it would be.

It was a memorial service. His. He saw the soldiers aim skyward and fire a rifle salute into the air. He saw a flag-draped coffin. This was no memorial service, this was a burial. He was watching his own funeral! How could they do that? Where would they get . . .

Josh felt his throat tightening, his mouth glued shut, his heart pounding high in his chest, aggravating the wound there from deep inside. In fact he felt as if his heart had been pierced instead of just a lung. He started to lift his hand which had been gripping his knee, as if to touch the television set to try to comfort the woman huddled over with her two children. He felt a burning sensation behind his eyes that was aggravated by the dull ache in his throat. For crying out loud, literally, he was going to tear up. He already had. A droplet of water fell down his eyelid and streaked across his cheek to the corner of his jaw, sliding into the groove of the scar that ran down into his shirt collar. He felt it tickle all the way as it trickled.

He hadn't realized it. He loved her. *Marilyn.* Now that he couldn't have her, now that he couldn't comfort those children. Jesus, he thought, what lengths would these people go to? What about him? Why did it take the image of his own funeral before he realized he loved somebody who really loved him.

Gates cleared his throat as a gentle signal. Vickers spoke. "The three of you died in a fiery automobile crash northwest of Fort Hood. It was a country road. Ingalls had been drinking. One of the bodies was burned beyond recognition. But they found your dog tags in the area of the crushed upper body."

"How . . ." Josh wanted to ask how Ingalls . . . how his own body and Breen's had turned up in Texas. But he knew how. He didn't need to ask.

Vickers shrugged. "Ingalls wasn't supposed to turn up in Texas. Then again we needed two identifiable bodies for realism. He and Breen were taken back there along with one of the other bodies that we policed up from the battlefield. Your proxy was burned beyond recognition."

Josh said, "You killed Ingalls just to keep this inhuman and inhumane project a secret? You'd murder an innocent man in the national interest?"

"We're soldiers. We take orders. Ingalls and Breen knew the risks when they signed on for the supersecret stuff. You knew the risks, too. You know damn well you have done some things that you wouldn't want to read about in the newspapers. Tell me, is it moral for you a fly a night mission on a South Pacific island and drop off a Special Operations team, then fly out only to find out two days later that seventeen communist guerilla leaders and sympathizers have been assassinated? Don't give me any lectures about morality, Avery."

Josh bit the inside of his lip to hold his tongue. Vickers, the bastard, was right. At least he didn't make any pretense about hiding behind morality.

"Just one thing I want to know . . ."

"*I'm* asking the questions." Vickers held up a scrap of yellow paper. "Maybe you could tell me how this came to be found in your clothing after the surgery."

Josh squinted at the paper. Then he remembered. "Oh, that's a telephone number."

"Right," Vickers growled sarcastically. "Just tell me how you got it."

"What does it matter? It's been disconnected. I tried to call. All I got was one of those recordings."

The tone in Vickers's voice became ominous. "Where did you get the goddamn thing?"

Josh saw how serious this was to Vickers. "From Breen," he said. He told Vickers the truth, including confronting the army major out on the day rerun of the night course.

When he was finished, Vickers said, "I almost believe you, Avery. You tell one hell of a good story."

"It's not a story, it's true. Exactly as I told it." As he spoke, his voice became more earnest, taking on an angry tone now that Vickers had challenged his honesty again.

Vickers looked at Gates and shook his head. "He really doesn't know. I actually believe the SOB." He turned to Josh. "If you had let that voice repeat the recorded message ten times, somebody would have answered. You may not have gotten any information out of them, but you'd have found out that this is not your ordinary telephone recording. It's a set system. It's a contact. It's a contact with a force of people that is inimical to the interests of the United States."

Josh slumped in his chair. "My God, I had no idea. Breen?"

"Evidently."

Gates finally spoke up. "Lieutenant Colonel Avery, we would like your assistance. It has been reassuring to discover that you are not responsible for contacting this group of saboteurs. You might be interested in knowing, however, that law-enforcement agencies have been successful in tracking down a part of this network of terrorists. At this moment we have a pair of them in custody. But for now the operative question is: Are you going to assist us in running this project?"

Vickers growled, "Or do we have to find someone else?"

Josh had no illusions. Now that they had killed him, now that they had buried him, there was no way that he could be resurrected. If he didn't cooperate, the reality would surely match the pretense. He had only one possible answer: "I'll do what I can. Can you assure me that the project that we're involved in is sanctioned by the highest authorities in the land? By that I mean the president and the leadership in Congress."

"Absolutely," said Gates without even the flicker of an eyelid. Josh knew he was looking into the face of a practiced liar.

"The president himself, goddammit," Vickers said, protesting too much.

"I suppose I'll have to be briefed in a little more detail about exactly what we're dealing with here."

"You'll be given a thorough orientation, including a tour—a good deal of which, I will personally conduct," said Gates. "As soon as your health and strength have approached normal, that is."

"A couple things," said Vickers, that threatening tone creeping back into his voice. "We'll be giving you the run of the place except for one wing of the building that you will never be allowed to go into. And we won't be giving you a pistol to carry. Other than that, it's no big deal. You've grown pacifist on us, anyhow. I hardly think you'll mind. If you screw up, Avery, the deal's off."

Josh didn't have to ask what it would mean if the deal were called off, now that they'd declared him dead. He was as good as forgotten by his military service and his government. He hoped not by Marilyn, for all that would matter. Josh shrugged. He stood up and asked, "When do we begin?"

"We'll begin with a complete physical examination for you in the morning," Gates said. "When you're sound, we'll take you on a tour of our training facility and explain some things that you must understand before you start your own training curriculum, which is going to take several months but cannot take longer than half a year."

. .

Clumsily, PJ pulled tangled stands of her blond hair off her face and tried to roll over onto her back. She felt leaden, and time moved slowly. She felt as if she were underwater, moving against the drag of a heavy current. Exerting as much effort as she could without becoming nauseated, she was barely moving at all.

After a tiresome struggle she sat up on the edge of her cot, her elbows on her knees, her head cradled in her hands. She stared down at the floor, blinking to arrest the spinning tiles. For a long time the edges of her vision were closed in by a ring of blackness, so all that she could see were her knees and her toes pointing outward at what seemed a half mile away. As the blackness receded, she saw two pairs of shoes at the edge of her vision. Her head snapped up, drawing a second cloak of darkness over her eyes. She had to steady herself to keep from toppling off the bed. Finally, she could clearly see a slender man and a bulky woman standing before her. She looked around the room slowly so as not to aggravate the dizziness. Her room had no windows. A cell. Yes, she remembered, she'd been captured. She had been in a cell before—one with bars and not nearly so clean. But this was confinement, nonetheless.

Before anybody spoke a word, she realized that she wore only a pair of loose pajamas. She looked at the squat woman and hoped that she had been the one who had undressed her. Not that it mattered. Not now.

"I have some clothes and shoes for you to wear," said the matron. The male attendant left the room and the woman briskly and impatiently helped PJ dress. When PJ's leaden fingers failed at manipulating the buttons on the blouse, the woman slapped her hands away and fastened them herself. Then the two attendants propelled her down the hall, each one grasping a wrist with one hand and her biceps with the other hand to support her. She barely felt her feet touch the floor. The pair took two or three steps for every one of hers. Although she tried to keep up, she was dragged into a spacious but stark briefing room and propped up before a man that looked like a circus clown dressed up in a lab coat. His hair was a horseshoe-shaped ring of fluff.

"My name is Quist. I am the chief researcher here. And you are PJ Larson." As he spoke, wattles of skin jiggled at his neck.

"Payne." PJ stiffened in the grasp of the two attendants and felt their hands tighten. "My name is PJ Payne." She spelled it. "P-A-Y-N-E. You may have killed my husband, but I still have his name. You bastards can't take that away from me."

Quist shrugged his shoulders and exposed the palms of his hands in front of his belly. "I know about your husband, Mrs. Payne, but I assure you our research operation had nothing to do with that . . . tragedy."

PJ spat an obscenity at Quist. Again the grip on her arms tightened momentarily. She relaxed, and they relaxed.

Inside her head, her thoughts whirled, spiraling into a central spot of blackness in the back of her conciousness—a part of her memory she hated to revisit. She felt as though she might be sucked down into that spot, entirely imploding into herself. The mention of her husband again, the fact that she had been captured by these people, the possibility that she would be helpless against them—this all made her even more furious and frustrated. She began shaking and felt alternately weepy and violent. Then all at once she just seemed to fold up.

"Please let me sit down. I feel very . . . weak and unsteady."

Quist nodded his head and the two attendants led her to a chair and gently lowered her, keeping their hands on her arms. She shuddered and did her best to hold her composure.

The chief researcher continued with his briefing in a clinical tone. "In case you don't recall, Mrs. Payne, your husband's brother-in-law was the researcher who first found the practical method for lowering the barriers that prevent the mingling of the species. Of course, his research methods and laboratory technique were very crude compared to what we are able to do here. Plus we have greater security than in the past."

He waved his hand and a section of the wall behind him slid into a pocket. The opening exposed a giant cage inside another larger room. With the sight of the

. . . thing inside that cage, she put a fist to her mouth and bit down on a knuckle.

• •

In the cage crouched the link missing from man's past, something like Neanderthal but with a more pronounced forehead. Hair covered its body, giving off a blue-black sheen from the overhead lights.

"This is, in a sense, the king of the subspecies we have created," said the chief researcher. "Admittedly, it does not look like much. But in fact, its brothers were gelded soon after birth and without the production of their unique hormonal testosterone, they developed into hairless, more upright, more manlike beings."

PJ had seen the earlier generations and shuddered at the recollection. She had seen the monsters that had been created in the beginning of this genetic research gone awry. This thing might have been a waxen image . . . except that it moved, showing interest in the humans, particularly PJ. Embarrassed, she couldn't help noticing his prominent genitalia. "The earlier beasts . . . they could fertilize any female of any species. . . ."

"Quite." said Quist. "These Decendants, as they are called, have the same capability. However, our security measures are much more stringent than any in past experiments. We have total control, I can assure you. There won't be any breeding accidents here."

PJ felt herself pressing back into the chair. She felt herself under that stare of the animal inside the cage even from a distance of thirty-five feet. It showed an excited interest in her, pacing upright before the bars, never taking its eyes off her. It thrust an arm through and reached out to her. She cringed, biting down on her knuckle again, harder.

The animal stared as if it had the capability of looking through her. She felt bewitched, drawn involuntarily into its control. The animal's breathing was loud and labored, as if it had grown excited. It opened its mouth, exposing permanently descended fangs. Suddenly she realized what this briefing must be about. Inside her head, the mental sinews that anchored her mind began to be stretched. In the distance she heard snatches of the chief researcher's conversation. He was saying: ". . . breeding stock . . . stud . . . Descendant . . . the king of his race . . . mixing the species . . . arriving at the perfect combination . . . future generations . . . incredible intelligence . . . yet subhuman. . . ."

She began breathing faster and faster. She felt her vision cut down again by that tunnel of darkness closing in on her, leaving only a narrow pipeline of vision connecting her and the beast. The Descendant wanted her. And she knew that the reason these people were here was to let him have his way with her. The mental sinews snapped. Her jaw muscles knotted with the effort of biting down.

"Mrs. Payne! What are you doing? Get her hand out of her mouth!"

PJ was unaware of Quist pointing at her and shouting, for the beast had mesmerized her in its lustful glare. She became vaguely aware of the two attendants yanking at her hand, tearing it from her mouth. She felt pain only for a moment and barely tasted her own blood drooling down her chin.

PJ heard the agonized shriek that paralyzed everyone in the room. The Descendant in the cage had seen

the blood, had perhaps smelled it. He began yelling
and screeching, tearing at the bars and rattling the
cage door, drawing everyone's attention to his hateful
stare, which had never released PJ's attention.

"Shut the goddamned door," ordered Quist. "Get
her out of here."

Whatever had snapped inside PJ's head energized
her.

She exploded out of the chair and ran toward the
cage.

"Stop her!"

As she ran into the room, the Descendant battered
on the cage and reached out for her. For a second she
thought she would fly into his arms. "Mark!" she
shouted. But it was not Mark, of course; this animal
did not have the gray eyes. And Mark had died. She
had watched him die. So she did not run to the beast.

She whirled and saw them pulling pistols from their
coat pockets. She threw herself against the wall inside
the room. She pressed herself into the wall, closing her
eyes, adding her own screaming to that of the beast.
She didn't see the switches that looked like a garage-
door control, a two-button affair. She didn't feel herself pressing into them.

"The lock, the electronic lock!" Quist shouted. The
lock clattered, and the beast fell out onto the floor, still
bugling.

Quist and his security people added their bellows of
alarm to the pandemonium. The two attendants
turned and ran. Quist hollered at them, "Get back
here and start shooting, dammit." He had his own
pistol out, and in seconds the trio began firing.

PJ jerked at every pistol report as if the slugs were
ripping into her. She slid down the wall, cringing,

holding her palms over her throbbing ears. Still she shrieked.

The Descendant clamored to its feet and sprang at her. It stumbled, splotches of red blossoming in its fur. It fell on its face and tried to drag itself across the floor. But it had been struck with a dozen bullets. It finally dropped its leaking head on the tile and stopped struggling.

Quist and his staff continued firing until their pistols were empty. For a moment it was silent except for wet, gurgling sounds from the furry carcass on the floor.

Then PJ began screaming anew, her voice cracked and hoarse.

"She's over the edge," said Quist, his own voice hoarse. "Put her in a straitjacket and get her out of here. Goddammit, when Gates sees this we're all going to fry."

• •

"You did *what* ?" Gates grasped the edge of his desk and half leaned out of his chair as if he might come over the top of the desk after Quist.

Quist held up his palms and stepped back out of Gates's swinging distance. "I thought it would be a good idea to brief her fully. I never thought she would get the idea we intended to mate her with that stud beast."

Gates flopped back in his chair. "What on earth were you trying to prove?"

"Mr. Gates, it was an orientation, nothing more. We have been parenting our Descendants using female animal breeding stock and sperm from human males to reach closer and closer to the proper genetic combination. All along we've had a contingency to use a human female, harvest her eggs, and fertilize them with the sperm of a Descendant male. The thinking is that perhaps some of these defects, like the bloodlust rages that our Descendants fly into and the limited-intelligence barrier might be overcome. We never intended for her to believe that she would be mating with one of these Descendants. We merely wanted to tell her that her ova would be fertilized in vitro, that it would be her contribution to the security of the country."

Gates slapped the palm of his hand on his forehead. "If you're any indication of the common-sense intelligence of all our PhD's, I'm worried about the future of this project. She's a woman, for crying out loud. To her what you're proposing is rape, even if it happens in two stages on the surgical table and in a glass test tube. Where is she now?"

"She's locked in a protective cell. Under constant surveillance. I'll suspend the experiment."

Gates raised a finger, pointing it at the ceiling. "I never said that, did I? I simply said not to tell her about it. If she's gone over the edge mentally, there's no reason why we need to worry about her consent or why we have to inform her. Sedate her. Keep track of her cycles and make sure that she's given fertility drugs. When the time is right, start the harvest. Run the experiment to see if we can overcome the bloodlust and other defects. I have a few ideas of my own that I'd like to try. Mrs. Payne can surely have no objections to becoming the mother to our country's newest breed of warriors."

8

· · · · · · · · · · · · · · · · · · ·

It had been weeks since Josh had been outside the walls of the compound. He and Vickers strode from the building. A jeep awaited them, sitting in the sun, vibrating at an idle. Vickers drove so they could be alone to talk. Josh savored the hot, dry air in his face.

"I want you to see the security around this place. I want you to get a feel for the kind of situation we're involved in here. I won't bullshit you, Avery. I don't trust you and I won't ever again. But I believe you can do the job, and you *will* do the job. There's a hell of a lot at stake here. I don't have to get explicit with any threats, do I?"

"If you're referring to Marilyn . . . if you're trying to convince me you can be a ruthless bastard, don't bother. I believe you."

"Fine."

As they drove along the perimeter inside the wire, Josh studied the security measures. Triple-security fences ringed The Ranch. The innermost ring was a dog run, a tunnel of wire patrolled by pit bulls, one every quarter mile or so. At the top of each wire, concertina coils intermeshed. Inside the dog run were wall-less shelters so that the dogs could escape from the sun. The dogs ran to and fro snapping at the fence, biting the wires as the jeep drove by.

"Pit bulls. Ever heard of them?" Vickers asked sarcastically.

Josh studied him, trying to figure out just what kind of man this was. He didn't respond to Vickers in any way. Not in words and not with the sneer that threatened to creep across his face involuntarily.

"Guard towers, too," Vickers said. "Constant line of sight between them. Searchlights. White and infrared. You never know when you might need them. There's a few passive detection devices, too. And a few surprises."

Josh nodded almost imperceptibly.

"And in the unlikely event that you should . . . that anybody should get beyond the dogs, the outer space between fences is laced with antipersonnel mines. Now and then you'll hear one go off when a badger tunnels under the wire."

"What kind of mission am I going to be training these things for?"

Vickers, talking over the whining of the jeep engine, said, "I'm a patriot, Avery. You know that. So are you. It's just that we have a different threshold for what we are willing to do. I tell you, pal, there is nothing I wouldn't do for this country. I mean, we have enemies and they are ruthless. It requires us to be ruthless, too. None is worse than those goddamn terrorists in the Middle East."

"We also have laws, Colonel. They become the rules of the game."

"I understand rules." He threw a fist in the air and

bashed it down on his thigh. "You can let the rules of the game be dictated by a bunch of wimps in the press and in the Congress and courts. Or you can let the bad guys determine the rules of the game and do a little bit of one-upsmanship . . . or 'one-downs-manship.' Remember in the Middle East? Remember when the Soviet diplomats were kidnapped in Lebanon? Remember when that happened, and the terrorists demanded a ransom by sending the ear of a KGB man? The Russians didn't negotiate, did they? They kidnapped their own Arab terrorists and sent back the bodies with the A-rab genitals stuffed in their A-rab mouths. Remember what happened?"

Josh nodded. He did remember. The kidnapped Soviets had been released. Subsequently, Soviets were not often kidnapped anywhere in the world.

"And how many Americans and other Westerners have been kidnapped in the meantime? And what do we do in the West? We negotiate. We pay ransoms. We make empty threats. And we just keep letting people get kidnapped again. I'm telling you, we gotta make an impression on these bastards, Avery."

"So instead of the Soviet brand of brutality—cutting off a few genitals—you're going to make an impression with these . . . Descendants?"

"You saw them in action. You know damn good and well they'll make an impression. We have just given America the capacity to be ruthless."

"So now you're a philanthropist, one who just happens to have your own terrorist squads."

"You're cracking wise, but you're exactly right. When did you become such a bleeding heart, Josh? Wake up. You're a smart boy, Avery. We've got to work out a few bugs, yes. Maybe the current generations of these Descendants aren't going to be the ones who carry it out. Maybe we're years away from a solution. Or maybe it's just a few months. We're going to give it a try. We're going to find out by the end of the year."

Vickers drove the jeep up to a high spot and stopped. He got out and swept his arms in a giant circle, surveying the land as he turned around.

Josh uncoiled his body from the cramped jeep cockpit and took off his hat, welcoming the heat of the sun on his head. He felt like baring his chest to soak up the healing rays. He couldn't take a deep breath without feeling the constriction inside his chest. The outside stitches had been removed, but the skin itched hotly. He felt stiff and stale from being shut up for so long. These few minutes in the sun were a balm to his wounds. Not even Vickers's fanatical scheme about American terrorists of subhuman species or the perpetual agony of missing Marilyn or even the vacant feeling of knowing that in the eyes of the world he was dead could keep him from enjoying the glorious freshness of a bright sun and a dry, warm desert breeze. Somehow they cleansed him. But then the other things kept intruding on his mind, including one deduction.

"That's why he wanted us to use Vietnam-vintage Hueys, isn't it? That's why those soldiers had such a mixed bag of weapons, isn't it? There were communist weapons and neutral uniforms and American weapons. . . ."

Vickers puffed out his chest and rested his hand on his hips. "Ain't it wonderful? These Descendants can't be identified as Americans. Not even by the language they speak. These bozos can't even be questioned. They're trained to respond to interrogation in any number of languages including Hebrew, Arabic, Bulgarian, Russian, and even one of the Chinese dialects. Truth serums, torture—nothing works on them to get them to talk."

"They're almost human, aren't they?" Josh said, barely keeping the irony from his voice.

"Yeah . . . ain't it something?" Vickers bridled. His face darkened in response to Josh's sarcasm. "You bastard. You can't piss on my parade. If you would just learn a little bit more about it, you would understand that this is the perfect weapon. We've got us a soldier that will fight to the death, one that will absolutely refuse to be captured. We have our own damned Kamikazes. Even if they could be subdued and kept alive, it wouldn't be for long. Because when they eat, man, they chow down." Vickers whistled. With his hands, he diagramed a mountain in the air. "You should see the piles of food that these somebitches eat. They need so much protein that no enemy force would even know how much to feed them until it was too late. Pretty soon they'd be munching on each other. . . . Well, you've seen them."

Josh shook his head. "Yes, I saw them. I saw them chowing down on my copilot, Cliff Breen. You remember Breen, don't you? He was a man, not a pile of chow, remember?"

Vickers had gotten his enthusiasm up. He ignored Josh's protest. "Even if they were kept alive by some miracle, they don't have a life span of more than a couple of years, anyhow. These things don't have any long-term memories, Josh. They don't have a childhood, they don't have any recollection of where they were trained except that they were out in a desert and that they were trained to shoot rifles and attack places and to speak languages. That's all they know. They don't think they are Americans because they are not Americans. They're nobodies. They are just like those dogs I was telling you about that are trained on the battlefield to sniff out tunnels or to attack saboteurs." Vickers grew agitated with his excitement. Josh saw little flecks of spittle collecting at the corners of his mouth. His eyes had grown wild with his enthusiasm. "Dammit, Josh, they're the *perfect* terrorists. They can't ever give away their government, their trainers, their sources. Can't you *see*?"

Josh shook his head. But he *could* see. He could see that the only way that he could influence this action was to be part of it. If he were to back out, somebody else would be doing what they needed done. They'd never let him live to tell about it no matter what they promised. Besides, he wasn't entirely sure that there wasn't some bit of good at the bottom of his mission somewhere. There had to be! If it was, in fact, sanctioned at the highest levels of government. Of course he couldn't know that for sure. He couldn't know anything. What in his life could he depend on? he wondered. Only one thing came to mind. Marilyn. "I can't see it," he said. "But I'll do it. What's the mission? What raghead do you want killed?"

Vickers burst out laughing. "Raghead? That's better. How do you know that it's an A-rab?"

Josh spread his arms out, indicating the desert all around them.

"Yeah, pretty obvious. North Africa mean anything to you? A dictator who has sponsored terrorism worldwide?"

"Saddiqi?"

"You got it, Avery. We're going to drain every drop of that bastard's blood into the sand of the desert."

Josh was stunned. "What the hell would I know about an operation like that? I'm just a pilot. You want me to fly into North Africa? In a damned old Huey?"

Vickers smiled and answered, a crooked grin on his broad lips. "Right on both counts. You are a pilot. And you are dumb if you haven't figured out yet what you'll be contributing. You're not going to be flying at all, Avery. You're going to be teaching a couple of these bozo Descendants how to fly a helicopter."

9

. . . .

Vickers drove the jeep at top speed down the graded road, leaving a dust plume to billow into the sky behind them. Vickers shouted over the noise of the jeep. "Me and Gates talked about it. I decided that there's no way I could let you fly into North Africa and deliver those Descendants. There's just too many ways you could sabotage the mission if you ever got an attack of conscience. But you could train the Descendants to fly the helicopter same as I train the Special Ops team. And we could train them how to navigate. We don't even have to make it a round-trip training mission. All we have to do is train them where to go and land the helicopter. Then they can just stay there. While the suicide team attacks."

Josh mumbled under his breath.

"Stop grunting at me, Avery. My ears are a little bad from being in tanks so long."

"You've got everything figured out, don't you?"

"Yes. Now, one more thing I want to show you. Flip that switch on the dash." Josh thumbed the switch that Vickers pointed to. Nothing happened.

"Now watch this." Vickers yanked the wheel to the right and drove toward the security fence.

Still nothing.

"So what?" said Josh.

"Watch." A button-sized amber light began flashing on the dash of the jeep. Then, as the jeep's bumper nearly touched the fence, a siren began yelping from somewhere under the hood. Vickers reached over and slapped the switch off.

He stopped the jeep and said, "That leakage is from the transmitters stationed just on the other side of the fences. Can you see that one over there?" He pointed. Josh didn't see anything except the wires and the dogs, two of which had gone insane with vicious excitement jumping at the fence, biting the wire diamonds. One began climbing the wire toward the concertina.

"See that dog climbing the wire? Look just beneath him outside the outer fence. See that cone? With the beacon on top of it? That's a vertical transmitter. It has a range of two to three miles. It shoots straight up in the air. Think of it as an invisible fence that goes up for three miles."

Josh was calculating altitude of two to three miles—somewhere between ten to twenty thousand feet. He wondered what good such a transmitter would be if he were flying in a helicopter and simply crashed through it and continued flying out over the ranch. Did they have something that could catch him? An Apache gunship, maybe, that would chase him and shoot him down? An airplane?

"Actually, it's not nearly so vertical. Think of it as a beam of light that's expanding outward. You know, like a cone that's on its point of light shooting up into the air. The whole goddamned ranch is covered by a vaulted ceiling of electronic signals sent out by those transmitters all the way around."

Josh just looked at Vickers and raised an eyebrow in question. "Is it radar?"

Vickers laughed. "Better than radar. Every helicopter we have is equipped with a receiver in it that is sensitive to those signals. And you've got an amber light on your dash just like the one in the jeep. If you should ever be flying and see that light flash, you'd better turn around immediately or drop yourself in altitude. You've got to get out of those signals as soon as possible, because if you get close enough to the transmitter's direct rays you'll cross over the threshhold. I don't mean you'll get a siren going off in the aircraft like this jeep. The light would stop blinking and it would burn continuously. Of course, you'd never see that happen. By then, the explosive inside the airframe of the helicopter would go off and blast you right out of the sky. Get the message?"

Josh nodded slowly, demonstrating that the message had indeed begun dawning on him.

• •

"Descendants are like men without souls, without true human personalities," said Quist, the chief researcher.

Josh barely listened. His mind was still on the videotape he'd just watched—the "Gregor Munn tape" they had called it. The bloody battle between the man and the pit bull had sickened Josh. He'd been in combat. He'd seen aircraft crashes and had pulled bodies and parts of men he had known very well from the flaming wreckage, but he'd never seen the kind of bestial display they had captured on videotape with man and dog fighting to the death. "They aren't men," Gates had reminded him. "They are Descendants."

Descendants. Men. What difference did it make? As Josh's mind tried to grapple with the issues that boiled up inside him during the screening of the tape, his ears kept hearing snatches of Quist's nonstop orientation as they marched four abreast down one of the hallways that all looked alike to Josh. He tried to concentrate on orienting himself in case he ever needed to get down this way.

". . . limited common sense and apparently no real reasoning ability. They are entirely without emotions. They do, however, accept training with a fairly advanced capacity. They can accomplish complex tasks. While your mission is to teach a pair of Descendants to fly a helicopter, a further advancement on our part would be to develop an airplane—perhaps even a jet something like an advanced drone. We would use the Descendants to fly it like a true Kamikaze pilot. Although that caliber of sophistication has not been reached yet, we are eager to see it someday. Perhaps during our lifetimes." He smiled broadly, even warmly at Josh.

Josh returned a crooked, quizzical smile. At moments like these, he still believed he must be dreaming. The fantasies these people were . . . participating in. He fingered the weapon on his belt. Vickers would only give him a stun gun, still showing a reluctance to fully trust him. "Maybe someday I can restore you to a full position of responsibility," the colonel had said. He had grunted ironically, adding, "Maybe someday we can even restore you to life."

They had just come from the infants' nursery. There, Quist continued to talk as Josh watched in horrified fascination as the little Descendants—beasts, as he thought of them—were fed. Quist explained the anatomy and the life span. Josh could not believe that these creations could achieve such an enormously fast growth rate, that they could eat so much. He began to believe that this was truly a remarkable science being developed at this clinic. He could not help but be impressed with the advances he was seeing in genetic research, although the dark purpose of that research was absolutely abhorrent to him.

"For now, Descendants can be trained only for a limited number of tasks. It might be easier for you to think of them as computers, at least in the sense of their learning powers."

Gates spoke up. "A computer. Now, that's an analogy that suffices for me. Yes, think of a computer with a limited memory. You can teach it step by step—like programing that computer—and it will execute the function exactly as programmed."

Quist's head bobbed up and down emphatically. "Yes, Mr. Gates, you have it. As you can imagine, Colonel Avery, the language training is limited to only that which is necessary to carry on a conversation and to proceed with training. Basically it's a conversational language program. Their vocabularies are limited and they are not capable of the nuances of colloquial speech. The reason for this is quite practical, actually. You see, like a computer with a limited memory, every bit of instruction that we feed into these creatures is accumulated in memory banks of the Descendants."

Vickers jumped into the conversation. "You mean these bozos stop learning once they're filled up?"

"No, Colonel Vickers, they can continue to learn.

But for each unit of learning that they acquire after the memory is filled up, the Descendant will lose memory from the very first tasks he accumulated. Think of it as packing peas into a straw. You can continue inserting peas at one end indefinitely. But sooner or later, out of the other end of that straw, the peas you put in first will start falling out."

Josh stopped suddenly in the hallway and the others took a couple of steps beyond him and turned.

"You mean you expect to teach these things how to fly a helicopter when they have a limited memory? Have you any idea what physical requirements, manual dexterity, reasoning powers, adaptability are—"

Vickers sniffed impatiently. "C'mon, Avery. Don't get overblown with your own self-importance about flying one of those stupid choppers. They've built spacecraft that a monkey could fly."

Josh began walking again. "Yes, but they haven't built the helicopter a monkey could fly. I doubt if even you have done that."

"We'll see, Colonel," said Quist.

"You bet your ass," added Vickers.

Gates resumed the briefing. "Now we're at the adolescent holding area, Colonel Avery." He stopped before a pair of stainless-steel doors without windows. Quist stepped up to a calculatorlike keypad and shielded it with one hand from the group as he punched numbers into it with his other hand. Josh felt Vickers's stare burning into the side of his face like cigarette coals. *Still suspicious,* he thought. *Trying to see if I'll cop the combination.*

"Last month we had an incident that forced us to change from electrical door locks to these electronic combination locks."

The doors slid open into pockets in the wall, letting loose a cacophony of shrieks and bellows, releasing a powerful smell. Josh stepped back and put his hand on the stun gun attached to his belt. He saw the other men put their hands into their pockets.

"Keep your weapons handy, gentlemen," Gates said without really having to. Together, they entered the jungle of sounds and smells that was the adolescent boarding and training area, a collection of classrooms running down either side of a boulevard of a hallway that ran the length of the wing. Each room had been fitted with a six-foot-wide window at the rear. The group stopped to observe as Quist continued briefing.

"These classrooms will handle up to sixteen Descendant juveniles," he crowed like a proud elementary-school principal acting as tour guide to newly elected education board members. "However, we have found that a class size of twelve is the maximum for an instructor to handle."

Josh frowned. "It takes four people to feed these things in small groups? Yet only one instructor can handle a dozen at a time?"

Quist and Gates exchanged patronizing smiles.

The chief researcher said, "These classrooms have been constructed like no other you have ever seen, Mr. Avery. Take a look."

He did. He saw that the desks and tables, like other furniture in the building, were formed of stainless steel, with no sharp edges. These had been bolted to the floor. As usual, the bare concrete sloped to a central drain. Josh assumed that accidents here must require the room to be cleaned by hosing everything down.

At each student position, the Descendant eunuch,

dressed in a blue uniform coverall, was chained by the ankles and wrists. In addition, each chair was fitted with an automobile seat belt, which strapped the juveniles firmly in place. No wonder they needed fewer handlers here.

"This classroom training begins in the seventh to tenth week of life and is the equivalent of elementary school for human children. Only here, these juveniles are humanized."

Josh snickered at the word. "How? You beat them into humans?"

Quist smiled indulgently. "No, but our reinforcing measures run along those same lines. Watch." Quist made a twisting signal with his hand. The instructor at the front of the room touched his control panel and turned on an audio switch.

"This is a conversational English class," Gates explained in a stage whisper. "It combines language training with no-nonsense discipline."

The instructor, a frail man with the dimpled face of a twenty-year-old and the receding hairline of a man twice his years, said, "I must raise my hand before asking a question, sir." He delivered the words in the singsong voice of a kindergarten teacher.

The class repeated the phrase back to him in exactly the same tone, sounding like any group of youths. Josh thought of Marilyn's two children and felt a pang of longing for them.

Quist made a combination twisting-jabbing motion with his hand.

The instructor nodded and barked a command. "Raise your hands!"

About half the class responded in singsong. The other half raised their hands, some the left, some the right, a few raised both, rattling chains on the metal furniture.

The instructor's youthful face contorted into a savage grin as he laid his weight on a palm-sized button on his control panel. Instantly, the students went into convulsions, chains vibrating on furniture, arms flying out, bodies trembling in a mass seizure.

Josh shook his head in disgust. "Wired."

"Mildly so, yes. Nothing serious, to be sure," said Quist.

The Descendant children were released from the grasp of electrical currents. They slumped in their chairs, collapsed over their desks, tongues lolling from their mouths, drool running from their mouths.

The instructor moved from Descendant to Descendant, lifting up each head to inspect the dozen mouths in the classroom.

"To see that they haven't choked," said Gates.

Josh sneered at the shorter man. "To see they haven't bitten into their tongues, don't you mean? Avoiding the bloodlust rages?"

"Quite," said Quist. "And you can be assured that by day's end, these will have learned the difference between repeating a phrase and responding to a command with similar words. Gradually, the clues, such as the tone of voice from sweet to demanding, as you witnessed here, will diminish. Within a few days, the Descendants will be able to discriminate between a statement, a question, and a command merely by the words, which will be spoken in identical tones of voice."

"How many do you lose?"

"Attrition, as we call it, is running at about ten percent. But we have seen evidence in recent generations of improved intelligence, a quicker grasp of this very basic humanizing. Mind you, the early versions of these creatures did not even possess the physical requirements of the larynx to generate speech as we know it. Now we have reason to believe they'll be able to handle quite complex tasks . . . including the one you're about to embark upon."

"You aren't even sure they can do it, are you? I hope like hell you don't expect me to electrocute these things as a way of teaching. I had some pretty evil instructor pilots in my day, but no one ever tried to light me up in the cockpit."

Quist and Gates shot him a simultaneous look expressing their disappointment in him for thinking such a thing of them. "Hardly, Colonel Avery. This is a technique required only in the earliest stages of training. It's a conditioning to language. After that, the training for each Descendant's life task is quite conventional. With continued improvements in breeding we may even be able to eliminate electro-conditioning altogether. The aim in future generations will be to eliminate the feeding frenzies and violent outbursts at the sight of blood and also to enlarge the intelligence of these descendants even further. Soon—"

"Soon," Josh barked, "you won't be able to tell them apart from yourselves."

10

. . . .

Josh Avery sat on the deck of the cabin, his feet tucked up inside so that his boot tops wouldn't be in the sun. Already he'd learned his toes would bake uncomfortably after only a few minutes in direct sunlight. Vickers had dropped him off half an hour ago. Then the colonel had gone back to pick up Josh's charges. He would meet them out here for the first time. His stomach roiled. He could hear the gastric fluids and bubbles agitating in his intestines. Already he had performed the pre-flight inspection of the aircraft. Today would be merely an orientation so that the two Descendants could get an idea of the helicopter they were to learn to fly before Josh took them into the classroom for a few days of ground school.

"Don't get too damned theoretical with this aviation crap," Vickers had told him. "It'd be like teaching a pig to sing—wastes your time and annoys the pig. You just treat these bozos like a couple of basic trainees—only dumber—and you'll be just fine. Oh, and don't forget: if you shed any blood be prepared to be gobbled up like a Christmas goose."

Vickers had enjoyed a belly laugh over that, although Josh denied him the satisfaction of even a chuckle. He felt too anxious for that, his guts twanging with cramps. Part of his anxiety was, of course, the notion that he would be participating in a clearly unethical and even outrageous project. If the press or the public ever got wind of a story like this . . . Then, too, there was the challenge of it. How would he ever teach two . . . monkeys—that's what they were, he'd decided—how to fly something as complicated as a helicopter? Of course it had occurred to him that there were a thousand different ways of cutting the protective shield of the human skin, allowing blood to be exposed. Every time he thought of that, his last image of Cliff Breen's torn, partially consumed body trespassed upon his consciousness.

The next picture that flashed on the screen of his mind was the color of hot red flashes as the pain of fangs stabbed him in the chest, punctured his lungs, broke one rib, and cracked two others.

. .

There were the snags of metal on the helicopter, the clipped ends of safety wire—hundreds of them, each one a little jagged needle ready to puncture or tear at his skin. He wondered whether a simple drop of blood could incite the violence that he'd seen in the Gregor Munn video. He might absentmindedly scratch a pimple and draw his own blood. He checked his whole body for scabs and was grateful that he had not found any before pulling on his boxer shorts and the rest of his clothing this morning. When he shaved, he paid so close attention to avoiding getting cut that he nicked himself, under the nose, probably because he was being so meticulous about it. He wore a bandage on his upper lip just to be sure that he wouldn't accidentally scratch himself and reopen the tiny cut. God, he thought, what a miserable existence. What if he just blew his nose? In the dry desert air, with chapped lips and cracked nasal membranes, it was inevitable that blood would show somewhere on him sooner or later.

He cursed himself and shuddered, shaking off morbid thoughts like a dog shedding water. He decided to kill some time by walking around the helicopter. Being out in the sun would ward off the chills brought on by thinking about spending his next weeks, and very possibly months, with those Descendants. Absently, he jumped down from the cabin floor. On the way out of the craft, he banged his head on the roof of the cabin. When he hit the ground, his knees buckled and he almost went down. Frantically, he began feeling his forehead, searching for signs of bleeding. *There,* he felt wetness! A truck wavered through the shimmering heat waves, traveling toward him. He waved at the driver, hoping that Vickers would see him and turn the vehicle around. Then he realized that the wetness was just sweat. He dried off his head, reaching as deeply into his scalp as he could with his handkerchief. No blood. He felt relieved and foolish all at the same time. Great start, he thought. He imagined he'd never survive months with this training. Not if he failed to survive the day.

• •

The truck Vickers was driving was a pickup with a camper top. He crunched the tires to a halt in the gravelly road. He jumped out of the pickup and went around to the back and inserted a key in the padlock. *It must be more than a hundred degrees in there,* Josh thought.

Vickers pounded on the back door and shouted, "You bozos all right in there?"

An unrecognizable voice answered from inside.

"Fine, then get your asses out here." Vickers pulled the door open and two young Descendants jumped to the ground.

Josh was amazed that they truly looked like two basic trainees: young, even boyish in appearance, except for their thick necks and heavy jaws. The pair were dressed in military fatigue uniforms. Josh immediately thought they should be wearing flight suits in case they crashed. The retardant material would keep the Descendants from burning. But then he realized that if they crashed they would probably see blood on each other, so the precaution of flame retardant material was hardly a necessary one.

"You two bozos just stand here until I tell you to move."

The two immediately reacted, locking their heels together, pushing their hands down straight along their sides, fingers curled, thumbs touching the first joint of the first finger. They were standing in the hot sun at the position of attention as Vickers strode across the ten feet that separated them from Josh.

"Colonel, they're not gonna last five minutes in the hot sun standing at attention."

"Yeah, I suppose." He turned around. "You bozos relax." One of the men slumped, putting his hands on his hips.

"You, too, asshole."

The other Descendant obeyed.

"Get into the shade, you two."

They did as Vickers ordered. Then Vickers strode up into Josh's personal space. "Well, here they are. I'm

going to leave them with you. Remember, you don't
have to treat them in any special way. You don't even
have to be nice to them. You can kick them around,
kick them in the balls if you want—that's right, they
don't have any balls. Only two things you have to
remember. One you can't let them see any blood. If
they do start to fly off the handle, your only defense is
to use that stun gun. Then use a pair of handcuffs and
ankle cuffs to immobilize them, and keep them that
way until the effect of the hormone subsides about half
an hour after the sight of blood is removed from their
field of vision. The best thing to do is just tie a ban-
danna around their eyes once you have them subdued
and wait till they settle down."

Josh sniffed sarcastically.

"Yeah," said Vickers. "Like you're going to be able
to subdue a pair of these things and get cuffs and
blindfolds on them."

"And the second thing?"

"Three hours, tops. That's all you have with them
at a time. They're used to eating every four hours
around the clock. Once these little beastie boys get
hungry, there is nothing you can do but feed them or
get the hell out of Dodge City, 'cause they are going to
start eating something before long, including each
other or you." Vickers broke into one of his character-
istically savage laughs. Josh had noticed that any time
the idea of cannibalism occurred to him, Vickers got a
sadistic delight in mentioning it.

"I don't know about this, Tommy."

"What's not to know? You been around idiots before. You just treat these particular idiots like a couple
of moron warrant officers. When they don't do what
you say, you knock them on the side of the head.

Other than their eating habits, they're pretty decent. They will learn, Avery. You'll be amazed at what you're working with here. Just try to stop thinking about morality and all. Just think of them as fairly simple-minded people, but people who are way smarter than you think. And one more thing. Be careful about what you say, because they will take you literally."

Josh cocked his head. "For example?"

Vickers barked one of his sadistic laughs. "For example, don't tell one of them to kiss your ass, or you're liable to find him dropping down behind ya." Vickers laughed again and Josh simply rolled his eyes, too jittery either to laugh or to be angry.

"Come on over here, you two. I want to introduce you to Colonel Josh Avery, best damned helicopter pilot in the Newnited States Army."

The two Descendants approached briskly and stood before Vickers. They looked him in the face, waiting like dogs in training for their next instructions. Vickers pointed. "This is Josh Avery. He's your new boss. You listen to him. You look at him."

The two turned toward Josh exactly as they were told. They stared at him and listened, waiting for something. Josh felt even more queasy at their blank stares.

"Well, say something, Avery, or they'll stand there all day staring at you until it's time to eat. And when chow time comes, if you happen to be the menu that they are gazing on, you're lunch."

Josh felt antsy under the gaze of the pair. He barely heard Vickers laughing at his little joke. He took a step forward and thrust out a hand, saying, "Hello, I'm Josh. . . ."

Vickers reached out and slapped Josh's hand down. "Remember, these are trainees, you idiot. Treat them like privates or warrant officers or something. Don't treat them like human beings, for chrissakes." Vickers turned on a heel and began walking toward the truck.

"Where are you going, Tommy?"

"Back to the air-conditioning. You don't think I'm going to stay out here with three idiots, do you?"

"Aren't you going to monitor their training? Aren't you going to fly with us?"

"Funny, Avery. If I got up in the air with you and started flying toward that fence you'd have some leverage on me, wouldn't you? Now if you do, it'll just be suicide. You'll just be fulfilling in reality the fairy tale we created with that video of your funeral, won't you?"

Josh shrugged, taking a breath to argue with Vickers, but realized that would be useless.

"Well?"

"Well . . . Tommy, don't they have notebooks and pencils? How are they going to retain—"

"The stupid bastards barely know how to talk, you asshole."

Josh was startled by a sound from one of the Descendants. "Yes, sir?" He turned and saw that one of them was looking at Vickers.

"Not you, asshole. Avery, these two don't know how to write. We didn't use up any of their limited memory teaching something that wouldn't be worth a heck of a lot. Don't worry, son, they've got good memories. And, oh, by the way, you'd better learn their names. I thunk them up myself." He puffed up a little in the chest and said, "The one on your left there, the one with the crew cut, his name is Bozo." Vickers opened the door of the truck and stood atop the running board to look out the windshield. "The other one is Asshole." Vickers let out a long, whooping, sadistic laugh.

The second Descendant and Vickers spoke in unison, "But you can call me Ass for short." Vickers slammed the door of the truck and waved. "And don't bother trying to use the radio to call out," he yelled. "Those are special radios set up to our tactical frequencies only. Ain't nobody else on them but our monitors." Then he gunned the engine, cranking the wheel around, throwing up a huge plume of dust that blew over them. Then the truck was gone, bouncing wildly down the road back toward the compound, leaving the trio standing in the hot, still desert air.

Josh spat a dusting of grit from his mouth. He felt the eyes of the pair on him. The one with the crew cut, the one Vickers had named Bozo, had brown eyes and was about five feet ten inches tall, with a medium build. The other one stood an inch or two taller but was a little more slender. His head was completely shaved, making it impossible to tell if it was brown or black. He also had brown eyes. Neither had any facial hair to speak of, only a light peach-fuzz beard. He found he couldn't discern their ages. He guessed somewhere between sixteen to twenty years. Then he reminded himself that it was weeks.

"Jesus, what have I gotten myself into?" he said. Their replies startled him.

"I don't understand," they said in unison.

"What?"

"Who is Jesus? And what have you gotten yourself into?"

Josh shook his head. "Forget it." He watched the two as they squinted their eyes hard, until their eyelids fluttered.

"What are you doing?"

"We're erasing our minds. You told us to forget."

Josh smiled. What a ludicrous situation. "Kiss—" He broke into a laugh, realizing he had almost said what Vickers had warned him against saying. For an instant the absurd vision of these two moving around behind him and bending over nearly buckled him over with laughter. Then he realized the two were staring at him soberly. "Don't you two ever smile?"

In response, they pulled their lips back, baring their teeth. Obviously, they'd been trained to smile. But as Quist had said, they had no true emotions.

"Forget . . . I mean, stop smiling." The faces sobered up on command. "Smile," he said. The pair fidgeted for a moment, unsure of what to do. He had countermanded himself in consecutive sentences, telling them once not to smile anymore and then telling them to smile. He was beginning to see the kind of absolute logic that they would answer to. True enough, these two Descendants were like extraordinarily advanced computers complicated in capability but simple in logic.

Josh decided that sooner or later he was going to undermine this mission, but there was no reason he shouldn't learn as much as possible from experimenting with these two. His own sense of curiosity gave him the incentive for proceeding with the project until he could find a way to undermine it.

"Can you laugh?"

In answer the two drew their lips back in that exaggerated smile and let loose staccato sounds that might have passed for laughter. In those sounds, he recognized a touch of Vickers's training. It was so pathetic, so ridiculous that Josh began to laugh himself. He tried to stifle his laugh under a hand. The two mimicked him, in unison putting their hands to their mouths to stifle their own phony laughter. Josh threw back his head and let out a belly laugh. They did the same. Suddenly he was overcome in absurd, uncontrollable laughter. His knee buckled, and he nearly went down. When they mimicked him at that, too, he finally did fall to his knees. So did they, laughing in the same tone as he, trying to be ever-faithful students.

Josh put his hands over his face and laughed until he shuddered, until he felt chills. He laughed and laughed until his sides hurt and his throat was hoarse. Every time he thought he would get control of himself, he would open an eye and see those two looking between their fingers at him, trying to match him action for action. It occurred to him that if he ever told them to laugh again he would be seeing this entire scenario replayed again somewhere. Better not do it in flight, he thought.

Finally his sides, especially where he'd been wounded, hurt so badly that he had to stop laughing. By then he was sitting on the hot sand, sweating with the exertion of the laughter, tears streaming down his face. Finally, he could wipe his eyes dry and get to his feet, feeling completely drained of the emotions that had pent up all this time. When he stood up, he watched them wipe their eyes and realized there were no tears rolling down their faces. They were, in fact, humorless. He felt a cold chill and remembered their capacity for violence and the black seriousness of this project he was being forced to participate in. Those thoughts helped him regain his composure.

"Bozo."

"Yes, sir."

"You're going to be sitting in the pilot's seat first. I'm going to take you two on an orientation flight in a helicopter." He waved a hand at the UH-1H Huey. "I will fly it today. You will watch me fly it, then I will teach you to fly it. Do you understand?"

"Yes, sir."

"Asshole?"

"Yes, sir. You can call me Ass for short."

Josh bit his tongue until he had control, remembering not to draw blood inside his mouth. "I'm going to change your name. Do you understand that? Change your name?"

"Sir, I do not understand 'change your name.' "

"Asshole, you don't have to understand anything. Just forget the name Asshole." He waited as the eyes squinted and began fluttering. He imagined a mental eraser working. "Your name is Ace. When anybody asks you your name, your name is Ace. When I say Ace, you respond to me with 'Yes, sir.' Do you understand?"

"Yes, sir."

"Ace?"

"Yes, sir."

Josh strapped them both into the helicopter and spoke to Bozo. "Put your hands on your knees and don't move them from there. Don't touch anything in the cockpit except those knees unless I tell you to. Same for you, Ace."

• •

The sound of the Huey flying electrified Grayson Kirk, renewing his hope for escape via air. He hadn't heard a helicopter flying for weeks and had assumed the craft to be transient. Suddenly, the rotor slap of blades whacking the air, setting up the insistent, whining racket that resonated through the building, began to resonate inside him. It stirred his blood as if a motorized blender had been thrust whirring into the pool of his lethargy.

He sprang erect, sitting up on his cot. His head spun from the sudden rush, but he caught himself, forced himself to take deep breaths. He knew he ought to restore his sense of balance—not only of the moment, but to recover from the weeks of stuporous inactivity he'd let himself lapse into.

He began stumbling back and forth from wall to wall in his cubicle. Gradually he regained his circulation and a steady gait. By then, though, the sound of the Huey had faded in the distance.

Kirk flopped back on the bed, exhausted from a few minutes of walking. He thought he might cry in despair.

Then he heard the Huey returning, flying by within a mile of this building. He touched the walls with both palms to feel the vibrations. He then pressed his chest against the wall, letting his body soak up the resonance of the Huey, letting it invigorate him with hope.

• •

Josh flew a two-hour orientation flight. In the entire time, the Descendants did not remove their hands from their knees. The orientation was as much

for himself as for his pair of Descendants. It would
help him regain his control touch after several weeks'
layoff, but mainly, he wanted to see the lay of the land
inside the fences. He wanted to see the extent of this
place called The Ranch. Once again, he was startled
by the extent of this operation. The fence ran for miles
and miles. It took a full two hours for him to fly inside
the perimeter all the way around to the starting point.
Even at a thousand feet he couldn't see from one fence
to that on the other side. He couldn't even spot the
low mound on which that nightmarish battle had
taken place in the interior.

At the helipad, he called operations for a fuel truck
to be sent, then shut down the helicopter, and assisted
Bozo from the front seat into the cabin. He watched
the Descendant strap himself into the seat belt. After
only one demonstration of this elementary function,
Bozo had mastered it perfectly. He then led Ace to the
pilot's seat and strapped him in for demonstration,
because shoulder straps had to be pulled down, their
loops included inside the buckling apparatus of the lap
belt. This was different from the passenger's seat belt
in the cabin.

Ace also mastered it after one demonstration. Josh
made sure both their communications helmets were
plugged in. After the fuel truck had departed, Josh
filled in the logbook entries for the first flight and fuel
quantity. Then he climbed into his own seat and
started the helicopter. As he went through the start-up
procedure he told the Descendants to watch and try to
memorize the steps. They didn't ask what memorize
meant, so he could only guess that they understood.
He then flew the second Descendant on the same

route, cutting the flight short at an hour so that he wouldn't exceed the training time before feeding time.

Josh did not speak during the entire orientation flight. He, too, was busy memorizing—imprinting the layout of the land onto his recollection. Once or twice he ventured toward the fence at varying altitudes from one hundred feet on up, in increments of a hundred feet to a thousand. True enough, as Vickers had suggested, the signal radiated inward in a fan away from the fence. Each time he flew toward the fence at a higher altitude, the amber light blinked sooner, forcing him closer to the center of the ranch. Judging by the shallowness of the angle, it would be impossible to fly out of the protective umbrella of those invisible electronic fans, even at the center of The Ranch's mass.

He could not fly higher than five thousand feet anywhere without that damned light blinking. He didn't dare try flying any higher, certain they had a radar fixed on him. If they saw him climbing toward an altitude of ten thousand feet, they might send some interceptors up after him. Or perhaps there would even be a surface-to-air missile on a launchpad tracking him. Without SAM receivers, there was no way of telling. Vickers and his group seemed to be so thorough. There might be holes in the ozone layer, but Josh doubted a hole existed in the electronic umbrella above The Ranch. He knew he'd have to find a different form of escape. Ironic, he thought, that the freedom of flying could be restricted so effectively.

He studied the terrain. There seemed to be no agricultural reason for the enormous amount of land enclosed by the security road and triple-wire fence. He doubted if the barren landscape could support more than a handful of cattle. It looked like the kind of useless wasteland devoted to military training at bases and posts all over the country, which of course, it was. The Ranch headquarters constituted most of the compound with its main access road and a set of main gates with extra security, including a mazelike series of trenches and barriers. No terrorist could drive a truck full of explosives to the entry without zigzagging through a concrete labyrinth a quarter-mile long.

Beyond the man-made security features extended a vast, open range spreading out in all directions like a sea around the compound. No doubt there were also some infantry training exercises run in the central areas of The Ranch. That would explain the fencing being so secure even at the farthest reaches: if one of the Descendant soldiers couldn't be accounted for immediately, at least he would always be contained by the wire. If any of them tried to escape, they would have to encounter the wire, then the dogs, then the mines, and the guards. Josh was sorry he didn't have time for an interior reconnaissance of the training area. That would come later.

The compound building itself was far more extensive than he'd imagined from the ground. He guessed it would dwarf the Army Finance Center, the largest office building in the military, at Fort Benjamin Harrison, Indiana, which he'd once visited. Seven other buildings half as large squatted behind the main compound building, with its individual wings running off like rungs of a ladder. Two buildings with giant, three-story doors were obviously aircraft hangars.

A dozen helicopters—ten Hueys and two Kiowas—

were parked on concrete pads beside the hangars. Corrals and fencing surrounded another pair of outbuildings. The corrals and feeding lots covered at least a five-mile square. On both rounds past the compound, the herds of cattle drew Josh's attention. He'd never seen such a stockyard. Feed lots joined together to form a giant maze. All the lots were occupied by either black Angus cows or red-and-white Herefords.

Josh looked for a railroad—otherwise, how could all these massive amounts of building materials be brought in? And how could the supplies be delivered to an operation of this size? How could the number of cattle that must be consumed here by the Descendants be replenished? On his second trip around, he saw the faint trace of a straight line, a railroad bed scratched into the earth running past the stockyards, heading east. There had been a railroad at one time, but now it was dismantled. That was a disappointment—he couldn't jump a train. On the other hand, that meant trucks and trailers hauled in supplies. Maybe that would offer a way out.

For a second time, he put the helicopter into a descent to the helipad, situated about three miles away from the main compound. He saw the truck bouncing down the road about halfway between the compound and the helipad and realized that Vickers was already on the way out to pick up his two charges. He looked at his watch. Just like clockwork.

This afternoon Josh planned to spend time in the classroom with them, trying to teach them the start-up procedures from technical manuals. Vickers had already told him not to waste time on a ground school. Josh had persuaded the colonel to let him try. "It'll save some flying time."

"What's flying time?" Vickers said. "The only time we are concerned about is the time it takes these bozos to learn how to fly. If they can't learn it, we're going to have to use men . . . men with guts." He glared harshly at Josh, and Josh looked away, unwilling to get into a childish stare-down.

• •

After less than an hour in the classroom, Josh satisfied himself Vickers had been mistaken. He had gone through the checklist only once with the two Descendants. They had already memorized the entire start-up procedure word for word. Bozo could recite the items to be checked and Ace could call back the proper action to be accomplished. Their precision stunned Josh. He'd been running down the checklist with them when he said to Bozo, "Anti-collision light." Then he remembered they wouldn't be using them on any flight. "Strike that." Each time he repeated the checklist, though, Bozo would say, "Anti-collision light . . . strike that," until Josh finally interrupted to tell him to erase the item from memory.

Next, using a line drawing of the instrument panel of the Huey, he instructed them to go through the instrument checks. Again the lesson caught on permanently after only one time through. Both Ace and Bozo could walk up to the chart and recite the entire procedure in the exact sequence without a hitch.

So Vickers was wrong! Josh inwardy rejoiced. He liked the idea of being able to throw that tiny victory into his face. The little victories! If he could just accumulate a few of those, he might regain his former spirit. Then two separate thoughts struck him.

The first was that he actually enjoyed teaching these

two Descendants. Was that healthy? he wondered. He decided to let the mixed emotions percolate awhile before trying to come to terms with them.

The second thought crept into his consciousness as a note of caution. He remembered past experiences with computers. In dealing with machines in general, he'd been burned a few times with breakdowns. So he generally adopted the attitude that it was always safer to assume things wouldn't work. Better to have that idea and to run tests that disprove it than to boast that something did work and be embarrassed in the attempt to prove it.

He devised a simple test. Josh picked up his Styrofoam coffee cup and drained the lukewarm, bitter contents. "Bozo, what is this?"

Bozo raised his hand. Josh was growing tired of that habit, apparently instilled in Descendant trainees from their earliest days of programming. He'd decided he would teach them to forget it first, checking with one of the researchers to see it had no other importance.

"Yes, Bozo, what is it?"

"A cup."

Josh set the cup on his desk. Then he pulled the center drawer of the teacher's desk completely out of its tracks and turned it around, pointing to the polished aluminum knob. "Bozo, and what is this?"

The Descendant raised his hand, and Josh repeated the question.

"I don't know."

"Bozo, Ace, this is a knob. Can you say *knob*?"

They repeated the word in unison. Josh reached down and unscrewed the knob from its drawer. He set it on the desk next to the cup. "Again, now. Bozo, what is this?" After the bothersome repetition of hand raising, the Descendant answered, "A cup."

"And what is this?"

After repeating the question, the Descendant stared at the detached knob for a long time, puzzled by it, apparently having a faint recollection of having seen it before. But finally he said, "I don't know."

"It's a knob. Say *knob*."

"Knob." The Descendants' eyes jerked back and forth from the knob to the place where it had been on the drawer as though not entirely convinced that what had been connected to the drawer was the same thing that now rested on the desk top.

Josh bit his lip. The Descendant had been ordered to say *knob,* so he did. But he could not see that the knob detached was the same as the knob attached. Josh felt a pang of worry.

He went to the chalkboard and drew a relatively accurate picture of a Styrofoam cup to actual size and with a three-dimensional look, tilted slightly at the viewer to that the opening was oval. He carefully shaded the drawing with chalk and rubbed out highlights. Next to that figure, he drew another depiction, this time of the knob. Then he painstakingly explained that the drawing represented the cup. He pointed at one and held up the other. Next, he repeated the explanation about the knob. He was met with blank stares, and his pang of anxiety began to turn into a dull ache of disappointment. He knew that his test was going to fail.

"Bozo, I want you to come to the board and do as I do. Place the knob inside the cup." He drew a dotted curving line that led to the oval. Then he drew intermediate knobs representing the knob moving across the air and into the cup, each time erasing the previous drawing. The Descendant walked to the chalkboard and repeated the demonstration exactly.

"Now, Bozo, I want you to do the same with these two items." He held up the cup and the knob.

The Descendant looked at the two for a long time and then took a piece of chalk and began scratching ineffectively on the foam. Impatiently, Josh said, "No, do this." He demonstrated picking up the knob and dropping it into the cup. The Descendant did it. Josh put the two pieces back on the table and instructed the Descendant to go to the board and redraw the act of putting the knob in the cup. The Descendant named Bozo did so. "Now, do the same thing with the two items on the desktop; put the knob inside the cup."

Bozo hesitated a second, then went to the desktop with his chalk again and began drawing the figure on the flat surface.

Josh stopped him and directed the pair to sit at their desks and wait for further instructions. Most of an afternoon wasted, he realized. These two would never be able to apply the lesson he had painstakingly taught them on paper to the actual machinery. They would be able to recite the checklist from rote. But if they'd never conceptualized an object from a drawing, there'd be no possibility they'd relate a mental abstraction to an activity. Maybe an expert in this kind of learning could teach the Descendants. He could not— he had to concede failure. He was glad Vickers had not been able to see his pathetic attempt to teach ground school to a couple of . . . bozos. He decided there was something learned this afternoon, after all—

not by the Descendants, only by him. He wondered whether that proved him any more intelligent than these beasts.

He pressed the call button in the classroom to summon security, but instead Vickers strode into the classroom. "Problems?"

Josh could see by the triumphant grin on Vickers's face that he already knew about the failure, probably with the help of electronic eavesdropping. "You were right, Colonel Vickers. This ground-school idea was a lousy one," he said, hoping to preempt ridicule.

Vickers's grin faded into a disappointed smile. He seemed satisfied by the admission, though, and did not rub in the defeat. "So what are you going to do?"

"I'm going to try to teach these guys how to fly a helicopter by making it strictly a mechanical procedure."

Vickers didn't resist saying, "I told you so."

Before Vickers released the two Descendants to the care of a pair of security guards, he told Josh to refer them to the charts on the tack board and to the drawings on the chalk board, telling the two to forget all they had learned about these items. The two Descendants went into a long semi-trance with their eyelids fluttering, erasing the afternoon's training.

Josh wondered how something so abstract as language could be so easily learned by these Descendants, when an idea as nearly concrete as the drawing alongside the object could not be connected. He made a mental note to talk to Quist about the parallel reasoning channels of the Descendants and the possibility that the two concepts would ever connect. If they ever did, he wondered if that would be so much a characteristic of human intelligence that the Descendants could no longer be considered members of a subhuman species, but in fact an equivalent to human species.

Through the night, Josh wrestled with the problems of making helicopter flight solely a mechanical operation. In doing so, he had to analyze his own flying techniques and habits. How much of what he now knew about flying had become instinctive, intuitive? One of the things he remembered about flight school was that very often, those men and women who approached flying as a strictly mechanical, procedural process washed out of the program first. It wasn't enough to know the academics and physics of flight precisely. It wasn't enough to have memorized everything in the operator's manual, including the details of every procedure and even the redline readings on the instruments. Sooner or later, physical and instinctual performance had to adapt to the characteristics of helicopter flight. The human being had to become one with the machine so that flying became not an act of a pilot strapping into the helicopter, but the pilot strapping the helicopter onto his back and buckling it on like an article of clothing.

The next morning he talked to Vickers and outlined a brief plan for teaching the Descendants to fly. Vickers wasn't interested in the technique, only in the result. And he was a little skeptical of that. He reminded Josh that he had a backup plan, anyhow, that of using American helicopter pilots. "And you're the first on my list, Avery. If I have to sit in the back of that helicopter and hold a pistol to your head, we're going to deliver a squad of those bozos to the desert. Did I ever tell you the CIA has discovered that Saddiqi suffers from acute hemorrhoids? Probably from riding too many camel humps—I don't know. We're going to cure his hemorrhoids with a case of hand grenades up the old wazoo."

Josh smirked tiredly. His immediate problems didn't have anything to do with the desert mission. His immediate concern was getting Vickers's cooperation.

"Colonel, I need your help," Josh said. "We have to standardize exactly the way that our helicopter is wheeled onto the helipad every day. It must be left in exactly the same position every single day. Each helicopter that is set up must be done so in exactly the same way, with the same number of blade tie-downs and covers and logbooks and fuel. . . . Everything has to be done exactly the same way every day. I don't have to tell you that the Descendants are not very adaptable. So once I teach them how to do things in a routine or sequence, they're going to do the same thing over and over again. If they find something out of order, they're going to become confused. They're going to screw things up."

Vickers nodded. He understood that. "Okay, Avery, you've got it."

Josh asked for a device to be built as a special kind of wind vane, a substitute for a wind sock on the helipad. "My guess is, it will be next to impossible to teach these Descendants how to land and take off into the wind. So I'm going to use this device so they don't have to learn." He gave Vickers a diagram that he sketched during the night, and Vickers promised that it would be ready by the next day.

At the helicopter with Bozo and Ace, Josh abbreviated a brief pre-flight checklist that concerned the barest of essentials. Once the helicopter and crew were moved to the desert, somebody human would have to set up the helicopter for flying conditions. It might as well be done properly. If he understood this mission correctly, it was going to be a one-way flight, anyhow. So Josh concentrated on showing the pair how to untie the tail rotor blade, how to take off the exhaust and air-intake covers, and how to remove the pitot tube cover from the front of the helicopter. After that he showed them how to untie the main rotor blade and swing it perpendicular to the axis of the fuselage. He let them practice the procedures over and over again while he used the checklist himself, accomplishing a pre-flight maintenance inspection.

As he went, he kept meticulous notes on how he wanted the helicopter set up each day for flight.

When he finished several pages of notes, he put the notebook inside the helicopter and called to the two Descendants to stop their practice of tying and untying the craft. "Come here," he said. As they approached him, he looked at the Huey and realized he'd made another mistake. They had left the Huey as they found it this morning. All the covers were in place, and all the blade tie-downs were knotted with precise bow knots. In effect, he had taught them that in order to prepare for flight, they should untie everything and remove all the covers, then replace them. What he actually intended was to teach them to untie all the covers, remove them and stow them inside the helicopter. Then, after a flight, he knew he would have to teach them to remove the covers from their stowage and to secure the helicopter again. Both activities could not be taught sequentially to Descendants because they would simply go through the motions and leave the helicopter as it was in the end. He decided to stop trying to teach Descendants as he would people.

After he had erased their memories and taught them how to untie the helicopter and stow the tie-downs, he began teaching them how to dress for flight, complete with gloves and helmets. He wasn't sure how far this afternoon's training would progress, but he hoped he could get through to the complete start-up of the helicopter.

First he went through the start-up sequence himself, then he taught it to Bozo, who was becoming his lead Descendant in everything. He actually liked the guy— or whatever he was.

The mechanical steps of starting came quickly to the Descendants. Furthermore, there wasn't any point in teaching them how to check the various electrical generators, voltmeters, instruments, and circuit breakers. These two weren't going to be able to reason the significance of a needle that failed to move, anyhow. All he had to do was to teach them the most abbreviated start-up procedure that he could imagine, reducing the entire sequence to a series of mechanical steps and no more. He demonstrated to both of them the entire start-up all the way to the point when the pre-takeoff check was accomplished, before lifting the helicopter to a hover. When he was done with that, he told them to close their eyes while he shut down the helicopter and returned all the instruments, switches, and controls to the pre–start-up position. He didn't want a repeat of the earlier fiasco with the tie-downs, with them thinking that the start-up procedure meant getting ready to lift off to a hover and then shutting things down.

When the main rotor blade stopped moving, he unstrapped himself and told Bozo to get into the pilot's seat in the cockpit and strap himself in. Bozo began fumbling around, feeling his way around the cabin, practically stumbling out onto the helipad. Josh had forgotten an intermediate command again, he realized.

"Open your eyes, Bozo," he said, disgusted with himself. "You, too, Ace."

Josh was startled to see that Bozo went through the entire start-up procedure without a flub. He was able to duplicate every move Josh had made, including the act of scratching an itch in his crotch before running the throttle up to full RPM.

Josh made them cover their eyes again and shut off the helicopter's engine, returning the controls back to the pre–start-up positions. Then he had Bozo repeat his start-up procedure. Again, Bozo did it flawlessly, again scratching his crotch at the exact point in the modified checklist as he had done before.

He repeated the procedure twice with Ace. Same results. No matter how dumb these two seemed to be —in comparison to humans, that is—Josh marveled at their own brand of intelligence and abilities. Again he felt the momentary push and tug of his conscience. Again he forced his guilt back into the dark, silent reaches of his mind. Although they had mastered the start on the first try, he made them repeat the exercise until he felt sure they had it cold.

During these repeated start-ups, he grew tired of hearing the boinging of the low-RPM audio alarm, the device that sounded off in the intercom headsets at any time when the engine's RPM fell below 6,600. Even as he was pinching and pulling out the low-RPM audio circuit breaker, an idea hatched in his head. He began to formulate a plan for sabotaging this mission if the need should ever arise.

11

In the ensuing weeks, Josh grappled with the moral and ethical problems of the Descendants' project every evening. His anxiety caused him to lose a considerable amount of sleep, but he also entertained anxieties besides morality and ethics. Whereas he had taught the Descendants to conduct a minimal pre-flight and to start up a helicopter in just a matter of hours, he had not yet reached the point after more than three weeks of training where it seemed likely that either of his charges would ever learn to hover the helicopter.

Vickers, true to his word, had the wind vane installed at the center of the oversized helipad the very afternoon of the day Josh had requested it. Josh's diagram called for a simple arrow three feet long with a rudder for the tail. The arrow was fixed on bearings at a pivot point about six inches ahead of center, so that when a slight breeze blew, the point of the arrow would point into the wind. On the bearings was a latch. Each day as a part of the pre-flight, the last thing Josh would do before stepping into the cockpit would be to tighten a wing nut on the bearing to lock

the arrow in place in the prevailing wind direction.
This was to prevent the arrow from spinning from the
down wash and turbulence of the helicopter's rotors as
they began to pick up to a hover. Josh's idea was to lift
the helicopter up to a hover and land behind the wind
vane so that the nose of the helicopter pointed in the
same direction as the arrow of the wind vane in the
center of the helipad. This enabled the Descendants to
unerringly make all their mission takeoffs into the
wind. Then, just before actual takeoff, he ordered the
Descendant not at the controls to go out and release
the wing nut. In this way, when they were up in the air
and returning for landing, they could always land to
the tail of the arrow. Landing and taking off into the
wind, a crucial skill of helicopter flight, could always
be accomplished.

• •

It hardly seemed worth the trouble of inventing
the arrow. If these two Descendants did not learn to
hover, there never would be a takeoff, let alone a landing.

Hovering a helicopter had seemed difficult to Josh
when he was first given the opportunity in flight
school. But he'd mastered it by the third flight hour.
Other students averaged as many as ten hours. Instructor pilots didn't let it go much longer. Even a
student who might eventually fly couldn't be allowed
to monopolize an instructor and aircraft too long. Josh
had often felt sad for somebody a little slow. He believed that eventually, given enough time and individual attention, anybody could learn to fly—until now.
It never occurred to him that it could be absolutely
impossible for some people. The longer he tried to
teach the Descendants to hover, the more names came

to his mind of men and women in his flight class who had been washed out in the very first weeks of training simply because they could not learn how to hover. Maybe those hard-assed IPs had been right, after all.

Day after day, night after night, he puzzled over the issue. He studied the flight-characteristics manuals. He tried to devise a method of understanding the mechanics of hovering so that he could communicate it to the Descendants. In reality, the fuselage of the helicopter was bolted to the transmission, held by five mounts in an upright position. From the top of the transmission extended the mast. On top of the mast, the rotor-hub assembly was attached and held by a single huge mast nut that kept the blades from spinning off like a Frisbee. The hub rocked in all directions on a universal joint. In flight, the helicopter was, in effect, suspended by that single point beneath the turning rotor blades.

Of all flight attitudes, Josh reflected, hovering was among the most difficult to master because of several characteristics: First, hovering deprived the helicopter of the effect of streamlining as in forward flight, where moving through the air added stability. At a hover, the prevailing wind acted like the current of a stream that kept trying to wash the helicopter off its spot.

A second force kept a helicopter stable in forward flight. Each rotor blade was a rotating wing. Fixed wing craft must be propelled into a wind fast enough to create lift. The helicopter created its own wind, spinning its wings. As it did, decreased air pressure on top of the wing added a lift component that pulled it upward. When the rotor disk is tipped forward, the blades screw into the air, adding a directional component, which, when combined with lift, gave directional flight. At a hover, the air compacted between the rotor blades and the earth. So the helicopter in hovering flight was both lifted and balanced over an invisible column, or ball, of air. Irregularities in the earth's surface, the slope of the ground, even grass affected the efficiency of that ball. Naturally, the prevailing winds blew against the fuselage of the helicopter. And they also tried to push the ball of air away, again affecting the stability of the helicopter at a hover.

These natural forces of physics made hovering a task not easily mastered. Then there were the human requirements.

The pilot at the controls sat with his feet on the anti-torque pedals, his left hand on the collective pitch lever, the "up-down" stick.

The grip of the collective lever was actually the throttle, a twist-on grip like that on a motorcycle. Fortunately, when the throttle on a Huey was set at operating RPM, it was coupled automatically with the collective-pitch lever. When the collective was lifted, increasing the bite of the main rotor blades, thus demanding more power from the engine, the automatically governed throttle provided it. But that was about all that was automatic in the flight controls. Little else automatically aided the pilot in establishing a hovering flight. Everything else had to be accomplished by the pilot.

The pedals controlled the anti-torque rotor blades, which spun in an eight-foot-six-inch disk on the side of the vertical tail fin. Just the friction of the turning rotor disc itself would cause the helicopter to begin spinning in the same direction as the blades—counterclockwise. The tail rotor would counter that tendency. The variable pitch of its blades was controlled by the pedals. Adding left pedal increased the pitch, pulling the tail to the left, turning the nose around the mast to the right. Every power change, every increase or decrease in the collective-pitch lever placed a demand on the engine and the transmission, increasing or decreasing the torque. So the pilot had to use anti-torque pedals continually at a hover. All these adjustments must be made simultaneously, instinctively. They became second nature to an experienced pilot.

Then there was the cyclic control lever, the stick that rises vertically from the floor of the helicopter between the thighs of the pilot. At a hover, discounting wind, the helicopter would move in the direction the cyclic is tilted: backward, forward, or sideways. To keep the helicopter over one spot on the ground, the cyclic must be tilted and adjusted to compensate continually to account for the prevailing winds, gusts, irregularities on the earth's surface, out-of-balance load conditions, and power changes.

At a hover all these controls must be used at once to maintain altitude and position. The preponderance of the pilot's attention must be focused outside the aircraft to ensure the helicopter did not drift in the breezes. This was because without a visual relationship to the ground, there was virtually no physical sensation of movement. Each control input was followed by an instant's delay. And if the input was too strong, then its overreaction must be compensated for ahead of time.

All in all, learning to hover required an extreme of the same kind of total body coordination involved in balancing on a unicycle while rubbing the stomach in a circle and patting oneself on the head, occasionally switching from that to patting the stomach and rubbing circles on the head.

Josh remembered the victory in flight school when he discovered the "hover button." Then came landings from, and takeoffs to, a hover. From there the student went on to learn how to move the helicopter about the parking and landing areas at a hover. More advanced requirements involved learning how to turn the helicopter, in turn using the nose as a pivot point, depending on the requirements of confined landing areas and parking zones.

Four weeks into his own flight-training program, Josh was almost totally discouraged. He had already taught the Descendants how to fly straight and level at altitude. He was able to trust them almost completely in maintaining level altitudes while flying on a heading dictated on the needle of the helicopter's directional compass. The Descendants were actually able to take over the controls once he had established a climb, maintain proper climb angle and rate of climb, then level off at the proper altitude. They could also descend at a regular angle at a steady rate.

But they could not hover for more than a few of seconds. All else was rendered useless if the pilot was unable to hover the helicopter after taking off or before landing.

He shared his frustration with Vickers, who for once was not sarcastic, but sympathetic. "I know you're upset, Avery. I've been following you and those dumb-asses. They ain't progressed an inch. When do we toss in the hand and re-deal?"

"Colonel Vickers, I honestly don't know. There are moments when they are there hovering, where for five or ten or even fifteen seconds they can stabilize the helicopter and even begin moving in the direction I tell them. There are times when they can pick it up, hold it steady at three feet for three seconds, and set it down. But any deviation whatsoever causes them to get behind the aircraft, and they go into a kind of panic."

"Panic? I ain't never seen emotions from one of them . . . unless chowing down like wolves is an emotion."

"It's not panic, really. It's confusion. If the slightest gust of wind comes up and blows them off their spot, they will fight the helicopter, practically painting the inside of the cockpit with the cyclic, overcontrolling and moving back toward that spot over the earth. Then, once they've passed it because they've overcontrolled, they induce an overcontrolling movement in the other direction. Usually by then I have to take over the controls from them before they set up mast bumping."

"What the hell is that?"

"Uncontrolled flapping of the blades so the rotor hub starts rattling off the mast. . . ."

Vickers grimaced. "Speak English, Avery. You shitbirds are all alike with that aviation babble."

Josh bit his lip to keep from retorting with an epithet of his own. He knew he had to win the confidence of Vickers rather than his spite. He had to keep him off his guard if he ever expected to catch him unawares. "Mast bumping happens with violent movements of the cyclic. It can lead to a crash, especially in slope landings."

Vickers smirked. "Fine. How're you going to overcome it with those two bozos?"

Josh shrugged. "Fortunately, I've trained them to

give up the controls the minute I say so. There's been a dozen times a week in the last three weeks when we could have been killed by those guys. God, it amazes me. They don't get the least bit excited. They don't sweat. They don't show any fear or anxiety about the possibility of being killed."

Vickers smiled wickedly. "That's what we've bred these degenerates for. That's why they're such wonderful terrorists. They can be trained for anything. They're afraid of nothing."

"Correction. They can be trained for anything but flying, or anything that requires reasoning. Tommy, I just don't know how we're going to be able to take these Descendants into the realm of night training."

Vickers slumped a little and bowed his head thoughtfully. "I'll bring up the problem with Gates. He and Quist have been continually pumping me for information about how this is going. We've established a D-day for our operation. It's about twelve weeks out. That's all you've got to get these pilots ready."

Josh wagged his head abruptly. "I don't know, Tommy."

"Okay. If these two bozos don't work out in the next couple of weeks, I'm going to suggest we try two of the newer generation. Maybe we can train them as pilots faster. You said yourself that they pick up things by rote very quickly. If these new ones have the slightest bit of natural instincts toward adapting beyond just learning the rote, that may be our answer."

Vickers lifted his head and cocked it to one side, indicating a change of subject. "Suppose we finally can get a pair of these degenerates to learn how to take off and navigate. You think there's another way we could make this work if we didn't have the requirement to make the night landing? I mean, how else we gonna land our special teams?"

Josh's eyes came open a little wider. "Fact is, I thought about it. Maybe parachutes . . ." Suddenly Josh realized how deeply he had invested his intellect in solving problems that should have been morally reprehensible to him.

Vickers bulldozed on with the idea, neglecting to notice Josh's hesitation after he had blurted it out. "Yeah, that would work! Damn! We could hook those bastards up on static lines and teach them to jump out at about a thousand feet. That way the helicopter could just fly on by and we could even activate a re-mote-control jump light."

Vickers was nodding his head, his eyes fixed on some far-off point, visualizing a night sky with Descendants jumping out of helicopters as they flew over a desert encampment. "Yeah. Then it wouldn't matter about the helicopter landing. They could just continue flying straight on past. Then the helicopter would run out of fuel or the ragheads would send up an intercep-tor. Don't look at me like that, Avery. We're solving a problem here. Quit trying to inject your morality onto everything. Have you ever heard our Middle East ana-lysts talk about how we try to interpret Arab and Ira-nian motives and actions through the filters of our own cultures and sensations? It's a mistake to do that, pal. Don't try it with these degenerates. Don't try to impose your values on them. They're animals, dam-mit! Did you know dogs are color-blind? Did you know it doesn't matter to them what color their food is? Dogs-food makers package their products to please owners, not dogs. We're not dealing with human be-ings here, Avery. We're dealing with animals, and if you can't get that through your thick head, goddammit, you're going to be stuck forever, paralyzed until you die of a guilty conscience."

• •

In the following three days of training, Josh was preoccupied with his dilemma more than ever. He was nearing the point where he'd decided to quit. What could they do to him? Send him to Vietnam?

Of course, he knew what they could do to him. He knew they could kill him. But he'd reached a point where the bleakness of the situation, like the bleakness of the surrounding terrain, seemed larger than his requirement for living. Why did he care again? Why did he care whether he lived or not?

Marilyn.

Marilyn, of course. Marilyn and her children. That's why he cared. On the afternoon of the third day, when this conclusion finally burrowed its way from the dark turmoil within him to the surface—into the light of his consciousness—he renewed his vigor at teaching the Descendants to fly. At times he worked so hard he forgot about their viciousness. So every day like a mantra recitation he forced himself to remember the Gregor Munn video. He remembered the mouth-to-mouth combat between man and dog, pushing his stomach to near nausea. Then he'd begin working with the pair and forget they were animals.

One day, he decided to try something new. Before the afternoon flight, Josh set his two charges in the cabin's shade. He knelt on the floor before them. He spoke to them earnestly. He leaned forward and put a hand on each of their shoulders, trying to communicate his earnestness, his caring and concern. They stared blankly at him as always, seeming not to grasp the point of the pep talk. If he'd read from the Bible, they'd have had the same expressions, he realized.

He stopped talking and stared back at them.

As an instructor pilot, Josh had tried everything in the midst of his frustrations to teach them to fly. He had encouraged and cajoled, and on a couple of occasions even shouted obscenities at the two, trying to touch any button within their limited sensibilities that would get them to master the art of hovering the helicopter. Nothing worked. Nothing fazed them. Their emotions reminded him of those spiky heart-rate monitors that went flat on medical TV shows when the patients died. On the emotional monitor, these two projected straight lines.

But he hadn't tried earnestness before because he hadn't felt it before. His own reserve toward this project kept him from being at any distance closer than arm's length from these two. But now, after three days of deep funk, he'd had that moment of revelation. He realized he wanted the project to succeed. So what if it was for selfish reasons? So what if it was only because he wanted to see Marilyn and the girls again? It was, he realized, a tiny spark of enthusiasm. That spark would have to ignite his fire for survival. And this afternoon, as he knelt on the pebbly floor of the Huey cargo deck, he spoke with emotion and earnestness and felt a small flicker inside him.

"Boys," he said into their blank faces, "you have just got to learn how to hover this helicopter today—tomorrow at the latest. I know you two are trying. And I know you know I'm trying. But we're not getting anywhere with it. You've got to apply yourselves. You've got to dig deep down within yourselves. Boys, it's . . . gut-check time." He blushed at himself.

It occurred to him how ridiculous he sounded. He would never have made this speech to a high school football team if he were the coach. But he knew it really didn't matter what emotions he was expressing or what words he was using—at least not to the Descendants. It mattered to him. He had to get this out of himself. So he clenched his fists and twisted them in front of his own gut, as if that were how one made a gut check. Unaccountably, although he had not told them to do it, the pair of them mirrored his maneuver, contorting his faces into the plastic replication of earnestness.

"Boys, you've got to win one for the Gipper." He nodded his head at them. "Do you understand me?"

They grimaced with the same kind of emotion that he was showing, or at least that he felt he was showing. "I don't understand," they said in unison.

"The Gipp, boys. Win one for the Gipper. Win one for me. God, mom, apple pie, America. God almighty, you boys can win one for your own self-respect."

"I don't understand."

"Win one for the Gipper. Say it."

They did.

He ordered them to shout it, and they obeyed.

Although his heart sank at the contradiction between their words and their plastic expressions, Josh said, "Good. Good. Now, boys, let's get this helicopter untied and strap it on. We're going to start it up. Then we're going to hover. Understand me?"

Josh was still nodding. And so were the two Descendants.

"Great," said Josh with undaunted enthusiasm. "Just super. Really goddamned great." He patted them on the shoulders and ordered them to get the helicopter ready for flight.

As he was going through the run-up, Josh felt a growing sense of enthusiasm. He actually felt excited for the first time since he could remember. It wasn't because of these two. It was because of himself. He'd inspired a bit of vitality in himself today. There had been a stirring that had lain dormant inside him for decades. Only Marilyn had ever generated such feelings. He'd forgotten that he could generate vigor within himself.

He knew he would probably never get these two dummies to hover this helicopter. But he was proud of finding within himself a willingness to live. A willingness to love. He thought about Marilyn for a moment. Then he put her and the two girls carefully away on the shelf of his mind and feverishly went to work trying to touch his flight students.

It couldn't have been the pep talk, he knew. That went against all reason. But Ace, the first to fly in the pilot seat on the afternoon training session, had succeeded at hovering within the first half hour of flight. Something had clicked. Maybe the newfound success was from all those weeks of training. Probably if he hadn't said a word, Josh would have seen them both learn to hover today, anyhow. He needn't have made that Gipper speech—but no matter. First Ace, then Bozo nailed the helicopter at a steady altitude of four feet over one spot on the ground for a full minute, then two. As the sweep second hand of the clock heralded a third minute, he realized that first the one Descendant and then the other, would be able to sit here and hover until they ran the fuel tanks dry and the damn helicopter settled to its skids. Sure, the air had becalmed the helipad. And, yes, maybe another day with the most gentle gusts would upset all he'd gained today.

But for now, dammit, he'd taught a couple of very dumb humans or very smart animals—depending on your perspective—to hover a damned helicopter.

By the time the security truck arrived at the helipad at the end of the afternoon session, the two Descendants had been capable enough to make full pedal turns slowly in either direction. Josh also taught them to stop at each point of the compass long enough to stabilize the aircraft. Once they learned it, he had to admit they were better than most human pilots he'd seen in making the helicopter stay glued to that one three-dimensional coordinate over the earth's surface. He appreciated the difficulty. Even in a calm, some movement of the air was inevitable. And as the helicopter turned from nose into the wind, where it became streamlined to either side, the persistent wind would try to push the helicopter off the spot. With the tail into the wind, the helicopter became most unstable. Any kind of moderate breeze would threaten to kick the tail around because of the helicopter's natural tendency to streamline.

Josh knew he'd have another day with wind gusts to complicate matters. Another afternoon, the dust devils would send his spirits crashing. Those tiny tornadoes that sometimes crept up out of nowhere and spun across the ground, blowing sand and creating turbulence, would certainly upset an inexperienced pilot; would almost certainly cause these two to have difficulty.

But that was another worry for a different day. Today, Josh had a victory. He had already begun instructing them to hover sideways and forward. For tomorrow, he would have them hovering flight forward, and then he would transition into the climb-out, which they had already learned. If this kind of progress kept up, he knew he would have them making approaches to a hover, and then landing from a hover.

Josh was overjoyed. After the blade had stopped turning and Ace had tied the helicopter down, he assembled them on the helipad and clapped them both on the shoulders, congratulating them for their jobs. He was laughing and happy. They stood looking at him blankly, as always, emotionless.

He felt stupid, but he said it, anyway. "Smile."

They bared their teeth.

"Laugh," he ordered.

They held their bellies and rollicked around, making phony laughing noises, mimicking Josh's own genuine hearty laughter. The more they laughed in their phony way, the more hysterical he got.

When Vickers arrived at the helipad, he was amused because he enjoyed pulling sadistic little stunts on the Descendants. For a moment, he thought that Josh was engaging in one of those antics.

Finally, when the Descendants had been ordered to stop laughing and had been put away in the security section of the pickup, Josh had sobered up. He shared the good news with Vickers, who brightened considerably.

"Great goddamn job, Avery. I believe you're beginning to appreciate these goddamn degenerates."

The next morning, however, Josh went out to the helicopter, his guts wormy with anxiety. He'd not slept well. Once the excitement of his success had worn off, he felt the nagging doubts about the morality of the enterprise again. By morning, his concern was

replaced by doubts about whether his pair of charges
would remember to hover. He thought of a thousand
different ways the mission or the project was going to
fail because of the doubts that had cropped up in his
mind overnight. Mostly he doubted that they would be
able to duplicate the proficiency at hovering that they
had shown yesterday. It worried him that he was more
concerned about his proficiency as an IP than the ethics question.

At least he was wrong about their flying. He demonstrated the takeoff and the climb-out to level flight for
Bozo. Then, instructing them to hold their hands over
their eyes, he landed to a hover, then set the helicopter
down. Then he told Bozo to duplicate the takeoff to a
hover, the stabilization at a hover, and the gentle slide
forward into the takeoff run.

He stayed close to the controls as Bozo began his
work. He felt the collective coming up, the cyclic moving forward slightly. The helicopter grew light on its
skids, but Bozo made enough of a pedal compensation
so that it did not begin scraping one way or the other.
The collective kept coming up, the cyclic moving in a
tiny circle about the size of a silver dollar. Then the
tips of the skids came up as the helicopter rocked back
on the heels of the skids. The cyclic moved forward to
counteract the movement, and the nose of the anti-
torque pedals adjusted slightly to keep the nose
pointed straight ahead. The lifting of the collective
continued almost imperceptibly. The right skid came
clear of the ground, leaving only the heel of the left
skid in contact with the earth for an instant longer.
Finally, it came up and the helicopter swung gently
for a second, like a pendulum beneath the rotor disk.
The helicopter continued to rise to about four feet,

then stopped rising at that altitude. Josh marveled. Somehow Bozo had exactly duplicated his own human takeoff. With almost no hesitation, he felt the cyclic moving forward an inch, then two. The helicopter began coasting forward on its ball of air. Then as the airspeed indicator first showed a reliable reading between ten and twenty knots, the helicopter rolled off the ball and out of the turbulence of its own downwash. The helicopter settled a foot or so toward the earth. Josh felt the collective come up to counteract, the helicopter swooped into a climb at seventy knots, five hundred feet a minute.

It was all he could to to prevent himself from letting out a scream of joy. When the helicopter reached a thousand feet, Bozo leveled off and set the aircraft up for a straight and level course, exactly on the heading they had used so often. The airspeed indicator and altimeter may as well have been nailed to ninety knots and a thousand feet.

"I've got the controls, Bozo," he said.

Immediately, the Descendant relinquished the controls and said, "You have the controls."

So mechanical, yet so perfect. Josh immediately took the helicopter back to the helipad to see if Ace could do the same. As he reached the altitude of fifty feet in his descent, he told them to put their hands over their eyes. He didn't want them to learn the landing part just yet.

After they had switched seats, Ace repeated the takeoff to a hover and the stabilization and climb-out exactly in the same manner as it had been demonstrated by both Josh and Bozo. *Cripes,* Josh thought. *Cookie-cutter pilots.* Was there really a practical use to this? Still, he could not come to grips with the idea of these genetic creations performing military missions. But he could not deny his excitement.

Once they had reached altitude perfectly, he took the controls again and turned it around, flying the downwind leg and landing on the helipad. This time he allowed the Descendants to watch him make the landing. He wanted to try something with a minimum of additional training. He wished he could put his finger on exactly what it was that made these two pick up their new skills so quickly. Whatever that key was, it was crucial to this project and future operations.

"Do it again, Ace," he told the Descendant. "Do it exactly as I did, including the landing to a hover." And the Descendant did. Josh talked gently over the intercom as he began the final approach, and talked him down to hover exactly over the spot from which they had departed. The Descendant did it perfectly.

Josh decided to push the session one step further. He ordered Ace to watch him as he executed another takeoff and landing. This time, though, he continued his approach directly to the ground without stopping at a hover. Learning this technique would prove valuable in landing with heavy loads at high-density altitudes.

"Now you do it, Ace," he ordered the Descendant.

Ace performed the maneuver. Although setting the helicopter down directly from the approach could be difficult for beginners, the helicopter touched down exactly as it would have under the most experienced hands, never coming to a complete hover, continually moving downward until the heel of the left skid, then the right, touched, then the toes rocked downward and the helicopter stopped.

"Nice job, Ace," he shouted into the intercom. Josh

could hardly wait to shut the helicopter down. He was impatient for the blade to stop turning to get back to the compound with the news for Vickers. By the time the security pickup was about a quarter of a mile away, he had gotten the pair assembled in their positions, waiting to board. He was still clapping them on the shoulders, telling them what a great job they had done. "Smile," he told them. Bozo's face contorted in that imitation of a smile.

Josh felt his heart's rapid pace stumble. Ace stood stock-still, staring straight ahead. Josh waved a hand before the Descendant's eyes. No reaction. Ace gazed through him, staring even more blankly than usual.

"Ace, smile." Nothing.

"Laugh." Bozo went into his contortions, holding his belly, eventually buckling his knees until he lay sideways on the ground, kicking a foot into the dirt. Josh stood in front of Ace. He called his name several times, but the Descendant did not respond.

For the first time in weeks, Josh put a hand on his belt where he usually fastened his stun gun. Suddenly a jolt of adrenaline set his pulse racing at double time. *The stun gun.* Where had he put it? He realized it was in his flight bag, and, keeping his eyes on the Descendant, he reached down inside and grasped the gun. He hoped it would work the way it had been demonstrated to him. He brought it out and wished that the pickup truck was already here, that somebody would be here to assist him, perhaps to advise him.

"Bozo, stop laughing." Instantly, the laughing fit ceased. "Stand up." Bozo did as he was ordered. When the truck came, Bozo jumped into the back of the van of the pickup as ordered. Ace had to be directed by one of the security men, who flipped off the strap that kept the pistol in its holster. He assisted the Descendant toward the truck while loosening the pistol. Vickers, too, put a hand on the grip of his pistol until the door of the pickup cover had been latched and locked.

"What happened?" he demanded.

"I don't know, Tommy. At first I was overjoyed. I taught Ace and Bozo how to take off. I had just finished teaching Ace how to land the damn thing. Then, when he got out, he didn't respond to his name. And when I told him to laugh, he didn't do it. It was like he forgot."

He looked into Vickers's eyes and a recollection passed between them.

"Forgot. He must have used up the last of his memory. The first thing I did for him was change his name. Then I taught them out to laugh. I never erased that part. God, I must have pushed the first of those memories right out of his memory bank. Do you suppose I overloaded him?"

Vickers grumbled. "I don't know, goddamn it. What the hell do I look like, one of those goddamned PhDs? All I know is you messed up the silly bastard's mind."

Josh felt a pang of despair. *Damn! What had he become?*

Back at the compound, Quist confirmed that the Descendant's memory had exceeded its capacity. "But it happened in a way we've not yet experienced. Don't look so glum. This is not necessarily bad, Colonel Avery. Just because something new and unexpected happens does not mean that it's a bad sign. We're going to learn something from this experience. Tell me all about your morning."

Josh did. When he finished, Quist said, "Learning to hover was a breakthrough. I'm not sure it had anything whatsoever to do with your Gipper speech. More likely, the attempt to teach them to hover was an enormous demand on their ability to acquire and store information, and you overcame it."

"But the other flying tasks were more numerous. And they managed them all right."

"Would you say that hovering flight is a more demanding skill?"

Josh nodded.

"Then think of it this way; you could write a four-hundred-page novel on a computer and store it on one double-sided, double-density floppy disk. That's not very much when you think of it. That's because the keystrokes that are used to make letters and so forth do not use a great deal of information in the computer's memory. On the other hand, if you had a scanner device attached to your computer and scanned an ordinary five-by-seven black-and-white photograph, and converted it to computer memory so that it could be reproduced on the screen and perhaps even be printed through a high-resolution printer, storing that same information as dots collected from that photograph might require four floppy disks. Mastering the art of hovering was probably one of the most complicated things our Descendants have been asked to do. But once they did master it and accumulate that, it dramatically reduced the capacity of their memories. The one you call Ace just went over the edge. I would suspect that Bozo is very close to overload as well."

"Why didn't they forget some of the things they were taught earlier in training? Why did they forget just the name change that I gave him and that simple instruction? Why didn't they forget how to speak or reason or listen at all?"

Quist shrugged. "Colonel Avery, there are many questions that we are unable to answer about this project. I have a hypothesis or two but I don't think that speculation gets us very far right now." He turned to Gates and said, "Mr. Gates, I recommend we take Ace out of the flying program. I suggest we provide a replacement to Colonel Avery."

Vickers growled, "What the hell good is that going to do? Have you got a degenerate with a bigger memory in him?"

"No, not yet, although we're improving every day," said Quist. "We will be capable of spawning a new generation of Descendants with several more advanced capacities. In the present instance, we are armed with new information. Perhaps, we can make some adjustments in the training."

Josh sat up straight in his chair. "I think I have an idea." The others gave him their attention. After a second's hesitation, he said, "I'm not going to teach Bozo anything more. He's mastered the art of taking off and hovering and flying to straight and level. When I get the new one, I will teach him how to hover and I will teach him how to descend to land. One of them will take off . . . and . . . I'll teach them to transfer controls in the air. Then the other one will land. That's how it will work."

"But *will* it work?" asked Vickers. "Why not just start out with a whole new pair of the higher-grade-intelligence degenerates?"

"That's still a contingency," Gates said. "For now, let's go with the plan Mr. Quist has suggested and the execution that Colonel Avery recommends."

• •

The next morning Josh changed his routine. Instead of riding out to the helicopter early to await Vickers or a security team to bring the Descendants, he worked in his combination room and office until he had a sketch for his ideas to train the new Descendant today. Then, when the telephone call came upstairs, he hurried down to ride out with Vickers, the Descendants in the back of the truck.

"They don't want you giving them names, you know that?"

"No, I didn't know that, Tommy."

Vickers grunted and was silent for a while. "Yeah, they decided that the names humanized them too much. So this new one in the back has got a number."

Josh gave him a "so what?" look.

"Delta Two-two-seven. That's his name . . . number, handle, whatever. . . . I guess you'll probably give him a name."

"I think I will."

"What are you going to call him?"

Josh looked at Vickers, waiting to see if he was joking. He looked serious. "I think I'll call him Ace, too."

"Pretty original."

"Not Ace T-W-O. I mean 'Ace, too,' as in Ace also."

Vickers began to nod slowly, thoughtfully, then nodded more rapidly as he began to understand. "I get it. What's the difference what you call them? They're basically all the same, right?"

Josh asked the question that had been bothering him. "What are they going to do with the first Ace?"

"I ain't exactly sure, Avery. You shouldn't worry about it, though. He was a burnout case. It's like he got his wires crossed or something. They'll study him, you know, ask a bunch of questions, and retrace the history of his training. They keep great records on these things. They'll see how much he's retained of his entire training life. Those little after-action reports you've been writing each day on these guys as pilots . . . they've been keeping track of everything that the guys learned. They put all that shit into a computer, you know. Nothing gets done without computers these days. They'll find out what he's stopped learning. They'll put some other training demands on him, you know, to see how far his memory or intelligence or whatever it is has disintegrated."

Josh noted that Vickers had ended his sentence on something of a middle pitch, as though he had more to say but had decided against it at the last instant.

"Then what?"

Vickers grimaced. "What do you care? What do you think? They'll probably turn up the heat until his pea brain boils a little bit. He's just a lab animal. Don't forget that. Think of him as a big white rat or something. As soon as they get finished with him, they'll put him to sleep. They'll do it humanely, a lot of these degenerates won't be as lucky as this one. Imagine what kind of story he'll take to degenerate heaven, for chrissakes. He's the first ever of his kind to learn how to take off and land a helicopter. Can you imagine that? *I* can't even do that."

Vickers looked at Josh and saw that he hadn't changed his expression. He shrugged. "Then they'll do an autopsy. Then they'll get rid of his body. You know the routine." Josh looked as steadfastly as he could at the side of Vickers's face as the truck bounced along the security road toward the helipad. He knew that

Vickers must be aware that he was staring at him. He was ignoring him. Josh refused to be ignored. He kept staring.

Without turning his head, Vickers said, "What are you gawking at? You're not getting sweet on me, are you?"

"Look at me, Tommy."

Already the truck was coasting to its normal stopping point near the helipad. Josh held Vickers's gaze with his own and said, "Tommy, does any of this—any of it at all—sound familiar to you? Can you ever remember reading about any similar kinds of experiments on actual human beings? Isn't there a spot somewhere inside your conscience—however small that is—a spot that gets tender to the touch when you think over the ideas that you've just mentioned, the things they are going to do to Ace?"

Vickers's gaze flickered for a second, but he did not look away. "You mean like Hitler and the Jews?"

"They called it eugenics—and things much worse."

"Well, bullshit is what I call it. This ain't a Nazi camp. This is a fucking lab. These ain't Jews or Catholics or Poles or Cambodians. These ain't people, damn you. I told you. They're lab rats. You ever see what they do to monkeys and cats and dogs and lab rats? What goes on here is pretty damned humane, considering the species that we're dealing with here. We ain't looking for a master race, remember?"

To Josh, he sounded as if his dogmatic convictions had been touched. Perhaps, a spot in his consciousness was not as small as Josh originally thought.

Vickers finally broke the lock of their gazes and shut off the ignition. "Now, let's get to flying this new bastard. You get him every day, just like you asked.

All by himself. Every other day, we'll bring Bozo along. One day you'll have just one to train, next day you'll have both. We don't want the first guy forgetting everything you trained him. And don't take forever with it, understand? Old Bozo is aging fast, in case you hadn't noticed."

Josh had noticed. Right before his eyes, Bozo had passed from young adulthood into middle age in the weeks of learning to fly. Wrinkles had creased his face and the bristly hair always cropped short had begun to glisten in spots on his head where the white began showing. It made Josh dizzy just to think about it.

But the new Descendant, the new Ace, was again a youngster somewhere in his twenties.

Josh let the Descendant stand in a position of attention until Vickers had turned the truck around and driven away.

In the weeks that followed, Josh found that simplifying the flight training was extremely easy. He had already made all his mistakes once or twice with the two original pilots. Now he worked hard at avoiding those same mistakes. He found that this Ace learned faster than the previous one. He seemed to have inborn instincts for flying, although that would have been impossible. He actually began to learn to hover in less than four weeks.

In the fifth week, Josh summoned Vickers to the side of the helicopter to stand in the late-afternoon shade after the two Descendants had been locked in the back of the pickup.

"Tommy, I'm ready for these two to solo as a team."

"What? Are you kidding? You mean to say you're ready to let those two go up alone?" Vickers's eyes were so wide open in astonishment, Josh had to lean forward and look at him closely to make sure he wasn't mocking him. But Vickers was serious.

"That's what solo means, Tommy. Of course they're ready. Isn't that the purpose of this exercise? Didn't you want to train these two to fly by themselves? Surely you didn't yet trust me to fly with them into North Africa? And *you're* not going, are you?"

"No . . . yes . . . I mean, no. I'm not going. But yes, these two degenerates are going to fly alone. I just didn't realize that they would be ready so soon. You didn't tell me."

"Until today, I wasn't sure. Now I'm fairly confident that these two can do it. Tomorrow is forecast to be a calm day. We can give them a try. The only trouble they've had is when they get unusual turbulence on the ground on a windy day. Whenever that happens as they are beginning to land, I've been able to tell them to make a go-around . . . I mean to abort the landing and go around to try again when there's less turbulence."

"I know what a go-around is," Vickers said.

"I want to try it tomorrow, if you'll agree." Vickers squinted hard at him and cocked his head a bit to the side and back, sighting down his nose.

"What's wrong?"

Vickers shook his head and cleared his face of the intense look. "Nothing's wrong. We'll give it a try. I'm not going to tell Gates and Quist because I don't want them around. . . . What are you smiling about?"

"I've already tried it, Tommy. It works. They can fly."

Vickers bristled. "What the hell do you think you're

doing? You mean you let these stupid bastards fly solo?"

Josh shook his head vigorously and held up a hand. "No, I wouldn't do that kind of thing unless I had the ability to keep in touch with them. What I did was sit behind them on the cabin floor. I was ready to take the controls if necessary. But I didn't have to. They flew the takeoff, the course, and returned to a landing to a hover and shut the helicopter down all by themselves without me saying a word. If I'd had to, first thing I would have done would be to give them directions over the intercom. Next, I could have taken the controls and stood there while one of them jumped over the seat or threw himself out the door or some other thing. I was in control of the situation all along. I practiced jumping over the console into the seat a dozen times on the ground."

Vickers was visibly relieved. "All right, then. We'll try it tomorrow. What do we need? Some kind of radio or something?"

"Yes, we'll need a ground-to-air radio so that if something does come up, I can talk to them and give them directions." Vickers nodded, but Josh noticed he was getting sighted down the nose again. "Let's do it in the morning, Tommy. That's when the density altitude will be the lowest. Once it gets later in the day, and gets hotter, it's a little tougher to fly. I want to give them every advantage for success."

Vickers simply grunted. "You're going to give them a course to fly and everything? They know how to navigate?"

Josh was puzzled. "Of course. I taught them a simple course. That's the point of the exercise, remember?"

Next day, Vickers and Josh stood behind the
pilots' seats as the two Descendants went through the
start-up by themselves. Vickers wore a headset so that
he could listen to the instructions that passed between
the members of the crew. Josh did his best to stay out
of the pre-flight conversations. His stomach churned,
and he didn't want to inject anything new into the
exercise. They had done it already. He had watched
them do it several times from his spot next to the
console behind and between them. There had been no
hitches. He wanted none now, so he tried not to do a
single thing differently. As far as he could tell, everything was going to be standardized.

Finally, he instructed Vickers that the pair were
ready for takeoff. "Now, let's jump down and get in
touch with them on the radio. I'll give them instructions from there."

Vickers shook his head. "No. You get down and
take the radio out there away from the helipad and
you give them a few instructions from long distance.
I'll stay in touch here and watch. When it's time for
me to get off, you wave your hand back and forth and
I'll unplug and jump down. We're not going to leave
these two alone until the last possible minute, got
that?"

Josh raised an eyebrow but he did not protest.

A minute later, he stood a hundred yards away and
realized that Vickers was probably right to stay back
and guard against any last-minute screw-ups. But
what could the colonel do? He wouldn't be able to
make any corrective maneuvers if the Descendants
screwed up a flying procedure. Besides, there was
nothing left to say to those two. He didn't plan this to

be a complicated exercise. All he planned was to tell them to begin their takeoff.

Josh waved his arms. Inside the Huey, he saw Vickers's arm and his thumb pointing up, violently pumping.

Finally Josh realized that Vickers wanted him to tell the Descendants to take off. He hoped the colonel would have enough sense to get the hell out of the helicopter as soon as he gave the order, because those two weren't going to waste a lot of time pulling pitch. Furthermore, if they had begun to lift off, his jumping around might upset their routine, as the helicopter would rock around, suddenly lightened by two hundred pounds.

Josh cursed Vickers for messing with his project. Then, as always, he felt an immediate surge of hot anger and a prickling of embarrassment that he'd taken this enterprise so seriously . . . so personally.

He put the radio to his lips and said what he had been saying without deviation for the last five flight-training days, "You are ready for takeoff. You may proceed to take off." He wanted to order Vickers to get the hell out of the cabin. He wanted to call him an obscene name. But he dared not inject a single new word into his instructions. The Descendants had been trained to listen to a certain set of phrases. By now he knew enough not to add any deviations at all. He sighed in relief as he saw Vickers lean forward to pat the pair on the back, then quickly jump out onto the helipad and run with his head bent low. Vickers pulled up panting when he reached Josh.

By then, the helicopter had lifted to a hover and had begun its takeoff run into the wind. Josh decided he wouldn't be taking any chances with these two. He positioned the helicopter into the wind before they had arrived. He didn't want them fooling around with that arrow on the helipad. He held his breath as the helicopter moved forward, visualizing the ball of air that it was balanced on, realizing that it was picking up speed as it was falling off the ball of air, settling. Finally, the rotor blades began screwing into undisturbed air. The Huey passed through the translational lift boundary between disturbed air and fresh air, and began an immediate climb-out. He was amazed at how steadily the helicopter rose and felt fully relieved when it had reached one hundred feet.

"They're going to make it, Tommy. They've got it. So far it's a success. They've gotten through the worst part of it. Next is the goddamned landing."

"Have you taught them how to make an emergency landing?"

Josh didn't take his eyes from the helicopter. Yet he hesitated a second before answering. "You know I didn't. What's the point? They have already shown that they can't take too much in the way of complicated maneuvers. If you think hovering a helicopter is difficult, try making an autorotational landing sometime. Worse, try teaching a human being to put one of those babies down without power, let alone a Descendant."

"Yeah. Now tell me about the course. What course are they going to fly?" Josh took his eyes off the helicopter for a second to see if Vickers was joking. He was not. "I already showed you the course. What the hell is going on with you, Tommy? They're going to fly straight out. They're going to make a simple series of right turns. They're going to fly back over the helipad toward the compound. Then they're going to make another simple, gentle turn and come back and land into the wind. They're going to fly this course, and they're not going to deviate from it. *What the hell is on your mind?*"

Vickers sighed as if in relief. "Then I guess this whole mission is going to be a success."

Josh shrugged. "As far as teaching monkeys to fly . . . I guess you could say we did that. But you know there's a hell of a lot more to flying than just doing what those two are doing. There's nap-of-the-earth flight. How do you suppose that helicopter's going to take off, fly to a thousand feet, and land exactly at the right place in the desert? Don't you think Saddiqi has any antiaircraft weapons, surface-to-air missiles, air cover of some kind, jets on alert? You know, I've heard it said that he's a madman. But I've never heard anybody say that he was a *stupid* madman."

Vickers guffawed, restored to his usual coarseness. "Let's just take one thing at a time, okay, Avery? Let's just see if those two degenerate bozos can bring that thing back and set it down in one piece."

Josh was already preoccupied with watching just that. The helicopter had flown back over the helipad and was headed toward the compound. "Start your turn now," he muttered under his breath. He heard Vickers sigh just as he saw the helicopter begin banking right.

"They're coming back to the helipad," Vickers said, almost in delight.

Josh's eyes traced the path from the sky down the invisible angle of approach, checking the flight path of the helicopter. He looked at Vickers. "You're surprised, aren't you? Why?"

An expression of concern crossed Vickers's face. He

pointed beyond the helipad. Words trying to form in his throat came out as grunts and groans.

Josh followed the point of the finger to a dust devil growing up about an eighth of a mile away, whirling into a tiny gray tornado of dirt, blowing toward the helipad.

Vickers said, "They'll probably miss is. It will go by before they have to land."

Josh thought the observation was spoken too hopefully.

"I'm not going to take any chances, Tommy. They're already in a descent. Those things are so erratic. If they were hovering when the thing came by . . ." He picked up the radio and put it to his lips.

"Don't bother," came the shaky voice of Vickers.

"Descendant flight, abort your approach. Go around, go around." They had practiced it before. Immediately, the nose of the helicopter would tilt forward, he would hear the whopping of the descending rotor pop hard, then swish into action, screwing into the air. The helicopter would intercept its original takeoff path and refly the entire route again. Ace, at the controls, would come around for another landing.

Josh watched in horror. "They're not going around," he moaned. "They're landing anyway." He put the radio up to his lips and began shouting his commands all over again. Then he felt a hand on his forearm.

"Don't bother."

"Don't bother? What the hell do you mean, Tommy? If they hit that dust devil, they could get . . ."

The realization suddenly dawned on him. "You turned the radio off. Goddamn you, Vickers. You turned the radio off, didn't you? Why? You didn't trust me? What did you think I was going to do?"

Vickers shrugged helplessly, raising the palms of his hands outward. Then they both were mesmerized by the sight of the helicopter approaching to the helipad and the dust devil now growing in strength, erratically blowing itself left and right, stopping, standing, starting. But inexorably, the sum of all of its movements added up to a single prevailing movement toward the helipad. Both men began leaning, tensely applying their own body English to the dust devil and to the helicopter in hopes that they would not arrive at the ground at the same time.

They did not. The helicopter arrived first.

"Put it down, put it down," Josh whispered.

"Put it down, you stupid bastards!" groaned Vickers.

The heel of the left skid began tap-dancing on the ground.

"Lower the collective," Josh ordered.

The Descendant at the controls, Ace, was performing the ritual exactly as he had been trained. He lowered the collective steadily, and the right skid's heel also touched. But instead of settling downward it, too, began tap-dancing. The dust devil was getting beneath the rotor disk from the opposite side of the helicopter. It began lifting the helicopter.

Both men watched as the helicopter leaped four feet into the air, its right skid at least a foot higher than the left. Vickers muttered an angry oath. Josh simply wheezed in despair. He knew what was about to happen. He knew that Ace would continue to lower the collective and possibly not even be able to correct with a cyclic.

Josh saw the helicopter's fuselage swing violently to the left underneath the rotor disk as the Descendant tried to correct but did it erratically, inducing the bumping of the rotor hub against the mast.

"Mast bumping," he whispered.

"What the hell . . . ?"

Both men stared in awe as the sound of crackling, like heavy gunfire, came from the helicopter. The rotor plane flipped back toward the left as the fuselage swung under it to the right. The helicopter emitted another series of crackling noises, and then the rotor plane dipped down. One blade struck the helipad on the downswing. That blade broke in half immediately and the upper blade, now unbalanced, yanked the transmission out the right side of the fuselage and forward, buckling the helicopter up in the middle. An instant later the helicopter hit the ground on its left side, the tail rotor slapping into the earth like a weed-whacking tool, flying apart, scattering buzzing pieces of wreckage in all directions. Vickers hit the ground as if he were under fire from a sniper.

Josh stood watching, paralyzed in grief.

The engine flamed out with a bang; like an explosion from a small cannon firing. A puff of white smoke evaporated into the air around the engine compartment, but there was no fire. The helicopter seemed to scrunch itself up into what resembled a fetal position. A final screech of metal—or was it one of the crew members?—rose out of the wreckage.

Josh took it as a cry of one of the Descendants and began running toward the helicopter.

Vickers jumped up from the ground and in two strides made a flying leap, barely able to make a shoe-string tackle to bring Josh down. Then he clambered up over him and held him, screaming at the back of his head as he forced him down to the earth, "Are you fucking crazy? If one of those things is alive, do you suppose it doesn't have a cut or scratch on it? What are you going to do, run out there and throw yourself into the wreckage with one of those bastards and get yourself eaten alive, too?"

Josh immediately stopped struggling beneath Vickers. He remembered the videotape that he'd seen. Gregor Munn had turned into an animal on screen.

Josh dropped his forehead onto his forearms and relaxed on the earth. Vickers pushed against his back to stand up. He drew his pistol and walked toward the wreckage slowly, cautiously, in case something should come flying out. Or in case the Huey might catch fire.

Josh heard a shriek; a rending, angry scream. He wasn't sure if it had come out of the depths of his own soul or if it came to his ears from the crash site. He looked up, suddenly feeling an enormous headache— or was it a pain in the neck? What had he become involved with? What kind of men were these? He pushed himself up as though he were suffering from a belly-dragging, toilet bowl–hugging hangover.

One of the Descendants—Ace, he thought—tried to crawl out of the wreckage. He was dragging himself over the top of the fuselage when the second Descendent rose up behind him suddenly, darting out of the wreckage like a jack-in-the-box, grasping him across the shoulders and pulling him back downward, simultaneously biting into the back of his neck. The scream repeated itself, and Josh realized it had come from inside the aircraft, not from inside himself. But there was a sympathetic resonation in his chest. He watched dumbly as Vickers, his pistol drawn, approached the top of the cabin and leaned over the opening into the fuselage. For a second, the colonel recoiled, then leaned back over, leading with his pistol, and fired three quick shots.

The reports of the pistol galvanized Josh. He stood up, feeling all at once angry and energized by all that had happened before his eyes this afternoon. Without warning, the dust devil hit him from the side and took his hat off, shooting it skyward and flinging it out of its vortex. The pebbles and grit in the tiny tornado forced his eyes shut but he did not try to defend himself against the ravages of the wind. He let it sandblast him. In seconds, it was gone, dancing mischievously across the desert. It had done its damage on the Huey just as quickly, he realized.

Perhaps a half hour later, Vickers stood beside him. He spoke gruffly, but his pale expression belied the bravado. "The one somebitch was eating the other. Straighten yourself out, Avery. Pull yourself together. You look like shit."

Josh brushed sand off his face absently. "You turned the radio off, didn't you?"

"I looked at the azimuth of your downwind leg. I saw that it was on a straight line with the compound. I didn't know, maybe you were going to try to make them go back and fly into the headquarters or something . . . so . . ."

"You shut the radios off? You mistrusted me and ended up killing my . . . those Descendants? And you expect me to work with you? You want my trust? How is that possible?"

Vickers for once did not have a response.

Josh turned away. Already three fire trucks, an ambulance, and several trucks packed with security forces raced down the road from the compound toward them. Vickers reached over and took the radio that Josh still held and changed frequencies. "Slow those trucks down, everything is under control here. No fire. No loose Descendants. No injuries among the humans."

"Well, I guess it's over," Josh said in a mixture of relief and despair.

"What's over?"

Josh smirked. "The mission. The project. How are you going to fly a crew and to kill Saddiqi when your crew just tried to eat each other up?"

Vickers sniffed loudly. "We'll just start again. I'll bring you another crew to train. Gates and Quist are practically wetting their pants over this new generation of degenerates, anyhow. They're still a little young, but they're smarter than the previous ones."

"But we've got less than a month—"

"That's enough time."

"And I'm not going to do it again."

Vickers laughed harshly. "Yes, you are. You're going to do it all over again. And we're never going to run out of these bozos, so if something happens to the next pair, you're going to have to train two more. And you'll keep doing it for as long as we tell you to, Avery. I'm not bullshitting you. You're going to do it and you're going to do it well."

"How can you force me? . . ."

"I've got three things in my favor, not just one. Let me count the ways." He held up a forefinger, "Marilyn." He held up a second finger. "Jill." The third finger went up. "Katy."

Josh stood and stared at Vickers for a long time. Something showed through in the clarity of the dry

sun. Maybe it was the altitude. Maybe it was the stark-
ness of what he had just seen, the naked brutality that
Vickers had shown. First his complete lack of trust,
and now this threat.

He squinted for a second, trying to think exactly
what it was. What was the saving grace that he could
ascribe to Vickers? When he was botching his first job
as a company commander, one of the senior captains
had dragged him aside and said with extraordinary
wisdom, "Stop looking for the worst in everybody,
Josh. Every goddamned five-percenter has a bit of evil
in him. And every single person on the face of the
earth—even the worst piece of shit—has some bit of
good in him. If you look for it, you'll find it. When you
find it, then find a use for that good in your unit. The
people who have the most good in them will carry the
weight of the unit, but everyone will be contributing.
That's how you build a team, goddammit."

He'd adopted that philosophy. But now he'd found
a man who defied the simple logic. He thought he'd
seen a shred of conscience in Vickers yesterday. But
now—

"What are you looking at, you somebitch?"

Josh decided. "Sorry," he said, mustering every
ounce of self-control to keep his voice and expression
neutral. Keeping that dispassionate expression on his
face, he made a silent vow to sabotage this mission. He
would do it with the next set of pilots. And he would
also bide his time and find a way out of this godforsaken place. He'd find a way to bring down this operation, even if it killed him.

"I'm only one man, Tommy. I'm going to need
some help if I'm going to train a new crew in a
month."

12

· · · · · · · · · · · · · · · · · · ·

The next morning, Josh stood on the helipad next to another Huey, one of the fleet of a dozen helicopters parked near the compound's hangar. He studied a gouge in the earth less than fifty feet away. Only the disturbed sand, darkened by fuel spills, testified to the terror of yesterday. The first windstorm would erase even that evidence. Only a handful of people on earth would ever know what had happened on that spot. Josh would be one of them. He renewed his vow to share that knowledge with some form of authority rather than this renegade bureaucracy running The Ranch.

He watched the truck plowing through wavering heat columns rising from the desert already at eight o'clock. Vickers drove the truck up and stepped out to release the latch in the back. "All right, asshole, get out of there."

A man poked his head from the truck's mobile cell, squinting in the sunlight.

Vickers didn't exchange a word with Josh. He climbed back to the cab, put the truck in gear, and

shot gravel at the man stepping down from the back of
the truck, his foot barely touching the ground before
the pickup pulled away. Josh looked him over and
said, "Come on over and climb inside the cabin." The
man stood looking at him defiantly. Josh spoke civilly,
"Grayson Kirk, isn't it? I didn't know you existed till
yesterday."

Kirk said nothing, did nothing. Josh climbed up
into the cabin and sat down on one of the fabric passenger seats. He patted a spot beside him and waited.
Gradually, Kirk's look mutated from defiance into
confusion, and he sauntered toward the helicopter. He
stopped with his thighs against the edge of the cabin
floor and spoke.

"They said I might be able to fly." It sounded like a
question.

"Come on up here and get out of the sun. I'll give
you a briefing."

Josh consulted his notebook and told Kirk everything. He made a lengthy checklist because there was
so much: the background behind the terrorist mission,
the genetic-engineering experiment that had produced
the Descendants, the security precautions around the
compound and the entire Ranch perimeter, and the
deadly quirks of the Descendants themselves. He
ended with the crash of the day before and repeated
his vow to bring down the operators of The Ranch.

When Josh had crossed the last item off his checklist, Kirk gave an account of his own. He told how he
had been involved in an earlier generation of genetic-
engineering experiments—experiments that had created monsters. He revealed that he had been hunted
by the earlier generation of government outlaws, and

how he had gone underground, supposedly protected by a witness-assistance program.

When Kirk had finished, Josh said, "We'd better get flying. They're probably watching. They'll be suspicious of us chatting out here in the wilderness. I'm supposed to be giving you orientation flights to bring you back up to speed in the cockpit. Then we're going to be training a new pair of Descendants. They needed you to help get it done quickly so they can pull off this mission against Saddiqi."

"How do I know I can trust you?" Kirk asked, the contorted right side of his face twisting his expression into a perverse grin.

Josh shrugged. "I'd ask you the same question. But who has time for tap-dancing around? Sooner or later, I'll know whether you're one of them or not. If you are, I'll bring you down with the rest of them."

Without waiting for a response, Josh clambered down and began untying the rotor blades.

As soon as they had gotten into the air and Kirk had his hands on the controls, he said, "There was a woman with me when I was captured. I haven't seen her since they brought us here. Have you seen her? Do you know anything about her?"

Josh shook his head. "As I said, I didn't know about you, either. Tell me about her. I'll try to find out something if I can."

Kirk told him that PJ Payne had been married to one of the first victims of the genetic nightmare. She had watched him be destroyed inch by inch until finally, mercifully, he had died. "From that moment on," he said, "she became consumed by revenge. She even established her own network of people snooping around all over the country looking for evidence of continuing genetic-engineering experiments inside the government and out."

"Cliff Breen." Josh stiffened and looked over at his new copilot.

Kirk met his eyes and nodded. "He was the jackpot when he got assigned to your project. One of her sources in Washington tied a guy named Gates to Vickers. It seems they had quite a few Washington meetings outside the Pentagon. When Breen drew an assignment to Vickers's detachment, PJ got in touch with him. Breen was a war buddy of Mark Payne's. She just asked him to let her know if he made any moves away from Fort Hood. And the rest, as they say, is history."

Josh took the controls and made a quick circuit of the entire perimeter of The Ranch. He pointed out one area they were never allowed to fly over. "That's where I suppose they are doing the infantry training for the Special Operations team that will attack the Saddiqi encampment. But I've never been over that way once, so I don't know much except that they sometimes train with live ammo."

Josh also explained that he had not been into more than a quarter of the entire compound. He didn't know all that went on in the outbuildings or in most of the wings of the main building. He tried to familiarize Kirk as quickly as possible so that they could begin their training of their new Descendants immediately, so that they could begin their plan to sabotage the mission.

After they had landed, shut down the helicopter, and tied the blades down, they watched the truck drive toward them.

Suddenly Josh said, "Kirk, I'm going to ask you to

do something. If you do it, I know it will be a sign of good faith on your part."

Kirk stiffened. "What is it?"

"It just occurred to me that only two kinds of creatures in this area are unarmed. One kind is the prisoners. The other is the Descendants. They're always talking about a new generation of those things. . . ."

"You think I'm one of those Descendants?"

"I don't know. And you don't know whether I'm one. But there is a way to find out. These animals have been castrated. And there is a stump at the base of the spine. It's the place where they cut off a vestigial tail."

"You want to pat me down? Feel me up?"

Josh nodded. Kirk shrugged. So Josh patted him down and was satisfied that he was intact, that he was a man. Kirk did the same to Josh perfunctorily. "Now all we have to do is figure out a way to throw a monkey wrench—no pun intended—into this operation."

Josh smirked. "I've already got a plan."

"Plan for what?"

"A plan to sabotage this mission."

Kirk lifted his head and waited for Josh to continue.

"We modify the start-up checklist, leaving the low-RPM audio off. Pull the circuit breaker so the Descendants never hear it in flight. And don't forget to push the breaker back in during the shutdown. Later, I'll tell you how we use that."

"It's not enough."

Josh looked at Kirk closely. He saw a hard, bitter diary recorded in those black eyes. Kirk's face, like Josh's, contorted by surgery and injuries from some past helicopter mishap, looked comical, but he exuded a deadly seriousness. "What do you mean?" said Josh.

"I mean it's not enough to undo this mission. We've got to destroy this entire operation. She wants it."

"PJ?"

Kirk nodded emphatically. "It's all that matters to her. I had hoped once she might learn to love me, to get revenge out of her system—but never mind that now. She's made a convert of me. Now I want the same vengeance that she does. The first thing we do is to destroy this place. Second—and this is for me—I want to try to save her. To get her out of here. I doubt she could ever return to any semblance of a normal life-style after all she's been through. I'll never know unless I try. If we fail on the second item, at least we will have accomplished the first. If we fail on the first . . ."

"It won't matter, anyhow." Josh suddenly realized that he had been elevated to a new plane in this contest between himself and the people in the compound who ran The Ranch. His vision had virtually been compressed into the boundaries of the cockpit of his helicopter. Kirk, who had engaged in much more deadly confrontations with this group, had now placed at the very top of his priority list the destruction of the entire group. What ruthlessness that must require, he thought.

When they had returned to the compound, Vickers ordered them sent to separate quarters. Josh protested, saying that they would need to collaborate on setting up training to finish their job on time. He also insisted Kirk be given quarters with as much freedom of movement and ability to exercise as himself.

Vickers refused, citing Kirk's history. Josh insisted that he needed somebody alert and fresh. He asked that the training sessions be increased daily to three, instead of two. Vickers thought awhile and finally granted this request. "Only because it makes sense," he growled.

Josh knew he'd won the point only because he had volunteered for more work. If any request had seemed evasive in the slightest, Vickers would have denied it.

Even at that, he had to get in the final word. "But the damned degenerates are still going to have to have their feeding breaks," he added. "They still get hungry, you know."

Josh shrugged. "I want a second helicopter after the first few days of Grayson's cockpit orientation."

"You can want in one hand and piss in the other, Avery. All you're gonna get out of that is a wet hand. No way do I trust you guys with two helicopters."

"Be reasonable, Tommy. I need Grayson to train one Descendant while I prepare the other. Two pilots, two aircraft. Three sessions a day for about three weeks with individual attention will nearly triple the capability we've been using so far with just me in two sessions and only one of those Descendant in the cockpit at a time."

Vickers, ever the analyst, screwed his mouth up thoughtfully. Josh knew in the first second of the red-faced colonel's hesitation that he'd won his demands because they all seemed entirely practical.

"But I'm not letting you two room together," Vickers finally growled, as if he had given too many concessions. "I don't want you two cooking up some kind of shit."

Josh shook his head. "We don't need to share a room. But you've got to let us have some time outside the cockpit so we can plan away from the Descendants. Whenever they're around, we always have to be on the alert that somehow somebody is going to nick themselves and let loose some blood. We always have to be watching them just so they don't do it to themselves. It takes too much out of our concentration. We need a time and a place where we can sit down and compare the day's notes, make out a report, and plan for the following day's operation."

Vickers muttered a curse under his breath, a curse that indicated he would grudgingly give in once more. "All right, dammit, you can have a conference room, but you have to schedule it in advance so we know when you're going to be there. You'll be monitored. By cameras. And by microphones. Maybe we'll even have somebody standing in the room." He raised an eyebrow, waiting to see what resistance this would bring from Kirk and Josh.

Kirk remained noncommittal, deferring to Josh, who knew he dared not defy a security measure without a training reason. He simply said, "Thank you, Tommy." He nearly choked on his own civility. He felt Kirk squinting at him, momentarily wondering why he showed such deference. Maybe he'd overdone it.

The idea that Josh seemed to be so cooperative, so willing to accept such things as he had just proposed, seemed to bother Vickers. "One more thing, I'm going to get a set of your helicopter books. I'm going to start reading up on those damn things. I don't want you two pulling any shit on me, hear? I'm going to ground school."

Josh lifted an eyebrow into an expression that said, "who cares?" and led Kirk off to lunch.

• •

The next morning, Vickers dropped a new pair of Descendants at the helipad after Josh and Kirk had already concluded a thorough pre-flight check. As a security guard unlocked the truck, Vickers said, "Their numbers are—"

"It doesn't matter, Tommy. I'm going to give them names, anyhow."

Vickers's lip curled in a sneer. "Let me guess—Bozo and Ace, right?" Josh smiled his answer. Vickers muttered a string of obscenities as he got back into the truck and drove off, leaving the foursome standing in a cloud of dust under the sun.

Just in the process of erasing numbers and giving names to Bozo and Ace, Josh saw differences between them and the previous Descendants of the same names. As he introduced everybody all around, he was startled to find that the Descendants already knew the practice of shaking hands. "Grayson, these boys are way smarter than the previous ones I've been acquainted with. I want to try something. Bozo, can you smile?"

A smile spread across Bozo's face, exposing gleaming teeth, as if from a toothpaste ad. Josh's neck and head pivoted backward as he squinted, examining the smile.

"What's wrong?" Kirk asked.

"Nothing. That's what's wrong. Ace . . . smile." The Descendant did as he was ordered, the smile as natural and wholesome as Bozo's.

Josh shook his head slowly. "There's almost nothing wrong. These two are too close to being human beings for comfort. This whole project makes me sicker by the day. We'd better get started." He turned toward the helicopter to pick up the checklist from the cabin floor.

"Wait." Kirk grinned foolishly, his face averted from the pair. "You better get these two to stop smiling."

Josh looked back. The two stood like mannequins, natural smiles still pasted on their faces. Maybe the two weren't so human, after all. "Wipe those smiles off your faces," he said. In unison they pulled handkerchiefs from their back pockets and wiped their faces roughly. The smiles disappeared.

Kirk burst into laughter.

Josh did not. His previous experiences had made him a little tougher toward anything that might have been humorous in his past life; his life before The Ranch, when he could go home to Marilyn at night.

The human pilots devoted the morning's session to a ground orientation, untying the helicopter and preparing it for flight. Josh stuck strictly to the mechanical essentials. Once they'd trained the Descendants to the steps in a sequence, he explained to Kirk, they would never leave out a step.

Next, Josh gave them an orientation flight, beginning with hover training. He selected Bozo first as his student. He told him the first step would be learning to hover, then to take off, climb out, and finally fly a specified course.

Into the intercom he said, "Ace, you'll be picking up the flying midway along the course, then you'll be responsible for landing. Got that?"

Josh was surprised to hear the click of the intercom button. "I have it, sir."

Josh wondered if they were Descendants at all. The very idea caused him to feel a jolt of adrenaline. Sure, what if Vickers had arranged for a couple of sandbaggers to sit in and determine whether he was going to try to sabotage the mission? *Chrissakes!* He hadn't even thought of that. He had no doubt that that was what Vickers was up to. His real Descendants would come later. He didn't know how to get the word to Kirk, but he hoped that Grayson would have enough sense not to say anything in front of these two Descendants—or whatever they were. Yes, they were men. They'd been told how to act. And they weren't very damn good at it. Their smiles weren't plastic enough for them to be Descendants.

After they had landed, Josh instructed the pair to tie down the helicopter in exactly the manner they had been taught earlier in the morning. Without hesitation, the two went at it. Josh yanked Kirk by the elbow as he stepped out with the pair. He told him in a whisper of his suspicions. Kirk nodded thoughtfully. "Well, you should know. Until today, I've never seen one of the damned things. What should we do?"

"Check them out the way I checked you."

"Feel them up?"

Josh smirked sheepishly. He ordered the two to line up and patted them on the shoulders then patted them on the behinds like a coach sending a couple of football players into a game with encouragement.

As Vickers and the security man were loading the two into the back of the truck, Josh murmured, "They're Descendants, all right."

Vickers ambled over to them, puffing out his chest. "Pretty sharp, aren't they? I been knowing West Point graduates that ain't as clever as these two. We used to get cadets for summer training. Had to hang a sign on all our urinals: West Point Cadets, Please Don't Eat the Big Pink Mints."

Josh squinted at Vickers without a trace of a smile. "Tommy, you're exactly right. Those two aren't . . . animals. This new generation is more like men. They might have some of the qualities of those Descendants, but they're closer to men than a lot of men I have known." He kept a stone-faced expression.

Vickers's own face darkened. "Think so, smartass? Get your butts in the truck. I hope you two ain't hungry."

On the drive back to the compound, Vickers's mood returned to normal. He began telling one of his nasty parables. "When I was on my third wife—not literally —she was giving me a hard time about my drinking. So one night I come home a little soused and she starts riding my ass. So what'd I do? I broke down crying. I told her I had finally seen the error of my ways because of the awful things that had happened to me that very day. Course she was just delighted, but so damn curious she had to ask what it was that had caused me to turn that way. I told her I got a pair of underage twins pregnant, and their mother, too. I told her I caught all kinds of crud. Told her there was a good likelihood that she was probably infected with gonorrhea, syphilis, and AIDS all at once. Stupid bitch believed me. Then I told her that there weren't no twins or mother pregnant, there weren't no prostitutes. All it was was that I was a little bit drunk from being out with the guys. She didn't know whether to shit or go blind. Of course I *was* out with a prostitute getting drunk. By that point, she wouldn't have known whether to believe that if I told her."

Grayson Kirk looked straight ahead out the windshield, his permanent wiseacre look tinged with disgust. Josh stared at Vickers expectantly. He wanted to ask for the point of the story, but he didn't. He refused to give Vickers the satisfaction of asking for a punchline.

Back at the compound, Vickers drove the truck down a passageway between two wings of a building that Josh had never seen from the ground. A maze of fences lined one side of the passageway. Josh saw that each fence was broken into compartments that led from a gate to the building. Vickers backed the truck up to a gate constructed so that the back of the truck fit exactly into it, forming a seal.

Vickers crooked a finger at them, indicating they should get out and watch the unloading. The security guard climbed up on top of the truck and used a stick to reach down and unlatch the back gate of the truck.

"This is how it has to be done when we get close to feeding time. We can't take a chance that they might have undereaten at their last meal. I think you remember how violent they can get when they haven't eaten in a while."

The door slid into a pocket and Bozo stepped inside. After he had gone in, a green light flashed above the door and the security guard pulled a ring on top of the truck that Josh had never seen before. This released an inner cage and let Ace into the enclosure. Ace stepped up to the door, pushed a button, and went inside just as Bozo had.

Josh shrugged. "So what?" said Kirk.

Vickers crooked his finger at them again and led the way, striding the self-important rolling walk of the little man trying to make himself taller. Beyond the maze of cages was another door with a combination lock on it. Vickers shielded the keypad with one hand and punched in a sequence. The door slid open. They came face-to-face with a video security camera. "This is Colonel Vickers with two righteous observers, the helicopter pilots. Total of three humans." A green light flashed beside the camera lens. Vickers beckoned them to step inside the door. They stood in a compartment between doors. When the outer door had slid shut, the inner door opened, letting them into a stairwell. Vickers marched upward nosily, his boots clumping on each step. Everything about him radiated arrogance. Josh wondered how he'd ever called the man a friend.

They found themselves on an observation deck shielded with dark glass, probably a one-way mirror, Josh realized. Vickers said, "I had this set up special for visitors, you know—skeptical VIPs and shit. So far we ain't had no VIPs. I just had a feeling you'd react like this, Avery. You know what? You're just like one of those damned bleeding-heart liberal bastards who make it so hard for us to carry out the national security interests of our country. I'm going to show you a little reality right now. It's time you put your feelings and emotions into perspective. Perspective. That's what this little lesson is all about today."

So that was his punch line of the story of the pickup, Josh thought. Before he had time to mull it over, Vickers grasped a microphone and spoke into it. "Run the bovine demonstration."

The choice of words startled Josh. He remembered bringing up cattle the day he'd eaten salad with Vickers back at Fort Hood. He'd used the word *bovine*.
. . . How long ago was that? Vickers laughed, seeing the recognition. "For a second there that day, I

thought you knew something you weren't supposed to. But now you're going to really see what the bovine demonstration is."

Below them a series of partitions formed half a dozen segments like locks through the Panama Canal. Below their feet, Josh felt the slamming of a door as he heard it. Bozo and Ace stepped into the first compartments of their separate channels and began undressing. Their fingers were fumbling, as if they were extremely nervous, or suffering withdrawal symptoms from drugs—or hunger pains.

Josh felt his stomach tighten. He knew what was to come. He'd seen the feeding demo with the juveniles.

"This isn't necessary, Tommy."

"Your ass," Vickers snarled. "You watch, you bastards. You watch and don't you never forget what you're seeing."

The pair of Descendants undressed hurriedly and poised naked before the next lock, each with a knot at the base of his spine. They had lost the composure they had shown this morning. Now they pounded on the barrier to the next opening. Bozo even jumped up and hung from the wire of his enclosure so he could swing his feet and bang his bare heels into the doorway. Vickers looked at him, then glared at Kirk and Josh, who were transfixed. He muttered an order into the hand mike and the second enclosure opened. The two Descendants rushed into their enclosures, separated by a partition. The doors behind them shut. The two bellowed in unison. Josh saw that each of the enclosures had a drain hole in the center of the floor. He knew why. He looked up above the cages and saw a sprinkler system.

Suddenly doors clanked at the far end of each enclosure. Josh saw two men, each holding a halter on a calf. Each used a knee to force the calves into the next enclosure. The calves needed more than a little encouragement, for they must have scented old blood or new terror. But the animals were heaved into the enclosure and tied. Before each man released his calf, he dragged a fist down a flank of the animal.

Josh shuddered, seeing what he hadn't seen before. In the hand of each man was a utility knife, the kind used to slash open cardboard boxes. This time the men had used them, not on cardboard, but to open a gash in the calves' flanks. The men dashed back to safety and pushed buttons so that their enclosures were cut off from the animals by a sliding gate.

The two Descendants began shrieking.

"Still think they're human? Avery? Kirk? Got any ideas about these bastards being your brothers-in-law or something?"

Josh turned away. "I've seen enough of this, Vickers. You don't have to give me any more of your reality conditioning."

"Turn around, you whining bastard. You're going to watch this reality, somebitch. You're going to see something about relativity. You're gonna learn a lesson in perspective." He barked into his communications mike. Josh couldn't hear what he said over all the noise from the very two Descendants he'd named this morning.

The door slammed. Instantly, the Descendants jumped the calves, slashing with extended fangs. Before the animals could even stop struggling against their halter ropes, the two had begun consuming flesh.

"Every four hours, boys," Vickers said bitterly. "That's how often these things have to be fed. We don't often send live animals in. We try to be at least a little humane about it. But you two needed a little reality conditioning. You two needed to see things in perspective. Now you know why we insist that you never exceed the training periods."

Kirk stood staring unemotionally at the sight before him. "This is nothing, Vickers. I've seen worse bestiality than this. But I get your point. And the first point is that you people are all lowlifes, pulling this kind of shit in the name of science and national security."

Josh looked at Kirk in wonder. To have seen worse than this, what had the man gone through? For himself, he felt his stomach lurching. He knew he was going to be sick soon if this wasn't over.

"Seen enough?"

Josh had already turned away, his stomach clenching higher.

"Things got voracious appetites. Eat anything. Eat anybody," Vickers said menacingly, displaying his yellowed stubs of teeth. "Even their relatives. Even you two boys if you screw up. First thing you boys got to realize is they don't have friends, so don't try to be friends with them. If they didn't have fresh beef to eat, they'd eat each other. If they didn't have each other, there would always be you. Don't forget that, girls."

• •

An hour later, a shaken Josh and a quiet Kirk stood beside their helicopter as a security truck delivered the two Descendants. They were in fresh uniforms, calm and sedate as ever. Josh and Kirk traded knowing glances and went about their business. But as they turned to the helicopter, both touched their belts, feeling for their stun guns as if to reassure themselves that they could at least make an attempt at defending themselves should anything go wrong.

Compared to dealing with the earlier Descendants, this flight training went remarkably fast. The Descendants picked up hovering in only three days, each having the advantage of three training sessions a day with just one pilot. Then Kirk and Josh began to fly separate courses, one teaching the takeoff, climb-out, and navigation techniques, the other teaching return navigation, descent, and landing.

As the training progressed, Vickers became more and more interested in the manuals, the maps, and training procedures, although he still refused to fly on any of the training missions.

"I'll know how you're doing by the results I see. Don't you worry. Don't you try anything funny."

As always, Josh answered Vickers's suspicions with a wry, sarcastic expression, as if the very suggestion were preposterous. But trying something funny was exactly what was on his mind.

"When are we going to pull this off?" Kirk asked one afternoon as they stood alone outside the helicopter watching Bozo and Ace untie the blades.

"Any time now. What I've got in mind involves the start-up procedure."

"The low-RPM audio?"

"Yes. When the helicopters are set up for the solo missions, all the circuit breakers are going to be in. And since we've abbreviated the checklist, they've never made an audio check. But now I'm going to start teaching my Descendant—" He caught himself and blushed. "I mean *the* Descendant to begin bleeding off engine RPM with his governor increase-decrease every time the airspeed reaches a hundred knots."

Kirk squinted one eye and nodded slowly, waiting for the rest of it. Josh continued. "You teach Ace a new step in his descent to landing. Before he begins lowering the collective, have him start his descent by nosing the helicopter forward with the cyclic so the airspeed exceeds a hundred knots—actually it'd be better if you'd have him go to a hundred five."

"I got that. I don't know why, but I'll start with it this afternoon. What then?"

"When Bozo sees the airspeed indicator going over a hundred knots at any time, he'll reach over and begin lowering the RPM with the button on his collective switch. When it falls between sixty-one hundred to sixty-three hundred RPM, what happens?"

Kirk lifted his chin. "The audio alarm sounds."

"You teach Ace to shut off the fuel switch every time he hears the audio wailing in his headset."

"Screw you, Jack." Kirk burst into bitter laughter. "I guess you hadn't figured it out, Josh. The first time I teach him that I get to land the SOB without power. Or else I get to crash. Boy, that'll teach Vickers a lesson, eh?"

Josh laughed. "You don't have to teach him that as you are teaching him to land. You'll teach him that during the run-up procedure. We practice it on the ground a few times so we won't have to do it in the air. Look, we'll do it right now in my helicopter. Come on."

Josh put Bozo in the left seat and Ace in the right. "We're adding a new procedure," he said. He pointed to the audio switch on the console. "This switch stays off during run-up, right?"

Bozo raised a hand.

"You have a question, Bozo?"

"No, sir. Not a question. An observation. When we reach normal operating range on the N2 power turbine, about 6400 to 6600 RPM, I observe that this switch always comes on."

Josh stared breathlessly into Bozo's face.

Ace raised his hand.

"Yes, Ace . . . you noticed it, too?"

"Yes, sir."

"Yes . . . yes, it does come on. . . . Yes . . . Grayson, outside. You two sit here. Just sit with your hands on your knees until we come back."

A hundred yards away from the Huey, Josh kicked angrily at the sand. He cursed into the afternoon's hot wind. Kirk hung his head and patted the gravel with his boot, waiting for the momentary storm to pass.

"How can we do this, Grayson? Those two are smart . . . They're almost—"

"We just do it, Josh. You saw them eat those calves. I saw them. Vickers made a pretty heavy impression that day, remember? They're not human, Josh. *Dammit, remember that!*"

"I've been at this for months, Grayson. I've never seen one of those . . . things express an independent observation yet. I mean, until today, until just now. They do have an intellect, Grayson. They're not just animals. *They are almost human!*"

"Tell that to their calves. Go pick a scab in front of one of them and see what happens."

"Okay, so they're humans with animal eating habits. So they're humans that can be incited to violence. I tell you, these things are more human than animal. I don't know if I can just coldly murder them."

Kirk rested a hand gently on Josh's shoulder. "You ever been driving along and see a squirrel dash in front of your car . . . or a dog or cat?"

Josh nodded his jaw muscles impatiently. "Of course."

"So what did you do? Did you swerve to avoid the animal or did you try to hit it?"

"Avoid. I always tried to avoid them."

"Naturally. Most humane people do. But would you swerve into the path of a truck and kill yourself to save the damned squirrel? Or would you run down a couple kids on the sidewalk to avoid hitting an animal?"

"You think this is the same thing? You think that's Chip and Dale sitting in the cockpit over there?"

"It's the same thing, Josh. It's them or us."

Josh mulled it over for a long five minutes. Finally, he sighed and wordlessly led the way back to the Huey.

From behind him, Kirk said, "Chipmunks."

"Huh?"

"Chipmunks. Chip and Dale aren't squirrels. They're chipmunks."

Neither of the men laughed. Josh saw that his friend looked as ill as he felt.

Back inside the cockpit, he instructed Ace. "Any time you hear this sound"—he flipped on the audio switch at flight idle—"I want you to reach over and shut off the fuel switch." The Descendant acknowledged that he understood the procedure. Josh demonstrated. The helicopter engine quit.

"Now let's test it out with you two," said Josh.

Bozo went through the start-up completely, the low-RPM audio switch off. When the throttle had been twisted to operating RPM, Josh instructed them to change controls so that Ace, in the right seat now, had his left hand on the collective and his right on the cyclic. Josh reached over to the collective at the co-pilot station and began working the governor increase-decrease switch to lower the RPM. The alarm sounded over the intercom system, a boinging sound, a varying, oscillating frequency, starting low and building up to a high pitch every two seconds. The signal was intended to startle pilots in flight before they lost the ability to continue flying as their RPM decreased. The instant the first signal sounded in their headsets, Ace reached over and shut off the fuel, exactly as Josh had demonstrated minutes earlier.

Josh talked to Kirk on the private circuit of the intercom, which the Descendants had never been taught to use. "Okay, now all we have to do is teach them another step in flight. I'll teach mine that any-time he sees the airspeed passing a hundred knots he'll reach over and began lowering the RPM audio. That will keep his half of the instructions inside my cockpit and it will keep it safe for me. Then all you have to do for your part is introduce a new step to the pre-landing procedure. Instead of beginning descent at ninety knots, increase the airspeed to a hundred knots plus. From there, begin the landing as normal. When my guy sees your guy going over a hundred knots, he'll begin reducing RPM. When your guy hears the low-RPM audio come on, he'll shut the fuel off. End of mission."

"Great, but how do you expect them to land in everyday practice?"

"The Huey will fly at six thousand RPM."

"As long as there's no load. And in the afternoon, the high DA will make it dicey."

Josh bit his lip thoughfully. "Okay, you teach him to land safely at six thousand in the mornings, when it's safer. In the afternoons, you take the controls, make him cover his eyes, and land it the right way. We just have to hope Vickers never asks to fly along and check us out. So far he's been afraid I'll take him on a Kamikaze ride and run this thing into the headquarters. I'm sure he won't screw up this operation. I'm not worried about him. I'm worried about me. I wonder if I've got the nerve."

"Don't get cold feet on me now, Josh. I owe it to PJ."

"I won't get cold feet. The only thing we're going to have to deal with here are our consciences."

"Now's not the time, Josh. Maybe later, if we get out of this alive."

"Grayson, just by looking at you it would be hard for me to see exactly how ruthless and hard you are. You must have had a hell of a lot of experiences. But just suppose . . . suppose that these people are acting in the service of our government. Do you know what it is to undermine a project like this against an enemy of the nation? It's high treason."

"No, goddammit, *no*! You may have an attack of conscience of any kind you want. But don't you ever believe these people are operating with the authority of our government. Believe me, they are operating all by themselves, and the result is going to be to undermine our country. The only thing they are interested in is looking out for themselves, perhaps to make a little money, maybe to grab some power. This is a black-budget operation that's out of control, Josh. If anything is treasonous, it's this ranch operation."

The instructor pilots began to develop plans for teaching tactical flying. They told Vickers that it might take two more weeks to instruct the Descendants on the capabilities of flying nap-of-the-earth and low-level navigation. Among other things, they'd have to learn to make high-speed landings, Josh explained. As he did so, he looked knowingly at Kirk.

Vickers accepted Josh's explanations. He bragged about his own learning of the aerial navigation systems so that when it came time to draw a route for the Descendants to fly with their terrorists on board, he'd be able to do it.

"I won't have to trust you two bastards," he said, gloating.

A jab of alarm spiked inside Josh's chest. "You mean we're going to fly some practice exercises here with your Special Operations team of Descendants?"

"No. I'm not putting all those degenerates together in a helicopter until they're actually going to pull the mission."

Josh was relieved that Vickers wouldn't be around before a takeoff. Neither Josh nor Kirk could take a chance that the low-RPM audio switch would come on during flight, so one of the men had to pull the circuit breaker before takeoff and leave it out until the flight ended.

Every day, under the scrutiny of the men, the Descendants practiced the separate steps that would sabotage the aircraft.

Satisfied that they had planted fail-safe steps that would ruin the mission, Josh and Kirk continued to advance the training skills of the Descendants. Next on the schedule came night flying. The men flew up front during the first orientation. The two Descendants strapped themselves into jumpseats, chairs of fabric and tube. They sat behind and between the pilots so that they could observe night cockpit procedures. This was to be an orientation as much for the humans as for the Descendants. Neither of the pilots had done any night flying for weeks. In Kirk's case, for years.

The staleness showed in the flying of both men, but Josh decided he should practice the first landing in the inky blackness of the desert night. He dropped the collective and set up for a normal approach.

Kirk momentarily set up their intercom switches to speak on the private circuit so that the Descendants could not hear. "Better nose it over to a hundred knots so our boy Ace won't question why our initial approach speed is seventy and his has to be a hundred."

"Damn, I forgot about Ace. Bozo and I always fly a normal approach. Grayson, this is going to be a hot approach. You keep a lookout for the ground, will you?"

"You got it. Watch out for a wind change. We're supposed to have a frontal passage sometime within the hour. Expect some gusts."

The only lights in the desert blazed around the compound headquarters and at the entrance gate. Josh could see the dusty halos around the lights, indicating the breezes had kicked up. He set up so that the lights would be at his back, minimizing their blinding effect on his night-vision goggles. At altitude, he tried to pick out the general area of the helipad, but could not. But as they approached within a hundred feet of the ground, the night-vision goggles began picking up the ambient starlight and faint, reflected glow from the compound security lights. Josh saw the wind arrow first and slowed his approach speed rapidly, adjusting his flight path to the helipad.

He felt a great surge of relief when the helicopter bobbed twice and settled into a hover at six feet. Kirk had been right. The wind had shifted direction about ninety degrees, giving him a gusty crosswind to deal with. The helicopter bucked, fighting his control movements. He hoped they would not have to train in this kind of tricky wind with the Descendants at the controls.

"Want to try this once to get your nighttime control touch back?" he asked Kirk.

"Truth is, I'm nervous about it."

"Roger. Me, too. Tell you what, Grayson, I'm rough as a cob. I think we'd better leave Bozo and Ace at home for a couple nights until we get the hang of it. I . . ."

Josh thought his night-vision goggles had experienced a short circuit.

"Take the controls, Grayson. I can't see . . . malfunction." Suddenly the helicopter's tail slashed left, then right.

"Chrissakes, tail-rotor failure . . ."

Josh nearly cut the throttle to pull a blind hovering autorotation. But he held off as he realized his pedals worked. They still controlled the anti-torque rotor. So he pulled power, then released the collective for an instant and tore off his goggles, trying to glimpse the instrument panel. "Hit the instrument lights. . . . I'll try for an instrument takeoff." He struggled to keep the creeping panic from his voice.

"No, there's nothing wrong with the goggles. It's a

dust devil. Look out!" Kirk shouted, making no effort at all to keep his terror in check.

Josh felt the helicopter shuddering, rocking on all its axes, shaken by invisible hands and shoved backward. He resisted the movement by pushing forward on the cyclic, continuing to pull power.

"Are you sure it's a dust devil?"

Kirk didn't answer. He fumbled around and finally found the rheostats that controlled the instrument lights. He twirled them all.

The dust storm had locked them into the center of a cloud where he no longer knew whether they were up, down, or sideways. He couldn't see to navigate. He couldn't tell whether they were still, gliding backward, bumping downward, or lifting up. Their only hope lay in those instruments. He checked the artificial horizon on the instrument panel and saw that it was banking severely to the left, although he couldn't feel the helicopter drifting right. Against the instincts of his body, he leveled the wings on the instrument of the artificial horizon and felt as if he were in a turn in the opposite direction. He pushed the nose below the horizon and pulled all the power he could, watching the torque meter to ensure he didn't overstress the helicopter. All his body sensations told him nothing was happening. The helicopter felt as if it were twirling, flipping like a leaf. He realized that feeling came from the sand and gravel being blasted across the windshield inside the cloud of dirt.

It had been only a few seconds, but they should have broken free of the ground dust by now. Unconsciously, Josh braced for an impact.

"Holy shit, we're going to die," Josh hollered.

"God help us," Kirk added breathlessly. But Josh was not giving up. He pulled sharply on the power, keeping the wings level, watching for an indication of a climb. The instruments at this altitude and airspeed were completely unreliable, but if the gyro compass was not spinning and if he could keep that artificial horizon squared off, he might be able to take off. He barely remembered how it was supposed to be done. Something occurred to him as he was starting his climb-out. "Keep your night-vision goggles on so you can see when we're out of this shit."

Kirk responded, "I already have them on, buddy. I tell you it's worse when you can see outside. Keep climbing out. I'll let you know when I see something, then hand the controls over to me."

At about a hundred feet in altitude and forty awkward knots, Kirk said, "I've got the controls."

Josh felt the hands lightly touching the controls and released them. "The fence, make sure we're not headed toward the fence."

"I've got it under control. We're pushing it up to ninety knots, climbing out to five hundred feet, and leveling off. Then we'll go around and try it again. This time we use the white landing lights."

The wind blew as strongly on the next approach, but was not so laden with dust.

Finally they were down, congratulating each other and slapping each other on the back. The Descendants joined in the small talk, copying the jubilant cursing from the cockpit, Josh hadn't known Ace and Bozo were capable of such conversational patter. They smiled and joked as if capable of emotions, although he knew they were not. As human as they seemed to be, something inside him kept insisting that they were not human at all. They could *not* be. If he allowed himself to believe these two were human, how could he participate in their murders?

13

. . . .

In subsequent night-training sessions, they experienced no further emergencies, either with themselves or with the Descendants. When there was only a week left in the schedule of training, Kirk and Josh began to feel confident that the Descendants would be able to conduct night tactical flying. But now they faced a new problem.

"We're pretty damned smart, Grayson. We've figured out how to foul up the assassination in North Africa. Now all we need is a plan for taking out the entire organization. You have any ideas about how to get off this damned ranch?"

"Something will occur to us. You know what they say about necessity as the mother of guys like us."

"Right. I'll give you necessary. If we don't necessarily get out of here about the time that mission fails, we're necessarily going to be executed. They'd never let me go anyhow."

"Quit your bellyaching," Josh said.

"I don't want to be lunch for the Descendants back here. We've trashed this mission, and we've trashed ourselves. Unless we develop a plan, they're going to take me out, then you. Are you prepared to follow me—"

"*That's it!* We can go out tomorrow evening."

"How?"

"God, we're dumb. We've had the two helicopters all along. We could have been gone. We could have put Bozo and Ace on a low-level flight path at one of those transmitters outside the fence. When the Huey blows, it takes out the transmitter. We fly out . . . get some help. Easy as hell."

"Right. And if it doesn't take out the transmitter?"

Josh merely shrugged at the rhetorical question. "Yeah. You're right. But it's worth a try."

•   •

The next evening both men were edgy from excitement over their escape plan. But when they stopped outside the building to meet their ride to the helipad, there was nobody there to meet them.

Instead, Gates approached them on one of his unusual forays outside the building, a self-satisfied grin pasted onto his face.

Josh could see Gates gloating from a distance of fifty feet.

"Something's gone wrong," he murmured under his breath to Kirk, keeping a smile pasted on his face.

"I see that," said Kirk through his own uneasy smile.

"How in hell could they have found out? You've never told the Descendants we'd be flying a different mission, have you?"

"Hell, no. I'm certain those two are debriefed every night after flying. Only person I told was you. Did you go running off to tell Vickers?"

Kirk grimaced. "Not funny."

Gates began talking before he'd even closed the last dozen steps to them. "Vickers is gone. He's taken the crew and the aircraft away."

Josh and Kirk answered in unison. "How? . . ." They looked at each other and at Gates, each of them trying to prevent their astonishment from being broadcast as fear; fear that the sabotage would be discovered before the mission could be aborted.

"We're not ready," said Josh lamely. Meaning as much that they had not attempted their escape from the compound as much as anything.

"Vickers said it was close enough," said Gates. "Close enough for government work. Besides, our intelligence has learned that Saddiqi will be coming out of the desert to attend an OPEC conference. We can't afford to miss him this time, not during the holy month when he spends his time in the desert. We'd have to wait until next year and do this thing all over again. There isn't time."

"Why did he leave us in the dark?" asked Josh.

Gates shrugged. "Mind you, this is Vickers talking, not me. He said he didn't want any funny stuff out of you two. He didn't want you to do anything to ruin the mission. So he did this suddenly to throw you off your guard."

"But who is going to get the aircraft ready to fly? Those Descendants need somebody to help them with the run-up procedures, the pre-flight—"

"Don't worry," said Gates. "Well, naturally, you know we do have civilian maintenance technicians who must ready the helicopter for flight. And Colonel Vickers has been studying the technical manuals, as you know. He'll be as helpful in the start as anybody. So our . . . boys can get off the ground."

NORTH AFRICA

Vickers noticed almost immediately that the deserts of North Africa seemed almost exactly like the deserts of Nevada at night. They had moved by truck as close to the border as they could without causing an international incident. The jump-off spot was far enough away to remain undetected by Saddiqi's border patrols. It would be little more than an hour's flight. He had plotted it, calculating the existing winds. He knew perfectly well that he would have those Descendants set up for one takeoff and one landing. He hadn't plotted a return route. Instead he had drawn a line, using Josh's techniques for communicating with the Descendants. The line would direct the crew to fly the helicopter closer to the interior of the country. With a little bit of luck maybe the thing would run out of fuel and crash in one of the populated cities. It wouldn't matter whether it crashed or whether anybody was captured. This mission was never going to be traced anywhere. That was the beauty of the thing.

He was confident about his pilots as they began the run-up procedures in the helicopter. He watched them as they progressed and followed along with his own copy of the checklist. Now and then, as he leaned over the console to observe them, he looked back at his Special Operations team sitting huddled over their weapons in the cabin. He had trained one hell of a crack fighting team. They were much more intelligent than the earlier Descendants, just one generation removed. No telling what the possibilities a fighting outfit like this might exploit. Tonight would be a dress rehearsal of the first order. If this worked, they might try more daring operations. They might set a few of these Descendants up for a visit to Red Square.

He watched as they went through the procedure, dragging his finger down the checklist. His head jerked up when they skipped over the RPM audio. *Maybe they aren't as good as Avery bragged them up to be,* he thought.

He reached forward and turned on the low-RPM audio. Immediately the boinging alarm sounded in his headset. Next, one of the Descendants was to run up the engine RPM, using the governor increase-decrease button until the alarm went off in the normal operating range. Instead, the Descendant named Ace reached over and shut off the fuel.

Vickers was astonished. The two kept going through the remaining start-up procedures although the engine had shut down to a whistle, and the blades had begun coasting down.

Next thing you know they'll be pulling pitch for a powerless takeoff, he thought—and with the very idea, Bozo began to pull up on the collective.

Vickers cursed into the intercom, which had no effect on them. "No!" he shouted. "Stop pulling the collective. I want you two to go through the start-up procedures all over again."

The two Descendants did as they were told. Again they skipped turning on the switch. Vickers's face darkened, the veins bulging on his temples. His throat swelled against the collar of his jacket. Again he turned on the low-RPM audio. Ace shut off the fuel.

Vickers cursed under his breath. He knew what had happened now.

"Ace!"

"Yes, sir."

"Did Colonel Avery teach you to shut off the fuel when you hear the sound in the headset?"

"No, sir."

Vickers was stunned speechless for a second. He felt a moment's disappointment that he'd not caught Avery in a sabotage attempt. That could mean a more severe problem. What if the memories of these two Descendants had suddenly gone faulty like the earlier Ace?

"Then why did you shut it off?"

Ace stared at him a second. "I don't know, sir."

"You don't know why you shut it off, or you don't know why you were trained to shut it off?"

Ace said, "I don't understand, sir."

Vickers loosed a stream of invective, literally spitting his words and not a little saliva into the unperturbed Descendant's face.

Vickers bit his lip. This kind of fury only wasted time, he realized. He'd never have been able to summon the patience that Avery and Kirk . . . *Kirk!*

"Whoa, Ace. You said Colonel Avery didn't train you to turn off the fuel. Is that right?"

"Yes, sir."

"Well, did Mr. Kirk teach you to turn off the fuel when you hear that sound?" The Descendant didn't answer. "Did Grayson teach you to turn off that switch?"

The Descendant nodded. "Yes, sir."

So. They had been trained to sabotage the mission, after all. And if one pulled this kind of a trick, they both had to be involved. Those two guys back in Nevada would have a chance to explain. Then they'd be invited to dinner. *As* dinner, that is.

Vickers called over one of the maintenance specialists for the helicopter and explained the situation. "Obviously, these two are supposed to keep this mission from flying. Guess what's going to happen to the goddamned mission."

The technician shrugged. "No problem, Colonel. I know how to fix that."

"How long is it going to take?"

In answer the technician reached up to the circuit breaker panel on the console above the pilots' heads. He searched for a moment and then pinched one of the buttons hard between his thumb and forefinger and pulled until it popped out. "There. The low-RPM audio circuit breaker is off. You won't have to worry about that again."

"You mean that sound isn't going to come on at all?"

"Guaranteed, Colonel."

Vickers smiled viciously. He was half-pleased because he had sabotaged the saboteurs. Then again, he had the satisfaction of knowing when those two back in Nevada were removed from active duty, he would see to it that it would be done in the most violent, painful way imaginable. They would feel every excruciating tooth and nail mark as they served themselves up for a meal in one of his bovine demonstrations.

Vickers watched the helicopter take off, then went back to his control van to observe the night's proceedings on radar scopes.

• •

In the cockpit of the Huey, the Descendants navigated at an altitude of five hundred feet and an airspeed of ninety knots on a straight line.

In fifty minutes, exactly on time, the Descendants

neared their landing zone, about a quarter mile from Saddiqi's camp. Ace, at the controls, nosed the helicopter over to 105 knots and dropped the collective to begin his descent. The craft trembled as the airspeed climbed. Although it had been dark for hours, the air was still hot above the desert, owing to a cloud cover.

As the airspeed indicator pegged a hundred knots, Bozo performed his function exactly as he'd been taught. He thumbed back the governor RPM increase-decrease switch, holding the button down continually until the RPM reached 6000.

Because of the pulled circuit breaker, no audio warning sounded in their headsets, and Ace missed his opportunity to shut off the fuel and end the mission. However, the drop in RPM combined with the full load of troops and a high-density altitude caused the helicopter to sink rapidly. Ace, using the techniques taught him, began pulling up on the collective to restore the rate of descent from fifteen hundred feet a minute back to five hundred feet a minute. But the power wasn't there at six thousand RPM. The loss of ten percent of engine power proved too much. The more Ace pulled, the slower the main rotor blades turned, dragging the lift capability below three hundred RPM, lowering the engine RPM to five thousand.

The helicopter sank faster. Ace continued to try to compensate in the only way he knew how. Instead of regaining airspeed and flying out on recovery or thumbing the RPM back to normal as a human pilot would, he continued to pull on the collective.

Before the helicopter hit the ground, the vertical speed indicator had been pegged out—six thousand feet a minute. The rotor blades had come almost to a stop even as the collective pitch met its stops.

Back in the control van, the operator could read the excessive rate of descent on his scopes. "He's going to crash. Goddammit, he's crashing . . . he's . . ."

"Goddammit," Vickers whispered.

The green light disappeared from the screen, and Vickers realized the mission was over. Unless those two had crashed right on Saddiqi's bed, he would survive the assassination attempt. Vickers cursed and banged his hand on the table. He dashed out of the control van and headed for his own helicopter. The sooner he got back to the States, the sooner he could get his vengeance on those two.

• •

Inside the helicopter at the instant of impact, both serenity and terror had reigned. In the back the Special Operations team, whose weight had caused the helicopter to fall so fast the pilots could not recover, were perfectly calm, unaware of what was going on.

But in the cockpit, Bozo had shouted, "Holy shit, we're going to crash."

And Ace, hearing and seeing the panic yelled, "God help us."

After that the only sounds were of the impact, followed by the crackling of a blossoming fire. Descendants began frying and screaming in the wreckage. A few turned on each other and died attacking one another.

14

. . . .

THE RANCH

It had been two days since Vickers had vanished unexpectedly. Josh and Grayson had persuaded Gates to let them prepare another helicopter for the next pair of Descendants to be trained. They crawled all over the Huey, opening panels everywhere, engaging in the furious, thorough pretense of a pre-flight inspection. Josh read the checklist as Kirk performed the activities. Both of them tried to see into every cranny of the helicopter's fuselage.

Josh stuck first his flashlight, then his head and one shoulder into the rear battery compartment to look deep down the hollow tail boom, its oval ribs ever decreasing in size, giving him an exaggerated perception of perspective. He pulled his head out. "Nothing. There'd be no way to search any further unless we could actually pull some more panels and look behind some of those interior ribs. Gates isn't going to let us stay out here much longer. We've got no reason, nobody to train."

"I'm not going to let myself be locked up again.

Next time they turn the key on us might be the last. They're going to hear from Africa any time."

"You're awfully optimistic today, aren't you?"

"We're still not sure they're going to be able to pin that crash in North Africa on us. How are they going to know it just wasn't an engine failure or some kind of flub by one of those Descendant pilots?"

Josh lifted his cap with one hand and dried his forehead on his sleeve. He replaced the cap and said, "Look, Kirk, if you want to, you can go back up to your room and wait to see whether the North Africa flight ever came off, if it was ever sabotaged, if we're going to get the blame for it. Meanwhile, I'm going to steal a truck and a helicopter—the bigger the better. We'll drive the truck into one of those guard towers. Then we'll disable those transmitters and . . . what are you gawking at?"

Kirk stared over Josh's shoulder into the hangar, where three or four other helicopters had been parked. His face went pale. Josh looked back over his shoulder.

Kirk found his voice. "Looks like we're not going to have to worry about finding out how the assassination mission went. I think it would be a safe bet to say it was a flop."

As they watched, a squad of soldiers stepped out of the hangar, their rifles half-raised, muzzles pointed at the two pilots. "I think they suspect us of something, wouldn't you say?" The sarcasm in Josh's words was tinged with a note of bitter despair.

Kirk stepped up close to Josh's shoulder. "I meant it, old buddy. I refuse to land my ass back in another cell, Josh. Let's fight our way out. Are you game? I'll take the three on the left, you take—"

Josh stiffened. "Don't be stupid. We'll have to find a better occasion than this. These idiots aren't going to hold their fire for us." He felt Kirk release an exasperated hiss of breath against the back of his neck and relaxed a little, knowing he would not be forced into a suicidal fight against superior odds, at least for the moment.

The guards surrounded them and herded the pair toward the main building.

Inside the compound headquarters, they were ushered brusquely down a wing of the building they had never been allowed to see from the interior. A set of double doors opened up. Somebody behind shoved Josh, then Kirk into a room. Josh looked down into the cavernous room. He realized they stood on the landing at the top of an amphitheater. *The* amphitheater. He recognized it from the Gregor Munn video. Another shove in their backs propelled him reluctantly down the steep steps toward the cage.

Under his breath, Kirk said, "So, fearless leader . . . is *now* the time to put up a fight?"

Biting his lip, Josh looked around. Three security men had joined the outside guards, who had remained at the top landing. Josh knew each of them carried a pistol in his coat pocket. The odds were worse than before. Even so, when they were told to halt at the bottom of the stairs just at the padlocked gate of the cage, he braced himself to fight back. Getting shot down suddenly seemed a choice preferable to being chewed alive in hand-to-mouth combat with one or more of those dogs. As he began summoning his strength and courage, he heard the familiar voice of Gates.

"Well, gentlemen, suppose you tell us how it is that

our mission into North Africa had such a disastrous end." Josh and Kirk turned around to stare upward at the figure of The Ranch's director standing at the top of the stairs near the entrance to the amphitheater. Kirk groaned in exasperation under his breath, and Josh wished now that he hadn't been so cautious outside next to the Huey, their only possibility for freedom. If he had been thinking, he thought to himself in bitter recrimination, they might have flown the Huey out to the far reaches of the Ranch. No telling how long they might have just flown around the Ranch from place to place staying out of sight until something concrete in the way of an escape plan had occurred to them. Not that it made any difference now.

He shrugged, raising his palms. "Disastrous end?" he asked, feigning helplessness, knowing that such an act had been nullified by his hesitation in answering. But Gates's next words told him he needn't have bothered trying to evade the truth.

"I have been in touch with Colonel Vickers. From what he tells me about the manipulation of some switches inside the cockpit, there is no question that the mission was sabotaged. I don't suppose you two are prepared to tell me precisely how it was done."

Before either of the men had an opportunity to respond, Gates instructed one of the security people to open the padlock on the cage. Using a small key from a fat keyring of his own, Gates unlocked a metal door embedded in the wall at the top of the amphitheater. He flicked a couple of switches. The video screen above the cage fluttered in bright gray light. The men could hear the sounds of clanking. The screen flickered again and showed the same hallway as in the Gregor Munn video. As in the video, a pit bull, this one blacker and larger than the one they had seen on the television, burst out of the black hole at the end of the hallway and charged the camera. Inside the amphitheater they heard the clank of a body against the metal door, then the scratching as the dog tried to paw its way into the cage.

The security man unpadlocked the door. He pulled it open so that he could stand behind it, out of reach of the two pilots.

They stood welded to the floor.

He waved at them impatiently to no effect. Then he waved at the pair of security men.

Josh felt a shove in the back. He and Kirk exploded simultaneously. They each threw a shoulder into the ponderous iron door, pinching the security man violently against the bars of the cage. His breath blew like a sounding whale's, fogging Josh's sense of smell with the stench of fermenting onions. Josh felt something snap even as he heard it, and realized a bone must have shattered. The horrified, red-skinned, black-veined, breathless expression of pain on the man's face confirmed that something in the arm had given. The steamy dregs of breath bubbled from the bottom of the barrel chest, wrenching Josh's guts and gagging him.

Behind them, Gates shrieked a command at the other two security men.

For Josh, time suddenly came to a standstill. Every action stood out in cold, slow-motion relief. He heard Gates shrieking orders. He heard the clicking of switches on the control panel. He could even hear the other two security men pawing at their jacket pockets for their pistols. This man in front of them puffed up as if to burst, moaning as he gasped for a breath. Kirk grabbed hold of the cage wall through the bars and

pulled even harder to disable the man, to keep him
from reaching into his pocket for his pistol.

"Get his damned gun," Kirk wheezed.

Josh fumbled for the pistol. "Get the other two," he
yelled back. He felt a chill on the back of his neck, a
tingling spot that seemed to pucker up, telling him
that was where the first bullet would enter his body.
Then came the sound of that metal door at the back of
the amphitheater. He did not look. He did not need to.
He knew that the black pit bull would be bursting into
the cage any second.

"The dog!" Kirk yelled.

"Forget the dog! Get the other two . . ."

The amphitheater had erupted in chaos as everyone
heard the low, whining growl of excitement escaping
the throat of the charging pit bull.

Kirk shoved away from the bars, releasing the
guard, who pushed the bars back against Josh and
threw himself at the pair of security men, now pulling
pistols from their coats. The dog had captured the
men's attention, giving Kirk the second of time he
needed.

The security guard between the bars and the cage
lost consciousness. His dead weight pushed against the
doors as he slumped to the floor.

Josh saw the black blur streaking across the floor of
the cage. He practically screamed in his desperation to
get to that pistol.

The dog covered the distance across the floor of the
cage in four bounds.

Josh bellowed a curse and hauled on the cage door,
trying desperately to slam it before the dog could get
free. As he pulled, he knew he'd never make it. He saw

the sprawled, scrambling bodies of Kirk and the two security guards. The dog would be on that trio first.

The iron door hit the terrier in the snout, bringing a yelp and deflecting the animal's hurtling trajectory. The animal ricocheted into the steel doorjamb. Josh pushed again on the door, hoping to shut the beast inside the cage.

He failed. The dog lunged, squirming into the open space between the door and the jamb as the metal hit him in the shoulder. Josh tried to hold it, sprawled as he was across the floor, unable to get leverage. He pushed with his foot and dug at the security guard's pocket. He felt the gun. The weight of the foul-breathed slob lay on the pocket. Josh yanked in panic. His own whine mingled with the angry growl of the dog.

He heard Kirk and the security men cursing. At a higher pitch, Gates shouted orders from his relatively safe station atop the landing.

Josh felt he was losing every battle. He couldn't get the pistol. And he couldn't hold the dog any longer.

Finally, unable to do both, hearing the footsteps of men running, he threw a shoulder into the unconscious security guard and tore at the pocket that held the pistol.

The pocket ripped away. In a second, Josh had the gun in his hands.

It was a 9-millimeter automatic. He could tell by the size of the bore and the heft of it, although he did not spend any time examining it. In two quick movements he flipped off the safety and started firing: anything to get the security men to duck, any action that might freeze that savage dog. As he did so he was already throwing himself across the floor of the amphitheater to seek cover behind the seats. Through all of this Gates was screaming orders at his security guards to open fire. Finally, they responded to the first three rounds from Josh's pistol. The room, large as it was, contained the concussion of the pistols' explosions enough to hurt Josh's eardrums.

Josh hit the floor hard, banging knees and elbows on the tile, rolled once, and came up kneeling and ready to fire again. When he arose, looking over the pistol, he half expected to be greeted with a faceful of bullets. But the security guards above were firing down the stairway. Out of the corner of his eye, Josh saw why. The black pit bull had lunged out the cage door and ignored the men seeking cover among the seats. Instead, it had charged up the steps directly at the men at the top.

Gates was barely more than a dark-colored shadow flitting out the doors of the amphitheater. Josh drew down on two guards above and immediately fired five times. One of the security men spun away and smashed into the wall face first, pinned there by two more of Josh's rounds. The second guard crumbled, holding his abdomen. Falling forward even as he lost his balance and toppled toward the dog, he realized it and screamed, trying to get his pistol aimed at the dog. The guard hit the stairway at the same instant the dog hit him, catching him high on the shoulder and immediately yanking backward. The man whose balance was already gone was launched like a projectile over the top of the dog, bouncing and rolling like a downhill skier.

Josh immediately turned to fire at the other pair of security men, singing a volley of bullets along the tops of seats halfway up the amphitheater at the men's backsides, bobbing up and down as they tried to escape.

He then turned to see how Kirk was faring and was relieved to see that his companion had climbed halfway up the cage, avoiding the pit bull. He opened his mouth to express his relief, but Kirk held a finger to his mouth as he climbed down and pointed at the dog, who was still worrying the dead or dying body of the security guard. Josh nodded and the two of them slipped along the edge of the cage until they came to another set of stairs up the side of the amphitheater.

It was too much to hope that they could climb to the top of the amphitheater and get to the doors in the center of the landing before the dog noticed them, or before the other guards opened fire.

But they crawled along anyhow until the security men finally gathered their wits and rose up firing. Josh and Kirk flattened on the stairs and looked helplessly into each other's faces. Kirk smiled first and raised a finger at the sound he heard.

Then Josh heard it, too: the sound of the dog in the attack.

Then came cursing and panicked outbursts from the remaining guards. "Help me!" screamed one. "It's got me!"

"I can't . . ."

Josh sprang to his knees and fired twice at one man and brought him down screaming. He aimed at the other, but saw the dog burrowing into the juncture of the neck and shoulder of the man on his knees.

He froze at the horrid scene, mesmerized by the sound of throaty growls and the splashing of fluids on the amphitheater floor. Then he felt a jab in his kidney and turned reluctantly, following Kirk up the stairs,

padding as silently as he could to avoid diverting the
dog from its current preoccupation.

Kirk went into the hallway first, although he didn't
have a weapon. Josh shook his head, marveling at the
man's courage. He wished he had as much.

He stepped through the doorway and turned, ready
to slam the door. But Kirk held the door back. "It's
all clear in the hall," he whispered, and then ducked
back inside. He worked over the body of the nearest
security man slumped against the wall. He found his
pistol, but that was not enough for him. He continued
to work away at the man's shirt front.

"Come on!" Josh said, straining the words between
clenched teeth.

Kirk waved a hand at him to keep him silent, but it
was a wasted effort. The pit bull stopped chewing on
the security guard below and turned his attention to
Kirk. The dog charged upward without hesitation.
Josh leaned forward, pointing his pistol over the edge
of the landing down the stairs at the hulk of the attacking dog. As large as it seemed to be in real life,
this head-on vision looked to be too small a target. As
he was squeezing the trigger, Kirk jostled his arm,
sending the shot wild. He felt himself being dragged
backward out of the room and stumbled into the hallway just as Kirk threw his weight against the two
doors, shutting them. Instantly a crash on the other
side of the wall told them how narrowly they had
again missed being victims of the enormous dog.

Josh hollered, "Grayson, what in the hell were you
up to? Wasn't it enough to get the pistol? What were
you searching around for? Ammunition?"

"Not ammunition, my friend." He held up his prize.

"A necktie? You risked your ass being torn up by

that . . . that Tyrannosaurus rex for a goddamned necktie?" Josh screeched.

"It's a Gucci." Kirk jammed the pistol down beneath his belt and tied the necktie loosely around the two door handles to the amphitheater. He stood up and looked both ways.

"Which way to Gates, eh?"

"Forget Gates. Let's get to the helicopter and—"

"Josh, Gates has that ring of keys. . . . No telling what kinds of secrets those keys might unlock. And Gates himself might be suitable for a hostage. In fact, he's probably the only hostage that anybody around this hellhole would value."

It made sense to Josh. He remembered seeing the blur leave the amphitheater and turn. He pointed. "Come on, Grayson. This way," he shouted, and started running down the hall. He glanced back over his shoulder and saw that Kirk was finishing his knot. Then he came to a startled halt as he saw Kirk pull on the door handles, opening the amphitheater. Immediately the door thumped with the impact of the dog launching itself outward. The necktie held the doors together with only a gap of two or three inches, enough to let the dog's muzzle press through but no more.

Kirk flashed a sadistic smile at the stunned Josh and began running down the hall.

"Let's find Gates. Hurry. We've got to get the keys and get PJ out of here before that monster figures out how to gnaw through that necktie and get out."

"Are you crazy?"

"Move it, Josh. Once that dog chews through that necktie he'll be roaming the halls." Kirk half snarled, half laughed, "Imagine the pandemonium a dog like that can set loose on the reinforcements they send after us."

As he ran by, Kirk punched Josh's shoulder and whirled him around. "C'mon, let's find Gates before he calls in the calvary."

They began running down the hall, neither with a clear idea of where to look for Gates.

Josh admired Kirk for his boldness. He began to feel a sense of guilt for not having taken control of this situation at all in the weeks that he had been locked in this compound. He had been letting events drag him along. Even now . . .

"Think, Josh. Where would a corner be on the outside of this building from here? Gates would have a corner office . . . lots of windows. Where would that be?"

Josh automatically pointed. His instinctive sense of direction told him where to find such an office, matching the exterior aerial views with what he'd seen from inside so far. "To the left here."

They rounded another corner and saw a carpet runner at the end of the hallway. Josh knew they had found Gates's office suite. He was glad that his footsteps stopped clomping on the tiles when they hit the carpet. It would make their approach to the office a little more surreptitious. Not that it mattered. Not that Gates wouldn't already be on the alert for trouble.

Josh arrived at the door first and stopped. He reached slowly for the handle. But Kirk beat him to it. He yanked the handle and threw his shoulder into the door in one motion. He slid into the room on his knees, waving his pistol from side to side. There was nothing to shoot at because the door opened into an empty reception area. Kirk regained his feet and dashed for the doors to the inner office. Josh followed quickly, surprised at Kirk's boldness and decisiveness. He envied him again.

Kirk went through the inner doors as he had the outer ones. This time there was a target for his pistol to lock on to.

"Put the phone down!" Kirk shouted.

Gates stood behind the desk, a telephone to his mouth. He looked blank, not in the least concerned at the sight of the pistols aiming at him. "Send security to my office," he said. "Yes, this is Gates. . . . Yes, to my office . . . The two men have—"

A pained look splashed across Gates's face even as his blood splashed across the far wall behind his head. One shot. Two shots. Three. Gates toppled into his chair and then slid out of it, sending it rolling back against the far wall. His broken head smashed wetly against the carpet.

Josh had seen Kirk's pistol hand jump three times. "Christ!"

"Josh, you're going to have to develop a little ruthlessness if you want to get out of here."

The words that rose to Josh's mouth were *cold-blooded murder,* but he did not have time to speak them.

"Josh, get your butt out there and fire up one of those helicopters."

Josh raised his hands in question.

"I'm going to go look for PJ. You're going to start that helicopter. We're going to fly it out to some remote part of this desert and see if we can't find those explosives. If we can dismantle them we can fly right over the fence and put an end to this operation. Maybe we'll mount an air assault on one of those towers or something. I'm not going back into one of those cells, buddy."

Josh hesitated. Shouldn't there be some way to negotiate? He glanced at the bleeding body of Gates. Somehow everything had gotten out of control.

"Goddammit, Colonel Avery. Get your butt in gear."

Josh ran from the office, remembering the route, retracing his steps. As he ran, he grasped his pistol, remembering the pit bull restrained only by a necktie.

He made it by the amphitheater safely. He saw the dog had discovered the necktie and begun chewing on it. Before he walked out of the compound headquarters building, Josh unbuttoned his shirt front and jammed the pistol down next to his belly into his belt. As he walked down the front walk, he could see a dozen men scurrying at different parts of the outside area. At the three guard towers in sight, he could see men climbing up the stairwells. Reinforcements, he reasoned.

At the hangar, another group of men were pulling shut the giant hangar doors. Soldiers in formation were being marched toward their barracks. Apparently some kind of shutdown was in effect. He guessed that all the Descendants would be put under lock and key in their separate enclosures. And the human security forces would be sent out to look for him and Kirk —and PJ—if Kirk was able to set her free.

At first he walked casually in order to avoid drawing attention to himself. But then he realized that he was the only one not in a hurry to get someplace, so he broke into an urgent jog toward the flight line. He selected a Huey farthest from that hangar, farthest from any guard post he could see.

His pre-flight consisted of making sure that the battery had been connected and that all tie-downs and covers were removed. For lack of a better plan, Josh decided he would start the helicopter and move it closer to the building so that when Kirk and PJ appeared he could pick them up and head out.

By the time he pulled the start trigger, he hadn't been discovered. He nervously divided his attention between the gauges and the approaches to the helicopter.

The blades had finally whipped up to half operating speed when, from two different directions, he saw three men running toward the helicopter. He knew there wasn't much he could do to rush the start. It would take 6,600 RPM, and that wouldn't come until he could wrap the throttle to full.

At last, he felt the engine shrug off its sluggishness and respond to his twisting of the throttle. He hit full idle stop even as he was pulling up on the collective. He realized that the helicopter wasn't getting as light as it should have been for the amount of pull. Could it be that the skids were secured to the ground?

No!

The RPM increase-decrease switch! "Damn!" Even with the alarm boinging in his ears, he had neglected to beep up the switch. He'd practically sabotaged his own takeoff as he had sabotaged the flight that carried Saddiqi's would-be assassins.

He shoved forward hard on the button and glanced out of the cockpit. The three men had converged about three hundred yards away and had stopped to point in his direction. Now they started running again down each side of the line of helicopters ahead of him, two on one side, one on the other.

Their hesitation gave him a few more seconds to get to operating RPM.

He kept shoving the button forward even after the low-RPM audio went off and began pulling the collective-pitch lever up again until the helicopter jumped four feet straight into the air. Only a hundred yards away now, the two men stopped to point their arms at him. But this time Josh recognized pistols at the end of those arms. Instead of trying to fly broadside to escape, offering the best target, he jerked the cyclic to the right, then back to the left, and aimed at them. He kept pulling pitch as he lowered the nose, and the helicopter accelerated quickly, the nose dipping downward as he continued to press the cyclic forward and pull on the collective pitch. Josh saw one of the arms recoil sharply with the firing of a gun. He heard nothing. But he did feel a distant rap on metal—a strike in the blades, perhaps, but no hit in the fuselage as far as he knew.

Perhaps their aims were disturbed by what they saw coming toward them. Josh knew it would unnerve the coolest hand.

The Huey nosed forward excessively and presented the rotor disk the tips barely clearing four feet off the ground as they screwed forward into the air. One of the two men dived to his right, between the parked helicopters, sprawling full length. The second man tried to run in the opposite direction toward the opening. After four steps he realized it must be a mistake and tried to plant his heels. The loose sand everywhere on the parking ramp robbed him of his footing. His heels went flying out horizontally, and the man landed in a spine-jolting, spread-eagle heap on the tarmac. The fall probably saved his life, because seconds later the Huey swooped over him, its skids barely clearing three feet over his body.

In the wake of the rotor wash, all three men were pelted with sand and pebbles and were unable to get a shot at the rear of the Huey. Josh kept the helicopter low, not wanting to rise above the profile of other helicopters, minimizing his craft as target. All he could hope for was that Kirk had found PJ—or had given up on finding her—and had now left the compound headquarters. There wouldn't be a lot of time for waiting around here for him. As the Huey cleared the end of the flight parking and before flying past the hangar, Josh hauled left, hard on the cyclic, allowing the Huey to gain a little altitude so that the blades wouldn't strike the ground in the severe bank. Then he straightened out on a line toward the headquarters building.

And there he was! Kirk was running out one of the side doors, dragging a slight woman. *PJ!* He had found PJ Payne. *Christ, what were the odds?*

Immediately Josh lowered the collective and hauled back on the cyclic to rob himself of the forward airspeed. He let the helicopter fly up into the air again so as to avoid hitting the tail stinger on the ground. He glanced at the interior and saw that his airspeed was just passing downward through ninety knots.

As the helicopter began falling through, drifting downward in its own rotor wash, he added power and leveled the helicopter while there were still about ten knots of forward airspeed. His running landing dragged the heels of the skids ten feet, and the Huey was still sliding when he lowered the collective all the way so that the skids bit into the earth and stopped, the fuselage bobbing backward and forward.

For a second PJ and Kirk were lost in a cloud of driving sand. Then they began slapping the side of the helicopter, blindly feeling for a door. Only then did Josh realize that he had not opened the sliding cargo doors. He might have saved them a few seconds had he done so.

For some reason, the general alarm must not have gone out about the theft of the helicopter. No one ran out from the hangar, and the squads of security men he expected to stream from the building did not materialize. Josh could see that Kirk had draped one of PJ's arms around his shoulders and held her beneath the ribs with his other hand as he pulled her along, half stumbling, half running. He let go of her by the cargo doors and opened up the cockpit copilot door. Kirk started to climb in, yelling something at PJ.

Josh knew he must be shouting at her to open up the cargo door and jump in, but she did not.

Josh squirmed in his seat and shouted himself, although he knew it was impossible for her to hear him.

PJ just stood looking at the door. Kirk jumped back out and opened the door for her. Clumsily, she put her hands on the cabin floor and began raising a knee. She had difficulty getting her balance, as though she had been drugged. Kirk was none too gentle about helping her in. He caught her up, one arm behind her shoulder blades, the other under her buttocks, and put a knee into her back, throwing her forward and at the same time rolling her over into the cabin. She lay there, her face on the floor, drool spreading from her mouth. Kirk grabbed the cabin door and slid it forward hard until the latch caught. Then he appeared in the copilot's door again, one foot on the skid, the other inside the cockpit, a sick look on his face.

"Get in, Kirk. What are you waiting for?" Josh shouted.

Kirk stood rooted to his spot, as though he had been shot. A second later, he shook his head and stepped down from the cockpit. He shut the copilot's door and walked around the front of the helicopter.

Josh was furious. He began cursing and swerving in the seat, getting the helicopter light on its skids, ready to take off without Kirk if he had to.

Kirk walked completely around the nose of the helicopter and opened up the pilot's door. He stepped up on the skids, reached into the cockpit, and keyed the intercom button on Josh's cyclic control. He grabbed hold of the boom mike on Josh's headset and pulled it to his lips.

"Get out of the helicopter, Josh. I want to fly it."

Josh yelled in a rage that hurt his throat. *"What!* You can fly later, or you can fly in the left seat. Just get your ass in here, Grayson. We don't have time for any bullshit!" Josh caught his breath as he looked into the cyclops eye of a 9-millimeter pistol. Kirk spoke into Josh's intercom again.

"I'm flying this helicopter, Josh. You're going to have to start a second one. I'll fly by the compound and draw some fire until you have a chance to get it started. You follow me. We're getting out of this place."

Josh opened his mouth to argue, to curse, to accuse Grayson Kirk of having gone insane. Then it occurred to him that maybe Kirk wasn't insane, after all. Maybe he was one of them.

In any case, Grayson Kirk, a determined, angry,

even half-crazed look on his face, reached for Josh's belly and yanked open the lap belt. He patted Josh's belly and pulled the shirt out of his pants first, then the pistol. Kirk grabbed him by the collar and dragged on him. Josh stumbled out of the cockpit, barely able to keep from falling on his face. He gathered himself and braced for a roundhouse left hook that would catch Kirk behind the ear. He'd throw him into the cargo compartment beside the doped-up PJ. Maybe they had been gassed when they were inside. But his left hook never landed. Instead he was stunned by the butt of a pistol rapped across the center of his forehead, next to the scalp line. Josh crumbled, dropping to his knees. His hands went spread-eagle as he tried to keep from burying his face in the dirt. He shook his head to keep away the edges of unconsciousness that threatened to wipe his vision out entirely.

As he began to regain his senses, a heavy gust of wind blew him over, and he realized that the Huey had taken off without him, Kirk at the controls.

True to his word, Kirk circled the flight line firing his pistol, perhaps to draw the fire of the security people. Maybe by firing aimlessly into people and buildings, he was trying to vent his consuming anger at anything and anybody connected to The Ranch.

Stunned, Josh scrambled to his feet and staggered off on a diagonal. When he bent over to pick up the pistol Kirk had left behind, he almost continued downward to kiss the ground. He stumbled to the nearest Huey and began untying it. He climbed to the top to pull off the air-intake covers and untied the exhaust cover, feeling as if he'd been drinking too many tequilas back at Fort Hood.

It seemed like an eternity getting through the start,

but finally he discovered he was twisting the throttle to the stop. So far no one had seemed to notice the second helicopter start.

Kirk had continued to fly around the compound although Josh could no longer hear the firing of his pistol. Finally Josh mustered the remnants of his senses and began pulling the collective-pitch lever. As he lifted off, the shadow of the first Huey passed in front of him. Then he saw it heading directly toward the entrance of the compound.

By the time he was airborne, Kirk had a half mile head start. He was nearing the gate. Any second now he would put the Huey into a banking turn and fly northward toward the barren reaches inside the fenced area of The Ranch.

Josh watched in horror as Kirk failed to change his course. He was not attempting at all to steer clear of the fence. And he dropped in altitude as well.

Through the wire Josh saw one of those cones. Kirk was flying straight toward it. He'd adjusted his altitude to fly over it. It was a plan for which they'd considered training a Descendant.

Kirk had flown over the wire. For a second, Josh thought that maybe Kirk had been right about Vickers's bluffing. Maybe there had not been explosives in the helicopter all along. But that hope was shattered— literally—as an explosion scattered the Huey. At first it seemed to be no more than a puff of black smoke, not much heavier than that which sometimes appeared with a drastic power change. But then parts of the top of the fuselage separated, flying in all directions. Then the blades tore away, whirling off together with the hub in between like a baseball bat flung across the infield. Then the unbalanced blades began wrenching themselves to pieces. By then the fuselage had hit the ground outside the compound. It skidded and rolled like the ducks Josh had shot from the sky during hunting season. But this dead duck started burning. The flames were slow and orange, growing more angry by the second before the fuselage had even stopped rolling, tearing itself apart against the earth on the spot where one of the conical transmitters had been.

Josh yanked the cyclic to the right to avoid the crash site. But then he came back to the left, even as the words of Kirk came to him.

"Follow me." That's what Kirk had said.

He had flown toward that fence intentionally. He had taken out the transmitter so that Josh could escape.

Crazy. It was the only word that occurred to Josh. Kirk had taken out himself and the woman he loved— Josh knew from the way he talked about her that it could be nothing less than love—to save him. But why? Why would he sacrifice his woman and himself for that? Even before he could think of an answer, he was free of The Ranch. The Huey cleared the top of the fence with two feet to spare. Josh zigged and zagged to avoid overflying the flames of the Huey where his friend and PJ, the woman he had never met, had died. He gritted his teeth, waiting for the explosives aboard his own craft to be ignited by the random signal of a second transmitter. It did not come.

Now he was free. He was free to go tell this incredible story. He was free to bring down The Ranch. He sucked in the power with the collective-pitch lever and lowered the nose some more, pressing 120 knots, putting as much distance as quickly as possible between himself and The Ranch.

Book Three

"Woe to the inhabiters of the earth and of the sea! For the devil is coming down unto you. . . ."
—REVELATION, Chapter 12

15

. . . .

Killers of Men

Only seconds outside the visible and invisible walls of his prison, Josh was already grappling with his freedom. The Ranch behind him could not even be out of sight, he reasoned. He had not crossed any high ground or put enough distance behind him to have lost the compound on the horizon.

Suddenly he felt a chill and did a sharp 180-degree turn, banking the helicopter steeper than 45 degrees simply to look back and see if perhaps he was being followed by some fast mover or perhaps more helicopters. But no, he was alone, free to go his own way. He continued on the course that would take him to the west. He checked the fuel for the first time and realized that he probably had enough to end up somewhere in California. He could probably get to Barstow or Fort Irwin. Maybe it would be safer to fly further west, maybe to Victorville. He tried to remember what the map of California and Nevada looked like. Nothing concrete seemed to occur to him. The only thing that he remembered was the vision of that helicopter with Kirk and PJ rolling across the ground, the craft covered up by a sea of orange flames topped off with billowing black smoke.

An instant of grisly satisfaction occurred to him that Kirk had had his revenge. He had personally killed Gates—had even overkilled Gates. Josh remembered blood and bits of flesh splattered on the wall of Gates's office, the body lying there, its head seeping, staining the carpet. . . .

"Avery. Lieutenant Colonel Josh Avery. You can answer me. Go ahead."

The voice over the radio came across cruelly. It was mocking, bitter, threatening. And it was distorted by the electronic transmission. But he recognized it. It was the voice of Edward Gates. The man whose blood and smashed head he had just been thinking about.

But it couldn't be, Josh reasoned. As if to contradict him, the voice repeated itself even more loudly, more cruelly, more insistently.

Josh peeled off the headset and stared at it. No, it just couldn't be. The sounds had to be coming from a voice inside his head. But with the headset removed he could hear nothing but the sounds of the helicopter, the noises of the air, the roar of the engine, the rattles, the shakes. They were deafening. He looked down at his hands and his legs. They were vibrating. No, they were shaking. *Of course,* he told himself as if in reassurance, *you always shake when you fly.* But he could feel it, too. He was trembling. He jogged the cyclic and adjusted his flight path, flying toward a group of low dunes of gravel. He landed on the north side, setting the helicopter down, twisting the throttle back. At an idle, the Huey set up a sympathetic resonation between its vibrating parts and the firm ground. Although he was shaking even more than before, he was even more certain that his trembling was worse.

He put the headset back on.

The voice was still there. It was still Gates. "Come back here, Avery. Don't be a fool. If we don't see that helicopter coming back over the horizon in a few minutes, some people are going to die. I don't have to tell you who, now do I? There will be Marilyn. Imagine. Imagine what it would be like if I were to have Vickers —the furious Vickers—bring her and her children to this place. Imagine what it would be like to make her the mother of a whole new species of our Descendant people."

Josh shuddered again, uncertain that what he was hearing was real. *It must have been a recording—but how? How would they know in advance about flying a helicopter off The Ranch so that a recording could tell me to come back? Maybe it was the voice of a mimic, a Rich Little bureaucrat of something.*

The voice kept talking, but Josh's mind was swept up in a cyclone of feelings and memories. Was he going crazy? Had they given him something in the water? Why had Kirk gone berserk and deliberately flown over the fence—with PJ? Had he really been so sure there were no explosives on the helicopter that he would have risked her life, too? Was this all a dream? Maybe he had been given drugs all along. Maybe that night after his first contact with the Descendants, that night of combat out in the eerie darkness of The Ranch's landing zone, after he'd passed out . . . maybe he was still asleep. Maybe he'd been dreaming all this like some television melodrama. Maybe he'd wake up in the arms of . . . Marilyn.

"Surely you don't want any harm to come to Marilyn." Gates was still talking, still mocking. Yes, and it was Gates's own voice.

Josh remembered Gates lying there on the floor. He remembered handling the body, searching for the pistol and keys. But there had been no keys, they had been left on the desk. And there had been no pistol. Minutes later, Kirk had gone berserk. What had happened to Grayson Kirk? He'd been perfectly all right as he had half dragged PJ out to the helicopter. He'd nearly climbed into the cockpit and they had nearly flown away. But what happened to make Kirk freeze in the door of the cockpit? He remembered thinking that Kirk must have been shot. But no, he'd gone nuts right there in that instant. The next thing he knew, he had been thrown out of the cockpit and Kirk had taken off on his suicide flight. There was no other word for it. And what about PJ? Had she had anything to say about Kirk blowing them to bits? Did she agree? Had Kirk given her a vote?

"Josh Avery, answer me, please."

Josh was stunned even more by the woman's voice. She had identified herself, called herself PJ Payne. This PJ Payne's voice sounded weak and tired. She did not sound frightened, merely weary. Josh would not believe that it was PJ until she said what she did.

"Colonel Avery, don't come back. Keep on—" Her voice was cut off.

Gates came back on, cajoling, threatening.

Josh took off the headset before Gates could make any threats. He picked up the helicopter to a hover and moved it about five miles north, well off his original flight path. In ten minutes he found what he was looking for, a narrow ravine. He flew above it until he found a space where a flash flood had cleared a flat space. Watching the tips of both blades so that they would not strike the walls of the ravine, he set the helicopter down, leaving a foot of clearance on either side of the rotor disk. The helicopter rocked gently as it touched down. He kept lowering the collective, feeling for the craft to settle into place and stop rocking. Finally he shut the Huey down.

The concentration of landing in the ravine had given him the focus he needed. As the blades coasted to a stop in this sheltered spot, he sharpened that focus into an exact recollection of the shocking events witnessed in the last hour.

When Josh had finished retracing those frantic, feverish steps from the moment he and Kirk had left the amphitheater until he saw the Huey fly apart above the fence, it seemed as though his mind reviewed the whole situation in real time. He believed he had a clue. So he went over the entire process again. This time he reversed his mental projector, traveling backward in time from the moment he heard the startling calls. He pieced together every vision, every word, every feeling that he had experienced.

Real time passed too quickly, seemed too fragmented. So he tried to take it in slow motion.

The first significant thing in backward review was the explosion. The engine compartment had blown apart. The engine turbines rotating at enormous speeds of 6,600 revolutions per minute had disintegrated, tearing out the top of the helicopter.

Josh stopped the projector in his head. Leaving it in freeze frame, he climbed out of the helicopter and opened up the cooling, crackling metal access doors to the engine compartment of his Huey. He inspected it from top to bottom. He found no sign of the explosives like those that had killed Kirk. He knelt on the engine deck, his body baking in the last rays of the hot sun and the radiated heat from the engine. He ran those split seconds of his memory back and forth across the vision of his mind, watching it fly apart and come together. Fly apart. Come together. Time after time.

Then he saw it! The explosion hadn't come from the engine compartment at all. The puff of smoke had come from *atop* the engine compartment. Then, seconds later, the engine compartment had blown apart. The puff of black smoke had not come from the exhaust, but from atop it.

That was it, the key!

They'd never been allowed to use the beacons. They had been disallowed for tactical reasons. The wiring had been disconnected. So Vickers had said.

He stood up on the engine deck and studied the red globe of the anti-collision beacon. He'd looked at it closely before, but observed the glass had been painted over in dark green. *Of course!* Nobody asked about the paint. It would be assumed that they had been blacked out to prevent them being turned on by accident. But that wasn't the reason at all. There was no light assembly in there at all. Of that he was sure.

Josh used his pocket nail clipper to scratch off a spot the size of a quarter.

What he saw disappointed him. Nothing. No, there was something—an opaque white. The inside of the globe had been painted with a curdling white paint. Why paint the inside? he wondered. No reason, he decided, except to hide something.

Josh climbed down to find a fist-sized stone. He began rapping cautiously on the glass. No effect. So he rapped harder, almost angrily until the glass broke.

The fragments stuck together. He used his clippers to pluck a chunk away and touched the paint. The feel of it sent a chill down his sweaty back. It wasn't paint at all, but plastic explosives. In a minute the fear passed, and he began digging out the contents of the broken beacon. Inside the compartment he found an antenna and a receiver beneath the wad of explosives. Using his clippers, he cut all the wires from the receiver. He tried to pull out the antenna, but could not. He tried to find wires coming from another direction but could not. He decided not to mess with the device any further. He cleaned out all the explosives he could and decided to stop.

Josh buttoned up the helicopter again, feeling a grim satisfaction. But what had it earned him? he asked himself. Now if he wanted to, he could safely go back over the fences of The Ranch. Big deal.

No, he must not be negative. He decided he would apply the same kind of mental rigor to the process of examining what had happened to Kirk before he took off, before he went nuts. So he replayed that scene with PJ. He mentally watched Kirk pick her up and throw her into the cabin of the Huey. Then she rolled back into his arms and onto his knee. Kirk set her down again. Then he threw her back in. Out. In.

When he had replayed the scene completely to his satisfaction, Josh finally understood. Now he knew what had snapped Kirk. Now he knew why Gates had lain on the floor of his office dying without trying to defend himself. He now understood what was supposed to have happened to Grayson Kirk and Josh Avery. They were supposed to have died a gruesome death together. But it didn't happen. At least not to Josh.

Now he knew. He had not gone crazy, either. He had been perfectly sane when he flew into that fence, setting off the detonator. He had figured out that Gates had outsmarted them. He figured out that the only way to defeat the gruesome gang at The Ranch was to get Avery out of there alive. Josh Avery could bring down the group running The Ranch.

So Grayson would only have his revenge through the proxy of Josh Avery. He had set Josh free. Now it was up to Josh to put an end to the genetic nightmare that Gates and the others had initiated.

16

. . . .

DFW AIRPORT, TEXAS

Before the military cargo plane had even landed back
in the continental United States, Colonel Tommy
Vickers already knew about the fiasco of the escape.
His secure-voice radio call to The Ranch had erased
the last shred of doubt about who had sabotaged the
mission into North Africa. He wanted a piece of Avery
and piece of Kirk. He planned to conduct his own
personal summary court martial. He savored the idea
that the pair would not even have to be killed in an
"accident."

When he had landed, however, he was given a
change of mission to fly to Texas instead of returning
to The Ranch. Vickers was ordered to go to the home
of Marilyn in Copperas Cove. He was to set up surveillance around the home. He was to kill Josh Avery
should he try to make contact with Marilyn. If he did
make contact with the family, Vickers was to kill everybody.

Vickers had argued. "Why do that? Why would he
do that? If he were going to anything, it would be to
get on the blower and call the police or the Pentagon."

"If that happens, kill the family, anyhow."

"How long am I supposed to wait?" He could not disguise the disappointment of not being able to return to The Ranch to deal with Josh personally.

"Kill the whole family?" Vickers asked himself as he hit the interstate highway, heading away from DFW Airport, heading south toward central Texas. "How the hell did I get into the business of killing a family?"

THE NEVADA DESERT

Family. It was the word on Josh's mind. He'd gone into a burrow like a desert mouse in hiding from a sidewinder rattlesnake. He didn't know what to do. He reasoned that Marilyn and her two children would be all right as long as he didn't try to see them. They were leverage against him. So that gave them a measure of safety. Besides, if he did contact them, he would have to get past the shock that his ghost would cause. They thought he was dead. Besides endangering them, he would certainly shatter their mental stability. Then, if he got killed again, he'd put them through even more grief. No, trying to get to Marilyn would remain out of the question for now.

He also knew that every fuel stop, airport, flight service station, bus terminal, car-rental agency, highway stop, and train station would be watched. No doubt he would be described as a fugitive, armed and dangerous—which was true—and killed on sight. No doubt tomorrow would bring a day search of the desert within the entire radius of the Huey's fuel load. For all he knew, there would be infrared-capable Mohawks out tonight combing the entire region, looking for hot-spot imagery of the Huey on the ground.

His first conclusion came easily: whatever he did would have to be done tonight.

Where could he go? Wherever there were authorities, sooner or later they would check his identity as well as his story and find that he was supposed to be dead. He would probably be locked up first so that they could ask questions later. Then he'd be reported to military officials. They'd say he'd gone AWOL. They'd send somebody to pick him up and return him to military control.

Suddenly Josh felt very alone. It was not just the realization that their declaration of his death had cut him off from the rest of the world while not giving him the peace and satisfaction of an actual death. He felt enervated by the realization that his closest acquaintances—human and unhuman—were all dead. Kirk. Bozo one and Bozo two. Ace one, "too," and three. Besides Marilyn, the closest thing that he had for a friend was Tommy Vickers. He knew Vickers would return from Africa full of vengeance. Josh was adrift.

But wasn't that the way with him, anyhow? Had he ever had a plan in his life to point to? Could he ever say that he ever set goals and objectives? No. All he had ever done was drift along in the current of events. Where the army told him to go he went. His most uncomfortable moments were when the Pentagon assignment officer told him he would have to choose between options. Even late in his career he had waffled, postponing a decision until someone suggested it might be beneficial for him to try Special Operations. Special Operations had merely been a search for thrills. There was no purpose in it, just the satisfaction of satisfying desperate urges, taking risks, experiencing danger.

Finally, when he had reached maximum on the scale of risk and danger, when he was hijacked to this place they called The Ranch, he had been found wanting.

He could have resisted helping with the horrid genetic-engineering experiments and The Ranch. But he hadn't resisted. Only Kirk had put up a fight. Kirk had gone the distance knowing there was little or no chance at all to survive flying out across that fence. Kirk had done it, anyhow. Kirk had shown his courage.

Josh knew that up until now in his life he had been putting on a good act. But now he was revealed to himself, his most severe critic. He simply lacked the guts to take charge of a situation and do the right thing.

He sat hunched over on the cabin floor, feeling the discomfort in his tailbone and the strain across his back. He wrapped his arms around his legs and buried his face between his knees. He tried to fight off the feeling of sickness. Maybe it was the heat. Maybe it was self-disgust. But he felt ill, so he hugged himself tighter until the feeling began to go away. Then he seemed to be lost. When the sun finally dropped behind the mountains and the desert darkened suddenly, chillingly, he hadn't moved.

• •

After midnight the desert radiated most of its warmth toward the heavens, quieting the activity of most reptiles. Then the activity of mammals picked up. The rodents began scurrying about until the thin air distributed the sound of a turbine whining. Then came the popping of helicopter blades trying to snatch a bite of the air. Finally the roar of the engine and the noise of the Huey blades spewed out of the earth into the night. The Huey settled for a moment at a twenty-foot hover. Then it dipped its nose and cruised away from the ravine, settling into normal flight, climbing to an altitude of two hundred feet, and flying on a heading of north-northwest, away from The Ranch.

Josh had decided. He had tried to rest, but he found his spirit would not let him. Somewhere in the examination of his own conscience during those hours of sitting on the helicopter floor, chilling with the air of the desert, he'd found a vestige of himself that he had become unfamiliar with over the years. Perhaps it arose from the desperation of his situation. Or maybe it was revenge for what they had done to his friend, Kirk, and what they intended to do to Marilyn and her family. Or maybe it was a touch of the hot anger born of righteousness.

Whatever the case, he knew it would not be enough to tattle on this group that ran The Ranch. He wasn't going to leave it to the authorities to discover the insanity of subhuman creations carrying out terrorist missions in the name of patriotism. For once, he was going to take charge of a situation; to get a grip on events and to run them the way they ought to be run. He was going to do the right thing.

The right thing. It made him laugh to think about what his own warped sense of reality had made of this definition of the right thing. He was going to execute a bloody coup d'etat, taking over command of The Ranch and its genetic projects. Then he would destroy them.

The Ranch and all its occupants had been developed and trained on a completely offensive basis. The dogs had been trained to attack. The Descendants attacked instinctively. Vickers had developed a training program that emphasized the attack. Nothing Josh had ever seen except for those wires and mine fields around the fence had indicated a single thought given to defensive maneuvers as a useful tactic.

So maybe the best idea, he had decided, would be to attack.

THE RANCH

Inside the compound headquarters at The Ranch, Edward Gates artlessly packed his briefcase full of computer tapes. "Are these all the backups?"

The chief researcher, Quist, said, "Yes. All the important ones. There are no other copies. The originals are still loaded into the computers, and the system is set for an automatic erase, destroying all the records."

"What about hard copy? There must be file cabinets full of backup information on paper."

"Everything has been moved to the central vault." Quist lowered his head and wagged in disgust. "On your order the ventilation turns into a flue system. The vault becomes a furnace. It's programmed to burn for twelve hours straight. Everything in the room will be reduced to ashes and puddles of molten metal."

Gates shut the briefcase and set it beside his desk. "Remember the operative words are, 'on my order.' I don't want anything to be destroyed until we find out whether Avery has really gotten free and done something that might jeopardize our operation. Then I want to make our move incrementally. The first priority will be to save the breeding stock. I suppose the humane thing to do would be to euthanize the remainder. But failing that, we'll just have to let them starve —or consume each other."

"Do you suppose," Quist added hopefully, "it's possible that Vickers will be able to bring Avery back under our control before he is able to get to the press or Congress?"

Gates shook his head emphatically. "Avery is not that dumb. He may not get to the authorities right away, but eventually he'll figure out some way to prove that he really wasn't killed in that crash. When he does that, if he gains the confidence of just one authority, somebody will be out here looking around. No, I believe that if we should capture Avery, it's going to be pure damned luck. The only thing that we can do is sit here and wait to hear whether our teams in the field can spot the helicopter before he can make a report."

Both men looked around the room to confirm with their eyes what their ears seemed to be telling them.

The windows in Gates's office rattled, and a desk lamp began to tap-dance, sliding across the desktop in tune to a high-frequency vibration.

Suddenly the sound of the helicopter grew louder. The office began rattling violently. The ceiling vibrated. Bits of plaster and light fixtures fell down, smashing on the desktop. Quist cringed against one wall, away from the windows. Gates ran to the radio console in a wall cabinet to demand why security hadn't reported the helicopter. The answer to his radio call was the voice of Josh Avery.

The vibrations of the landing helicopter made the sound of his voice over the radio tremulous, but Josh's intentions came across hard and firm. "I'm taking over The Ranch, Gates."

Gates blew the plaster dust off of his radio transmitter mike and asked, "How?"

"I found the explosives in the anti-collision light. I disconnected the receiver and built my own bomb. I've reset it to go off on my command. I'm ready to blow this place down. If my calculations are correct, my skids are now about four or five feet directly over your head. That's how."

"You're going to blow yourself up? That's going to give you satisfaction?" A note of concern had crept into Gates's voice. He'd seen Kirk's helicopter explode earlier.

"No, you're going to invite me down to your office. I'm going to bring a portable bomb with me. I'm going to collect some information that will put the bite on this operation of yours. And I'm going to collect PJ Payne. Then we're going to fly out of here unmolested."

Inside the office, a heavy stillness reigned, despite the continuing vibrations through the top of the building and down the walls. Quist, still leaning against the wall, slumped in defeat.

But Gates displayed no sign of defeatism. He rubbed a knuckle against one of his temples hard, angrily, trying to think of the a response that would give him some time. He spoke crisply into the mike. "Come on down, Avery. We can talk about this."

"There isn't going to be any talking. You get on the horn right now and tell your security forces to stay put. Tell them you will not permit anyone to go on top of the building. Tell them to stop using the security radio net altogether."

Gates gave the orders. Then he said, "Avery, I'll have Mrs. Payne brought here by the time you get down to my office. As a sign of good faith."

"That's fine, Mr. Gates. But I also want to visit with your chief researcher, Quist."

"He's right here in the office with me. Come on down." He put down the radio mike and gave more orders over the telephone.

Josh decided he would let the Huey continue to idle. He locked the controls down, buttoning the strap onto the collective, twisting the knurled lock on the cyclic control. Finally he stuck his supposed bomb—his survival radio—into his shirt front, arranging it so the antenna stuck out. They would have to believe his bluff or this entire desperate attempt was going to end suddenly.

He switched his pistol from hand to hand to dry his palms on his flight suit. Then he gripped the doorknob to the stairwell and took a deep breath, knowing that once he walked into this building, he was taking the chance that he would never again walk out. He looked back at the helicopter vibrating at an idle. All he'd have to do was jump in and unlock the controls and pull pitch. He could still fly away from it all. Instead, he jerked on the doorknob.

Inside the stairwell he was startled by a pair of security guards. Immediately he leveled the 9-millimeter and four open palms flashed toward him to keep him from pulling the trigger.

"Don't shoot! We are here to guide you."

"Lead the way." Josh did his best to keep the trembling out of his voice. But he didn't sound all that secure and confident. So he repeated, "Lead the way, goddammit!"

The two sidled quickly down the stairs and into the hallway. As they burst from the stairwell, Josh saw four more people and could barely maintain his composure. A third security guard again held up his palms to ward off bullets. Josh's attention was fixed on the other three. He told the three security guards to get lost. The three men scuttled off in the opposite direction from Gates's office.

Then he turned to confront the three women standing before him.

He had figured it out in the desert. He knew why Gates had not died from being shot in the head. And he knew why PJ had not died in the helicopter with Kirk.

The three who stood before him confirmed it—they were all the same woman. Each said the same thing to him. "I am PJ Payne."

"These other two are clones . . . Descendant copies of me."

"No, I am the real PJ."

"No, I am."

"Kirk told me the real PJ had scars on her belly from being shot. And on her thighs."

Two of the women lifted up their shirts and showed white scars across their midsection. The third one lowered the pants of her sweatsuit for a moment to show shiny spots of scar tissue on one leg.

"They did surgery on those two."

"No, on the other two."

Josh remembered Kirk picking up the PJ Payne of this afternoon and tossing her into the cabin of the Huey. His hand had been beneath her buttocks. He had felt the vestigial tail and he had known that the real PJ had not come out. Gates had not been the man shot in his office this afternoon. Gates had allowed the Descendant image of himself to be killed. He had allowed Kirk and Josh to escape with a Descendant. He had calculated that they would fly out into the desert, that the drugs would wear off the Descendant before they would discover that it was not the real PJ. Sooner or later, the Descendant would become hungry, and Gates had expected the pair of them to be devoured by one of his creations. Only Kirk's act of desperation had prevented that.

Josh set his jaw angrily and gave an order. "Turn around. All three of you."

Two of the women turned full circle. The third one, the one on Josh's right, turned her back. And Josh had his answer.

"Face me." The woman on the right did as she was told. He pointed to the woman in the middle. "I choose you. You are PJ." The woman on the right slumped in despair. The two other women smiled. Josh reached out and at the last second closed his beckoning hand into a fist and smashed the center PJ in the nose. Blood immediately splashed across her face, and the PJ on the left leaped onto her neck. Josh grabbed the woman on the right and pulled. "Come on, let's get to Gates's office."

As they ran toward the office, PJ said, "You could tell by the absence of the tail?"

"Yes, even through the clothes I could see theirs."

"In case we run into any other look-alikes, you'll know me because I'll use the code word *Beastmaker*," she said.

"All right. We're going to talk to Gates." He patted his stomach where the transmitter bounced as they ran down the hallway. "I told them I have a bomb on me. We have to act as if we're afraid we'll have to blow ourselves up in order to destroy this place and these

Descendants. We have to make them believe we'll do it. So put on your best act."

"I don't have to act," PJ said matter-of-factly.

As they approached the part of the building where Josh remembered being this afternoon, he recognized the carpet runner on the hallway. He burst through the door as he had before, his pistol at the ready. It surprised him that only the two men were in the office. Gates sat calmly, even smugly, behind his desk. Quist had found a chair near the wall to the right. Josh pulled PJ into the room, closed the door, and locked it. He patted the radio under his shirt. "Believe me, I'll blow the whole goddamned place up if I have to. Kirk and I agreed. He drew the short straw this afternoon. He had to go first."

He heard a groan beside him. He glanced over at PJ and saw that she had gone pale, her face slack and filled with pain. "I'm sorry," said Josh, "of course you had no way of knowing that Grayson—"

Gates interrupted. "Fine and dandy, Colonel Avery, but the matter at hand? I surrender. What now?"

Josh stammered for an instant. What now, indeed? He hadn't thought it all out *that* well. He really never expected to have gotten this far so easily. He figured he might be able to land on the building. He thought there might be a firefight. He might confront Gates and get a shot at him. So he patted his belly again. "I'm placing you under arrest. . . . I'm taking you in to the proper authorities. Now give PJ your pistol."

"What pistol?"

"If you are really Gates . . . if you're not another one of those clones. . . ." Josh stepped up to the desk and looked over beyond Gates's shoulder. The black spot irregularly ruining the carpet had not been cleaned up. "You'll have a pistol on you. Give it to her."

Gates produced the standard-issue 9-millimeter from his pocket. PJ took it. Immediately a kind of murderous look crossed her face. Josh had no doubt she would use the pistol if provoked. She might even use it without provocation.

"What now?" said Gates, his eyebrows rising in exaggerated concern.

Josh felt a twinge of anxiety that Gates could act so calm.

"I'm taking you and Quist out of here with us. Before we go, you're going to lock this place down—permanently."

"And what's going to happen at feeding time?" A note of concern suddenly crept into Gates's voice.

Quist sat up in his chair and spoke for the first time. "They'll starve or eat each other . . . whatever. You know they have to consume extraordinary amounts of food, Mr. Avery. You can't lock them down. It's too cruel. . . ." Then he seemed to realize the irony in his reference to cruelty.

"You bet, Mr. Quist. They will have to consume extraordinary amounts of protein. Perhaps even each other. If they don't they'll die. It shouldn't take very long, should it?"

"You would be so ruthless? You would kill these . . . these . . . *almost* people?"

Josh laughed at the irony of Gates giving such a lecture. "This coming from you? You, Mr. Gates, the modern personification of Adolf Hitler?"

Gates did not react to the insult. On the contrary, he became even more smug. He pointed at Josh's belly. "You have your secret weapon. Now I would like you to meet mine." With a flourish, he indicated a doorway at the side of the room. "A mere closet, sir. But what miracles it holds. Come out of the closet, Colonel Avery."

The closet door handle turned and the door came open an inch. Both PJ and Josh pointed their pistols at the doorway. The door swung open completely. Josh opened his mouth, but no sound came out, for he was looking into a mirror of himself. A perfect Descendant copy of Josh stepped into the room. Finally the air escaping from his throat was shaped by his mouth into a word.

"How?"

"When you were first brought here after the combat fiasco that night. When you were wounded. We put you under anesthesia to repair the damage. While we were there we extracted some information and . . . certain body fluids. Among them, your semen. In truth we've made dozens of you. We've even killed dozens of you. You know, imperfect copies. We've experimented through several generations since you've been with us. Now you remember your manners and introduce yourself to our finest model of Mr. Josh Avery. This one we call Avery XL."

The Descendant called XL held out a hand.

Stunned, Josh held out his own automatically. "Excel," he mumbled.

"Stands for copy number forty," said Gates. "You know, Roman numerals. Actually we're breeding a whole new generation of fifties models. I think you'd like them."

Josh asked, "Secret weapon?"

"Imagine the possibilities, Colonel Avery. Imagine if certain Congressmen or other influential people in this country were to have certain body fluids extracted. Imagine what we could do with one of our Descendants casting votes on the Senate floor, for example. Or maybe we would have him giving orders to combat units."

Josh and PJ were shaking their heads at the same time.

"Well, yes, in fact it could be done. At first, we had been thinking just of the possibilities in having our own national brand of suicidal terrorists and counter-terrorists. But now we've been able to become more refined with our ideas. But to the matter at hand . . ." He waved a hand at XL. "He . . . *it* is trained to attack on my command. It's trained to attack you, as a matter of fact. It's just like an attack dog. But as I say, we are becoming more refined here. We call XL our attack colonel."

Josh stepped back away from the Descendant. "PJ, you keep your pistol on Gates. If necessary, I don't doubt that you will use it. I'll take care of . . . this one." He waved his pistol at the Descendant.

"Of course if any harm should come to XL here, we'd be severely disappointed. Actually he's been quite a breakthrough. You could put it down to superior breeding, I suppose. He has some improvements over the previous models, even over the two you trained for helicopter flight. Oh yes, and there are some earlier models still around the building. We have trained them to attack you on sight. You know, bring the nice Josh to us, Fido. Speak for your supper. That sort of thing."

"It's quite true," said XL, the Descendant image of Josh.

Josh was utterly stunned at the closeness of the Descendant's voice to his own.

Gates picked up on his reaction. "And as a matter of fact, he's got your fingerprints as well. The genetic makeup is identical. Can you imagine . . ."

"Shut up, goddamn you, Gates." As she gave the command, PJ poked her pistol threateningly at Gates. Gates did as he was told. He seemed to realize that PJ was less likely than Josh to be numbed by something new and horrible such as these clones. PJ Payne had been through years of surprises and pain. She had grown hard, even callous. Gates understood his own life was in danger.

Suddenly, the speaker on Gates's shelf crackled and a security outpost began inquiring about the progress of repairs on the breech in the fence that Kirk had caused in the afternoon. Gates stood up from his desk and yelled into his mike a repetition of his order that no one was to be using the security network. Then he angrily shut off the speaker and faced Josh. But the sound of the security outpost's apology leaked into the room. Everyone in the room stared at Josh's stomach. The sound came from under Josh's shirt.

Gates laughed. "Secret weapon, eh? Remote detonator? I call baloney on that, Avery."

Josh's pistol hand stiffened as he squared himself to face the Descendant.

"Excel! *On guard!*"

The Descendant hissed, crouching, brandishing his fangs.

"PJ, if this guy makes one move toward me, you make damn sure that you shoot Gates first. The sight of the blood will enrage this Descendant."

Gates shrugged, showing his lack of concern.

"Don't waste your time, Mrs. Payne. As I told you, this is a new, improved model of the Descendant. We finally bred that fatal flaw out of this generation. All future generations will be bred along the same lines." He pointed at the dark spot on the carpet. "You don't think we would have allowed one of the older generations of Descendants into this room with that spot on the carpet, do you? You should be proud of your superior genes, Colonel Avery. You'll be the father of a whole new race."

Josh said, almost hopefully, "You are bluffing."

"Here." Gates picked up a shard of glass from the floor. He pressed the glass against the back of his hand. A line of blood welled up along the edge of the shard.

"He won't bother me. You could decapitate me and not stir the slightest reaction from him—it."

Gates pulled open the top right drawer of his desk.

PJ uttered a cry of warning. Josh turned his pistol on Gates, fearing that he might be reaching for a gun. But the desk drawer was filled with wires and switches. Gates looked up and smiled. "Sic 'em, XL."

The Descendant erupted from his crouch and rushed across the room, covering the last six feet in a flying tackle. Josh turned the pistol quickly and fired, missing the Descendant, who'd planted a shoulder into his solar plexus.

Josh fell, gasping for breath, unable to turn the pistol into the Descendant. When they hit the floor, enough of XL's weight was on him to stun him further. Josh remembered the fangs from the Gregor Munn video. He renewed his fight and twisted from beneath the animal. He tried to swing the pistol at his head, but the Descendant caught his wrist and squeezed it hard.

Josh realized they had bred extra strength into this beast. The pain in his wrist brought a groan to his lips. The pistol loosened in his grasp and almost slipped away. With the other hand, the Descendant grabbed the pistol and tossed it across the room. It brought a knee up under Josh's ribs and threw him over. Josh kept rolling, gaining an extra yard of clearance as the Descendant leaped at him again. For an instant Josh felt the horror of wrestling with his mirror image. He was amazed to see the scar streaking down the Descendant's face. They had to have put that one on surgically. It was not exactly the same as his. But the mole behind the ear. That was his own birthmark there on this Descendant.

Josh felt his breath restored as he rolled up and regained his feet. Again the beast rushed him, its mouth wide open.

Josh threw a left uppercut smacking into the jaws, shutting the mouth, closing it with a clatter as the fangs meshed, cutting the animal's lip. The blow had no effect on the onslaught, and Josh found himself grappling with the stronger Descendant, avoiding those jaws.

"Which is which?" He heard PJ scream.

"The fangs," he shouted. They should have been enough to identify the beast. He heard her whine in frustration, unable to tell them apart.

The fangs, indeed. This battle was going to be over shortly, for the Descendent had the advantage of those two-inch-long fangs. He kept slashing, moving his head from side to side as he tried to bear down toward Josh's face. The only thing that kept them away was

Josh's stiffened arms against XL's throat. The thing was trying to lower its jaw and slash away at Josh's forearms. Josh threw up a knee under the body of XL, who was straddling him. He felt it land between the legs and hoped the blow caused enough pain to give Josh an edge. He remembered that these Descendants had been castrated. He threw up his knee again, harder this time, lifting his weight, bending his legs, falling back to throw the beast over his shoulder.

He felt the buttocks of his attacker rise into the air. He felt pressure on the pivot point of his hands against the animal's throat. The Descendant's hands tried to gouge his face. Up and over went the center of gravity of the Descendant. Finally he began toppling over Josh. As he did, Josh rolled free.

"Beastmaker! Beastmaker!" He shouted. "PJ, shoot the son of a bitch."

She needed no more than a foot's clearance between the two. She pointed the gun at the Descendant and fired four rounds, pinning it to the floor. It writhed for a moment, then fell still.

Josh leaped for his pistol and scrambled to his feet, pointing it at Gates. Only a shred of civility kept him from blowing away the man the same way that Kirk had blown away his Descendant image this afternoon. Gates stood silently, his arms crossed. Josh looked into the open desk drawer and saw that the switches in the drawer had been rearranged.

"It's over, Avery. You got your wish. This place is ruined. I've just hit all the self-destruct switches. I suggest you get to that helicopter and try to make your way out of here."

Josh shoved Gates hard, sending him toppling over backward into the damp spot on the carpet. Gates grimaced and rubbed the palms of his hands off on the dry part of the carpet. Josh reached into the drawer and reversed the position of every switch in it.

"It won't do any good. Once they're activated, the process is irreversible." Gates started to get to his feet and Josh let his rage overtake him. He planted a kick into Gates's face, knocking him backward again, back into the gore in the carpet. This time, when Gates tried to brush off the blood, it was his own, streaming from his nose and mouth.

Josh felt brutish, as if he had become one of the same savages as his enemies.

"Come on, PJ, let's get out of here. How much time before this bomb goes off?"

An explosion of air and a spray of blood escaped Gates's mouth. "Bomb? There's no bomb, Colonel Avery. Those switches have released all the dogs in captivity in the compound. And all the Descendants. I suggest you get moving. Or you could stay here. This office is secure against the arrival of either the dogs or the Descendants. There's a couple days' supply of food. . . . It won't take more than that for the self-destruction to be completed."

Josh ran to the door and peeked into the hallway. It was clear. "PJ, down this hallway to the left at the stairwell door. Go up to the roof. The helicopter's sitting at flight idle. Unlock the controls. Can you still fly?"

She nodded vigorously, then shook her head. "Yes, but I'm not leaving you."

He waved her out brusquely. "I've got to take care of something. You get moving. I'll be just a step behind you."

She hesitated a second. He shouted at her. *"Get moving!"*

Gates still sat dazed on the floor, blood streaming down his face. Josh walked around jerking desk drawers out onto the floor. He stumbled over the oversized briefcase. He picked it up and opened it. Before he had a chance to examine the rolls of tape inside the briefcase, he saw the look of panic cross Gates's face. He knew he had all he needed. He had the evidence to incriminate Gates and discredit this operation. He laughed, surprised at the wickedness he heard in his own voice. "If you follow me out that door I'll blow you down in the hallway," he growled at Gates.

Then he was gone.

As Josh began running down the hallway toward the stairwell, he heard shouting behind him. He turned and aimed his pistol but he didn't need to pull the trigger.

Gates stood in the hallway shouting commands, pointing, desperately trying to get the Descendants to attack the figure running down the hallway.

The Descendants did attack. They attacked the man standing agitated in the hallway, the bottom half of his face and the front of his shirt soaked in blood. Gates could barely let loose his screams before his own throat was ripped open and he died at the hands of his own creations.

Josh continued running toward the stairwell. As he neared it, he saw a group of four Descendants sprinting toward him from the opposite direction. He had no doubt they were Descendants because they were Joshes. He wondered if they were like XL, unaffected by the sight of blood. Or were they earlier versions that had just killed Gates? He raised a pistol and fired into the center of the group. One of them dropped, doubling in pain, a bloody stain spreading across the left side of his chest. The others kept running for Josh. Josh beat them to the stairwell and shot down a second Descendant. Footsteps behind him told him he was under attack from that direction, too.

• •

On the roof, PJ had the Huey at full takeoff RPM. She had removed the locks on all the controls to give herself complete freedom of movement. She wondered if she would remember how to fly at all, but as she pumped her feet back and forth on the pedals and worked the controls, she realized that she would have to do it. For practice, she picked up the Huey and turned the tail a full 180 degrees so that the open cabin door was nearest the entrance to the roof. As she turned the helicopter around she saw that there were two more stairwells besides the one she'd used. She put the Huey down so she could watch all three doorways. Then, suddenly, she saw two of the stairwell doors fly open. Men ran from each of them. In the glow of the security lights, she realized they were all the same man. Josh was running toward the helicopter from two different stairwells in groups of two.

Immediately, she knew that one of the groups of Descendants was the older generation that Gates had described because they attacked each other on sight, unable to distinguish the actual Josh Avery from his image.

Three other Joshes continued to run toward the helicopter.

From a distance of ten feet, one Josh struggled with the briefcase, trying to lift and throw it at the same time. She felt it crashing against the floor of the cabin and saw it sliding across. It was nearly at the point of going out the other door when Josh turned around and fired a pistol. One of the Descendants sat down awkwardly, holding his chest and screaming, his fangs bared viciously. The third one hit Josh, the pistol, and then the helicopter.

The 9-millimeter flew through the cabin and out the other open door. The two men landed in the back. Uncertain of what to do, PJ checked the rooftop. More and more Descendants, not all of them the images of Josh, streamed from the doorways. She heard barking dogs and saw three pit bull terriers burst from one of the stairwells, pulling down a figure from behind.

She decided there was only one thing to do, and pulled pitch hard. Better to be airborne with one or two monsters than to stay here and confront legions of them.

The Huey vaulted into the air. She shoved the cyclic forward, lowering the nose to give forward airspeed to the takeoff. Then she was off the top of the building.

Below her in the security lights of the compound, chaos reigned. Men and dogs milled around, dogs attacking men, men attacking dogs and each other. Men and Descendants mingled in battle with each other and the dogs. True to Gates's word, the place was destroying itself. Down toward the stockyards she saw surging waves of cattle flatten the fences of their pens and stampede into the barren spaces of The Ranch, pit bulls in pursuit.

Then the Huey shot beyond the fence and out into the desert. She didn't know which direction to take or where to go. She began pulling pitch into a climb.

Behind her, she felt the bodies rolling around on the

floor. She knew that the Descendant and Josh were still wrestling. Guiding the Huey with the cyclic in her right hand, she tried to turn awkwardly back with her left to fire her pistol. But the bodies rolling around on the cabin floor simply could not be sorted out. She could hear shouting, and knew that Josh was hollering *"Beastmaker! Beastmaker!"* But what was she to do? She needed to fly. She could not shoot blindly into them. She hit the landing light and searchlight buttons on the pilot's collective and began looking for a place to set down. Maybe if she got down on the ground she could release the controls and sort them out.

But landing was not to be. One of the two had finally overpowered the other. She saw the legs fly out into the night air and the body start sliding out of the cabin. One set of clawing hands tried to cling to the dimpled cabin floor, sliding, sliding. The other one stomped the first one's hands. The first one grimaced in pain, slipping, weakening, unable to withstand the onslaught of stomping boots. His mouth was open. He had no fangs that she could see.

Josh!

She whirled and aimed the pistol at a spot high on the back of the Descendant that stood, holding on to the edge of the cabin roof and stamping on Josh's hands. She shot once and saw the figure crumple, bounce off the cabin floor, and tumble out into the night. She felt a thump as it hit the skid on the left side of the helicopter. And then there was nothing but the figure of Josh trying to paw his way back into the cabin.

Trying to fly, trying to see, encouraging him to hang on, she started a descent. Maybe she could get it onto the ground and help him. But Josh struggled back into the cabin inch by inch, and PJ began shedding tears of relief. She put the helicopter into a steep climb, heading west. Somewhere in front of them were the mountains. She knew she needed to gain altitude to clear them. Maybe Josh would know how high.

She put her pistol down on the radio console and reached into the back for him. He knelt on the cabin floor between the two seats and smiled at her. He tried to speak to her but she couldn't hear over the noise of the helicopter. She pulled down the two headsets hanging from the roof of the cockpit and put one on herself. She held out the other to Josh. He held up his battered fingers in front of his face and she saw the problem. She put the headset on him and set their intercom buttons to talk. She motioned him to sit down in the copilot seat, so he climbed over the console and slumped into the chair.

"Thank you," he said, smiling sheepishly. "Thank you for saving my life."

"You're hurt," she said.

"Yes, but it's over."

"No," she said. "I thought that before. It's never over. They are still there. Gates is back there. They can't be brought down. Not unless we get evidence. Is there evidence in that briefcase?"

He smiled broadly and worked his fingers. "This is settled once and for all. It is completely over. I assure you. Honest, PJ, it is really over."

Tears welled up in her eyes.

"I'm sorry," he said. "I didn't mean to make you cry."

"No, don't be sorry. Mark Payne—my husband. And Grayson Kirk. Both dead . . . I can't believe

. . . oh, look at me. I can't even see anymore." She tried to wipe the tears from her eyes with her sleeve.

"Take the controls so I can blow my nose," she said. "How high do we have to go to clear the mountains?"

"Hmmm?"

"Take the controls, you big lug. Fly. Take us up and over the mountains. I can't see through all these waterworks."

"I . . . I . . . My hands. You do it while I fix you. Here." He held out a handkerchief and dabbed at her eyes.

She studied his hands. She saw his injuries were no more than some discoloration and swelling. His fingers manipulated the handkerchief just fine. Nothing there should prevent him from flying.

"Josh," she said, sniffing herself into a strained sobriety.

"Yes?"

She released the controls. The helicopter started into a nose dive, banking to the right. He did not react with alarm or any other emotion. He did not react at all. She took the controls and leveled the aircraft off again.

"You don't know how to fly?"

"PJ. My love. You are crazy, darling." He smiled stupidly.

"Beastmaker," she said.

"Huh?"

"Beastmaker, Josh . . . or whatever you are."

"I'm afraid I don't understand this . . . beastmaker." He smiled blankly.

"You are one of them."

He shrugged. "No, actually I'm kidding. I can fly, really."

She stared at him, again tears welling up in her eyes. But they were not tears of joy.

"Really, I can fly," he said.

"Put your hands on the controls, Josh." Her voice was choking as she gave the order. "I'm going to watch you fly."

He shrugged and put his hands on the controls. The craft weaved in the night.

Her face contorted in horror. She had shot Josh Avery. It was he who had tumbled out of the helicopter. She had saved the life of this . . . this . . . thing. She had known all along there would be no chance of ending this. She had known something would happen to extend the agony. She was right to feel completely in despair when she heard that Grayson Kirk had been killed. It was the second man that she had had any feelings for in the last few years. Then there was Josh. This heroic kind of figure who had come back to save her. She was wrong to have hoped . . . She looked over at the Descendant. He was still struggling with the cyclic control and the collective. The nose of the helicopter was flying up, then down, as the power changes became even more erratic. He looked over at her with absolutely no fear or concern showing in his face. He looked at her and smiled, his mouth going wide, fangs appearing, lowering from the upper jaw, rising from the lower jaw.

Her next act was instantaneous, certain, and irreversible. She reached down and shut off the fuel and governor. Instantly, the helicopter dropped.

She grabbed the collective to pull it up. For a moment, the craft would climb, the blades would bite into the air, the engine would be dead, and the momentum of the blades would carry only a few rotations before they stopped. The helicopter would tumble down to the earth, then she knew it would be over. She glanced at the altimeter and guessed they might be five thousand feet above the earth. Not too far or too long to fall. Then it would really be over.

She pulled hard on the collective but it would not come up. She looked to see if somehow it had become locked down. As she did so she looked over at the Descendant to see whether he was holding it down, if somehow he would know its effect. But no, the Descendant was still looking at her, still smiling stupidly.

She felt a boot on the collective. She shrieked and looked back. Josh Avery stood there, his foot forcing the collective to the floor, blood streaming from high on his shoulder.

"Take the controls!" he shouted. The Descendant looked back and literally leaped toward the console from his sitting position right at the muzzle of the pistol. Josh jerked three rapid-fire rounds into the head of the beast, who fell back onto the cyclic.

PJ struggled with the craft to keep it from nosing over as Josh grabbed the shirt of the Descendant and dragged him back into the cabin. Then he climbed over the console and put a headset on. He grasped the controls with her.

"Steady . . . steady, PJ, we're going to have to put this thing down together. I'm going to talk you through it. Seventy knots . . . Remember, seventy knots. We're out of trim. Give it some pedal."

"How did you get here? I thought . . . ," she murmured into the intercom.

"I caught the skid. It wasn't easy climbing back in

here. First you shoot me, then you start a climb-out so I'll have farther to fall. Then, when I finally get back in, you cut the fuel."

"I'm so sorry. . . ."

"Relax, PJ. Just help me fly."

The helicopter straightened out, descending level and streamlined. The landing lights showed that the desert floor here was relatively even and uncluttered.

"This is so . . . hard," she grunted between her teeth. "No hydraulics."

"Right. You just manipulate the controls as best you can. When it comes time to pull pitch I'll help you."

At about seventy-five feet he told her to begin pulling back on the cyclic. This was higher than normal for an initiation of the autorotational landing, but it was night, and he did not want to misjudge low. Besides, with the hydraulics off, it would take longer for an input to show its effect.

When the nose of the helicopter rose, they could no longer see the desert through the windshield. They had to watch between their feet as the landing lights showed brighter and brighter, a blinding white glow reflected upward. At ten to twenty feet he ordered, "Initial pitch!" Together, they jerked up on the collective-pitch lever and the freewheeling blades bit into the air and jerked the helicopter to a momentary stop.

"Forward cyclic." The helicopter leveled off. Simultaneously, they both applied left pedal to counteract the increased torque they had reestablished by putting a demand through the transmission to the rotor blades. The helicopter was slow in coming around, but the skids leveled off. The airspeed passed rapidly down through thirty knots.

The main rotor blades began to lose their inertia,

but at the last second at an altitude of five to six feet, Josh grunted a command and the two of them began hauling up on the collective, using up the last remnant of energy stored in those blades. The helicopter hit heels first on the skids and rocked forward severely. The craft skied about six feet onto the sand until the friction of the burrowing skids pulled it to a stop. The metal squeaked and screamed as in protest as the fuselage twisted.

Josh felt the helicopter crumple and realized that they had not landed squarely, that the skids had buckled from sliding in at an angle.

But the helicopter had stopped.

They were alive. The Huey bounced, and the blades slowed down, flapping erratically. Together they shoved the collective down. He looked back into the cockpit. The Descendant lay dead, his blood spilling over the cabin floor. They had in that briefcase and in that body all the evidence they needed to prove their case against those who had organized The Ranch. He looked at PJ. "It really is over, PJ. I believe it is finally over."

Her response to him was to cry. She put her hands over her face and shook her head, breaking down altogether.

"I doubt it, Josh. I doubt that it will ever be over," she sobbed.

He dragged the Descendant's body into the cabin and strapped it into a seat. She satisfied herself that the wound in his back was no more than a severe scratch. Then they climbed into the cockpit again.

Josh centered the pedals, then the cyclic. He began flipping switches. Within minutes the Huey's turbine whined in another start.

"I know it will be hard for you to believe that this could possibly be over. Grayson told me all that you have been through. I know about everything. But now there's a new factor in it. There's me. I'm going to take this matter into my hands. I'm going to do something about it. I'm going to get these pieces of evidence into the hands of the authorities. Tomorrow there is not going to be a Ranch. Tomorrow there's not going to be a Gates, a compound, a Descendant alive. If you help me, we can end it all for good."

She lifted her hands from her face and tried vainly to smile through her tears. He pulled up on the collective. The helicopter hesitated, unsticking itself reluctantly from the sand. The skids groaned as the weight of the fuselage was lifted off then, rising to a hover. The helicopter began rolling forward, falling off its ball of air. Then it was off into the night.

Epilogue

• • • • • • • • • • • • • • • • • • •

Vickers stood watching in the window. Marilyn sat reading to a pair of children who clung to her knees, drawing their comfort from that voice.

He, the tough soldier, had been given his marching orders. The time had come to kill these three, then to go on to The Ranch.

Killing terrorists, Viet Cong—even going after Avery—those tasks were simple enough. Those people could be called the enemy. Those could be killed for God, country, deadly career professionalism.

But children? Women? Soldiers didn't ambush innocent women and children, no matter what their reputations, no matter what their lack of morals in past lives had been. Already he had made these three feel the loss of Josh Avery. A would-be husband and stand-in father killed. They now thought that he made one of those sacrifices for the good of the country, the blessed rationalization that all loved ones feel to soften their grief as the kin of men and women who die in uniform, even senselessly in accidents.

These three had paid their price. They had paid with grief and a loss they couldn't reason. And they had been duped into believing that the corpse from that crash was their Josh. They didn't know about Descendants and such deceptions. They didn't know that a Descendant was buried in Josh Avery's coffin. And why should they? Vickers asked himself.

They shouldn't, was his answer.

He was beginning to understand why his country wouldn't sponsor terrorism. He felt that if ever there was a brutal man capable of abominations against other men, he, Vickers was it. Yet the idea of carrying out *this* kind of terrorist act sickened him. He aimed his pistol at the woman, the gently breathing bosom, placing the front sight between her breasts.

Kill her first? Then when she slumps, and the children cluster around her body screaming, give them their peace, too?

He balanced the younger girl's ear atop the site. Or should he do one child, then the mother, then the other child, moving efficiently from left to right?

His stomach lurched. He couldn't remember ever becoming so nauseated.

He'd killed before. Face-to-face. Hand to hand. He'd bitten, torn, strangled, shot, and knifed. Why, he'd even called in devastating artillery fire on his own . . . forces.

But this.

The idea of this act dragged him lower than he'd ever been before.

He shrugged.

Could he live with it?

He raised the pistol. Only one way to find out. He hesitated a long time, then his arm dropped to his side.

Hell with it.

He didn't need to know.

He holstered the gun and fought down his stomach. He remembered his own mother, his own lessons from the Bible at his mother's knee. He realized he did have a mother.

He decided he might someday be able to commit suicide, if in the interest of his country. But he could not kill the innocents in there, for those girls and that mother were part of himself that he thought had been excised by his rigid training, by his acquired brutality. But they had not been excised at all.

He turned and melted into the muggy darkness of central Texas.